THE
REVENGERS

Pinnacle Westerns by Terrence McCauley

The Jeremiah Halstead Series

BLOOD ON THE TRAIL

DISTURBING THE PEACE

The Sheriff Aaron Mackey Series

WHERE THE BULLETS FLY

DARK TERRITORY

GET OUT OF TOWN

THE DARK SUNRISE

THE
REVENGERS

A JEREMIAH HALSTEAD WESTERN

TERRENCE
McCAULEY

PINNACLE BOOKS
KENSINGTON PUBLISHING CORP.
www.kensingtonbooks.com

PINNACLE BOOKS are published by

Kensington Publishing Corp.
119 West 40th Street
New York, NY 10018

Copyright © 2023 by Terrence McCauley

All Kensington titles, imprints, and distributed lines are available at special quantity discounts for bulk purchases for sales promotion, premiums, fund-raising, and educational or institutional use.

Special book excerpts or customized printings can also be created to fit specific needs. For details, write or phone the office of the Kensington Sales Manager: Kensington Publishing Corp., 119 West 40th Street, New York, NY 10018. Attn. Sales Department. Phone: 1-800-221-2647.

PINNACLE BOOKS and the Pinnacle logo Reg. U.S. Pat. & TM Off.

First Printing: April 2023
ISBN-13: 978-0-7860-5004-8
ISBN-13: 978-0-7860-5005-5 (eBook)

10 9 8 7 6 5 4 3 2 1

Printed in the United States of America

PROLOGUE

Helena, Montana
November 7, 1889

US Marshal Aaron Mackey did not look up from his paperwork when Billy Sunday entered his office.

"I've got something to tell you," his deputy said. "And you're not going to like it."

Mackey continued to review a report written by one of his deputies. He had grown used to getting bad news since becoming the federal marshal for the entire Montana Territory. He doubted the news would get any better once the territory officially became a state at midnight that same evening. "Sometimes I think this job is nothing but one bit of bad news after the other. What is it this time?"

His deputy's silence caused Mackey to finally look up from the report. Billy was not just one of his deputies. He was his best friend and he had always been a direct man. Hesitation had never come easy to him.

And judging by the look on his face, the news was worse than usual. "What happened?"

"I'll tell you," Billy cautioned, "but I need you to promise me something first. I want you to promise you won't get mad like you do."

Mackey set the report to the side and pushed himself away from the desk. "You know I don't make promises until I know the details." He noticed the papers his friend was holding. They looked like official documents. "What is it?"

Sunday handed the papers over to him. "I can't read it, but Judge Hitchcock's clerk already told me what it says. The judge thought you should hear it from me first. Governor Owen has just pardoned Ed Zimmerman and Rob Brunet."

"He *what*?" Mackey snatched the papers from him and began to read. "That's impossible."

But as Mackey read the document, he saw his deputy was right. Governor Charles Mannes Owen had granted both outlaws a full pardon.

Mackey rose from his seat without realizing it. "He can't do that. Today's his last day in office. Jeremiah's got Zimmerman and Brunet dead to rights. I've already sworn out warrants on them. Halstead is about to arrest them, if he hasn't already grabbed them."

Billy held up his hands. "Easy, Aaron. You promised you wouldn't get mad, remember?"

Mackey read the pardon a second time, hoping he had missed a word or phrase that might prove him wrong. That this was just a misunderstanding. But a second and third reading of the document proved he had read it right the first time.

Governor Owen's last act in office was to grant a pardon to the two most wanted men in the Montana Territory.

Mackey crumpled the document as he stormed out from behind his desk. Billy followed close behind him into the hallway and toward the governor's chambers.

Mackey walked past the clerk's desk without stopping

and pushed in the door to the governor's wood-paneled office.

Governor Owen was standing behind his ornate desk as he examined various documents. "Afternoon, Marshal. I take it you've come to bid me a fond farewell."

"Hardly." Mackey threw the crumpled proclamation on the desk. "What's this nonsense about you pardoning Zimmerman and Brunet?"

The governor was tall and balding. He had a weak chin and the pale skin of a man who spent most of his time indoors. "I don't see how my reasoning is any business of yours."

Mackey felt his temper begin to rise. "Considering I swore out a warrant for their arrest and one of my men is about to arrest them, I'd say that entitles me to an answer."

Owen continued flipping pages of the document he had been reading. "Which deputy would that be?" He snapped his fingers as if he remembered something. "That's right. Your man Halstead, isn't it? The same rabid dog you cut loose on the good people of Silver Cloud a few months back."

Mackey did not like hearing his men run down, especially by the likes of Owen. "Jeremiah's got nothing to do with your pardon."

"No, I suppose he doesn't." Owen placed the document he had been reading on his desk. "I granted pardons to Zimmerman and Brunet because it's my right and privilege to do so as the territorial governor of Montana. Need I remind you that I *am* still governor until the stroke of midnight tomorrow morning? I suggest you address me with some measure of respect."

Mackey watched Owen slide the document into a satchel. "Now, if that's all you've come to discuss, I'd like you to leave. I still have a great deal of work to do."

But Mackey was not going anywhere until he got some answers. "Zimmerman and Brunet are murderers. They've been wanted for years. Why pardon them now?"

Owen picked up another sheaf of papers. "I don't have to explain myself to you or anyone else. My decision is final and the matter decided."

"That's true for now," Mackey agreed, "but if you don't answer me today, you'll answer me tomorrow as a private citizen. And you can bet I won't be nearly as cordial then as I am right now."

"Aaron," Billy cautioned from the doorway. "Easy."

Mackey watched Owen's Adam's apple bob up and down as he swallowed hard. "Fine. If it'll get you to leave, I'll tell you. A concerned constituent brought Zimmerman and Brunet's cases to my attention. I reviewed their records and decided they deserved to be pardoned for their crimes as they seem to have begun to do some good. They've moved into a forsaken town, Hard Scrabble Township, and are going to great pains to bring it back to life. They've even changed the name of the place to Valhalla. I decided they've proven themselves worthy of a second chance, as is my privilege as governor to do."

Mackey leaned on the governor's desk. "What concerned constituent, Charlie?"

Owen backed away from the desk. "I fail to see how that's any of your business."

Mackey continued to glare at him until he answered, "Zimmerman and Brunet's attorney."

Mackey's jaw tightened. "What's his name? I'll find out anyway when I lean on your clerk as soon as you're gone."

"Mark Mannes," Owen told him. "He represents both Zimmerman and Brunet."

Mackey pushed himself off the desk and slowly rose to his full height. Now it was beginning to make sense. "Mark

Mannes. Your middle name is Mannes. He's a relative of yours, isn't he?"

"He happens to be my cousin," the governor confirmed. "And before you embarrass yourself by making any charges about corruption, I want you to consider one important detail, Marshal. My cousin is an attorney who would stand to make a great deal of money defending Zimmerman and Brunet against these charges in a court of law. My pardon only serves to take money out of his pocket, not line it. He obviously felt a pardon was the proper course of action and I agreed with him based on the facts I had at hand."

Mackey folded his arms across his chest before he took a swing at him. "And you made it your last official act, so no one had the time to challenge it."

"As governor, no one has the right to challenge it, whether it was my first act in office or my last. You know that."

Mackey knew it but did not like it. "Is this really how you want to be remembered, Charlie? As the man who let two killers go free because his cousin asked him to?"

Owen laughed. "I doubt I'll be remembered at all once the new governor is sworn in tomorrow. This is the West, Aaron, and people in these parts have short memories. They have statehood now and have elected someone else to be their first governor. Montana is Joe Toole's problem now, not mine. You can take this up with him tomorrow if you wish, not that it'll do you any good."

Mackey knew he was right, which galled him most of all. "You'll be known as a man who cuts deals for his family at the expense of the people."

"Nepotism in politics?" He laughed. "Perish the thought. Frontiers are built on family, Aaron, and last I checked, Montana is still a frontier land. We won't immediately become a state just because some old men back in Washington have decided to admit us to the Union. Land isn't always settled by nice people. It takes grit and determination to make a life out here, and I can't think of anyone grittier and more determined than the likes of Zimmerman and Brunet. You say they're murderers and thieves. You're probably right, but they're also building a new town in the middle of nowhere. I'd rather have them put the darker aspects of their nature to work for Montana's benefit rather than seeing them rot behind bars or swing at the end of a hangman's rope. If Zimmerman and Brunet are to die, I say let them do so while doing something for Montana instead of dying simply because you and your wild, half-breed deputy hold them in contempt."

Mackey's eyes narrowed.

"Aaron," Billy cautioned from the doorway. "He's still the governor."

Owen smiled. "Listen to your Moorish friend, Marshal. He's right, you know. And don't think anything changes once I'm out of office. I've heard all about your barnyard tactics. The both of you. Mackey and Sunday, the saviors of Dover Station. I've never allowed myself to be intimidated before and I have no intention of starting now. I may not be governor anymore, but I still have many friends in Washington and throughout Montana. Friends who won't be happy if you lay one finger on me. Now, tomorrow, or ever."

Mackey kept his arms folded across his chest. Owen had all the answers. And, unfortunately, he was right.

Governor Owen slid another document into his satchel. "Don't look so glum, boys. My pardon only extends to Zimmerman and Brunet's past offenses. It doesn't offer protection under the law for any crimes they might commit in the future. I have no doubt you'll have good, legal reasons for arresting them soon." He flipped the cover over his satchel shut. "Now, if you'll both be kind enough to excuse me, I still have quite a bit of work to tend to before I surrender this office."

Mackey had never thought much of the politician, but he had not thought him capable of turning murderers free. Jeremiah Halstead already had Zimmerman and Brunet dead to rights. He did not like the idea of letting them go now in the hope of getting a better grip on them later.

He did not like the idea of being so powerless to stop him. "You're going to pay for this, Charlie. You and your cousin."

Owen rested his hands on the back of his chair. "If I didn't know better, I might take that as a threat."

"Take it however you want," Mackey said as he began to leave. "You'd just better hope I can get a telegram to Halstead before he finds Zimmerman. He's liable to kill him and Brunet on sight."

"If he does," Owen called after him, "I'll see to it that he's arrested and tried for murder! Do you hear me, Mackey? For murder!"

The governor's threat echoed through the hall as Billy followed Mackey outside.

Billy said, "Did he call me a Moor? What's a Moor?"

"Not now," Mackey told him. He had an important telegram to send and time was of the essence.

CHAPTER 1

Battle Brook, Montana
Several weeks later

Jeremiah Halstead saw the glint of a blade as the man slashed out at him from the alley.

Halstead fell back against the building, grabbing his attacker's wrist before he could plunge the blade into his neck.

Halstead could have ended it quickly had he been able to reach one of his pistols, but he did not dare weaken his grip on the man's wrist.

The stench of rot and filth from his attacker almost made him gag.

"I heard you're tough to kill." The man's voice strained as he put his weight behind the knife. "This won't hurt but a little and then it'll be over. I'll get my money and you'll get peace. That ain't so bad, is it?"

Halstead tried to bring a knee up into the man's ribs but was too close for maximum impact.

The assailant responded with a knee of his own that hit Halstead's inner thigh instead of his groin. The attempt had put the man off balance enough for Halstead to shove the man against the building, pinning his knife hand against the wall.

The stranger delivered a hard left hook that knocked Halstead back, breaking his grip on the knife. The man charged before Halstead could grab one of his guns.

The long blade of the bowie knife raked across his chest but failed to cut through the thick cowhide of his vest.

Halstead jumped backward to dodge the next slashing arc meant for his neck. A third thrust aimed at his stomach caused him to jump to his left as he pulled his Colt from the cross draw holster on his left side.

His gun fired as he slammed the stranger in the temple with his pistol. The man tumbled into the thoroughfare.

Halstead jumped down from the boardwalk and kicked the knife out of his attacker's hand, though he was clearly dead. The back of his head had been ruined by the discharge of Halstead's gun.

The dead man's face was as unfamiliar as all the others who had come before him. Desperate men looking to claim the bounty Ed Zimmerman had placed on his life. Ten thousand dollars was the latest rumor. Some said more, many said less.

The correct amount did not matter, for Halstead had given each man lead instead of gold for his trouble.

Halstead tried to catch his breath as he looked around the darkened street for anyone else looking to try their hand at earning the outlaw bounty. They usually came in pairs. Flickering oil lamps along the boardwalk offered just enough light to show Battle Brook was as deserted as it usually was at that time of the morning. Even the saloons were quiet now, given that sunrise was just a little over an hour away.

Yet in the silence of the slumbering town, he heard a boardwalk plank creak behind him.

Halstead turned as he dropped to a knee and raised his pistol. A bullet struck the rail of a hitching post several feet from his head. A stocky man half in shadow cursed and was about to fire again when Halstead cut loose with three shots from his Thunderer.

Each bullet struck the man in the chest. He fell to his knees as he feebly pawed at the holes through his middle.

Halstead kept his Colt trained on him as he rose and stepped up onto the boardwalk. The dying man looked to be in his late thirties and had the sturdy build of a farmer. His blondish beard had grown unevenly. His coat was patched in several places and the shirt beneath it looked threadbare. Another stranger.

Halstead saw a rectangle of pale light spill out onto the boardwalk from the jail farther up Main Street. His partner, Joshua Sandborne, rushed outside in his long underwear, his Winchester rifle at the ready. Halstead figured the gunshots must have woken him.

Sandborne lowered his rifle when he saw Halstead standing over the dying man.

The farmer, still on his knees, held up a pair of bloody hands to Halstead. "You shot me."

"You shot first." Halstead kept his Colt trained down on him. "Zimmerman send you?"

"Not directly." He looked down at his red hands, as if seeing them for the first time. "Good Lord, I'm dying."

Halstead saw no reason to ease his passing. "Yeah, you are. You got a name?"

"Glenn." He was struggling to breathe now. His lungs likely beginning to fill with fluid. Every beat of his heart only brought him closer to death. "Archer Glenn out of Deadwood."

The name meant nothing to Halstead, but their names never did. He placed a boot on Glenn's pistol and kicked it off the boardwalk. "Got any kin you want me to write to on your behalf, Archer Glenn?"

The dying farmer shook his head as he squinted up at Halstead. At the man who had taken his life. "I was supposed to get ten thousand dollars for you."

Halstead was glad to disappoint him. "You never had a chance."

Glenn coughed, then shuddered. "Never thought I'd meet my end by a no-good half-breed like you."

Halstead grinned at the insult. He was half-Anglo, half-Mexican but doubted Glenn would appreciate the difference. "We all die from something."

He watched another shudder go through Glenn before he pitched over on his left side. After a final wet rattle of breath, he died.

Halstead kept his pistol aimed down at him until the man's eyes grew vacant. He lowered the gun when it was clear Glenn was dead.

Halstead looked at Sandborne. "His name was Archer Glenn. A mighty fancy name. Shame to see it go to waste."

Sandborne kept his rifle low as he looked over the street. "How many were there this time?"

"Just two." Halstead opened the cylinder of his Colt. "The other one's back there in the street. He jumped me from the alley. Had a knife."

Sandborne stepped down into the street and checked the man who had fallen into the thoroughfare. "Mr. Fitzgerald's going to be happy for the business, but not the mess. You tagged this one pretty good to the back of the head."

Halstead knew Battle Brook's new undertaker was his biggest supporter. He had certainly kept the man busy. "Stopping men like that is our job, just as it's his job to bury them."

He plucked the spent bullets from the cylinder and

dumped them out on Glenn's corpse. "This one here said he was from Deadwood. Stands to reason his partner is from there, too."

"Guess that doesn't matter now." Sandborne picked up the dead man's bowie knife and carried it over to Halstead. It would bring a good price at the general store when he decided to sell it. "You hurt?"

"No." Halstead fed three fresh bullets from his gun belt into the Colt, snapped the cylinder shut, and slid the pistol back into the holster on his left side. "After Fitzgerald picks up these bodies, head over to the telegraph office and send word to Deadwood." He knew words were not Sandborne's strong suit, so he added, "Have the clerk help you write it."

"I will." Sandborne frowned as he looked down at the dead man on the boardwalk. "I thought this bounty business would've played itself out by now, but these boys just keep coming."

"And dying." Halstead decided he had allowed the dead men to take up too much of his time. He was late for his daily appointment but could still make it in time if he hurried. "I'll pass Mr. Fitzgerald's place on my way to the livery and tell him to haul these two out of here. Folks will be waking up soon and I don't want them seeing this mess first thing in the morning. Starts the day off on the wrong footing."

Sandborne watched him begin to leave. "You mean you're still going to take your ride? Even after all this?"

Halstead stopped. "They're as dead as they're gonna get, Joshua. Whether I'm here or not won't change that. Tell the mayor I'll write up a report when I get back. I know how he loves to have things documented properly."

Sandborne had learned the futility of arguing with Halstead once his mind was made up. He rested the butt of his rifle on his hip as he looked over the quiet street. "Battle

Brook sure is a funny place. I can remember when everyone would've run out in their nightclothes to see what the shooting was about. Now, they just sleep through it like it was nothing."

Halstead started walking toward the livery to fetch his horse. "Guess folks can get used to just about anything if it happens often enough."

Sandborne called after him, "If that's true, I sure wish you'd get used to Zimmerman being a free man."

Halstead did not bother answering. Sandborne should have known better than to expect the impossible.

CHAPTER 2

Jeremiah Halstead stood alone on the hill that overlooked the reborn town of Valhalla, Montana. By the time he had ridden there, ribbons of deep pink and blue had already begun to fan out across the eastern sky behind distant mountains.

Another day was about to begin. Another day that Edward Zimmerman would spend as a free man. As far as Halstead was concerned, it was one day too many.

The power of nature's glory was lost on Halstead, for he had not come to witness beauty. He had come to hold his daily vigil for those who would never enjoy another sunrise. The many victims of former outlaws Ed Zimmerman and Rob Brunet. The outlaws who not only called Valhalla home but had set about making the town a thing of their own creation.

According to the maps, the spot Halstead had chosen was legally on the edge of Battle Brook's jurisdiction. But his ongoing pursuit of Zimmerman had little regard for boundaries.

Halstead had chosen the spot for a more practical reason. It was just out of rifle range from the town, yet close enough to be seen by anyone who cared to look. And he knew Zimmerman always had someone watching. He guarded his freedom as jealously as he guarded the newfound power Valhalla had given him.

Being seen was part of Halstead's plan. He wanted Zimmerman to awake each morning knowing Halstead had not forgotten him or the crimes he had committed. Come rain or shine, wind or snow, Halstead had not missed a day on that hill in the weeks since Zimmerman had received his pardon. His attorney might have gotten his cousin, the governor, to free him from prison, but nothing would free him from Halstead's justice except death.

Halstead had spent many sleepless nights in bed with Abby wondering why he should not just ride into town and call Zimmerman out. Face him down with fists or guns. Halstead knew he could beat him with either, assuming it was a fair fight.

But men like Zimmerman never fought fair. Fighting dirty was why he and Rob Brunet were still breathing free air instead of rotting in a cell while they waited for the hangman to call their name.

Halstead took cold comfort in the knowledge that his daily presence on the hill galled Zimmerman's pride something awful. He was practically daring the former outlaw to try to kill him by making himself such an easy, predictable target. Halstead rode to the hill each morning hoping that Zimmerman would send some men to ambush him. That one of Valhalla's loyal citizens might try to collect the bounty their leader had placed on Halstead almost a year before.

But no one had come yet. He had heard from travelers between the two towns that Zimmerman would not allow it. No one in Valhalla disobeyed their leader and lived to tell the tale, so the stalemate continued.

And so did Halstead's vigil. Vengeance was expensive and had cost him a great deal.

For as he watched the morning sky begin to brighten, his mind drifted to his love for Abigail Newman. The woman who had managed to capture whatever still remained of his soul. The woman who had set her own safety aside to leave the comfort of Helena only to come back to Battle Brook to be with him.

He watched the sky take on the same deep blue of her eyes. The thin streak of white from the rising sun was the color of her skin. The deep red of the horizon reminded him of her lips, and he found himself wishing he was with her in their room right now.

He wished he was still the man she thought he was. The kind of man she needed him to be.

But Halstead knew part of that man he had once been had died the moment he was forced to allow Zimmerman to go free. Abby had insisted on remaining with him in Battle Brook even though she had no reason to stay. She often told him he was a better man than he thought. That he was strong and honest and good and everything she could ever want in a man in this world or the next.

But Halstead knew better. Any qualities she saw in him had been long submerged in a pot of boiling water he could only describe as hate.

Hate that had been born years before and over a thousand miles away. Hate for men like Zimmerman and their cunning. Hate for his own inability to stop them. Hate for allowing such men to go free despite all the men they had killed and the lives they had ruined.

Hate for himself for not being strong enough to kill Zimmerman when he'd had the chance.

He felt his old resentment return as he remembered the look of smug satisfaction on Mannes's face as the lawyer presented Halstead with Zimmerman's pardon from his cousin, the governor. As if words on a piece of paper could rewrite what was right and what was wrong. As if the ink of a governor's signature could wash away a man's sins. As if the dead could be forgotten with the casual stroke of a pen.

The law books might say differently but in Jeremiah Halstead's book, Zimmerman and Brunet still owed a debt. A debt Marshal Aaron Mackey in Helena expected him to collect. A debt Halstead still owed to Zimmerman's many victims.

Halstead tugged his hat lower to shield his eyes from the light of the rising sun as it began to shine down on the growing town of Valhalla. Zimmerman had used the money he had stolen from countless people and from the surrounding mines to transform the forgotten township of Hard Scrabble into a place that would soon rival Battle Brook in size and population.

And Halstead knew that as Valhalla grew, so would Zimmerman's influence throughout the new state of Montana. Mannes and Cal Hubbard's Valhalla Bank and Trust would see to that. Soon, Zimmerman's reach would extend far beyond the valley and he would become an important man. Too important for even a federal deputy marshal to touch.

Halstead could not allow all that to happen. The dead deserved better. Jack McBride, the late sheriff who had been killed during Zimmerman's robbery of the Bank of Battle Brook, deserved better. So did all the countless, unnamed others who had lost their lives and fortunes to Zimmerman's murderous greed.

Every new building erected in Valhalla was built on a foundation of blood and corruption. Every success a mockery of any notion of right and wrong.

When his hands began to ache, Halstead realized he had balled them into fists against his sides. He forced them open again. There would be a time and place where his anger might prove useful, but today was not that day. Battle Brook was still without a proper lawman and, for now, Halstead and Sandborne were all that stood between the town and Zimmerman's ambition.

And as the rays of the rising sun failed to warm him, Halstead renewed his daily vow to the dead that he would do everything in his power to stop Zimmerman by any means necessary. It was not much, but it would have to be enough for now.

Knowing one of Zimmerman's watchmen must have spotted him by now, Halstead walked back to the shrub where he had tethered his horse, Col, and climbed into the saddle. He had left Sandborne quite a mess back in Battle Brook. It was time to tend to it and leave Zimmerman for another time.

Chapter 3

Edward Zimmerman woke when he heard someone knocking at his door.

The former outlaw threw aside the heavy blankets and swung his legs over the edge of his bed. He stretched his long arms and basked in the warm sunlight streaming through the cracked panes of his bedroom windows. He was free and had an official decree from the governor to prove it to any man who doubted it.

"What is it?" he called out to the man who had knocked. He never closed the front door of the ramshackle house as a sign of the power he enjoyed over the town. There was no point in closing it because no one would dare enter without permission. Only the old heathen who tended to Brunet's wounds was allowed to clean the place and bring him a bowl of warm water for his daily shave.

"It's just me, sir," a young voice responded. "Randy. You told me you wanted me to wake you at first light."

Sir. Zimmerman closed his eyes, warmed as much by the title of respect as by the morning sun. He had insisted that all his men called him "sir" upon his return to Valhalla following his pardon. Randy was one of the new watchmen he had appointed to keep an eye on the town at night. Another group of young men kept watch during the day.

And while they were all young men eager to impress him, Randy had proven to be the most obliging.

"Thank you, Randy," Zimmerman answered. "Any sign of our mockingbird this morning?"

"Yes, sir," Randy reported. "He was right there in the open, same as yesterday and the day before. Just standing like an old scarecrow before he ups and rides away."

Zimmerman smiled at the news. Randy's description of Halstead was more accurate than he realized. Travelers between Valhalla and Battle Brook had told him how Halstead had become a different man since the governor's pardon. His spies reported that Halstead was not the same man. He was broken somehow. He had never been affable but had become distant and grim. He had taken to riding out to that hill each daybreak since as his way of making a point. To remind Zimmerman that he was still close. That he had not forgotten.

Zimmerman often wondered if Halstead realized he only rode back to Battle Brook each day because he had allowed him to do so.

The former outlaw stood up and stretched his arms and legs before pulling on a fresh shirt from his dresser. The new laundry that had opened the previous month did wonders for his clothes. Free of charge, of course. A sign of respect.

"Thanks for letting me know. Any trouble during the night?"

"No, sir," Randy reported, "but you've got a couple of men here to see you. Spotted them myself just after sunrise as they approached the town from the north. They're over in The Iron Horse right now, waiting for you."

The north? That was rough country. "Who are they? What do they want?"

"They told me they're the Riker boys. Said that you sent

for them. They're over at The Iron Horse right now, like I said. Blinky's keeping an eye on them."

Zimmerman had not expected the Riker brothers of Texas to be in the valley until next week at the earliest. He did not know what to make of their early arrival but would look forward to finding out.

"Thank you for telling me. Any other strange events?"

"No, sir. The town was quiet. Hardly a peep out of anyone, just how you like it."

Yes, Zimmerman thought. The people of Valhalla knew better than to defy him. Many of them were newcomers who had arrived looking to make their fortune in a new town. Outlaws and misfits, mostly, along with a healthy number of civilians to balance things out.

Those who agreed to live by the rules Zimmerman had set forth were allowed to stay and prosper. Those who refused were thrown out on their ear. He reserved his harshest punishment for those who intentionally disobeyed him. They were dealt with in a harsh and public manner.

It had been rough going when he first assumed control of the town upon his return, but the people soon fell in line. It was almost two weeks since he was forced to beat a man to death.

"That's a fine report, Randy." Zimmerman pulled on his pants and slipped his feet into his boots. "You may go now. Job well done."

He enjoyed giving compliments to his men almost as much as he enjoyed receiving them. His time riding with Darabont had taught him the value of tempering his rule with a certain degree of kindness. Everyone knew he was in charge. There was no need to remind them of it every time he opened his mouth.

But he was surprised when Randy persisted. "Can I ask you a question, Mr. Zimmerman?"

He did not encourage questions from his men, but he'd had a good night's sleep and was in a benevolent mood. He stood up and pressed his feet further into his boots. "You may."

"It's just that me and some of the other fellas were wondering why you don't just let us shoot Halstead for you? Seeing him perched on that hill like a buzzard each morning is downright unsettling. It's kinda like he's thumbing his nose at you. At this whole town and everyone in it. It just ain't right, sir. I sure wish you'd let us do something about it."

Zimmerman started for the door as anger surged through his body. But he quickly remembered Darabont's lesson that showing emotion was a sign of weakness. A true leader must always be seen to be above such things. To be better than those who followed him.

But Zimmerman knew men only followed if they were led. He also knew that silence could also be the loudest weapon when applied correctly, which was why he remained silent as he slowly stepped out of the bedroom and into the parlor.

Zimmerman was broader and taller than most men in Valhalla. Since his return, he had taken to shaving each morning to give himself a separate, cleaner appearance from the others.

But Randy, still standing in the doorway, was neither tall nor broad. He was ten years younger than Zimmerman, which put him at about twenty. He began to tremble and swallowed hard at his leader's slow approach.

Randy had backed all the way out onto the edge of the porch by the time Zimmerman reached the door. He clearly had realized his mistake. He wanted to run but was unable to look away.

Zimmerman drank in the young man's fear. He always

had taken great pleasure in seeing terror take hold in another man's eyes. It was one of the few habits of his outlaw days that he retained.

The boy flinched when Zimmerman finally said, "Are you questioning me, Randy? Do you doubt my orders? My wisdom?"

"N-n-never, Mr. Zimmerman," the boy stammered as he continued to back away. "It's really none of my business. I should've kept my big mouth shut. I didn't mean any offense."

"Offense?" The former outlaw threw back his head and laughed, though there was no humor in it. "You can't offend me, boy. You're not important enough to offend me, no more than Jeremiah Halstead is man enough to scare me."

Randy stumbled off the porch and almost tripped over his feet. "I never thought otherwise, sir."

Zimmerman kept walking toward him as fast as Randy backed away. "I haven't sent anyone to kill Halstead because I don't want him dead. I want him to live. I want him to see this town grow and thrive in the full knowledge that there isn't anything he can do to stop it. I want him to live so I can turn his own weapons against him."

Zimmerman picked up his pace. "Now do you understand, Randy? Does my decision sit well with you?"

The youth threw up his hands as he continued to withdraw farther across the street. "I don't need to understand anything, sir. I just need to do what I'm told. What you tell me to do."

Zimmerman was aware that some of the people on their way to work had stopped to watch them. *Good. Let them see.*

"Well, that's a relief. I'm so glad you agree. I don't know how I could sleep at night if I thought you didn't like one of my decisions. My whiskey would turn to vinegar and my cigar to ashes if I didn't have your approval. It would just about ruin my whole day. And you don't want to ruin my day, do you, Randy?"

"No, sir." The boy kept stepping backward. "I wouldn't. I would never."

Zimmerman continued to stalk the youngster, driving him back with the sheer force of his being until the boy bumped against the railing of the boardwalk at the far end of the thoroughfare. He felt the eyes of the townspeople and workers and knew they were watching. That was good. *They would remember. They would see.*

Randy cringed when Zimmerman bent to speak directly in his ear. "Thinking is for adults, Randy. For your betters. Do you understand?"

The boy nodded quickly. He was on the verge of tears.

"Don't ever question me again. Not to me. Not to anyone, not even to yourself. If you do, you'll defy me. You remember what happened to that drunk Meachum. You've seen what happens to people who defy me."

Randy choking back a sob. "Yes, sir. I do, sir. It won't happen again."

With the boy sufficiently cowed, Zimmerman withdrew to his full height and patted him on the shoulder. "Good boy. You'd best get yourself something to eat and rest. We want you ready for the night to come, don't we? No falling asleep at your post. We both remember what happened to the last man who couldn't stay awake, don't we?"

"Yes, sir. I'll never forget it." Randy continued to sputter gratitude as he slid away, putting as much distance between himself and Zimmerman as he could manage without showing any hint of disrespect.

Zimmerman met the eyes of the few people who continued

to look at him. Most had ducked their heads and gone about their business of making something of the town.

But a few of the newcomers dared to look at him longer than he deemed proper. His mild display of power had concerned them. He would make a point of dealing with each of them later in his own way.

"Show's over, folks," he bellowed to them. "Time to get back to work. This town won't build itself."

The stragglers who had remained quickly scattered, except for two strangers standing in front of The Iron Horse Saloon. Each man was tall and broad, though any resemblance ended there. One had long gray hair and an untamed beard. His slouch hat had lost its shape and color to sweat and the weather long ago. His long coat was faded and filthy. The man next to him sported a black mustache and his brown coat was in better condition than that of his companion.

He took them to be the Riker boys Randy had told him about. He made a point of not acknowledging their presence. He had sent for them, not the other way around. He would meet them when he was ready. Perhaps after his shave. Perhaps he would make them wait simply because he could. He controlled everything in Valhalla, including the time.

As Zimmerman walked back to his house, he was pleased to see the people on the street quicken their pace as he approached. Everyone in town always needed to look busy during the day or risk his displeasure.

That was true power. Leading outlaws was easy when compared to getting civilians to do what he wanted and getting them to do it freely. It was an art that took considerable skill. A skill he would need if he hoped to have influence beyond Valhalla and Battle Brook. And not the kind of influence that could make him a senator or even a governor. Controlling senators and governors was much more to his liking.

As he entered the crooked house he called home, Zimmerman was pleased to see the steaming bowl of water waiting for him. Brunet's Indian caretaker had brought it in while Zimmerman was teaching Randy a lesson.

As he pulled off his shirt and began to lather up the shaving cream, he decided it was a shame that Darabont had not lived long enough to see Valhalla. To see how the seed of an idea he planted in Zimmerman's mind years before had since taken root.

And while Darabont's ambitions of an outlaw Eden had been his ruin at the hands of Aaron Mackey, Zimmerman had learned a great deal from his mentor's failures. He would never fall beneath a lawman's gun again. In fact, he already had a plan to turn that gun on the very man who held it. Jeremiah Halstead.

"Valhalla." Zimmerman whispered the word as if it was a prayer. The stirring sounds of hammering and sawing and the shouts of work crews that began to rise outside sounded like a hymn. And this town was his sanctuary, built in his own image and by his own design.

He dabbed the brush in the shaving soap and began to apply it to his face. Once Halstead was disgraced and gone, Battle Brook would soon fall under his control. The Riker brothers would play an important role in making his dream a reality.

He would allow Halstead to live just long enough to see the inevitability of his success. His cunning—combined with Cal Hubbard's bank and Mark Mannes's legal maneuvering—would allow him to stand with men like Morgan, Rice, and Vanderbilt. Edward Zimmerman would show the world how a true Westerner did things. He would be a new man for a new time.

Once he had applied a thick layer of cream on his face, he picked up the straight razor and admired it for a moment. The same blade that would shave him could also be used to cut a man's throat. A tool that could also be used as a weapon. There was value in versatility here in the wilderness. And before he was through, this country would learn a Zimmerman blade was most versatile indeed.

"Valhalla." He smiled at his own reflection and used the razor to scrape away his stubble.

CHAPTER 4

Randy managed to hold back his tears until he reached the back of the laundry, where he finally allowed himself to sink to the ground. He drew up his knees close to his chest and wept quietly into his arms as his fear overflowed.

He was embarrassed by the way Zimmerman had treated him like a dog in front of the entire town. He was terrified over what Zimmerman might have done to him for being stupid enough to question him. And he was relieved that he had been allowed to leave with his life.

Randy was so proud of himself the day Zimmerman chose him to become one of the new watchmen in town. It was a position he cherished, for it was the first hint of responsibility he ever knew in his young life. Meachum, the man Randy had replaced, had fallen asleep at his post. Randy knew this because he was the one who found him and reported him to the constables. He stood by and watched while Zimmerman personally beat the man to death in front of the entire town.

Randy was one of the men chosen to carry the body away from town, though Mr. Zimmerman had forbidden them from burying him. He remembered how the buzzards picked at the remains for days. His stomach still turned whenever he saw one of the menacing birds.

Each time he blinked, he saw Zimmerman's terrible glare while he made an example of him. He thought it would be the last thing he saw in this world. All he did was ask a simple question.

Randy had come to Montana to make a name for himself in this world. There was nothing for him on his father's farm back in Kansas except endless, backbreaking labor and thankless toil. Here, he had become someone.

Other towns had sheriffs and marshals. Valhalla was different. New. It had watchmen and constables. Watchmen kept the town and its people safe while others slept. It was an important position because Mr. Zimmerman deemed it important. That meant Randy was important, too. He was honored to have been chosen to wake Mr. Zimmerman each morning. He always delivered his first report each morning. Randy even began to allow himself to hope he might become a constable one day.

Now he had put his dreams at risk over a stupid question he had not needed to ask. He should have kept his mouth shut and been happy that Mr. Zimmerman had been pleased with his work. He was only trying to help. To show Mr. Zimmerman he was worthy of doing more.

"Randy? You back here?"

He ran his sleeve across his face when Mule Wilson and Hec Garvey stepped into the yard.

Mule might only be eighteen, the same age as Randy, but he lived up to his nickname. He was already well over six feet tall, wide, and muscular. He was quiet when he first arrived in Valhalla, but people's deference to his size and strength had turned him into a bully.

Mule bent at the waist to take a closer look at him. "You ain't crying, are you?"

Randy dared not admit that he had. There was no place

for the weak in Valhalla. "My stomach's cramping up on me is all."

Hec Garvey laughed. "Mine would be, too, if Mr. Zimmerman yelled at me like that."

At twenty, Garvey was the oldest and most worldly of the three. His red hair and freckles had made him a target for ceaseless teasing from some of the others. Mr. Zimmerman forbade fighting within town limits, so Hec had to settle his scores outside of town. He never let an insult slide, and any man who dared mock him paid dearly for the insult. The jokes quickly stopped, especially after he was named a watchman.

Hec often defied Mr. Zimmerman's orders by sneaking out of town on his day off to visit Battle Brook. Randy knew the boss would skin him alive if he caught him, but Hec prided himself on his rebellious nature.

"I'm not laughing at you," Hec explained. "I would've wet myself on the spot if I was you."

Randy found no comfort in that. "I thought he was going to kill me. All because I asked him why he didn't let us ride out to that hill one morning and take care of Halstead for him."

Mule and Hec traded glances, with Hec saying, "He got mad at you for that?"

Randy choked down a sob. "I was just trying to show him I wasn't just some dumb kid staring off into space all night."

"Can't blame you for that," Mule said. "Did he tell you why he lets Halstead get away with it?"

"No. He just told me I'm not paid to think."

Hec said, "A man paid to watch a town in the dead of night's got to spend his time thinking of something or else he'll fall asleep and get himself beaten to death.

There's no shame in what you did, Randy, no matter what Mr. Zimmerman might say."

Randy had not expected such support from his friends. He wondered if Hec might be looking to goad him into saying something bad about Mr. Zimmerman. Hec was a cunning sort and not above using Randy's misfortune to his own advantage.

But misery loved company, and Randy was in no position to be choosy. "You really think so?"

"I know so," Hec said. "It also just so happens that I've been thinking the same thing myself. It's like Halstead's just standing over on that hill laughing at us each morning. Doesn't seem natural. In fact, it's downright insulting, and you boys know how much I hate an insult."

Mule said, "You heard what the boss told Randy. It's none of our business."

Hec hooked his thumbs into the edge of his trousers. "That doesn't mean we can't make it our business. Mule, why don't you help Randy here get back on his feet. I hate seeing a good man sitting on the ground like that old squaw who tends to Brunet."

Mule offered Randy his thick hand and easily pulled him up.

"Dust yourself off and tuck in your shirt," Hec told Randy. "You're a Valhalla watchman, by God, not a common laborer. Put some pride in your appearance and people will treat you different, even Mr. Zimmerman."

Randy felt a bit better after he tucked in his shirt. "Thanks for listening to me, boys. Let's go get something to eat. I'm hungry."

But Hec stopped him. "What if you were right just now?"

"He's right about getting something to eat," Mule said. "I'm starving."

Hec frowned. "Not that. I'm talking about what Randy said to Zimmerman about teaching Halstead a lesson."

Randy was embarrassed for even thinking it, much less saying it out loud. He had not only seen Jeremiah Halstead from the hill but had heard about his reputation. Everyone in Valhalla had, even though gossip was technically against Mr. Zimmerman's rules.

"That was just a dumb idea I had that's best forgotten," Randy admitted. "Halstead's a known killer. He's fast, too. Totes two Colts. One in a cross draw holster on his belly and the other on his hip. He'd dust the three of us before we even thought about shooting him."

Hec did not seem so sure. "You boys know how I like to sneak over to Battle Brook on my day off. I've seen Halstead up close plenty of times and he ain't nearly the pistoleer you make him out to be."

"But we ain't pistoleers of any kind," Mule reminded him. "Even if the stories about him are all lies, he's more of a killer than the three of us put together. Let's talk about this over breakfast, Hec. I want to get some of Mabel's biscuits before they're all gone."

But Hec remained where he was, causing the others to remain as well. "Halstead's got something none of us have. A reputation. So does Zimmerman, and so do the constables here in town. Tote, Gordo, and the others. I've been thinking a lot about that since getting this job. About how I could get myself a reputation, I mean. I've been thinking that maybe it's time for the three of us to make a name for ourselves."

Perhaps it was because of his growling stomach, but Randy was unsure about what Hec was getting at. "What are you talking about?"

Hec explained. "Do you think Zimmerman got to be who he was by waiting around for someone to give him orders? Do you think Tote or Gordo or the rest of those boys got themselves picked to be outlaws? Halstead sure didn't get his reputation out of thin air. A man doesn't get himself known by accident or luck. He gets a reputation by making it himself. And I don't see why the three of us should think we're any different."

Mule spoke before Randy had the chance. "I'm more interested in having a bed and a roof over my head than a reputation. Breakfast and supper, too. I've heard enough talk for one morning, Hec. I'm hungry."

Randy was about to agree with Mule when Hec said, "We only have food and a place to sleep because Zimmerman gave them to us. And he can take them away whenever he chooses. I'm talking about how we should have all those things for ourselves. On our own terms." He leaned in closer and lowered his voice. "I'm saying Halstead can be our way to set ourselves apart from everyone else in Valhalla."

Randy might not have been as worldly as Hec, but even he knew such talk was dangerous. "Halstead's a killer, Hec. Going up against the likes of him would be crazy, even if it was three against one."

"But I'm not talking about going up against him," Hec explained. "I'm not even talking about killing anyone because I've got it worked out so we won't have to. I've spent a fair amount of time in Battle Brook watching where Halstead goes and who he goes with. I've got a way we can hurt the man and put ourselves in Mr. Zimmerman's good graces without even firing a shot."

Mule seemed to forget about his hunger for the moment. "How?"

The freckles on Hec's face bunched up when he smiled. "If you boys will hear me out, I'll be glad to tell you. Here's a hint. It's somewhere that has even better biscuits than Mabel's. A fancy place in Battle Brook called The Standard Hotel."

Randy did not want to, but he listened to Hec's plan.

And by the time his friend was done explaining himself, the three young men were convinced it just might work.

CHAPTER 5

Although he was only twenty-five, Joshua Sandborne imagined he was already too old to ever be considered a learned man. But he always enjoyed learning new things.

He especially liked looking up new words he heard in the dictionary Katherine Mackey had sent back with Abby when she returned from Helena. He liked listening to people's conversations for new words, too, though he never considered it eavesdropping. A man could learn a lot about a place just by listening to idle chatter.

He had learned how to handle civilians by watching the way Aaron Mackey and Billy Sunday did it. They usually listened more than they spoke. When they were quiet, they watched a man closely to see if he was lying or telling the truth. There was an art to it that Sandborne hoped to master one day.

Sandborne figured Jeremiah Halstead must have spent a fair amount of time watching Mackey and Billy as well, which explained why he sat at his desk while Mayor Phil White got around to making his point. He had spent several minutes hovering around his meaning, like a bee deciding which flower to land on.

After several minutes of flattery, White got to it. "I know this might not be the most pleasant conversation we've ever had, Jeremiah, but in light of what happened this morning, I feel we need to set a few things straight."

Sandborne watched Halstead closely, for he knew Jeremiah did not like to dwell on the men he had killed.

"No sense in putting off the pain," Halstead said. "Just tell me what you've come to say and I'll tell you what I think."

The mayor of Battle Brook was a squat man whose natural countenance was one of permanent annoyance. He had a full head of white hair and a matching beard.

White began by saying, "First, I want you to know I've taken the liberty to write to Marshal Mackey in Helena. I've asked him to tell me when you and Deputy Sandborne might be moving on to handle other duties."

Sandborne had heard rumors that White and some other citizens thought it was time for Battle Brook to have some law of its own instead of a couple of federals filling in. Zimmerman's bounty on Halstead was beginning to make people nervous.

If Jeremiah was angry, he hid it well. "Did you send the marshal a letter or a telegram?"

"Both," the mayor admitted. "I even sent an emissary who happened to have business in Helena. Mackey refused to meet with him. He has not responded to my letters or telegrams either."

Sandborne was not entirely sure what an emissary was but would make a point of looking it up in Katherine's dictionary later.

But Jeremiah seemed to know what the word meant, which was all that mattered for the sake of this conversation. "Looks like he doesn't think much of you writing to him about such things. Sometimes silence is an answer."

The mayor licked his lips and cleared his throat like he

always did when he was nervous. "Yes, of course, but I'd still like to know when you boys will be moving on."

Sandborne watched Jeremiah take his hat from his desk and begin to examine it. He paid particular attention to the brim, something he often did when he was gathering his thoughts.

"I don't know Aaron Mackey's mind and neither do you," Halstead told the mayor. "He's good at telling people what he wants in no uncertain terms. I'm sure he'll get back to you in time. Now that we're a state, I'm sure he's busier than ever."

White scowled. "We're all busy. The good marshal does not have a monopoly on worries in these parts." White's chins waggled as he cleared his throat. "I speak for everyone in town when I say we're awfully grateful for all you've done for us since Jack McBride was killed. I don't know what might've happened to us if it hadn't been for the both of you. I'm personally indebted to you, but a fair number of my constituents feel the time has come for Battle Brook to have a lawman of our own."

"Sounds reasonable." Halstead slowly turned the hat in his hands. "No one's stopping you from hiring a sheriff. Deputy Sandborne and I will be happy to work with him."

Mayor White cleared his throat again. "Well, that's just it, Jeremiah. Battle Brook is growing, true, but we don't need three lawmen in a town this size. We need to stand on our own two feet. After all, we can't expect Marshal Mackey to be gracious enough to allow two of his best men to stay on here forever, can we? I'm sure he needs you elsewhere in the state."

Halstead picked some lint off the brim of his hat. "Sounds like that trouble I had this morning really spooked some folks."

The mayor showed a bit more grit than Sandborne had

expected from him. "So have all the others who've come to look for it. I believe the number is somewhere around ten or more."

"Nine," Halstead said, "including the two today."

White said, "And while I wouldn't go so far as to say we're frightened, I'd say 'concerned' would be a more accurate way to put it."

"I'm concerned, too, since I'm the one they're trying to kill." Halstead looked at him. "But you should remember I'm not the only man in Battle Brook with a price on his head."

The mayor's expression soured. "What's that supposed to mean?"

"It means that the second Sandborne and I ride out, Zimmerman and his bunch will swarm in and hang you from the balcony of The Standard Hotel. No one will lift a finger to stop him either."

Sandborne watched Mayor White sink back in his chair. "There's no need to be so vulgar, Jeremiah. This town has a right to defend itself on its own terms, and that includes dealing with the likes of Zimmerman, as we see fit. Battle Brook is our home and, like it or not, he is our neighbor. We must find a way to live with him. You don't."

"Assuming he lets you live at all." Halstead tossed his hat on the desk. Sandborne had heard that edge in Halstead's voice before and knew what happened next was usually not pretty.

Halstead went on. "You've got these sand flies buzzing in your ear about how reasonable Zimmerman can be. How he's a businessman now and can be reasoned with. That you can strike a bargain with him so nobody gets hurt and everybody wins."

"Some believe that's the case," White admitted, "and while I always want peace, I've never been a gullible man.

That's why it's so important for us to hire the right man to be our sheriff. A man who won't be afraid of anyone." He cleared his throat again. "That's why I've hired on a new sheriff. He comes with the highest recommendations."

Sandborne watched Halstead's dark eyes narrow. "Whose recommendations?"

"The honorable H. Calvin Hubbard, among others."

Halstead closed his eyes. "The man who ruined your bank a while back. Zimmerman's banker in Valhalla."

"Mr. Hubbard owns the Valhalla bank and kept the Bank of Battle Brook from going under. Some would say that means he's played as much a role in saving this town as you boys have."

Sandborne did not like the idea of following Hubbard's advice on anything, and Halstead clearly agreed. "Who did Hubbard tell you to hire?"

The mayor bristled at the idea he had been ordered to do anything. "A man out of El Paso named Emil Riker. He's due here in Battle Brook next week."

Sandborne thought Halstead looked like he had just been hit. "Emil Riker?"

Mayor White brightened. "I take it you've heard of him. That's good."

Halstead slowly rose from his chair. "I know him because his father put me in prison for three years."

Sandborne got up as well. He knew Halstead had spent some time in prison down in Texas, but they had never talked about it.

Mayor White said, "I'm sorry, Jeremiah. I wasn't aware of your history with the man. But I fail to see how it changes anything. Emil Riker has earned a solid reputation for himself and was eager to take the job."

When Halstead leaned on the desk, Sandborne feared he might fall over. He had never seen Jeremiah so shaken before. The mayor looked back at Sandborne as if he might be able to provide an explanation, but the young deputy had no answer for him.

Halstead looked down at his desk. "He has a solid reputation all right. A reputation as a thief and a bully. He's every bit as crooked as his father was, and that's saying something."

Mayor White raised his chins in defiance. "I've heard no such charges against his character. And Cal Hubbard vouched for him, which is good enough for me."

Halstead continued to look down at his desk. Sandborne braced for his temper to erupt.

Halstead said, "I take it you've heard that I've been riding out of town before sunrise every morning for the past several weeks."

The mayor cleared his throat once more. "Some of those who go to work at such times may have mentioned it to me in passing, though I saw no reason to ask you about it."

"I ride out to the hill directly across from Valhalla every single day. I do that because I like to keep an eye on what's happening over there. I want Zimmerman to know I'm doing it. You'd be amazed by all the work they're doing over there. Seems like several new buildings go up every week. Zimmerman's not the type who goes to the trouble of building something out of the goodness of his heart. He's not a businessman. Everything he does is meant to give him more power."

Halstead raised his head to look at Mayor White. "Cal Hubbard isn't your friend and neither is Zimmerman. He didn't tell you to hire Emil Riker because he cares about this town. He told you to hire Riker because Zimmerman thinks Riker can handle me." A new thought seemed to come to him as he watched the mayor's expression. "But you already knew that. You hired him, anyway, didn't you?"

White held up his small, soft hands. "I wasn't aware of your past dealings with Riker and I don't care either because you won't be here when he arrives next week."

Halstead's eyes narrowed again. "That so?"

"This jail happens to be town property, not federal. I'll need you boys out of here within the week."

Sandborne watched Halstead tense. "If you don't think Zimmerman will burn Battle Brook to the ground as soon as we're gone, you're a bigger fool than I took you for."

Sandborne watched the folds of the back of Mayor White's neck grow red as he stood. "There's no call for insults, Jeremiah."

"And there's no call for this town to run off the only men standing between you and the grave. Instead of asking Mackey to bring us back to Helena, you ought to be on your knees, begging him to let us stay. The wolf is at the door and what do you do? You've just opened the door and tossed meat on the floor to welcome him. I've known some stupid men in my time, but you take the top prize."

Sandborne may not have been well versed in the art of polite conversation, but even he knew Jeremiah had gone too far.

Mayor White stood his ground. "You may insult me all you like, Deputy, but my decision is final. I won't beg anyone for anything. Not Aaron Mackey and certainly not you. You might think you're keeping the peace here, but you break it every day you're in town. And yes, I was troubled by those killings this morning. How many more men must Mr. Fitzgerald pick up off the streets because of the trouble caused by your presence? How long until an innocent man or woman gets killed in the cross fire of one of your shoot-outs?"

Halstead started to move around to the mayor's side of the desk. "As many as it takes until Zimmerman is dead."

Sandborne knew there was no telling what Jeremiah might do once his temper got hold of him. He quickly got between the two men. "Let's keep it civil. We're all on the same side. Aren't we, Jeremiah?"

"I know what side I'm on," Halstead yelled down into White's face. "I can't say the same for the mayor, here. I'm not going to let you hand this town over to Zimmerman and Riker. I've seen how men like you bow and scrape to a bully. I saw it in El Paso and I saw it in Dover Station, but it's not going to happen here. You want us to leave? Good luck finding someone who'll make us, because it sure as hell isn't Emil Riker."

The three men flinched when a young boy's shrill voice filled the jail from the boardwalk. "Somebody better come quick! Some men have a gun to a lady's head down at the Standard. Hurry!"

The boy ran off before anyone could ask him any questions.

Sandborne watched all the color drain from Halstead's face. It took him a moment for him to understand why.

Abigail Newman lived at The Standard Hotel.

Halstead swiped his hat off the desk and pulled it on as he stormed out of the jail. "What were you saying about me being hard on the peace, Phil?"

Sandborne grabbed his Winchester from the rack and followed Halstead into the street. He did not have to lever a round into the chamber. They always kept their weapons ready to fire.

CHAPTER 6

Halstead took off at a dead run down the boardwalk. He heard Sandborne running right behind him. His argument with Phil White was already a distant memory.

He knew Abby had to be at the center of the trouble at the hotel. It was too close to that morning's shootings to just be a coincidence.

His stomach grew cold when he saw that a cluster of people three deep had already begun to gather in front of The Standard Hotel. He feared he might already be too late.

Halstead turned sideways without breaking his stride and knifed his way through the crowd. He knocked men and women aside without apology until he reached the clearing at the front door of the hotel.

He had just drawn his Colt from his belly rig when a hand reached out and grabbed hold of his arm.

Halstead tried to pull himself free but saw it was Earl Potter, one of Battle Brook's doctors. The short, frail man's grip was much stronger than it should have been for a man his age.

"There are three men with rifles inside," the doctor told him. "One of them has a gun on Abby."

Again, Halstead tried to pull himself free, but Potter held on. "He's got a coach gun to her back, Jeremiah. Bill

Holland was blocking the back door last I looked, but the men are threatening to shoot her on the spot if they're not allowed to ride out with her. If you barge in there looking for a fight, they'll kill her before you get three steps."

Halstead jerked his arm free from Potter's grip as he moved inside the hotel. "They're not taking her anywhere."

In the lobby, he saw the manager and some of the waiters hiding behind the front desk. He turned into the dining room and saw the scene Doc Potter had described.

Twenty tables had plates of food left half eaten and coffee undrunk. Napkins littered the floor and tables. Chairs had been overturned by diners making a hasty escape from the gunmen at the front of the room.

He saw Abby Newman standing in the middle of the dining room, held by a man with a kerchief over his face. That man quickly crouched low behind her when he spotted Halstead. He had the stubby barrels of a coach gun pressed against the small of her back. Both hammers were being held back by his thumb. If Halstead shot him, his hand would go slack and Abby would be cut in two.

Two men with kerchiefs over their faces flanked them, their rifles aimed at Bill Holland, the hotel owner, who was blocking their path to the back door, which led to the stables outside.

"Here's the deputy marshal now," Holland told them. "You'd better give up before someone gets hurt."

"Shut your mouth!" the largest of the three men yelled at him.

Halstead raised his Colt and aimed it at the top of the head of the man holding Abby. At that distance, it was far from a clean shot, but he could make it. "Let her go and you don't die."

Abby cried out when the man jammed the shotgun hard

against her side. "Tell him what I told you to say, missy. Do it!"

Halstead saw Abby was wearing his favorite dress—the dark blue one with the fancy lace frills. She only wore it on special occasions, and he wondered why she was wearing it now. He could tell by the streaks on her face that she had been crying, but her voice remained steady when she spoke.

"Everything's fine, Jerry. These men promise they won't hurt me if you do exactly what they say. They've got three horses waiting for them out back. They're going to take me with them. Once we get away, they'll send word to you with their demands. If you or anyone else tries to stop them . . ."

Her voice caught.

Halstead hated seeing her cry. He gripped his pistol tighter to keep it from trembling. He made a silent vow to make these men die slowly for this.

She began again. "If you or anyone else tries to stop them, they'll kill me. If you or anyone else follows us, they'll kill me. The sooner you give them what they want, the sooner they'll let me go unharmed. That's what they said."

Her eyes remained on his as she silently mouthed, *I love you.*

"Good girl," her captor said from behind her. "Unless you want to see what this pretty lady had for breakfast, you'd best do like she told you. My thumbs are getting awfully tired. These hammers could drop any second."

Halstead saw just enough of the top of the gunman's head above Abby's left shoulder. He might have taken the shot if he'd had his Winchester. It was trickier with his pistol but not impossible.

His Colt led the way as he took two steps closer. "Let

her go right now and I promise I won't shoot you in the belly."

The gunman pulled Abby with him as he took two steps backward. "That's just your pride talking." Halstead was close enough to see his face was filthy. "Tell that fella minding the back door to move out of the way."

Bill Holland looked at Halstead but did not move.

Halstead kept his pistol steady as he jerked his head to the right, signaling Holland to step aside. The hotel owner kept his hands up as he reluctantly obeyed.

Halstead saw the gunman smile behind his mask. His face wasn't filthy. They were freckles. "See how easy that was, Jeremiah?" He spoke to the man on his right. "Go outside and make sure the deputy, here, doesn't have anyone waiting for us out back. His friend Sandborne is somewhere close by."

Halstead was sure of it.

The larger of the three men kept his rifle on Holland as he backed up toward the door. He dug his rifle barrel into Holland's stomach and pushed him back into the hallway that led to the kitchen.

The big man opened the back door and stole a quick look outside. First to the left, then to the right. "Looks clear to me."

The man holding Abby at gunpoint said, "I don't care how it looks, dummy. Get out there and make sure."

Halstead watched the big man do as he had been told. He brought his rifle to his shoulder as he moved down the back steps. Again, he first checked the left side, then the right.

The big man was about to announce there was no one back there when Halstead saw a rifle barrel slide from the left side of the doorway and press against his neck.

The big man dropped his rifle and raised his hands

without Sandborne telling him to do so. Sandborne pulled the man's pistol from his hip and tossed it away.

The man holding Abby dug his fingers into her shoulder, causing her to cry out as he yelled, "Well? Is it clear?"

"No," the big man said.

Both remaining gunmen turned to look out the back door. The leader's grip on Abby's shoulder relaxed just enough to allow her to drop to the floor.

Clear.

Halstead fired four times at her attacker. The first shot struck him in the right temple. The other three hit him in the chest.

The coach gun fell to the dining room floor but did not fire.

The third man held his rifle over his head and hollered, "Don't shoot! I surrender!"

Bill Holland stepped forward and snatched the rifle from him and pushed him against the wall.

Halstead lowered his pistol and rushed to Abby's side. "Are you hurt?"

But she was already getting back on her feet. "I'm fine, Jerry. Just a little frightened is all. It's not every day a woman almost gets abducted, not even here in Battle Brook."

Halstead clutched her around the waist and pulled her close as the room began to spin around him. He could lose a lot. He could lose everything, but not her. Never her.

He let Abby go as his eyes fell on the man he had just killed. His mask had slipped down from his face and he could see he was young. Older than a boy, but not quite a man. Maybe twenty or so. Now he saw the freckles and the red hair that poked out from beneath his hat. He imagined they had caused him plenty of grief in life.

Taking hold of the woman Halstead loved had cost him that life.

He picked up the coach gun and cracked open the weapon. Both barrels were empty. He threw the gun aside in disgust. Had he known it was empty, he would have killed the kid a lot sooner.

The big man Sandborne was holding on his knees outside said, "Can I get up now?"

Halstead's head snapped toward him. The same man who had just held Abby hostage had the gall to complain about being on his knees.

Halstead began moving toward him.

"No, Jeremiah!" Abby shouted. "Don't!"

Halstead kicked out at him from the top step and caught the man on the jaw with the toe of his boot. Sandborne pulled his rifle away as the man pitched to the side.

Halstead walked down the steps and brought his boot down on the man's neck before aiming his Colt at the man's face. "Did you touch her?"

"Darn it, Jeremiah," Sandborne yelled. "Let him go. It's over."

"Somebody get him off me!" the big man cried out. "He's crazy!"

But Halstead put more weight on his neck as he thumbed back the hammer on his pistol. He could take attempts on his life, but not Abby's. Not her. But this would go on and on unless he stopped it now. Until he made an example of someone. Someone had to pay.

His Colt remained steady, aimed down at the big man's head. "Did. You. Touch. Her."

"Go to hell!" the big man rasped.

Halstead felt his Colt get knocked aside as the gun went off. The bullet buried itself in the ground about a foot away from the big man's head.

And Sandborne's hand was gripping his wrist. "Stop it, Jeremiah! Just stop!"

Halstead took his boot off the big man's neck and pulled his pistol free from Sandborne.

The two deputies stood less than a foot from each other. Neither man looked away.

Halstead felt his rage begin to subside, but only a little. "Don't ever do that again, Joshua."

"Don't do it again and I won't have to."

Halstead blinked first. There was no cause to be angry with Sandborne. He had just helped save Abby's life.

He pointed down at the man on the ground. "Get this one back to the jail. I'll question him later. I'm going to talk to the one inside."

Sandborne moved to block him. "I don't think that's a good idea just now."

"I won't touch him," Halstead said. "I'm just going to talk to him. I promise I'll bring him back to the jail in a bit."

Sandborne took a step back. "If it's all the same to you, I'll wait here until you're done. No sense in us making separate trips."

The big man on the ground moaned.

Sandborne nudged him with his boot. "Give me any trouble and I'll finish what he started."

Halstead stepped back inside the dining room. Bill Holland stood guard over the prisoner, who was now sitting on the floor. Abby had taken a seat at one of the empty tables.

He recognized the expression on their faces as they watched him. Fear.

Halstead spoke to the hotel owner first. "Thanks for standing up to them, Bill. I'm forever grateful."

"No need to thank me," Holland said. "It was the only decent thing to do."

"You can go on about your business," Halstead told him. "I'll tend to the prisoner."

The hotel owner looked at the pistol in Halstead's hand. "You sure that's a good idea, Jeremiah?"

Considering what had just happened outside, he understood Holland's concern. "I promise I won't ruin your carpet more than I already have."

Holland touched Halstead's arm. "Stains can come out. Carpets can be replaced. Good men can't be replaced." The hotel owner set the rifle aside and walked over to Abby's table. "Do you want me to escort you up to your room, Miss Abby?"

She shook her head. "Not right now, Bill. I'd like to stay here with Jeremiah for now."

He placed a comforting hand on her shoulder. "Then I'll have a pot of tea brought in to you immediately. It'll make you feel as good as new in no time."

Once Bill pulled the pocket doors of the dining room closed, Halstead turned his attention to the prisoner cowering on the floor. Now that his kerchief had been pulled down from his face, he could see he was probably even younger than the dead man at his feet.

"What's your name?" Halstead asked him.

The boy sitting against the wall began to shake. "Randy Meyers out of Valhalla."

Halstead refused to allow his temper to get the better of him this time. The kid had seen what he had done to his two partners. He would be useless if he terrified him any further.

Randy flinched when Halstead opened the cylinder of his Colt. "What are you doing here, Randy Meyers out of Valhalla?"

The young man pointed at the corpse at Halstead's feet. "It was all his idea. Hec Garvey. He wanted to impress Mr. Zimmerman by stealing your woman from you. Said we could do it without shooting anyone."

Halstead dumped out the spent bullets into his hand. "Kind of hard to shoot anyone with empty rifles."

"They were just for show. Mr. Zimmerman keeps the ammunition locked up separate from the rifles, and none of us had the right key. We're watchmen, and only constables have the keys to the bullets."

Valhalla had watchmen and constables. Zimmerman was getting fancy.

Halstead allowed each spent bullet to drop from his hand one by one. Each landed on Hec's corpse before rolling onto the carpet.

Randy shut his eyes and mouthed a prayer.

Halstead already knew the answer to his next question, but he had to ask it. "Zimmerman send you?"

"No. It was all our idea." Randy swallowed hard. "Hec's idea, mostly."

Halstead grinned as he pulled a bullet from his gun belt and slid it into the cylinder. "That's convenient. Blame it on the dead man."

"We weren't gonna hurt her," Randy implored. "Honest. We were just gonna bring her back to Valhalla where she'd be nice and safe."

Halstead plucked another bullet from his gun belt. "You think a lady friend of mine would be safe in Valhalla? With Zimmerman?"

Randy drew a ragged breath as he watched Halstead feed another round into his pistol. "I guess we didn't give it much thought. But we could've protected her."

Halstead loaded the last bullet into the gun and spun the cylinder before flicking it shut. "You? Protect her? I don't think so."

Bill Holland returned to the dining room from the kitchen. He was carrying a tea service on a silver plate. He also had a length of rope under his arm.

The hotel owner set the tray on Abby's table and held out two long lengths of rope to Halstead. "I figured you could use this to tie up the prisoners before you bring them to jail."

Randy sagged with relief when Halstead slid the Colt into his rig and accepted the rope. "Don't worry, Bill. I wasn't going to shoot him."

As Bill began to pour Abby's tea, Halstead told the prisoner, "On your feet and put your hands behind your back."

He tossed the second length of rope outside to Sandborne, who quickly tied the big man's hands behind him.

As Halstead bound Randy's hands, he said, "Later, you're going to tell me everything about what goes on in Valhalla. If you lie, I'll know it. I'll be angry and I'll hurt you. Understand?"

The boy choked back sobs as Halstead tied the knot tight. "Just please don't send me back there. To Valhalla, I mean. Mr. Zimmerman will kill me when he finds out about this. I've seen him do it."

Had the circumstances been different, Halstead might have taken pity on the boy. But he had been old enough to grab a rifle and try to take a woman captive. The woman he loved. Pity was in short supply.

He pulled Randy off the wall and made him face Abby. "Apologize to Miss Newman for ruining her breakfast."

"I'm sorry, miss."

"Now apologize to Mr. Holland, here, for scaring his customers and ruining his fine carpet."

"I'm sorry for the mess, sir."

Halstead shoved the boy out the door. He tripped and fell down the stairs, knocking the big man over. Sandborne helped both prisoners to their feet.

"Run them over to the jail and get started on your report," Halstead told his partner. "I'll add to it when I get back."

Sandborne pulled the prisoners close together and pushed them in the direction of the jail.

Halstead did not like the way he felt as Bill and Abby looked at him. As if he should be ashamed of what he had done.

He asked Holland, "You send for the undertaker yet?"

"Mr. Fitzgerald is on his way," Bill confirmed. "I'll see to it that you and Abby have privacy until he gets here. I imagine you two have quite a bit to talk about."

This time, he left the dining room through the hallway to the kitchen and closed the door behind him.

Abby was looking at Hec's corpse. "I feel like I'm in a Shakespearean tragedy. The two of us just sitting here talking while a dead man lies on the floor between us."

Halstead had never read Shakespeare. He sat beside her and pulled her close to him. "I'm sorry about this, Abby. They grabbed you because of me."

He closed his eyes when she placed her hand on his face. He felt that familiar warmth spread through him like it always did whenever they were this close.

"This wasn't your fault, Jerry," Abby assured him, "though I'd be lying if I didn't admit I'm worried about you."

"No need for worry," he told her. "I'm fine."

"You can tell Joshua you're fine and even yourself, but not me." She took his face in both her hands. "You're anything but fine. I've seen it for weeks now. This Zimmerman business has changed you, and not for the better."

Halstead knew she was right and cursed himself for it. "I know, but I can't just . . ."

She brought a slender finger to his lips. "I told you a long time ago that you never have to apologize to me, Jeremiah Halstead, and that still goes. But you need to take it easier on yourself. Being angry about Zimmerman's pardon won't change things. It's only going to hurt you.

Hurt us. Montana's full of men just as bad as him who'll never see the inside of a jail. You can't expect to fight them all."

He kissed her finger and held her hand flat against his cheek. He remembered his argument with Mayor White. It seemed like a month ago, though it had been only a few minutes before.

"I've seen what men like him can do once they sink their teeth into a place," Halstead said. "I'm supposed to be able to do something about that and I can't. They won't let me. They're even hiring a new sheriff to keep me from doing it. A man they knew would hurt me but did it anyway. Emil Riker."

She folded her hands on the table. "The same Riker family you told me about from El Paso."

Halstead frowned at the memory. He still had trouble believing it was true. "They didn't hire him by accident either. This was Zimmerman and Hubbard's doing. It's Zimmerman's way of proving he's already in charge of this town. He'll do anything to stick a knife in me, and this one is sharp."

"You need to remember you're not in this fight alone," she reminded him. "You've got people who admire you. People like Joshua. You've got people who love you like me." She smiled. "And you have people who want to help you like Aaron and Billy. You don't run Battle Brook, Jeremiah. You're only here to help. Who cares who they hire as sheriff, or why? Maybe they're right. Maybe it's time you let them handle Zimmerman on their own."

The warm feeling that had spread through him began to cool. "You mean you want me to give up?"

"Not give up," she explained, "but move on from this place. Montana's a big state and we could be just as happy in Helena as we could be here. I know you're worried that

Zimmerman will come after Battle Brook next, but it's not your battle to fight. Don't trade our happiness for the chance to see him swing. Someone will get him someday and that person doesn't have to be you."

No, he thought. *Not her, too.* "You've been talking to the mayor, haven't you?"

Abby slowly shook her head. "No, Jeremiah. A lot of people have been talking about it. Here in Battle Brook, and elsewhere, too. In Helena. You've already got a wonderful reputation on your hands and there's no reason to keep butting heads with Zimmerman any longer. It can only get worse for you from here." She caressed his cheek. "Worse for us."

Halstead gently lowered her hand from his face. "You want me to run away."

"The great Jeremiah Halstead? Run away?" Her smile grew wider. "I don't think it's even possible to say those words in the same sentence. But it's time for us to get on with our lives, and there's so much more to those lives than putting one bad man in prison."

Halstead had been watching as she spoke and heard a change in her tone. There was something off about her. She was holding something back.

"What's going on?" he asked her. "What have you done? If you haven't been talking to Phil White, you've been talking to someone else. Who is it?"

When she looked away, he knew he had been right.

Something had been nagging at the back of his mind since the moment he walked into the dining room. He looked at the clock on the mantel above the dining room fireplace. It was almost ten o'clock.

Abby never ate breakfast this late. She was usually an early riser, just like him.

Suspicion began to overwhelm him as details came

together. She was not only eating late, she was wearing her favorite dress. Yes, it suddenly made sense. "You were meeting someone for breakfast, weren't you?"

Abby's smile faded. "Now, Jeremiah, it's not what you think."

"Think?" He'd known he was right. "I wasn't thinking anything until now. I ran in here trying to save you but didn't wonder why you'd be eating this late. You're usually up in your room by now, writing to your parents or reading."

Her lower lip began to quiver. "Get ahold of yourself, Jeremiah. I'm not doing anything wrong. I'm trying to help you because you're in no condition to help yourself. You admitted as much just now when you first sat down."

He rose from the table and knocked over his chair as he backed away from her. The walls holding back his temper began to crack and weaken. Her talk of leaving Battle Brook. Of letting Zimmerman go free. Emil Riker becoming sheriff of Battle Brook. Everyone was working against him, even Abby.

It all began to make horrible sense. Was it Phil White? Cal Hubbard? Or was it Zimmerman himself?

The rising tide of rage broke within him when he heard a familiar voice say, "Calm down, Jeremiah. You're among friends here."

Halstead looked at the entrance to the dining room and saw Aaron Mackey, the US Marshal for Montana, standing in the doorway. Deputy Billy Sunday was right beside him.

Halstead had not seen them come in, but both men tended to move quietly. He could not believe they had come to Battle Brook.

Mackey had not changed since Halstead last saw him back in Helena. He was six feet tall, and lean, though his black, flat-brimmed hat made him appear taller. His coat and suit were black as well, save for the starched white shirt beneath his coat. The silver marshal star pinned on his lapel gleamed.

He stood at an angle, with his left shoulder toward the room. He often stood that way because it presented a smaller target to anyone who might try to shoot him. The butt of the Peacemaker holstered across his belly was facing away from whoever he was talking to. It made for an easier draw. Halstead had chosen a cross draw rig because Mackey wore his gun in similar fashion.

"Good to see you, Jeremiah," Billy Sunday said as he stepped farther into the dining room. The black man offered the same easy smile he always had, even since Halstead's childhood. "You're looking well."

"Aaron? Billy? You're here?"

"Yeah." Mackey looked down at Hec Garvey's corpse. "I see you've already had quite a morning for yourself."

Halstead leaned on a chair to keep from falling over. "Why are you here in Battle Brook?" He looked at Abby for answers to a question his mind had not been able to form yet. "Is this what you were hiding from me?"

Abby stood and took his hands in her own. "That's what I was trying to tell you when you got so upset, darling. I wrote to them about you. You're not in any trouble. They've come to help you set things right."

"Help? I don't need any help. Sandborne and me are doing fine."

"You're doing better than fine," Billy said. "How about you and me take a walk around town? Get ourselves some of that clean mountain air they boast about around here."

Halstead moved toward them like a man still half asleep. So much had happened so fast, he began to wonder if he might be dreaming.

But he realized he was not dreaming when Mackey shook his hand with his usual hard grip. "We'll talk later,

Jeremiah. Until then, keep an eye on Billy for me. I think he's getting touched in the head."

"A man would have to be touched in the head for riding with you for as long as I have." Billy threw an arm around Halstead and ushered him outside. "Come on. Show me what Battle Brook is all about."

CHAPTER 7

The cold Montana air served to restore Halstead's senses but answered none of his questions. "I didn't know you were coming."

"We didn't know it ourselves until a couple of days ago. We would've sent a telegram, but you haven't been too responsive lately."

Halstead had thought he had only fallen behind on a letter or two but realized it was probably more than that.

Billy pointed at two horses at the hitching rail in front of the hotel. "Here's another friendly face for you."

Halstead knew the bay gelding with a white star on his muzzle must be Billy's horse, but there was no mistaking the black Arabian mare tied beside him. Mackey had named her Adair.

The black horse did not look at Halstead but rather straight through him. She was one of the fastest horses Halstead had ever seen and never shied away from gunfire or blood. She stood completely still as Halstead held out his hand for her to smell.

"That's a good girl," he soothed before trying to stroke her muzzle. The mare withdrew and tried to bite his hand. She had never accepted anyone except Mackey and, occasionally, Billy Sunday.

"I see she hasn't lost her gentle nature."

"Don't take it personally," Billy said as he untethered his horse from the hitching rail. "She's just lost your scent is all. Give her a couple of days to remember you and she'll come around."

Halstead joined Billy in the thoroughfare as he led the horse along Main Street toward the jail. He saw the Winchester in the left scabbard on Billy's saddle. The .50-caliber Sharps rifle was in its usual spot on the right.

"Glad to see you're still lugging around that buffalo gun wherever you go."

"Still have cause to use it." The rifle had always been Billy's pride and joy. "Comes in handy now and then."

Now that he had gotten over the initial surprise of it, Halstead was glad Mackey and Billy had come to Battle Brook. Halstead had idolized Captain Mackey and Sergeant Sunday before his mother died and his father sent him off to missionary school. They were like older brothers to him. Billy taught him how to ride a horse, while Aaron showed him how to shoot a rifle. To a young boy, they were heroes who rode out in search of adventure on each patrol.

Much had happened in the years since the fort, but he had never forgotten the kindness they had shown him as a boy.

"It's good to see you, Billy. Awfully good."

"Awfully good to be seen." Billy nudged him in the shoulder as they walked. "You haven't been much for answering letters. Telegrams neither. What's going on with you?"

Halstead wished he had a good reason. "That why you came? On account of not hearing from me?"

"A visit was long overdue," Billy said. "Aaron wanted to come right after Zimmerman got his pardon, but things were awfully busy back in Helena after statehood. We began to worry about you when your letters and reports stopped coming, but we were able to track you in other ways."

Halstead stopped walking. He suddenly felt disgusted with himself. "Abby's been writing you, hasn't she?"

"She has." Billy beckoned Halstead to follow him, and he did. "Mayor White's written to Aaron a couple of times. Some other folks, too, but Abby's letters were all he paid attention to. Don't be cross with her, Jeremiah. She's just worried about you. We all are."

Halstead noticed the curious looks he and Billy drew from the people they passed on the boardwalk. He knew they would notice the star pinned on the lapel of Billy's coat and would wonder if he might be Billy Sunday. And where Sunday went, Aaron Mackey might be close by. The prospect of laying eyes on a couple of genuine heroes would thrill the people of Battle Brook to no end. The hero of Adobe Flats. The saviors of Dover Station. The men who had captured Darabont and stopped James Grant.

The people of Battle Brook might enjoy the company, but not everyone in the valley would give them a warm welcome.

Halstead began to share some of his bad news with Billy. "I had a run-in with Mayor White this morning. He's looking to push me and Sandborne out of Battle Brook. He wants to put his own man in as sheriff. Emil Riker."

"That the same Riker you had trouble with down in El Paso?" Billy did not need to wait for an answer. "Guess that's their way of sending you a message. No way that could be a mistake."

"Zimmerman's behind it," Halstead confirmed. "He's still got that bounty on my head, too. Two men tried to collect on it early this morning. And I wouldn't be surprised if he had spies all over town. That's part of the reason why I didn't respond to your telegrams. I didn't want the clerk at the telegraph office telling Zimmerman what I wrote."

"You could've written a letter," Billy said. "Even if Zimmerman's got as many spies as you say, finding a letter in all that mail is a tall order."

Halstead should have known better than to try that excuse with Billy. "Guess I was afraid of the response I'd get. I was worried that you'd order me and Sandborne back to Helena."

The two men kept walking in the thoroughfare as Billy led his horse. "You and Sandborne have been out here a long time, Jeremiah. We've got plenty of men who need hunting down besides Zimmerman. Your talents are needed elsewhere."

Halstead did not want to argue, but he could not let go of the point. "That's where you're wrong, Billy. Zimmerman might not be the worst now, but that's because I've kept him boxed in. He'll be a bigger threat than James Grant was back in Dover Station if we let him. He's not stupid or crazy. He's smart, and now that he's got himself a lawyer who can fix things with the politicians, there's no telling where he'll go next. We can't ignore him and hope he'll go away. We've got to stop him here and now while we can."

"Easy, now." It was the same tone Billy used to calm frightened horses. "No one's ignoring Zimmerman. That's another reason why Aaron wanted to come all the way out here. He wanted to get a look at the man with his own two eyes."

Halstead was encouraged by the news. "You didn't come out here just to bring me back?"

"No," Billy admitted, "but Aaron might still order you to leave with us. He figured there must be something special about Zimmerman if he's stuck in your craw this bad. Seeing as how he was able to get a pardon out of the previous governor, Aaron wants Zimmerman to know he's got his attention."

It was the best news Halstead had heard in weeks. "We'll ride out to Valhalla at first light. I've been making the trip each day just to remind Zimmerman that he hasn't gotten away with anything. Got a real nice spot picked out, too. He won't know what to do with himself when he sees the three of us on that hill come morning."

Billy was much less enthusiastic, though Halstead was too taken with the prospect of the three of them facing down Zimmerman together to notice.

They reached the jail and Billy quickly wrapped the horse's reins around a hitching rail in front. He was eager to get Halstead inside.

"I'll get some coffee going while you tell me all about what you boys have been up to. I hate to think what mud you've been passing off as coffee all this time."

On the back steps of The Standard Hotel, Aaron Mackey eyed the distant mountains while Abby Newman dried her tears. Mackey would have preferred to have this conversation inside, but the crowd in the lobby and the dead man on the dining room floor made that difficult.

Her description of Halstead's condition was exactly as bad as he had feared. "I was hoping you were exaggerating a bit in your letters. That news about Riker becoming sheriff will only make him worse. I never thought he could get this bad."

"He wasn't like this when I first met him, Aaron," Abby told him. "Jerry was tough but kind and capable. He had a way of being brave without being cold. But since Zimmerman got his pardon, all he can think about is how he's going to put the man behind bars or in the grave. He rides out to Valhalla every morning before sunrise just so Zimmerman's men will see him at first light."

Mackey winced. "That's bad."

He looked out at the scenery while Abby wiped away tears with a lace handkerchief. He remembered Katherine had enjoyed the young woman's company when she lived in Helena. She was impressed with Abby's strength and deep love for Jeremiah. She often said Abby had maturity beyond her years and Mrs. Mackey was not one to give compliments lightly.

Katherine's opinion of Abby was why her letters about Jeremiah's condition had troubled Mackey enough for him to make this trip. He had to see his deputy for himself. And now that he had seen him, he was sorry to admit that Jeremiah was worse than he had feared.

Abby dried more tears as they came. "Nothing I say or do seems to make him feel better. Maybe I should've just stayed in Helena instead of coming back here."

"Making him feel better isn't your job, Abby. Jeremiah's a grown man. You can't control him or tell him how to think. If you hadn't come back here, he'd be a lot worse."

"Sometimes I see him staring off into space during dinner," Abby said, "and he gets this look in his eyes that frightens me. Not of what he might do to me. I know he'd never hurt me, but I can't bear to think of what he'd do to Zimmerman if he had the chance."

Mackey remembered that melancholy ran in the Halstead family. Jeremiah's father had suffered from it after losing his second wife and daughter.

Since coming to Montana, Jeremiah quickly proved himself to be one of the bravest, most capable men Mackey had ever known. He was good with a gun, was calm under fire, and knew how to manage the peace. He had been everything Mackey could have wanted in a deputy. Steady. Smart. Reliable. But this business with Zimmerman had knocked him off-kilter.

Mackey had endured similar torments in his time with Darabont and Grant and Rigg. He had lost a great deal in his failed attempt to keep the slow, steady march of progress from reaching Dover Station. It had almost cost him everything. It had cost him a good friend, his own father, and, ultimately, the town itself. All that remained of Dover Station were burned ruins of buildings sitting in the ashes of his own hate. Even the name had been changed, and the town was already on the verge of being forgotten forever.

He knew Jeremiah was going through a similar trial in Battle Brook. He finally had come up against a man he could not defeat the way he had defeated other men. A man who had proven himself to be smarter than him. A man who was as tough, if not tougher.

Mackey knew Zimmerman's death would not be the answer to the questions that plagued Halstead. Jeremiah would have to find another way to make peace with his rage before it ultimately consumed him. Talking about peace of mind was one thing. Finding it took a great deal of patience and courage.

But Mackey had more immediate problems to handle. "That bounty Zimmerman's got on him doesn't help matters."

Abby used a lace handkerchief to dry more tears. "He had to kill two men this morning. And he almost killed one of the men who tried to take me just now. I thought he was going to shoot him dead right where you're standing. He was ready to murder that boy, Aaron. He might've done it, too, if Sandborne hadn't knocked his pistol aside."

Everything Abby had written in her letters, when combined with what she had just told him, convinced Mackey that he had to get Halstead out of Battle Brook before the young deputy did something they all regretted.

Mackey was no stranger to tears, but Abby's suffering got to him. Life with men like him and Halstead was never easy. Loving a dangerous man took an exacting toll on a woman's heart.

"You really love Jeremiah, don't you?"

A single tear ran down her cheek, but she did not wipe it away. "More than anything."

"Good, because he's going to need all the love you can spare to help him get through the days ahead. It's going to take a lot of work for both of you before he gets better."

Abby tried a smile. "Katherine already warned me of that before I left Helena to come back here, Aaron. I know what I'm in for and I'm not going to leave him. No man ever looked at me the way he does, even now. And nothing is going to make me leave him. I'll stay with him for as long as he'll have me. You've got my word on that."

Mackey was glad to hear it. "I plan on having all of us on the next train back to Helena. You, me, Billy, and Jeremiah, so you'd better start packing. Jeremiah won't be happy about leaving without Zimmerman, so I'll need your help to get him on that train tomorrow. Think you can do that for me?"

She smiled as she slid her handkerchief inside her sleeve. "I'll do everything I can to make him listen to reason. We'll get him on that train." She held out her hand to him and he took it. "Thank you for not giving up on him, Aaron. He'll thank you, too, in time."

Mackey had never been good at accepting compliments. He let go of her hand as he walked past Abby and up the steps to look inside the dining room. He saw a man in a black suit directing two orderlies as they placed Hec Garvey's body on a canvas stretcher.

"Stop what you're doing," Mackey told them.

"I beg your pardon." The man in the suit had longish brown hair and his beard was neatly trimmed. "Who are you to be giving us orders?"

"The name's Aaron Mackey."

The two orderlies exchanged glances before quickly backing away from the corpse.

The man in the suit straightened his tie. "Forgive me, Marshal. I'm Mr. Fitzgerald, the new undertaker here in Battle Brook. I'm afraid no one informed me that you . . ."

Mackey did not have time to waste on conversation. He pointed at the orderlies and said, "You two will pick up that body, carry it outside, and lay it across the saddle of one of those horses out in the yard."

The orderlies did not wait for confirmation from Mr. Fitzgerald to begin carrying out Mackey's orders.

The undertaker grew flustered. "Forgive me, Marshal, but I must say this is highly irregular. I wasn't told of any such plans for the remains."

"Consider yourself told as of right now." Mackey stepped aside as the orderlies loaded Hec Garvey's corpse onto the stretcher and carried him out the back door.

Abby had already gotten up from her seat on the steps and allowed the men to pass.

"Just drape him over the saddle," Mackey told the men as he followed them outside. "I'll take care of tying him down on my own." He looked down at Abby. "I'd say you've got some packing to tend to."

She surprised him by popping up on her tiptoes and giving him a kiss on the cheek before rushing through the dining room.

Mr. Fitzgerald scrambled to join Mackey as he watched the orderlies struggle to heave the corpse over the saddle. The marshal was almost embarrassed for them. He was tempted to just throw a rope around Garvey's middle and pull him across the saddle himself.

"Easy does it, boys," Mackey encouraged them. "Just pop him up there before the rigor takes hold. He'll be a lot harder to move then."

Mr. Fitzgerald said, "I must say, this is quite a peculiar situation, Marshal. I've never been ordered to surrender a body before. In my experience, lawmen such as yourself usually prefer me to take them away as soon as possible."

Mackey watched the orderlies finally figure out how to work together to drape Hec across the saddle. "Then I guess you learned something new today. Good morning to you and your men. You're excused."

But the undertaker was clearly not satisfied. "What do you plan to . . . do with him?"

"I'll be bringing him where he belongs." Mackey removed the rope coiled on the dead man's saddle. "He's going to help me to make a point with his boss."

He was glad Fitzgerald and his orderlies left without asking any more questions. Aaron Mackey was not accustomed to sharing his plans with strangers.

CHAPTER 8

At The Iron Horse Saloon in Valhalla, Zimmerman was enjoying the company of his unexpected guests. He normally did not like surprises, but Emil and Warren Riker were a welcome exception to his rule.

"I wasn't expecting you boys to get here for at least another week." Zimmerman poured the men coffee from the pot the bartender had brought them. "My compliments on getting an earnest start."

"We're not earnest," Emil told him. "We're just early. Smart, too."

Warren said, "A man can get himself killed by living up to what's expected of him. We find it best if we move at a pace of our own choosing."

Zimmerman was glad Warren Riker's appearance matched his reputation. The former army scout had long, gray hair that flowed out from beneath the shapeless slouch he saw earlier after teaching Randy his lesson.

"I take it that's a lesson hard learned from your years as a scout for the army," Zimmerman said.

Warren looked down at his mug of coffee. "Learned it when I lost my wife and baby girl to the Sioux."

Zimmerman feigned concern. "Mr. Hubbard told me

about your tragedy. That was thoughtless of me. Please accept my condolences."

"No need for condolences," Warren said. "I found a way to avenge them and then some. Now it's time for my brother and me to avenge our daddy."

Emil Riker was long-limbed and lean. His black mustache was trim and his square jaw was devoid of any hint of stubble. "After we got off the train at Wellspring, we spent a week riding around the valley to get better acquainted with the ground. It's a mighty unforgiving land you've got here, Mr. Zimmerman."

"Where you see unforgiveness, I see opportunity, Emil."

The incoming sheriff of Battle Brook winced. "Never much cared for my given name, Mr. Zimmerman. My brother Warren and you can just call me Riker. It won't confuse us any."

"Noted." He sipped his coffee. He always found it rewarding to drink coffee in a saloon. There was something defiant in it, as though he was breaking some unwritten rule. "What did you two learn while you looked over the land?"

Warren spoke on behalf of his brother. "It's mighty dangerous up in and around those hills. Lots of old, abandoned mines up there."

Zimmerman decided this conversation might have promise. "And?"

"And a man could find himself in a world of trouble if he got himself caught out there alone," Warren said. "Miners tend to be a solitary bunch, and there's no one around for miles anyway. No one to hear you call for help if you're in trouble. Could be days before anyone came along, if ever."

Zimmerman found this a most encouraging conversation. "You're thinking about Halstead, aren't you?"

Emil thumbed his hat farther back on his head. "On the train ride up here, Warren and I heard a lot of talk about all the men who've gone to Battle Brook to try to collect that bounty you're said to have on Halstead. We heard he's had to kill fifty men or more because of it."

Zimmerman laughed. "The real number is probably closer to twenty, but the truth serves each man differently, doesn't it? What do you boys have in mind as far as Halstead is concerned?"

Warren said, "That depends on if you've really got a bounty on him or if it's just rumor. We heard a lot of numbers along the way, but the most common was ten thousand dollars. That true?"

Zimmerman did not answer right away. He did not want to smother the fire of invention before it had a chance to start. "Ten thousand's the rumored amount, but I was thinking of a more modest sum. But why do you ask? Are you interested in more than just vengeance?"

Riker hooked his arm over the back of his chair. "Vengeance is mighty expensive work and we're always interested in making money, Mr. Zimmerman. My brother and I didn't come all the way from Texas out of the goodness of our hearts."

"No. You came here to become sheriff of Battle Brook and to kill Halstead. We've already reached an agreement, remember?"

"That agreement don't mean we're willing to leave money on the table," Warren said. "We know you're the boss, and we'll do what you say if it doesn't get in the way of us killing Halstead. But if you've got an open bounty on him, we'd like a shot at it ourselves if we can agree on a price."

Zimmerman could hardly blame a pair of thieves for being interested in money. Had they been honest men, he never would have picked Riker to be sheriff of Battle Brook. "I was thinking a thousand dollars would be a more appropriate sum."

Riker cut loose with a low whistle. "A thousand is a lot less than the ten we heard. You're lucky no one's been able to collect. They'd be mighty disappointed when you gave them a lot less than they were expecting."

Zimmerman's anger flashed. "They'd take what I gave them or they'd get nothing."

"A thousand might sound appropriate to you," Warren said, "but a thousand a piece sounds a good sight more appropriate to my brother and me."

Zimmerman enjoyed haggling as much as the next man, especially when he had a better offer to put on the table. "I was thinking more along the lines of two thousand for you, Warren, assuming you're willing to go after Halstead on your own and go after him soon."

Warren looked up from his coffee. "Mister, I made a living scouting Injuns for the army. I've killed more Comanche and Apache and Sioux than you'll ever see if you live to be a hundred. Full-blooded savages, every last one of them. I think I can take a lowly half-breed easily enough. And if my brother comes with me, Halstead's as good as dead."

Zimmerman saw no point in telling him Halstead was half-Anglo and half-Mexican. "I don't doubt your abilities, Warren, but I'd prefer it if you went after him alone. I'm a betting man who likes to spread his stakes across as many numbers as I can. Cuts down on my risk. Besides, I have big plans for your brother here. He's the new sheriff of Battle Brook, remember? How would it look if I lost him before he was able to take the oath of office?"

The brothers exchanged a brief glance and came to an unspoken agreement. Zimmerman envied them. It must be nice to have a brother one could trust. He had been forced to kill his own years ago.

Warren said, "Then I'll do it alone. You've got yourself a deal, Mr. Zimmerman."

Zimmerman smiled. "Now that we've agreed upon a figure, I'd like to know how you plan on killing Halstead."

Riker hesitated. "My brother and I don't like to announce our plans. It's bad luck."

"It may be your plan," Zimmerman said, "but it's my money. I want to know how I'm spending it." He held up a finger and employed a term he had heard Mannes use on several occasions. "And that's a point not up for negotiation."

Another look passed between the brothers before Riker told him, "The way we see it, it's best if we find a way to get Halstead away from town. To find a way to draw him out somehow. Warren and I found an old mine while we were riding around up in the hills around Battle Brook. A sign says it used to be called the Pine Branch Number One."

Zimmerman had heard of the old mine months before when he and Brunet were raiding mining camps but had never seen the place. "Go on."

Warren explained, "It's good ground, with some rundown old shacks scattered around it. My brother here was fixing to ride into Battle Brook and find some old drunk who's down on his luck. He'll pay him to deliver a message to Halstead that he just saw some of your men camped out up at the Pine Branch."

Riker added, "Halstead likes to avoid a fight in town whenever he can, so he'll be anxious to ride out and head off trouble before it starts."

Zimmerman began to lose some faith in their plan. "It's a risky proposition. What if he doesn't take the bait?"

"No harm done," Warren said. "But we know Halstead.

He's just cocky enough to believe he can take on five men alone, especially if he thinks he can get the jump on them. When he rides out, he'll find me waiting for him, and that'll be the beginning of the end for him."

Warren offered a yellow, crooked smile. "And our daddy will be avenged. Don't worry, Mr. Zimmerman. I'll be sure to take my time with him before I'm done. I want him to hurt the way he made our pa hurt. Come morning, you'll be able to add Halstead's scalp to the others I've heard you keep tied to your pommel."

Zimmerman was glad news of his scalps had reached as far down as Texas. What good were they if they did not add to his reputation? But he was far from convinced their plan would work. "Even if you're able to trick him into riding out there, Halstead's clever. He's been a hunted man for a long time, boys. He won't be that easy to trap."

Riker said, "We don't need anyone to tell us about Jeremiah Halstead. We had him figured out a long time ago. If he's on the sharp edge like Hubbard wrote me, he won't be able to pass up a chance to head off a fight, especially if it'll weaken you."

"Don't give it another thought, Mr. Zimmerman," Warren said. "He'll ride right into my bullet. That's when the fun will begin. And if he stays in town, we'll just have to figure out another way to get him. The place won't matter because it'll end the same way."

Zimmerman could see the brothers had already made up their mind. There was no point in wasting time trying to persuade them. It was not his neck they were risking, so why argue? Their plan might work. It only took one bullet to get lucky.

He raised his mug to toast them. "Here's to happy hunting, gentlemen."

The three men clinked their mugs together. The plan agreed upon.

Zimmerman said to Riker, "While Warren gets ready to spring his trap, I want you to remain here in Valhalla for the time being. I have some men I'd like you to meet. Men who are every bit as dedicated to Halstead's destruction as we are. I think you'll be impressed by what we've come up with."

Warren's eyes narrowed. "Seems like a waste of time to me. Halstead will be dead in a few hours."

"Oh, of course he will," Zimmerman agreed, "but as I said before. I'm a betting man. I don't like to leave matters to chance. You'd better go get yourself settled at the Pine Branch while your brother and I explore other strategies. Just in case something goes wrong."

Warren drank his coffee. "Just don't keep him here too long. I don't want to be twiddling my thumbs in one of those old mining shacks all day. I'm an impatient man."

"So am I," Zimmerman winked. "And a cautious one, too."

Now that he had set the Battle Brook part of his plan in motion, Zimmerman decided it was time to solidify his position in Valhalla. He had heard Hubbard use the term "solidify our position" once when talking about investments and thought it was an apt phrase for what he was about to do.

He strode along the new boardwalk past his own home to visit the ailing Rob Brunet a few doors down. After knocking on the door and waiting a moment, he let himself inside.

The boardwalk in front of the house may have been new, but the house was as dilapidated as the ruined building where Zimmerman slept each night. Canvas had been nailed over the cracked windows to give Brunet privacy while he healed. A weak fire burned among the crumbling brickwork of the fireplace.

Rob Brunet's condition had not changed in weeks. He watched him dozing in an old brass bed some of the men had salvaged from one of the other abandoned buildings in town.

Brunet had been a fearsome bear of a man in health. He had been wanted in several territories throughout the United States and Canada for murder, manslaughter, robbery, and other major offenses. Now he looked pathetic as he shivered beneath a small pile of blankets.

The old Cheyenne woman who had brought Zimmerman's shaving water earlier that morning tended to Brunet now. She wore her iron-gray hair in a long braid down her back and she had a colorful shawl draped around her shoulders as she placed cold towels on Brunet's head. A strap of leather around her face covered the gaping hole where her nose had once been.

Zimmerman doubted white men had marred her appearance. They would have just shot her instead. He figured a rival tribe had done it—and worse—after raiding her village.

He watched the old woman soak a rag in a bucket of water beside the bed and replace the dry one across Brunet's forehead. Brunet gestured weakly as he muttered a fever dream to her.

Zimmerman often wondered if Brunet was as sick as he appeared to be. The bullet or an infection would have killed him long ago. He tried to confirm his theory by coming at different times of the day but always found the old woman tending to him just as she did now.

"You told me he was getting better," Zimmerman said to her. "He sure doesn't look like it."

"Because the bullet's still near his spine," she said. "It's too deep for me to get and his body hasn't been strong enough to push it out. Not even the doctor will try to remove it. His fever is still high, but it's come down some over the past few nights. I think he might be able to eat a little today. Some broth, maybe."

Zimmerman was not encouraged by the news. Brunet was the only man in Valhalla who could challenge his authority. All the former outlaws he had elevated to the rank of constables—Tote, Weasel, Gordo, and Stoneman—thought of him as a hero. He had helped Zimmerman found Valhalla and was something of a legend to them.

Brunet may have been laid low by a bullet, but every day he lived he posed a threat to Zimmerman's plans of absolute control of the fledgling town they had started.

Besides, Brunet had played his part in Zimmerman's plans already. He had helped Zimmerman build a new gang after Jeremiah Halstead killed off his old one. He had led the raids on mines in the surrounding area that had paid for the creation of Valhalla. He had caught a bullet in the back after robbing the Bank of Battle Brook weeks ago but was too stubborn to succumb to his wound. Some men just did not know when to die.

Perhaps he needs help to complete his journey?

"Leave us," Zimmerman told her. "I want to talk to him alone."

But the Cheyenne woman did not budge. "He's out of his mind with fever, so it won't be much of a conversation. I am his woman and my place is with him. You can speak to him as if I am not here." She touched the leather where her nose used to be. "I didn't tell the Lakota where my people went and they took my nose for it. I know how to keep a secret."

Zimmerman was not accustomed to being defied, especially by an old savage heathen. "I'm the one who paid you and I'm telling you to leave us."

"My word to him is more valuable to me than money." She wrung out a strip of cloth in the basin of water and placed it on Brunet's head. "My place is with him."

He could throw her out easily enough, but there was something about the old woman that always gave him pause. He often thought the old medicine woman might put a curse on him and he had too many irons in the fire to run the risk of bad luck. There was no point in making another scene that morning. He could always come back to kill Brunet later. A pillow over the face would make it look like he had died in his sleep.

"I'll be over at Mannes's office if you need me. Be sure to come get me if he dies or wakes up."

The Cheyenne refused to look up at him. "You'd be happy either way, wouldn't you?"

Zimmerman did not care for her mouth but admired her grit. Not many people spoke to him with such scorn anymore. Perhaps he would take her tongue when he was done with Brunet. Or maybe her scalp. It would make a fine addition to the scalps he had tied to his saddle horn.

He left the house and stepped out onto the boardwalk. He stomped his bootheel on the wood to test the boardwalk's sturdiness. Not a shake. He knew the work crews thought him a fool for insisting the boardwalks be the first things repaired in town. The ground might be nearly frozen now, but come the thaw in the spring, people would be grateful for having safe, dry passage through the mud.

Such details were important when building an empire in the wilderness.

Almost as important as having the right men in the right places to help him maintain it.

He stepped onto the thoroughfare and took his time crossing the street to Mannes's office. He was early for their meeting and there was no reason to hurry, especially when everything—and everyone—he saw belonged to him.

CHAPTER 9

Sandborne was disappointed that not even the arrival of Billy Sunday in Battle Brook was able to improve Jeremiah's dark mood. He remained sullen and distant while his oldest friend demonstrated how to make a fine pot of coffee.

Sandborne imagined the events of that morning had taken their toll on Halstead. Having two men attempt to kill him was a difficult way to start a day. Being told the mayor was hiring a sheriff who was a bitter rival from his past was enough to drive any man to his limit. Having to save Abby from abduction had ruined any hope of salvaging the day. And it was not even noon yet.

Billy ignored Halstead's sour mood as he finished crushing a bag of coffee beans beneath the handle of his unloaded pistol. "It's always better to have the general store grind these into a fine powder for you, but since we don't have that here, we'll just improvise. A dash of cinnamon's my secret for a bit of flavor, but since you don't have that either, we'll skip it."

He shook the bag, which sounded much quieter now that the beans had been crushed, and smiled. "Hear that sound, Jeremiah? That's a good sound. Means we've got a good pot of coffee heading out way."

Billy opened the bag and inhaled, smiling widely before holding out the bag for Jeremiah to smell. "Take a whiff of that and tell me it doesn't smell like heaven to you."

Sandborne watched Halstead smell it and thought he saw a change come over his friend. "Does smell appetizing."

Billy beckoned Sandborne to do the same. He thought the beans smelled good enough but ground up was certainly better. "That's got me hankering for a cup right now."

"You'll have it in a bit, but we've got to work for it first." Billy creased one edge of the open bag and began to carefully tap coffee flakes from it into the pot. Sandborne had watched Billy reload spent ammunition with powder using the same care.

Billy said, "I learned long ago that brewing a good pot of coffee is a matter of measurements. The secret is to pound the grounds into powder before you pour them into the pot. It's a good way to get out the frustrations of the day without taking it out on someone."

Sandborne had a feeling Billy was talking about more than coffee, but Halstead was too lost in his own thoughts to notice.

Billy continued with his lesson. "Make sure you measure the right amount that goes in the pot. Too little and you'll wind up with brown water. I've seen men grow downright nasty if their coffee is too weak first thing in the morning. But if you put in too much, like most people do, you'll have a pot of mud on your hands. It'll be too strong and give you the jitters, not to mention make you run for the nearest privy. That's why measure is important. Just fill the bottom of the pot with the right amount of powder, then add a bit more to coat it."

Billy withdrew the bag and folded the top over on itself. "Keeping the bag nice and tight helps trap all the flavor inside. Leave it open and it's liable to go stale. I learned that the hard way, back when I was riding with your daddy, Jeremiah. Nothing will hurt the morale of a patrol more than lousy coffee."

Sandborne saw that not even mention of his father was enough to pry Jeremiah from the depths of his troubles.

Billy went on undeterred. He picked up a pitcher of water and poured it into the pot. "Now you add your water. Make sure it comes just short of the spout. That way, it won't boil over the top and make a mess when you put it over the flame."

He placed the full pot on the iron stove and clasped his hands behind his back while he let the heat go to work. "Now, all we do is keep an eye on it until it's ready. All that talk about a watched pot never boiling is just nonsense. It'll boil whether you watch it or not. It's what you do while you're waiting that's important. I find that it gives me a chance to think about the day before and the day ahead. Brewing coffee is a lot like life. It's all about grinding and measuring and timing. Take it off the heat too early, you lose the flavor. Leave it on too long, it'll not only overflow but turn bitter. Then you have a mess you've got to clean up."

Billy held up a thin, dark finger. "But if you tend to it properly, you'll have the perfect pot, and that's something to be proud of."

Sandborne waited for some sign that Jeremiah was paying attention, but it was no use. He was dwelling on all the changes about to come to Battle Brook. Sandborne kept hoping that Halstead would snap out of it. That he would be up to questioning the prisoners about Valhalla, so they could learn more about what happened there. They might know something that would lead to a reason to arrest Zimmerman.

But Halstead had not bothered to question them yet.

And given that Halstead had tried to kill Mule in the yard behind the hotel, he supposed that was for the best. He knew Halstead's temper could flare up in the blink of an eye, so distance was better for the moment.

The three men looked up when they heard Mackey call to them from outside.

"Hello in the jail. It's Mackey."

Halstead perked up faster than the coffee. It was the first sign of life he had shown since returning to the jail with Billy.

Halstead opened the door and Sandborne saw the marshal sitting atop Adair in the thoroughfare. Even though he had seen Mackey ride the black Arabian hundreds of times, it was still an impressive sight to behold.

The marshal had a horse with a body draped over the saddle. The arms and legs were bound together beneath the barrel of the animal. Sandborne recognized the red hair and freckles as belonging to Hec Garvey, the man Halstead had shot dead in the dining room.

Halstead surprised Sandborne by asking Mackey, "That took you long enough. What kept you?"

Sandborne knew the marshal did not enjoy explaining himself and was not surprised when he ignored the question. The flat brim of Mackey's hat cast his face in shadow, but Sandborne could tell he was looking into the jail. "Nice to see you, Sandborne. We'll talk when we get back. Get mounted, Billy. We've got some traveling ahead of us."

Halstead walked outside ahead of Billy. "That's the best news I've heard all day. Just give me a minute to get my horse and I'll ride out to Valhalla with you boys."

Billy slid past him and blocked his way.

Mackey said, "You're not coming, Jeremiah. Billy and I will make this trip alone."

Jeremiah laughed, as if Mackey was teasing him, but

Sandborne knew Aaron Mackey was not a jokester. And when he began to head for the livery again, Billy moved to cut him off a second time.

"Sorry, Jeremiah," Billy told him. "It's better if you stay here to help Sandborne keep an eye on those prisoners."

"Better?" Halstead slowly backed away. "How is me staying here better?"

Though he could not see his face, Sandborne could tell by the incline of Mackey's hat that he was beginning to get annoyed. He disliked waiting almost as much as he disliked having to explain his decisions.

Billy spoke for him. "There's a lot of bad blood between you and Zimmerman. The marshal and me are riding out there to make a point, not start a war. Things are less likely to get out of hand if you're not there."

Halstead looked at his two old friends. "You might not want a war, but you've already got one. You just don't know it yet. Another gun against Zimmerman won't hurt. Quit joshing me and let me get my horse."

Halstead moved and Billy blocked him a third time.

Sandborne looked away. He was embarrassed for his friend.

Halstead said to Mackey, "This really the way you want it, Aaron? Has living in Helena made you that soft?"

Sandborne closed his eyes. That was not the proper tone to take with the marshal.

Mackey raised his head a fraction of an inch. "You're not going. Get back inside and wait until we come back."

"Like hell I will. If you don't want me riding with you, I'll ride out in front of you. The three of us will show Zimmerman what he's up against."

Halstead stepped off the boardwalk and into the thoroughfare.

Mackey moved Adair to block his path like a cutting

horse blocking a runaway cow. When Halstead moved to the other side, the mare matched his movement and stopped him.

Mackey said, "I gave you an order, Deputy. Follow it or take off that star."

Halstead backed up onto the boardwalk. "You don't mean that."

The heavy silence that followed said otherwise.

Billy stepped forward to break the tension. "It's for the best, Jeremiah. And it's best if you don't press the matter."

Halstead remained where he was. Sandborne may have admired Mackey, but he knew there was always a line no man dared to cross without consequences. And Jeremiah Halstead was standing on the edge of it.

Halstead's shoulders sagged. "Guess that means I'll be here waiting for you boys when you get back."

Billy patted him on the arm as he unwrapped his horse's reins from the hitching rail and climbed into the saddle. Mackey handed him the reins of Hec's horse and rode west down Main Street at a gallop.

Billy tried a smile as he pulled his horse away from the jail. "Make sure you mind that coffee like I told you. We don't want it boiling over and making a mess, now do we?"

He tapped the horse's flanks and pulled the second horse on a lead rope as he went to catch up with Mackey.

Sandborne waited until Halstead decided to come back inside before he closed the door. He watched Halstead walk over to the stove and look at the pot of coffee on it. The water inside was already beginning to come to a boil.

"Measure," Halstead said. "Heat. Time." His eyes were as vacant as Hec Garvey's. "Billy wasn't just talking about coffee, was he?"

"No," Sandborne admitted. "I imagine he was talking

about more than that. Why don't you sit down, Jeremiah? I'll be happy to pour you a cup when it's ready."

Halstead went to his desk and sat down, but he looked anything but comfortable.

Sandborne pulled over a chair and placed it in front of the door leading back to the cells. He did not want Halstead to take his embarrassment out on the prisoners. He sat quietly and waited for the coffee to be ready.

Sometimes, waiting was the best medicine.

CHAPTER 10

Mackey tried to keep a firm grip on his temper as he and Billy rode west toward Valhalla. Hec Garvey's corpse bounced quietly across the back of the horse Billy was leading.

"That boy crossed the line," Mackey said. "He never used to talk back like that."

Billy rode beside him. "That boy is in such a lather, he can't even see the line, Aaron. He's blind with rage."

"Are you making excuses for him now?"

"No. I'm not saying he was right for testing you like he did. I'm just saying it's not all his fault. He's been through a lot and he's still just a kid."

Mackey did not see that as an excuse. "Even kids need to grow up sometime. I was a lieutenant at his age. Leading patrols."

"With four years of West Point training to lean on," Billy reminded him. "Jeremiah doesn't have the benefit of your education. And he hasn't had an easy time of it in Battle Brook."

Mackey knew arguing with Billy was pointless, usually because he was right. "I never should've sent him out here. Not after Zimmerman got away from him at Silver Cloud. I should've sent someone else to Battle Brook. It's gotten too personal between them. That bounty he put on Jeremiah has ruined him."

"No sense fretting over what's already done," Billy reminded him. "For what it's worth, I thought sending him here was the right thing to do at the time, too. Thought it would be good for both him and Sandborne to handle it on their own."

Mackey thought if there was any bright spot in this mess, it was the obvious progress Joshua Sandborne had made. He was different from the young kid he had dispatched from Helena weeks ago. He was nearer to a man now and seemed the better for it. "That doesn't make me feel better."

"It wasn't meant to," Billy said. "Just reminding you of why you decided what you did is all. The best thing for Jeremiah is for you to pull him out of here before he gets any worse. I take it you got Abby to come around to your way of thinking?"

"I didn't have to," Mackey said. "She's up in their room right now, packing their things. Katherine was right about her. That girl has a good head on her shoulders and she's not as delicate as she looks. She's tough. I just hope Jeremiah's not already too far gone to see her worth."

"He's not," Billy assured him. "A bit of time with us in Helena and he'll be back to his old self in no time. We'll see to that."

Adair tossed her head and quickened her pace until Mackey drew back on the reins to slow her down. "Looks like everyone's fighting me today, even her."

Billy kept riding beside him, leading the horse carrying the dead man. "She's just getting anxious because we're getting close to Valhalla. She always knows when a fight's coming."

Mackey hoped that would not be the case. He knew

Zimmerman had literally gotten away with murder. He had the territorial governor's pardon to thank for that.

But he and Billy were not riding to Valhalla to start a fight or avenge a wrong. He was looking to plant a flag in the ground. The flag of the United States of America. He wanted to remind Zimmerman that he might not be in prison, but he was not free. He wanted to make it clear that the next time he crossed the line, he would have to contend with Aaron Mackey.

Billy cut loose with a low whistle as they crested a hill and the town of Valhalla came into view before them. "I can smell all that fresh-cut timber from here. I'd say it looks like Zimmerman's been keeping himself busy."

Mackey brought Adair to a halt as Billy did the same with his mount.

Mackey saw how the road dipped down a bit before rising to the plateau where the town was situated. New buildings in various stages of construction rose into the sky, while older, damaged structures were being pulled down. Even from so far away, the sounds of hammers and saws echoed across the open valley.

And for a moment, Mackey felt as if he was riding toward another town that had undergone a similar transformation.

"Remind you of anyplace?" Mackey asked Billy.

Billy said, "Dover Station was a different town and Zimmerman's a different man, Aaron. The outcome could be different, too."

But Mackey was not so sure. He had seen the damage one man's greed and ambition could bring to a town. Halstead had seen it, too. He had been in the middle of the fire that destroyed Dover Station. Maybe his deputy was right to be blind with rage. Maybe there was only one way to deal with men like James Grant and Ed Zimmerman.

Billy had always been able to read Mackey's moods and this time was no exception. "We stick to the plan, Boss. You ride down there, make your point, and come back."

Mackey looked over at his friend riding by his side. "And what'll you be doing while I'm down there talking?"

Billy nodded toward the hillside to the left. "Saw a spot over there that looks awfully peaceful. Has a good view of the town, too. It's shaping up to be a beautiful afternoon, so I thought I'd head over and rest a while."

Mackey knew Billy's true intention had nothing to do with rest. "Guess I'll be seeing you on the way back to Battle Brook."

Billy handed him the reins of the horse bearing Hec Garvey's body and tapped his horse's flanks before riding onto the grass. "You most certainly will."

Adair raised her snout and caught the scent of something on the wind. She threw her head again but remained perfectly still.

"I know, girl." He patted her neck. "Me too. Let's go."

He let up on the reins and let the mare move toward Valhalla at her own pace. He led the trail horse with the dead man upon it behind him.

CHAPTER 11

Not even the bland expressions of Mannes or Hubbard could dampen Zimmerman's joy as he read the document a second time. Emil Riker sat off to the side and looked bored.

"You're sure it's real?" Zimmerman found a better word and used it. "Legal, I mean."

Mark Mannes, the attorney, said, "This murder complaint you're about to swear out against Halstead is entirely legal and justified." His voice managed to be as lifeless as his eyes. "We have an abundance of evidence and testimony that Halstead killed sworn deputies of Valhalla while they accompanied you to the station in Wellspring. And since they were not breaking any laws at the time of their respective deaths, we have a strong case for murder."

Riker leaned forward in his chair. "Is this the big plan you've been talking about all morning? A lousy warrant no judge in his right mind will sign?"

Cal Hubbard, the banker, answered for the others. "We don't need a judge in his right mind to sign it. We already have a well-placed jurist who is more than willing to do it."

Zimmerman was usually coy around strangers, but he told Mannes, "Might as well let Sheriff Riker in on our plan, Mark. He's going to play an important part in seeing it's a success."

Mannes said, "My cousin appointed the attorney general of Montana when he was still the territorial governor. Now that we're a state, my cousin was forced to find another line of work. He's now a state judge. I can practically guarantee the attorney general will indict Halstead and my cousin will be glad to sign the warrant for his arrest. He has some resentment toward Mackey and will welcome the opportunity to embarrass him. Getting a jury to convict him will be nearly impossible, but even a trial will prove troublesome for Mackey and Halstead."

Zimmerman laughed as he flicked the paper. He was holding power in his hands. Real power. A knife was good, a gun was better, but he was beginning to understand that the pen was the mightiest weapon ever devised by man.

"It'll apply pressure," Zimmerman added, "which comes at a most opportune time. And should your efforts fail this afternoon . . ."

Mannes spoke up. "Efforts neither I nor Mr. Hubbard know anything about."

Zimmerman hated to be interrupted and waved for the attorney to be quiet. "Should your efforts fail this afternoon, we'll have this warrant in our back pocket." He set the testimony on the desk out of fear of wrinkling it. "First, Hubbard got that simpleton White to hire you as Battle Brook's sheriff, now this. I can't wait to see Halstead's face when Riker slams his own cell door on him." The mere thought of it brought him joy. "Halstead's troubles are only just beginning, gentlemen. He won't know what hit him until the train has already passed."

But Hubbard was far more cautious. "I'm afraid Halstead won't be as easy to get rid of as that."

The Honorable H. Calvin Hubbard looked exactly the way Zimmerman thought a bank president should. Round-headed, with a slight double chin, thinning white hair, and an impressive set of thick, white muttonchops and mustache to match. He looked to be about sixty or so, though he had the energy of a much younger man. The walking stick he had begun to carry added to his aura of an important man.

"You've managed to stay one step ahead of him so far," Hubbard went on. "You've kept him off-balance, but it won't always be that way. When he finds out about this complaint, it will cause trouble."

"Only for him." Zimmerman smirked. "And if he pulls any of his nonsense here in Valhalla, I've got enough men around who'll make him regret it. Plenty of witnesses who'll swear it was legal, too."

When Mannes and Hubbard looked away, Zimmerman knew something was wrong. "What is it? Is a plague of locusts about to descend on our humble valley?"

"In a manner of speaking," Hubbard told him. "We have it on good authority that Aaron Mackey is on his way to Battle Brook."

Riker groaned and crossed his legs.

Zimmerman blinked. "What?"

Hubbard said, "One of our men at the railroad sent a telegram that reached us just before you came here. The conductor said Aaron Mackey and Billy Sunday were on the last train that stopped at Wellspring. In fact, they may already be in Battle Brook as we speak. We would have known this earlier if you'd been willing to pay to have the telegraph wire extended here from Battle Brook, but . . ."

Zimmerman held up his hand to silence him as he

absorbed what he had just heard. "Mackey and Sunday here? Are your men sure?"

"Mackey's well-known," Mannes offered, "and there aren't many black deputy marshals in Montana, Ed. It's them, which certainly changes things. At least in my view."

Zimmerman resented being spoken to as if he were a child. "Your view is from behind a desk, Mark. Mine is on the horizon. Always."

"As it should be," Hubbard agreed, "which is why it's important that you listen to our advice when we offer it. We're not telling you to forget about the murder complaint entirely. We just think it would be prudent if you waited to dispatch Mark to Helena to file it officially. We should find out why Mackey is here before we do anything rash."

Mannes added, "For all you know, he might be coming here to bring Halstead back to Helena with him. It would be much better to file the complaint once he's left town than to risk even more trouble while he and Sunday are here."

Riker's expression soured. "Meetings. Nothing good has ever come out of a lousy meeting."

But Zimmerman was already thinking on a much grander scale. He had never thought Mackey would come to Battle Brook. If his pardon had not been enough to bring him out of Helena, he doubted anything would.

But if the report was true, it was better news than Zimmerman could have hoped. "Imagine that. The great man himself coming all this way just for little old me."

Mannes folded his hands atop his desk. "I don't think you're taking this news as we intended, Ed."

Hubbard pitched in. "Aaron Mackey coming to Battle Brook is hardly a welcome development."

Riker spoke to Zimmerman. "I can go find Warren. Give us a couple of your best boys and we'll make quick work of Mackey and the rest of them."

Zimmerman waved for all of them to be quiet. So much chatter at once made it difficult to think. "No one's doing anything unless I tell them to do it. Mackey being in Battle Brook isn't nearly the problem you think it is. Don't you understand what this means? Mackey hasn't ridden out after anyone since he became marshal. I'm the first one to force him to do that. Me. That means something, boys."

The lawyer swallowed hard. "He brings a considerable amount of authority with him wherever he goes. Legal authority."

"A *considerable* amount of legal authority," Hubbard emphasized.

But Zimmerman understood that. "Great men aren't born out of easy times, gentlemen. They're forged from the heat and fire of trial and tribulation. Their reputations are sharpened against other great men. Where you see trouble, I see an opportunity, for if I play my hand well, Mackey won't be my end. He'll be my grindstone."

Hubbard sank back in his chair and ran his hands over his face. "This is hopeless."

"No," Zimmerman told him. "This is a chance at becoming something more. Valhalla is now officially on the map." He pointed at the document that controlled Jeremiah Halstead's fate. "And this is how we use the law's own weapons against it. If we're successful, we'll beat Mackey and his men once and for all. They won't dare cross the likes of me once Mark files this complaint in Helena. And he *is* going to file it. He's going on the next train to Helena, just like we planned."

Zimmerman enjoyed the look of confused despair on his lawyer's face. His time in Valhalla had taught him that the most valuable education rarely came from books.

Riker said, "It'd still be a whole lot quicker and easier if you just let me and Warren handle it our way."

"Your time will come," Zimmerman assured him as he picked up the document. "What do I have to do to make this official?"

Mannes frowned. "Just sign on the line as indicated right there at the bottom of the document." He gestured at the pen and inkwell on the desk. "Sign all three copies. I'll retain one for my records and bring a second with me to the state prosecutor in Helena, which I will deliver personally."

"And the third?" Zimmerman asked.

"I was planning on delivering it to Aaron Mackey's office, but if he's here, we don't have to wait. Though we can't expect him to arrest Halstead without the actual signed warrant from a judge."

Zimmerman shoved aside some documents on the lawyer's desk and quickly signed all three pages. Ink splattered as he dipped the pen, but he did not care about neatness. He only cared that this was the first step on his journey to destiny.

He glanced up at Riker, who still looked bored by the proceedings. "Cheer up, Sheriff. You're a witness to history in the making. You'll be able to tell your grandchildren about this. Killing Halstead and Mackey would be quicker, true, but death has a way of making a man a legend. Just look at what it did for those preening fools George Custer and Bill Hickok. What we're doing here today might not seem like much to a man like you, but I'm salting the earth forever and for all time. A man like Halstead won't be destroyed by death. The only way to destroy a man like that is to kill the legend in its crib. To grind him to powder beneath the wheels of the justice he values."

Zimmerman finished his signature on the last document with a sweeping flourish of the pen. "That is how to destroy a man, Riker. Any fool can kill; only a thinking man can truly destroy."

He tossed the pen aside and eagerly handed the documents back to Mannes. "You're on the next train to Helena, Mark. I want that complaint filed and official as soon as possible."

The attorney placed the signed papers on top of a pile as he replaced Zimmerman's pen in the inkwell.

Hubbard sighed as he folded his hands across his considerable belly. "You're nothing if not consistent, Ed. I'll grant you that."

Zimmerman laughed as he slapped the banker on the shoulder. "Cheer up, Cal. With Mannes's connections, your money, and Riker as sheriff of Battle Brook, we'll have this valley sewn up tighter than a spinster's purse in no time."

Riker asked, "You want me to go back to Battle Brook and look things over?"

Zimmerman thought it was a good idea. "I'll send Mule with you. That big oaf has been sneaking over there for weeks as if I didn't know about it. He'll bring back any messages you have for me. He might just make a good deputy one day."

"Not in Battle Brook," Riker said. "Warren's gonna be my deputy."

Zimmerman looked around when he heard a loud rapping on the glass of Mannes's back door. He saw through the window that it was one of his constables, Tote. Zimmerman gave the tall man his name because his flat, long face resembled one he had seen on a totem pole. He had never seen the man smile, but he had never seen panic in his eyes like he saw now.

Zimmerman got up from his chair, went to the door, and opened it. "What's wrong?"

The tall man beckoned him to come outside. "We've got a lone rider outside of town, Boss, and it sure ain't Halstead. This fella's just sitting there right out in the open for the whole world to see. Has a packhorse with something draped over the saddle. I can't tell for certain, but I think it's a body."

Zimmerman, Riker, Mannes, and Hubbard followed Tote out into the alley and looked in the direction he was pointing.

Zimmerman saw a lone rider in the near distance. He could only see the silhouette of the man but knew it was not Halstead. This man was tall and lean and appeared to be dressed entirely in black except for a white shirt. His flat-brimmed hat cast his face in shadow, but the silver star pinned to the lapel of his coat was clear enough for any man to see.

And although he had never laid eyes on the man before, Zimmerman knew this had to be Aaron Mackey.

Zimmerman steadied himself against the building. "The mountain has come to Muhammad after all."

"Whatever his name is," Tote said, "he sure don't look friendly to me. That's why I figured I ought to come get you once I saw him. What do you want me to do?"

Zimmerman heard Hubbard and Mannes take a few steps backward, while Riker remained where he was as he asked, "Want me to go out there and meet him?"

"No. I want you to stay here in case something goes wrong out there. Tote, get over to the livery. Have someone saddle my horse and bring it here to me. Make sure they use the saddle with the scalps on it. This is a formal occasion and I want to look my best."

Tote went off to carry out his orders, but Zimmerman grabbed him. "Make sure no one goes out there to talk with him without me. Get some of the boys mounted. Constables only. We'll ride out together and see what he wants."

Tote dashed off to do Zimmerman's bidding.

Zimmerman realized Mannes and Hubbard had moved

a fair distance behind him. The attorney looked like he might get sick to his stomach.

"That's him, isn't it?" Mannes did not wait for an answer. "That's Aaron Mackey out there."

Zimmerman laughed. "Don't worry, Mark. I'm not going to make you ride out to meet him. You can start packing after you give me Mackey's copy of the complaint. I plan on taking this opportunity to deliver it to him personally."

As Mannes scurried back into his office, Hubbard said, "I'm needed back at the bank, Ed. Come get me if you need me for anything."

Zimmerman did not acknowledge him as he moved away. Like Brunet before him, Hubbard had already played his role in his plan. Let him hide. This was a matter for real men. Men like him and Mackey.

Now that it was just the two of them, Zimmerman said to Riker, "Get on your horse and ride as fast as you can to Battle Brook. Take the road to the south. Try to draw Halstead out of town before Mackey gets back. I'll do my best to stall him for as long as I can. If Mackey arrests me, I want you in town, ready to help get me out. Stop by The Athens Saloon first. If you're looking for a messenger, you should have your pick of the litter in that dive."

Riker headed for the livery, climbed on his horse, and sped off on the south road to Battle Brook.

Mannes came back outside and handed Zimmerman a copy of the signed murder complaint before stepping back behind the cover of his office.

Zimmerman folded the document in three and slipped it into the inside pocket of his coat. "See that packhorse he's got with him, Mark? Looks like the marshal has brought us a gift." He patted the pocket of his coat. "Fortunately, I have one for him in return."

CHAPTER 12

Edward Zimmerman sat tall in the saddle as he and his constables slowly rode out to meet the man standing alone at the edge of town. He kept their pace slow but constant. This was an important moment for Zimmerman. He had secured the attention of a man who was almost a legend. He did not want to spoil it by rushing.

Tote and the roundish Gordo rode at his left. Pinch-faced Weasel and Stoneman were on his right. Weasel was a talker with a penchant for malice, while Stoneman had earned his name due to a chiseled expression that never changed despite the situation.

Each man was a killer to his core. Outlaws who would not blink under the marshal's steady glare.

As he and his men drew closer to Mackey, Zimmerman could not help but admire the marshal's calm. He sat with his hands draped across his saddle horn. He appeared as relaxed as an idle traveler pausing at a crossroads while he decided which path to take on his journey.

And the black horse he sat upon was obviously Adair. He had heard a great deal about the Arabian mare. A majestic animal worthy of her reputation. Swift and powerful and brave. The muscles beneath her rich black coat gleamed in the morning sun. As true a warhorse as any man could hope to have.

The kind of horse Zimmerman would have one day.

She stood as stock still as her rider. She did not nose the ground like the packhorse behind her, but instead kept her head high, watching the men and beasts as they drew nearer.

And although Mackey's eyes were still in shadow, he could feel the marshal taking in every detail of each man riding toward him. He was undoubtedly judging which one might cause trouble first and who would run if trouble started. He was studying the types of guns they carried and the condition of their horses.

Zimmerman had made sure the scalps tied to his saddle horn were on the right side of his mount so Mackey would be sure to see them at his current angle.

"Why's he just sitting there like that?" the ever chatty Weasel asked aloud. "Why didn't he just come into town like a normal fella?"

Zimmerman remained unfazed. "Silence, Weasel."

Mackey remained still until the riders were thirty yards away, when he called out, "That's far enough."

Zimmerman held up his hand to signal his men to stop. "You've caught me on a good day. I don't usually take orders from strangers on my land."

Mackey's hands remained crossed on the saddle horn, though Zimmerman noticed his right was only an inch away from the handle of the Peacemaker jutting out from the holster on his belly.

The marshal said, "We're still in the United States of America. That makes this my jurisdiction."

He's a proud man, Zimmerman thought. *Such bearing and poise. He must've gotten that at West Point.*

Zimmerman raised his chin. "And who might you be?"

"Aaron Mackey."

Zimmerman had not told his men who they were riding out to meet, so the name landed with great weight as they traded glances among themselves.

"I suspected as much. I'm Edward Zimmerman."

"I figured." Mackey inclined his head toward the pack-horse behind him. "Brought you something that belongs to you."

Weasel inched his horse forward. "You really Aaron Mackey?"

The marshal did not look at him. "I am."

Zimmerman would run the loudmouth through with a hot poker in the belly for ruining this moment for him. "Get back in line, Weasel."

But the constable kept the horse inching forward. "You ain't Mackey. If you really was Mackey, you'd have that colored deputy with you. Sunday's his name, ain't it?"

Mackey remained still. "He was here a minute ago. Don't know where he got off to."

"Weasel!" Zimmerman failed to keep the anger from his voice. "I said that's enough."

But Weasel moved another inch closer. "This fella ain't Mackey. Everyone knows he don't go nowhere without his ni—"

The left side of Weasel's head disappeared in a cloud of red mist, followed by the unmistakable echo of a Sharps rifle that thundered through the valley.

Weasel's body dropped to the ground as all the horses of Zimmerman's men jumped. Weasel's mount kept its footing as it dashed back into town.

But as he brought his own horse back under control, Zimmerman noticed that neither Mackey nor Adair had moved an inch.

Mackey grinned. "That would be Billy Sunday."

Zimmerman saw Tote reach for the gun on his hip. Stoneman too.

But Mackey's Peacemaker was already in his hand before any of them cleared leather.

The men wisely kept their hands in plain sight and away from their guns.

"Unless any of you boys want to join your dead friend down there, I suggest you stay right where you are. Billy's already reloaded by now and has your boss in his sights."

Zimmerman jerked on the reins as his horse continued to fuss over the dead man at its hooves. His grand moment ruined by that idiot Weasel. "What do you want, Mackey? You didn't come here just to pick off my men one by one."

"I already told you. I'm here to return something you lost." He pulled the packhorse forward. "I think you'll recognize it when you see it."

Mackey tossed the end of the rope to Zimmerman and the horse kept moving forward. None of the men moved until the animal was close enough to grab without crossing the invisible line Weasel had violated.

Zimmerman handed the rope to Tote, pulled the horse toward him. "It looks like Hec Garvey, Boss. One of the watchmen."

Zimmerman knew who Hec Garvey was. "I take it we're looking at the result of your handiwork."

"Not mine," Mackey said. "Jeremiah Halstead finished him off when he and two of his friends were dumb enough to try to grab a woman in Battle Brook. During breakfast, no less."

Zimmerman's eyes grew wide with rage. He knew who the other two must be. "Mule and Randy."

"I believe that's what they call themselves."

Zimmerman looked back at his men, who seemed as

surprised by the news as he was. "Bring Hec back into town. The rest of you should wait for me there."

Stoneman kept his horse steady. "You sure, Boss?"

"I said move. Now!"

The three remaining constables obeyed, leaving Zimmerman and Mackey alone.

And Mackey's Peacemaker was aimed directly at him.

When he was sure the men were well out of earshot, Zimmerman said, "I had nothing to do with grabbing that woman, Marshal. You must believe that."

"If I thought otherwise, you'd be down there next to Ferret, and so would your men."

"Weasel, but that doesn't matter now. Are Mule and Randy still alive?"

"They were last I checked, but Jeremiah's in a dark mood. They might be dead by now."

Zimmerman saw this as a way he might be able to garner some goodwill with the marshal. "You can do whatever you want to them as far as I'm concerned. Let them rot in jail or shoot them. I'll be happy to do it for you if you want."

"We'll handle it our way," Mackey said. "Not yours."

"Well, my offer stands. I'd gladly kill Halstead if I had the chance, but I don't need to go through a woman to do it."

"I figured."

Zimmerman was beginning to grow frustrated with the short answers. *He doesn't give up much, does he?* "Though I must admit I'm curious about something. You didn't come all the way out here from Helena on the off chance one of my men might do something stupid. That tells me you've come to this valley with another purpose in mind."

Mackey remained still and his Peacemaker was steady. "This town used to be called Hard Scrabble until you came along, didn't it? Got abandoned when the mining company started building up Battle Brook."

Zimmerman began to relax a little. He was talking and talking was always good. "We call it Valhalla now. It's my pride and joy."

"Built on stolen money. Blood money."

Zimmerman shrugged. "Ever see a town that wasn't?"

"You managed to get yourself a pardon from the territorial governor, too."

"My attorney did, yes, but I hope you won't hold that against me as much as Halstead has. After all, the French pardoned Napoleon, didn't they? Twice, or so I've heard."

"You're not Napoleon and this isn't France," Mackey said. "It's Montana. We're a new state now, with a new governor. The law says you're free, and you'll remain that way if you don't break the law."

Zimmerman tried a smile. "That's awfully good to hear, Marshal."

"But this business between you and Halstead ends here," Mackey told him. "Today. Right now. You make of this place whatever you're going to make of it, but you'll put out the word you've dropped that bounty you've got on his head."

Zimmerman grinned. He had not only been important enough to bring the great Aaron Mackey to the farthest reaches of the state. He had just forced him to beg for mercy. Zimmerman had won.

No one was around to see it, but Mackey would remember it. And so would Zimmerman.

"While I'm considering it, I'd like to give you something. A piece of paper." Zimmerman pinched the lapel of his coat between his thumb and forefinger. "But I'll have to reach into my coat pocket to get it."

"Send it later. Tell me the bounty's dropped so I can be on my way."

"This piece of paper I want to give you concerns the bounty."

Mackey's Peacemaker remained aimed at his chest. "Move slow. I see anything besides paper, you die."

Zimmerman eyed the hillside as he slowly pulled open his coat. Billy Sunday was still out there on the rocky hillside.

Zimmerman slowly plucked the murder complaint from his pocket and handed it over to the marshal.

Mackey took it with his left hand while his right kept the Peacemaker trained on Zimmerman. The marshal shook the paper open. His eyes narrowed as he read it.

"A murder complaint?" Mackey asked aloud. "Who are Brian Allum and Alfred Pike?"

"They were sworn deputies of Valhalla who Jeremiah Halstead murdered in cold blood when he tried to abduct me at Wellspring Station several weeks ago. The day *after* I was pardoned. He gunned down those men in cold blood even though I was a free man at the time."

Mackey crumpled the paper. "He didn't know that."

"The date on the pardon was clear. As was the telegram you sent, notifying him to that effect. My attorney assures me that we can produce records from the telegraph office to verify that claim."

Mackey balled up the letter and tossed it away. "You send your complaint to Helena yet?"

"No, but I will."

"Don't."

"Why?"

"Because it'll turn out to be a big waste of time for everyone. It'll stir up a lot of problems none of us need or want."

Zimmerman's smile broadened. "Especially Jeremiah Halstead."

"For him. For you, too."

"That sounds like a threat. I don't take kindly to those."

"Then you'll hate what happens if you keep pushing. Think long and hard before you file anything formally, Zimmerman."

"I already have. My mind is made up and my attorney is already on his way to Helena." He held up a finger. "That is, unless we can reach an understanding. Something that benefits us both equally."

Mackey's jaw tightened. "Such as?"

"You allow me to take over Battle Brook," Zimmerman explained, "within the sacred confines of the law, of course, and allow me to spread my influence in Helena. I'll agree to not only tear up the complaint but to rescind my bounty on Halstead. The bounty and any ill will between us will be buried forever. As long as he leaves me in peace, of course."

Mackey remained quiet long enough to lead Zimmerman to believe he might be considering it.

"Just like that. A truce."

"Honor saved for all sides. What do you say? Do we have an agreement? Do I dare offer my hand to you without fear of Deputy Sunday shooting it off?"

"Your hand can stay where it is," Mackey told him. "As for taking over Battle Brook, that's between you and the people of this valley. If they let you in, that's on their head, not mine. Any influence you get in Helena is between you and anyone foolish enough to deal with you. Go ahead and file your complaint if you want. I won't try to stop you. But the next time you break the law—and we both know you will—I'll come down on you like the wrath of God."

Zimmerman felt a jolt of excitement course through

him. He had certainly gotten to the great man, hadn't he? "And the bounty on Halstead?"

"If you don't pull it, I'll be disappointed. You won't much like what happens after that."

"No, I imagine I won't." He leaned forward in the saddle. "But I bet we'll both have fun finding out."

"I will," Mackey said. "You won't."

"At least we understand each other."

Realizing he had already gained more than he could have hoped, Zimmerman touched the brim of his hat and pulled on the reins to make his mount step backward.

Mackey's Peacemaker tracked him the entire way. He was certain Billy Sunday's Sharps was doing the same.

Yes, Aaron Mackey was as cold and steady as a mountain stream.

"Have a pleasant day, Marshal. I've enjoyed our conversation."

He brought the horse around and heeled it into a gallop into town.

Zimmerman expected to catch a bullet in the back for his trouble but made it to the livery without incident.

CHAPTER 13

Billy rode out from the hillside to catch up to Mackey on the road back to Battle Brook.

"You and Zimmerman talked for a long while down there."

Mackey kept his eyes on the trail as he tried to order his thoughts. "We said a lot of words at each other, but I wouldn't call it a talk."

"What was on that paper he handed to you?"

Mackey hated to give Zimmerman's murder complaint any credibility, but Billy needed to know. "He's swearing out a complaint against Jeremiah for murder. He claims the men Halstead killed in Wellspring a few weeks back were his deputies."

Billy may not have been able to read or write beyond making his mark, but he knew the law as well as Mackey. He knew how it could be twisted to fit a cunning man's purposes. "He's got the record of that telegram you sent Jeremiah, hasn't he? The one Halstead didn't get until the next day."

"Yeah." Mackey cursed himself for having sent it. The telegram was the only proof Halstead might have known about the pardon a full day before Mannes returned with the physical document. He knew Halstead had not received the telegram before arriving in Wellspring, but it might take a trial to prove that.

Billy continued to ride beside him. "Sounds like Zimmerman's lawyer is a dangerous man."

"Capable, too. And that's bad news for Jeremiah." Not too long ago, Mackey would not have been worried. He would have been confident Zimmerman would never find a judge willing to hear his complaint. But that was before the outlaw had gotten a governor to grant him a pardon.

Montana was a state now and times were changing. It only took one judge to agree to swear out a warrant for Halstead's arrest and bring the matter to trial. And anything could happen during a trial. They had a habit of stirring up facts and emotions best left buried.

"We can't tell Jeremiah about this," Mackey decided. "Not until Zimmerman's lawyer files it formally in Helena. He said he's already got a man on the way to the capital, but I'm not sure I believe him. All I know is that we'll need to get Jeremiah out of here before he does. We'll be able to protect him better back home."

Billy rode beside him in silence for a mile or so before saying, "The next train for Helena leaves tomorrow. If Zimmerman's lawyer is in on it, we could have a long talk with him."

Mackey gripped Adair's reins tighter. He hated being forced to move quicker by a man like Zimmerman. "No. We need to get Jeremiah out of here. We can handle everything else after that."

Billy kept pace with Mackey. "Arresting a lawman for doing his duty? I can't see any judge worth the name signing an order like that. And he wouldn't be long for the bench if he did."

Mackey was not as confident as his deputy. "It'll depend on how much Zimmerman is willing to pay for a warrant.

A judge could earn himself a nice pot of money for his trouble. Besides, Mannes has relatives all over this state. He's bound to have a cousin or two who are either judges or are married to one."

He knew the sooner they got Jeremiah out of Battle Brook, the better. "As soon as we get back to town, I'll have Sandborne help Abby finish packing. I'll need you to find us a stagecoach that'll make a special trip to run her and her trunks down to Wellspring as soon as possible. We'll send Jeremiah with her. You and me will hang back to protect the town and head for Wellspring after dark."

As soon as he said it, Mackey saw the holes in his plan. Holes Billy was quick to point out. "It's a long ride to Wellspring from Battle Brook, Aaron. Word's bound to get back to Zimmerman and he'd send some men to ambush Jeremiah along the way. And with Abby at his side, he'll be more concerned about her safety than his own."

Mackey clenched his jaw. Zimmerman was already having a poor effect on him. He was rushing before thinking through a notion. That would only lead to mistakes that would get more people killed.

But he remembered sometimes the best way to learn how to do something was by making mistakes. Or at least appearing to make mistakes.

"Let's go about getting that stagecoach anyway," Mackey said. "And make sure plenty of people know you're doing it, too. That owner of the hotel, Holland, might be able to help you spread the word."

Billy caught on quickly. "You want Zimmerman to think we're using the stagecoach."

Mackey had not thought that far ahead, but he would use the rest of the ride back to Battle Brook to devise a plan. Zimmerman was not the only clever man in this part of Montana.

"While you do that, I'll have a talk with Jeremiah. Set him straight on a few things before he hits the road."

"Let's just hope he's in a better frame of mind than he was when we left."

But Mackey did not care about Halstead's state of mind. He was leaving Battle Brook. That much was final. The rest may very well be up to Zimmerman.

Upon reaching Battle Brook, Emil Riker saw The Athens Saloon was every bit as run-down as he had expected it to be. He pushed through the batwing doors and a thick cloud of dust hung in the sunlight like fireflies on a summer's night. Each of the tables scattered around the place were empty except for gouges from the initials carved on them.. Every chair was warped from years of rough use by drunken customers.

The few men standing at the bar looked like they were holding on to life by their fingernails. Two of them shook enough to spill their whiskey as they tried to bring it up to their lips.

It was exactly the kind of place Riker was looking for.

"Welcome to The Athens Saloon," greeted a thin bartender with a long, drooping mustache as dark as Riker's own. "My name is Ted Purdy, owner of this fine establishment."

Riker looked over the place. "Doesn't look too fine to me."

"I'll admit we're not as fancy as The Blue Belle or some other places in Battle Brook, but our prices are fair and our whiskey isn't watered down. I like to think of us as a diamond in the rough. What'll you have?"

He made the mistake of placing his hand on the bar but recoiled when he felt tobacco juice. "I'll try a beer."

Purdy went to the keg behind the bar and filled his glass.

"Don't recall seeing you in here before, mister. What brings you to town?"

Riker figured a chatty bartender was better for his purposes than a sullen one. "I'm not sure yet. Just getting the lay of the place first."

Purdy placed the mug of beer in front of him, and Riker could tell he was in for a story. "The Athens Bar is a good place to start. When I opened a few years ago, I wanted a place where philosophers and important people could come to discuss important things. My name is really Theodore Pertesis, but since no one could say that properly, I just go by 'Purdy' now."

Riker was glad it had not been much of a story. "A man's got to be willing to change to survive out here."

"Like Plato said, 'Nothing ever is, everything is becoming.' I always liked that one. It's a bit too deep for the men who come in here, but I like it."

Riker looked past the two old drunks standing closest to him and watched the other men spread along the length of the bar. They were solitary drinkers, which was good. In his experience, it was hard to cut a drunk out of a herd of drunks. Misery loved company. They often formed a bond between them as they peered over the doom that awaited them at the edge of the world.

Riker sipped his beer and was surprised it was not half bad. "What kind of crowd do you cater to?"

Purdy used a faded towel to wipe the bar. "This is pretty much it. This time of day, it's usually the men who work nights. Hotel clerks, a liveryman or two. Freighters waiting for goods to be ready to haul. And some who don't have anywhere else to go. We get a lively crowd at night, though. Even have a couple of sporting ladies you might find interesting company. They're out back sleeping now, but I can see if one of them is available if you're interested."

But Riker had come to The Athens in search of a different kind of company. "I might have a job for a man who can set a horse properly. Anyone in here who might fit the bill?"

Purdy gave it a moment's thought. "The pickings are a bit slim at the moment, but I think Chuck Corrigan's your man. He's the sandy-haired fella in the middle. Works odd jobs here and there. Did a bit of mining a while back if memory serves. He's got the thirst something awful and can't seem to keep a job under him. Been here about a year. Said he rode up here with a cattle outfit out of Texas, but he had a falling-out with the trail boss. I can't speak for his reliability, but he's friendly enough."

Riker had never laid eyes on Chuck Corrigan before, but one glance told him the whole story. He had been around such men all his life. Rangy and bowlegged, just like his brother. And, like Warren, Corrigan was a man who tumbled through life, one day fading into the next without a thought of what might be on the horizon. A forgotten man who would work a job just long enough to get money for whiskey. And if he had enough left over, maybe a little company to help him pass a long night. His life would continue that way for years until, one morning, he didn't wake up. And when that day finally came, maybe the undertaker would spare a few moments to say some words over him before they stuck him in an unmarked grave.

Riker did not pity the man. He thought he was perfect.

He picked up his beer and brought it over to a spot next to Corrigan.

The cowboy looked him up and down before returning to his drink. "Go away. I'm busy."

Riker looked at his glass. "I can see that. How about another?"

"No thanks," Corrigan said. "I pay my own way."

"An independent man. I'd expect nothing less from a fellow son from the sovereign state of Texas."

Corrigan rolled his eyes. "Save that down-home nonsense for the old drunks over there. Whatever you're peddling, I ain't buying."

"No, you're not. I'm the one who's buying." Riker placed a double eagle coin on the bar as he called out to the bartender, "Ted, give us a bottle. My friend and I have business to discuss."

He was glad to see the ten-dollar piece got Corrigan's attention and softened his disposition.

"Haven't seen one of those in a long time," Corrigan admitted. "Not in here."

"I've got another one just like it. It's yours if you'll hear me out."

Purdy pulled the cork from a full bottle of whiskey and filled two fresh glasses for them. He took the coin with him when he moved back down the bar.

"You're a tough man to ignore, mister. What did you say your name was?"

"I didn't say and I won't. It's part of the deal."

Corrigan looked at the bottle, and Riker could tell what he was thinking. Ten dollars could buy a whole lot of whiskey. It could get him a nice room for a couple of nights, too. No sleeping in a hayloft or in an alley. It might last him a week if he was careful.

"Make it twenty dollars and I'll kill a man for you."

"We'll keep it at ten because I don't need you to hurt anyone. You won't even have to lay a hand on them."

Corrigan became cautious. "Sounds like you're willing to pay a lot for something you could do yourself. Things too good to be true usually are."

Riker placed a ten-dollar coin on the bar. Seeing money was much different from talking about it.

Corrigan quickly pocketed the coin. "Tell me what needs doing."

Riker picked up his drink. "It's the easiest money you'll ever make. All I need you to do is walk over to the jail, look nervous, and tell Deputy Halstead a story."

"Halstead?" Saying the name sobered him up a bit. "That man's a killer. I'm not getting my fool head blown off for a lousy ten dollars."

Riker steadied him down. "He won't shoot you because you won't have a gun and you won't be trying to hurt him. I just need you to talk to him. That's all."

Corrigan dug the coin out of his pocket and handed it back to Riker. "I'm not sure about this, mister. My memory ain't what it used to be. Too much whiskey, I guess."

Riker refused to take the coin. "The beautiful thing about this story is that it's easy to remember."

Corrigan put the coin back in his pocket. "What kind of story?"

"The kind I want you to tell. Here's what I want you to say."

The drunkard listened while Riker laid it out for him.

And by the time the new sheriff of Battle Brook was done, Corrigan agreed to repeat it.

As a boy growing up in a mission in El Paso, Halstead heard stories of men who had lost limbs in the War Between the States. He learned how men still felt pain in limbs they had lost even years after Lee's surrender. How men who were blinded in battle had improved their sense of hearing and smell after losing their sight.

He was never able to understand how such a thing was possible until he found himself a hunted man. He lost his sense of security, which forced all his senses to improve out of necessity. Even when he was lost in thought, as he was when Mackey and Billy left for Valhalla, his ears were always listening and his mind alert for any threat.

Which was why Halstead set down his mug of coffee when he heard someone stop walking just outside the jail. As the attempts on his life had increased in Battle Brook, people often sped up when they had to pass in front of the jail. Most crossed to the other side of the thoroughfare. Men seeking to collect Zimmerman's bounty had struck at all hours of the day and night. No one wanted to risk being caught in the cross fire between the deputy and an assassin.

Which was why the sound of footfalls stopping on the boardwalk in front of the jail—especially during the day—struck Halstead as odd. Dangerous.

From his chair in front of the door to the cells, Sandborne noticed his partner's concern. "What's wrong? You hear something?"

"No." Halstead drew his Colt from his hip as he stood. "And that's the problem."

Sandborne reached behind the desk and brought up his Winchester as Halstead moved to the door. He opened it as he raised his pistol, ready to fire at anyone outside.

He saw a lanky man with sandy hair standing on the boardwalk, hat in hand. Upon seeing a gun aimed at his belly, he dropped the hat and threw up his hands. "Sorry, Mr. Halstead. I ain't come for trouble and I ain't armed."

Halstead could see he was telling the truth and lowered his pistol, though he did not holster it. He recognized the man from around town. A harmless young drunk named Chuck Corrigan. He did odd jobs for shopkeepers and at some of the mining camps around Battle Brook. He was usually in a saloon during daytime hours when he had the money to drink.

"What are you doing out here, Corrigan?"

"Came to tell you something, but I was trying to get up enough nerve to tell you. Something important. Mind if I pick up my hat?"

Halstead eyed the street in case he was being set up to take a bullet, but no one was around. "Go ahead."

Corrigan picked up his hat and continued to fiddle with it in his hands. "I just rode down from the Buster mines up in the hills and saw some men camped out at the old Pine Branch mine. You know it?"

"I do." Halstead kept looking over the street. "Go on."

Corrigan began. "I normally wouldn't think anything of it. Lots of people camp out in an old mine for a day or two to rest their horses and such. But when I stopped to look them over at a distance, I counted five men, and I remembered seeing one of those fellas before. A big, ugly fella named Tote. I wasn't close enough to swear it was him, but I'm pretty sure it was. We'd worked a couple of claims together before he went over to Valhalla and joined up with Zimmerman's bunch."

Halstead had heard the name before. He was one of Zimmerman's new constables. "Why tell me?"

"Because the wind changed while I was looking them over from the tree line," Corrigan explained. "I heard them say they were getting ready to ride down here and take a run at you. They didn't say when, but I saw them loading up. Rifles, pistols, everything. Thought it was only fitting I tell you before trouble started."

Halstead was suspicious. Men like Corrigan cared more about being able to drink in peace than keeping peace in town. "And you're just telling me this out of the goodness of your heart?"

Corrigan blushed and fiddled more with his hat. "Well, I was kinda hoping you'd be grateful enough to appreciate the gesture. You see, I'm a bit short on money right now on account of the boss up at the camp didn't pay me what he owed me. Said I didn't earn my keep."

Halstead knew the toll drink could take on a man. He had been tempted to it himself more than once since his trouble with Zimmerman started. But even one drunken evening might lead to his death, so he resisted the urge. He only wished Corrigan—and men like him—could do the same.

He took two one-dollar coins from his pocket and handed them to him. "I appreciate you stopping by to tell me, Chuck. Have one for me and thank you."

There may have been a time when Corrigan would have been insulted by the gesture, but that time had long since passed. He quickly pocketed the coins. "Thank you, Mr. Halstead. And good luck."

Halstead shut the door, knowing he would need more than luck against Tote and his fellow constables.

Sandborne stood up from behind the desk. "Sounds serious, Jeremiah."

"Yeah." Halstead slid his pistol back into its holster on his hip. "I'd better ride up there and look them over myself. Maybe stop them before they get around to coming down here."

"I don't think the marshal would like that," Sandborne said. "One of us has to mind the prisoners, and Aaron told us to stay here until he gets back. We'll be able to fight Zimmerman's boys together here in town instead of you going up there alone. Besides, I wouldn't put much stock in what Corrigan says. That old drunk is liable to hear and see all sorts of crazy things."

But Halstead was not as sure as his partner. Randy might have been lying about not being sent by Zimmerman to take

Abby. And a group of Valhalla men hiding on the outskirts of town on the same morning would be too much of a coincidence for Halstead's liking. They could be part of the same plan. They might be waiting for Randy, Mule, and Hec Garvey to return with Abby. And when they did not show, they might ride into Battle Brook to get them free.

Mayor White had already tried to force him out by hiring Emil Riker as sheriff. Another battle on Main Street would turn the town more against Halstead.

He was surprised by how quickly his mind had become cluttered with possibilities and indecision. *What's happened to me? I always knew what to do before. Why am I like this now?*

There was only one person in town who could help him make sense of it. To help him see it all clearly before he acted.

Sandborne moved closer to him. "You feeling all right, Jeremiah? You look just about ready to fall over."

"I'm fine," Halstead lied. "I'd better go check on how Abby's doing. We didn't part on the best of circumstances back at the hotel." He took his hat from the desk and put it on. "Keep an eye on things here until I get back."

Sandborne said, "You're just going to the hotel, right? Not to the livery to get your horse."

Halstead appreciated his friend's concern. "If I do anything stupid, you'll be the first to know."

The people Halstead met on the way to the hotel put decent effort into hiding the concern in their eyes as they tipped their hats or offered curt nods as he passed by. But their eyes hung on him longer than usual, as if they expected him to start shooting at any moment.

It was not too long ago when they looked at him and Sandborne with something closer to grateful reverence. They had stood up when Jack McBride was killed. He and Sandborne had kept the town safe.

But now they looked at him like he was a rabid dog, foaming at the mouth in the middle of the street. They respected the danger instead of him. They were afraid.

He could not blame them. Killing three men before noon was not normal, even by Halstead's standards. Battle Brook had not seen such violence in some time. They had grown used to a certain degree of civility. Civility Halstead and Sandborne had given them by keeping criminals in their place.

He was also aware that most of the town probably knew Emil Riker had been hired as their new sheriff. Mayor White would have wasted no time in telling them about his bold action despite the bad blood that existed between Halstead and Riker.

The people he passed did not know trouble might already be waiting to ride down from the hills at any moment. If another large fight broke out in Battle Brook, the fear in their eyes would quickly turn to angry scowls. They would no longer whisper about him among themselves but would demand that Aaron Mackey send him elsewhere.

Halstead could not allow that to happen. Not until his business with Zimmerman was finished.

He entered The Standard Hotel and looked for Bill Holland. There was no sign of the owner, but one of his clerks was at the front desk, sorting letters for the guests.

Halstead asked him, "Miss Abby up in her room?"

The clerk did not look up from the envelopes. "I should hope so. Clara is supposed to be helping her pack. And if that girl is off somewhere loafing again, I'll see to it she's docked for it."

"Packing?" Halstead asked. "Why would Miss Abby be packing?"

The clerk seemed mildly annoyed by the question. "I imagine she's probably going somewhere. Why else would somebody go through the trouble of packing their things?"

Halstead took the stairs two at a time as he rushed up to her room. He pushed in the door without bothering to knock and found her trunks open. Her luggage and clothes were on the bed. Clara, the hotel maid, was bringing dresses from the wardrobe to the trunk while Abby was folding one of his shirts.

"Jerry!" Abby exclaimed when she saw him and ran to give him a kiss on the cheek. "I thought you'd still be over at the jail, guarding the prisoners with Sandborne."

But Halstead did not care about the jail or its prisoners or the Zimmerman men up in the hills. "You're packing."

"Of course." She said it as naturally as if she was breathing. "We've got a train to catch tomorrow and Mr. Holland was kind enough to allow Clara here to help me get everything in order. You know how much I hate packing and she's been invaluable."

The maid offered a quick curtsy and placed another dress in the open trunk.

Halstead was as confused as he was down in the dining room that morning. "Where are you going?"

"With you, silly. Back to Helena." She wrapped her arms around his middle and hugged him tightly. "You didn't think you'd be able to get rid of me that easy, did you? Isn't it wonderful? You and me finally in Helena. Together at last. And you're going to have yourself a good long rest before the marshal sends you away again, even though he doesn't know it yet. I'll have a talk with Katherine once we get there."

But Halstead felt lost. "We're going back to Helena? Tomorrow?"

Abby slowly stepped away from him. Her smile quickly fading. "Didn't Aaron tell you? He told me he would. I thought you'd be happy about a new start."

"No. He didn't tell me."

Mackey might not have told him, but everything was becoming all too clear. Billy had kept him busy while Aaron plotted with Abby. They had not come to Battle Brook to help him take on Zimmerman. They had come to bring him back to Helena, like a convict. To take him out of the fight before it was done.

Abby took his hands in hers. "What's wrong, Jerry? This is wonderful news. We're going to make a new home for ourselves like we've always wanted. We'll be with your friends and leave all this nonsense behind us. Isn't it exciting?"

Halstead felt the room begin to close in on him. Aaron, Billy, and Abby had joined together to work with Mayor White against him. He had not expected loyalty from the mayor. He could even understand why Abby had been taken in by the idea of going back to Helena.

But Aaron and Billy? They knew the fate of Battle Brook hung in the balance. They knew better than anyone how Zimmerman would spread like weeds throughout Montana if somebody did not stop him.

But they did not care about that, did they? Battle Brook was a long way from Helena. They had an entire state to think about. They did not care if Zimmerman took over two towns in the middle of nowhere. They had no idea about the kind of man Zimmerman was. They would not know until it was too late.

Abby looked like she was about to cry. "Jeremiah, what's wrong? Don't be upset. I thought Aaron already told you about this. I thought that's why you came here. To celebrate the good news."

Halstead backed into the stair railing. Poor Abby had no idea what this was about. She had returned from the safety of Helena to be by his side and still did not know him. What he had to do and why.

But Halstead knew. Today was the day when Zimmerman had pushed his luck too far. He had sent men for Abby and now they were coming for Battle Brook. He could not afford to hide in the jail until Mackey and Billy returned.

It was time to bring the fight to Zimmerman's men.

Abby called after him as Halstead broke for the stairs and ran down to the lobby. He barreled through the front door and weaved through strolling citizens as he dashed to the livery. Time and distance were everything now and he did not have a moment to lose.

He ignored the old liveryman, who had offered to help him with Col. The mustang accepted the bridle and bit and Halstead quickly saddled her himself. The man was wise enough to step aside as Halstead pulled her from the stall and climbed into the saddle as soon as she cleared the roof of the livery.

He rode Col out onto Main Street and sped around the wagons clogging the thoroughfare as he made his way to the jail. There was no sign that Mackey and Billy had returned, so it was worth the risk to get his rifle.

When he got inside the jail, he found Sandborne consoling a weeping Abby. Halstead's heart sank when he saw her face was swollen and streaked with tears.

Sandborne gently moved her aside and went to Halstead. "You've got to calm yourself, Jeremiah. You're getting worked up into a lather over nothing."

"You call getting pulled out of town before the fight's done nothing?" Halstead took his Winchester down from the rifle rack and pocketed a box of bullets. "Not me. I'm going after those Valhalla men up in the hills and finishing this before it gets started. Tell Aaron I'll be back when it's done."

And as he headed out the door, Halstead stopped when he heard gunmetal clear leather.

Abby sobbed.

Sandborne had drawn his pistol.

Sandborne said, "I'm gonna need you to move away from that door, Jeremiah. Back up and put the rifle in the rack where it belongs. Aaron told us to stay here until he gets back, so that's what we're going to do. I don't know anything about going back to Helena and neither do you. It's best if you wait to talk it over with the marshal yourself."

Halstead hung his head. *Not Sandborne. Not him. Not after all we've lived through. All the good we've done.*

"You going to shoot me, Joshua?"

"Only if you make me." The quiver in Sandborne's voice was small but there. "And I hope you don't make me."

Abby's voice cracked as she cried, "Please listen to him, Jeremiah. You're not yourself, honey. No one wants to hurt you. We all want to help you. To keep you safe."

Halstead had faced unlikely odds before, but not like this. He had been beaten to the draw by his best friend. The woman he loved was weighing him down, preventing him from doing what he knew in his soul was right.

He was not angry with them. In fact, he felt a small amount of pride in Sandborne.

"You picked your moment well, Joshua. Both of my hands are full and my back is turned. There's no way I can drop all this, turn, and pull without you getting me first. You're learning."

"I don't care about learning anything. Just put the rifle back and sit down. Aaron knows what he's doing. So does Billy. We can talk about all this when they get back. They'll be here soon. What difference will a few minutes make?"

But Halstead knew Sandborne was wrong, just as Aaron and Billy and Abby were wrong. No one knew Zimmerman as well as Halstead knew him. The outlaw would sacrifice anything and anyone to get what he wanted. Sandborne was not at Silver Cloud. He had not seen Zimmerman sacrifice his own gang for the sake of his freedom.

He was not in El Paso when Riker's father goaded him into killing a man only to turn on him later. Sandborne had not lost three years of his life to the whims of clever men. More powerful men.

No, Sandborne had not seen enough of life yet to know how dangerous it could be. He did not know what people were capable of when faced with a difficult situation.

But he was about to learn.

"I'm walking out that door, getting on Col, and riding up to take on Zimmerman's men. You can shoot me if you want, but you're going to have to shoot me in the back if you do."

Abby sobbed as Halstead stepped outside and slid his rifle into the scabbard on his saddle. He climbed atop Col and could not bring himself to look back at the jail. He did not want to see the love of his life begging him not to go. He did not want to risk seeing his friend aiming a pistol at him. He did not want to think less of him if he was not ready to do his duty.

And he did not want his instinct to cause him to kill Sandborne.

Halstead brought the mustang into a gallop and sped along Main Street.

Sandborne did not shoot, so Halstead kept on riding as the sound of Abby's plaintive wails filled the street behind him.

CHAPTER 14

Mackey heard what Sandborne told him but could not believe it. "What do you mean, he's gone?"

Billy placed a hand on Sandborne, who was slumped at the desk. "I mean he's gone, Boss. Just flat-out gone. Chuck Corrigan stopped by to tell us he spotted some of Zimmerman's men up in the hills waiting to jump us."

"Who's Corrigan?" Billy asked.

"An old drunk who's been hanging around town for the past month or so. Does odd jobs here and there so he can spend the rest of his time drinking. Jeremiah took the news well, but he didn't like it. He was thinking about going up there after them but wanted to check on Abby first to see if she was all right after what happened this morning. I thought she'd calm him down, like she does. But when she came in here crying, I knew it hadn't done any good. Next thing I know, he came barging in here to get his Winchester and some bullets. He said something about you taking us back to Helena, but I told him to stay here and ask you about that himself. Me and Abby practically begged him to stay. I even held a gun on him, but he just wouldn't listen. He told me if I was going to shoot him, I'd have to shoot him in the back."

Sandborne raked his fingers over his face and hair. "I

guess I could've winged him, but I couldn't bring myself to do it, Boss. Not even Abby's tears were enough to stop him." He pounded the desk. "I guess I'm still just a fool kid after all."

"Get that thought out of your head right now, Deputy," Billy scolded him. "No one expected you to shoot him, least of all the marshal. If Abby couldn't get him to listen to reason, no one could. Tell him, Aaron."

"Of course not." At least he knew how Halstead found out about his plans to take him back to Helena. He cursed himself for not telling him about it before riding off to Valhalla. "If Abby couldn't stop him, neither could you. Did this Corrigan tell you where Zimmerman's men were supposed to be hiding?"

Sandborne dropped his head into his hands. "The Pine Branch mine. It's an old mining camp up in the hills about an hour's ride from here."

Mackey was glad Halstead had not headed straight for Valhalla, but riding out alone on the word of the town drunk was not smart. The Jeremiah Halstead he had once known would have been wise enough to wait for help. The broken man he had obviously become was a total stranger to him.

Billy gestured for Mackey to follow him outside while they left Sandborne alone with his regrets.

When they were out on the boardwalk, Billy said, "This is a mess, Aaron."

Mackey knew he could not change what had already happened, but he could do something about it. "Think you can track him?"

"I probably can, especially now that I know where he's headed. I don't know where the Pine Branch is, but I'm sure I can find it."

Mackey stifled a curse. "I should've kept my mouth

shut about going back to Helena until we got back from Zimmerman. If I hadn't told Abby to start packing, Jeremiah never would've run off like that."

"I told you, the boy's not in his right mind," Billy reminded him. "The only way to have kept him here was to lock him in a cell, and neither of us thought there was any cause for that. Besides, the chance to take on Zimmerman's men would've been tough for him to resist."

Mackey knew what had to be done and knew all the wishing in the world would not change things. If Zimmerman had men up in the hills, Halstead would be riding into trouble. If it was a lie, he would be riding into a trap. Neither outcome would be good.

He looked back into the jail and asked Sandborne, "Got any idea where Corrigan might be right now?"

"He usually drinks up at The Athens this time of day. I saw Jeremiah give him a couple of coins, so he's probably over there spending them right now."

"Let's go talk to Corrigan," Mackey said. "Get him to tell us where the mine is so you don't waste time trying to find it."

"I'll pay him a visit," Billy said. "You'd best stay here with Sandborne. If Zimmerman's men really are up in those hills, there's bound to be more of them coming from another direction. I don't think that boy's in any condition to handle them alone."

"Fine," Mackey said, "but I don't want you riding into anything alone. If you find Jeremiah before he gets there, bring him back. I don't care if Zimmerman's got fifty men up there, we'll make a stand here in town together. Knock him out and tie him up if you need to."

Billy climbed on his horse and rode along Main Street toward The Athens Saloon. Mackey hoped his friend came back with good news. He hoped but was not hopeful.

He walked back into the jail to try to get Sandborne to calm down. He would need him steady for whatever challenges might lie ahead in the coming hours.

Chuck Corrigan staggered into the alley behind the saloon to relieve some of the burden of his celebration. He could hardly believe his good fortune. First an El Paso dandy shows up and gives him ten dollars to feed Halstead a two-bit lie. And after he delivered it, Corrigan managed to guilt Halstead into giving him money for leading him to his own death.

Corrigan always knew the best whiskey was bought with another man's money, but fooling a man to get it made the liquor taste that much sweeter. He had found a way to profit from both sides and come out ahead. Yes, sir, it was shaping up to be a memorable evening and the day was hardly half over yet.

He unbuttoned his fly and steadied himself against the side wall of the saloon as he began to make water. He was already mighty drunk and intended on getting drunker still if his money held out. And when he sobered up, he'd drink some more. His mama used to say a beggar would ride to Hell if you gave him a horse. Corrigan planned on shaking hands with the devil before the last of his money was spent.

He was still in the process of relieving himself when he was slammed hard against the wall. He tried to fire an elbow back at the man who had hit him, but two hard shots to the kidneys brought him to his knees.

His attacker grabbed a handful of hair and yanked his head backward. It was a black man holding a bowie knife and he brought that knife to his neck. "Tell me where you told Halstead to go and I might not cut your throat."

Corrigan had never seen this man before, but the look in

his eyes and the star on his chest meant this must be Billy
Sunday. He had heard he might be in town and now he was
certain of it. He searched his besotted mind to remember
Riker's lie as best he could. He needed to stick to that lie,
for the truth might cost him his life.

"I just told him what I saw on my way into town. Five
men holed up by the Pine Branch mine, looking to jump
him here in town. I was trying to do something good. I
should've just kept my mouth shut."

Billy kept the edge of the knife against Corrigan's neck.
"And where's this Pine Branch mine supposed to be?"

Corrigan struggled to remember the way and told the
man what he could remember. One mine blurred into the
other in these parts, especially now that his mind was awash
in whiskey.

He hoped it would be enough for the man to let him go,
but the grip on his hair tightened. "If you're lying to
me—and I think you are—you'd better not be here when I
get back."

Billy let go and Corrigan fell over. Whatever numbness
he had felt from drink was gone. The front of his pants was
soaking wet.

Maybe the time had come to get out of Battle Brook
while he still had a few coins in his pocket. If he played it
right, he might be able to steal a horse and ride out of town.
His luck had held so far, but he knew it was changing for
the worse.

CHAPTER 15

Considering that Jimmy Warstler was not given to telling tall tales of any kind, he was annoyed that his friends did not believe him.

"Quit laughing at me, boys. I tell you, I know what I saw with my own two eyes. There's something going on over at the jail that ain't quite right."

Taylor Richards, who had ridden with Warstler on many cattle drives between Texas and Montana, spoke through his laughter. "You're so drunk half the time, you don't even know what you saw."

Warstler shoved his beer mug away, though not hard enough to cause any of it to slosh over the side. "This is my first beer of the day and I know what I saw. I was as sober as a judge when it happened."

"Depends on which judge you're talking about," said Doc Higgins, who was not actually a doctor. "I've known a few who were even bigger drunks than you."

The four other men standing at the bar resumed their laughter, which only caused Warstler greater consternation.

He looked around at other patrons who might be willing to take him more seriously than his trail partners, but they were too interested in their card games to pay him any notice.

But there was one man who might be able to support his story. A stranger drinking alone at a back table of the saloon next to the window. He had been sitting there when Warstler first came into The Blue Belle over an hour ago. A man with deep-set eyes and a full black mustache who had hardly touched his whiskey. He just kept looking out the window at the jail directly across the street from the saloon.

"Hey, mister," Warstler called out to him. "You've been sitting there a while. Tell them what you saw so they know I'm telling the truth."

The man did not look away from the window. Warstler was going to ask him again, but there was something about the stranger that made him think better of it.

Doc Higgins resumed his teasing. "Can't expect him to admit to seeing something that never happened, you old drunk."

"I only get drunk when I'm bored," Warstler complained, "and I'm neither right now. I'm telling you, we could have a genuine chance at making some easy money here and none of you fools are wise enough to see it for what it is."

"A poor man's pipe dream is what it is," observed Wally Moses. "You really think Aaron Mackey and Billy Sunday have come all the way here from Helena just for a visit? You think Halstead would just ride off without them two knowing exactly where he's headed? It just doesn't make a lick of sense."

Warstler could not have agreed more. "And neither does me seeing Halstead's pretty lady slumped in the doorway overcome with grief when Halstead rode off. Sandborne had to practically carry her back inside. That might sound normal to you fellas, but I know a sorry sight when I see one."

"You should," Wally said. "You see one every time you pass a mirror."

The men laughed again, except for Lou Johnson. He was always the quietest and most serious of the group. "You saw his woman do that? Collapse, I mean."

Warstler was glad someone was finally paying attention. "Like her man was going off to war and she didn't think she'd see him again. Saw it plain as day while I was passing on the other side of Main Street not hardly an hour ago." Warstler raised his hand as if taking an oath. "May I be struck dead right here and now if I'm lying to you boys."

His solemn tone and the gesture served to dampen their laughter. Such oaths were not taken lightly among these kind of men.

Warstler could not be certain, but the man at the back table seemed to have taken notice.

Lou said, "That doesn't sound right to me. They could've had a fight, but I've never heard Halstead say a cross word to anyone. I've seen him kill a man, of course, but that's different."

Warstler was glad his story was finally beginning to reach them. "That's what I've been trying to tell you boys. This wasn't just some squabble. It looked like Halstead was taking off for good and neither Sandborne nor the woman could stop him. If he was leaving on Mackey's orders, why would she be that upset? And if he was traveling somewhere, how come he didn't have any provisions on him when he left? I didn't see as much as a bedroll on the back of his saddle. And why didn't Sandborne go with him?"

"To guard the prisoners," Eddie Richards offered. "I heard they've got a couple of Valhalla boys locked up for trying to steal Halstead's woman over at The Standard Hotel this morning."

Doc Higgins added, "There's nothing standard about that woman. I can tell you that right here and now. She is one fine-looking gal. If Halstead's thrown her over, I might bring her some flowers. Show her how a real man can treat her."

"You'd have to bring a real man with you if you did," Warstler said to the laughter of the others. He was glad the boys were laughing at someone beside him for a change.

But Warstler wanted to keep them focused on the subject at hand. "Who cares about her? I'm more interested in Halstead leaving town in a rush. He's still got a price on his head and he's up in those hills all alone. I hear Ed Zimmerman's willing to pay a handsome sum for him."

Wally Moses was about to drink his beer but stopped when the mug was halfway to his mouth. "I heard two boys tried to collect that bounty this very morning before sunrise. One got his head caved in and the other got shot full of holes for his trouble. If you're saying what I think you're saying, you can count me out. The five of us put together ain't much of a match for a man who can kill as easily as Halstead."

Lou Johnson did not seem as certain. "Two against one is a lot different than five against one. The odds are even better if we jump him at night."

Warstler was encouraged by what he was hearing. They were finally beginning to pull in the right direction. "That's what I was thinking. We wouldn't even have to get close to him to do the job right. All of us are fair hands with a rifle, aren't we?"

He looked around the saloon to see if anyone was listening. The man at the back table continued to nurse his drink as he looked out the window, but he did not seem as bored as he had earlier. He thought the stranger might be listening to him. He hoped that meant he was curious. He might even throw in with them. Six against one were better odds.

Warstler beckoned his friends closer as he began to lay out his plan. "I say we head out now and track him while the light's still good. Once we find him, we hang back and wait for night. If he camps somewhere, we spread ourselves out in a circle and get him between us. When we're ready, we all shoot at the same time. I don't care how fast he is; he won't be able to get all of us before we get him. He'll never have a chance! Afterward, we'll take him over to Valhalla and collect our money from the big man himself."

Warstler did not recognize the voice of the man who said, "That's big talk coming from the likes of you."

Warstler looked up while the others turned around to see who had spoken. It had not come from the direction of the back table, but the front of the saloon. They saw the silhouette of a tall man in the doorway. Warstler might not have been able to make out his face, but the silver star pinned to his coat was easy to spot.

It was US Marshal Aaron Mackey.

"Afternoon, Marshal," Warstler said. "Me and my friends here are just having ourselves a friendly conversation."

"Nothing friendly about conspiracy to commit murder." Aaron Mackey stepped into the saloon. "Especially when you're talking about killing one of my men."

Warstler had no idea how long Mackey had been standing there, but it must have been long enough to hear what they had been saying. He glanced at the back table where the stranger had been sitting, but he was gone.

"We're just having what you might call a little barroom banter, Marshal. You know how it is. Big talk over a round of drinks. We didn't mean any harm by it."

"That so?" Mackey took another step toward them. "Loose talk like that can get a man killed. Men like you."

The small group of cowboys began to break up and drift to other spots at the bar when Mackey came even closer. "I didn't say you could move."

The men froze in place.

Mackey took another step, which made the conspirators move backward against the bar, Warstler included.

He tried a smile. "We're just a bunch of poor cowpunchers running cattle up from Texas. We're not looking for any trouble. Just have big dreams."

Mackey stopped three feet away from them. "Every man whose been foolish enough to try his hand at Zimmerman's bounty has been a man like you. Dumb men. Desperate men. Greedy men. Now, they're dead men."

Warstler noticed Mackey's hand was on his belt buckle, less than an inch from the pistol butt jutting out from his belly holster.

The marshal went on. "If any of you want to take a run at Halstead, you'll have to go through me first. Right here. Right now."

Each of the four other men lowered their heads, unwilling to meet Mackey's glare. Warstler placed both hands on the bar, as far from the pistol tucked in his belt as he could manage.

Mackey looked at each of the five men in turn. "No takers?" He kept looking at them as he raised his voice so it filled the saloon. "What about anyone else in here? Doesn't have to be these five. Anyone else have dreams of Zimmerman making them rich?"

Warstler wished someone—anyone—would say something, but the saloon was as quiet as the grave. No one made a sound. No one moved. Even the cardplayers lowered their heads as they kept their cards covered while they waited patiently to resume their game.

"Guess that's settled." Mackey pointed at the bartender. "I'm telling every saloon owner in town the same thing I'm telling you. Collect the gun and rifle of every man in here. No one gets it back until after dark. No exceptions. You ignore me, you'll answer to me. Any man refuses, you come to the jail and get me. Is that clear?"

"Clear as a bell," the bartender confirmed.

Mackey nodded toward Warstler and his partners. "Keep a close eye on this bunch right here. Any of them leave, I don't care when it is, you let me know."

"Consider it done."

Mackey made a point of looking over Warstler and the others a final time before he began to back out of the saloon. "Any of you boys get brave and change your mind about my offer, you know where to find me."

None of the men breathed until the marshal stepped outside and walked away.

Doc Higgins sagged against the bar. "If that don't beat all."

Johnson gulped down his beer and called for the bartender to give him another. "I thought he was going to gun us down right on the spot. Lord, I'd hate to meet my end in a place like this."

The bartender pushed their empty glasses aside. "You heard the marshal. If you want to drink in here, you'll hand over your iron. I'll give it back after dark." He looked up at the other customers. "That goes for all of you. Come on. Hand them over like the marshal said."

Warstler put his gun on the bar while Wally Moses asked, "It won't be nightfall for hours yet. What if I want to leave before then?"

"And go where?" the bartender asked. "A prayer meeting?

Go wherever you want, but your guns stay here. You don't like it? Take it up with Mackey. He gave me an order and, by God, I'm not crossing a man like that for the likes of you."

Moses was the only one who grumbled as the men undid their gun rigs and placed them on the bar.

Warstler had survived stampedes and lightning storms and led herds through parched land without a drop of water. But he could not remember a time when he had felt so close to death than just now, when he fell under Aaron Mackey's glare. Any notion of collecting a bounty or killing Halstead left his mind.

He did not like feeling so weak. He did not like feeling powerless and afraid. He knew his friends didn't either. They might have been poor, but they were proud. Mackey's warning proved Warstler was right about something not being over at the jail. And he had the rest of the day to watch what happened next. To watch and wait to see what transpired.

To see if he was right.

CHAPTER 16

Halstead slowed Col's pace as he reached the hills where the Battle Brook mining district began. If Corrigan was right about Zimmerman's men being at the Pine Branch, they were up a steep, rocky hill and around a bend to the left.

When he was hunting Zimmerman and Brunet through the mining camps months before, he heard about the Pine Branch, an old gold mine that was tapped out years before. It was one of the first of its kind in that part of the state. It had caused a brief gold rush to the area, with some selling all they had just to make the trip, with dreams of making their fortune in the hills of western Montana. Without enough money to go elsewhere, the unlucky travelers decided to ride out the winter on a nearby plateau that offered sweeping views of the valley. That was how Hard Scrabble Township was founded. Now they called it Valhalla.

The Battle Brook side of the site was the back of the mine. The Valhalla side of the mine was at the top of the hill and had an easier entrance to reach. But with Zimmerman's men hiding out up there, he didn't have time to take the easy way.

The area had become overrun by overgrowth since it

was abandoned. The mossy soil among the rocks was loose and slick, making it difficult for Col to get her footing. After trying several times, and with the horse almost slipping, Halstead decided to walk.

He climbed down from the saddle and wrapped the reins around the largest bush he could find. He pulled his rifle from his saddle scabbard and stroked the horse's muzzle. "Stay here, old girl. I'll be back in a bit."

The incline was slippery for him, too, but his boots found purchase among the rocky moss. Young trees gave him something to grab on to as he pulled himself up the hill.

Halstead stopped to look and listen before he risked cresting the hill. He would present an easy target for anyone who was paying attention. The rocks at the top of the hill were more jagged, which gave him better footing while he looked over the site.

The mine camp's layout was more spread out than he remembered. The mine entrance sat atop a hill with a gradual slope down to a larger encampment. Sloped roofs of buildings that were dug out of the hillside stuck out among the rocks. Wooden shacks dotted the area as well. Such buildings needed less material since most of the wood in the area was needed to shore up the mine.

Four narrow railbeds for carts were laid into the gradual incline that ran from the mouth of the mine down to the building below, where rocks were broken apart to get at the gold within it. Narrow shacks cobbled together with spare wooden planks littered the area, their windows long since broken.

There was no shortage of places where men could hide up there, but Halstead did not see any signs of life. He listened carefully for any human sounds but did not hear anything except for the wind rustling through the trees.

Have Zimmerman's men already gone? Were they ever here?

He would not know the answer until he searched the place. He scrambled up to the top of the hill and moved at a crouch to the mouth of the mine. He was careful to keep his footing among the loose rocks while he looked for any hint of movement among the structures below. He knew he made an inviting target for anyone keeping watch.

He had almost reached the entrance of the mine when a rock behind his head shattered, quickly followed by the sound of a rifle shot. Another rock was struck at his feet as Halstead ducked into a narrow wooden shack. More shots echoed on the hillside as round after round struck around him. Halstead was forced to lie flat on his stomach as the air was filled with splinters and dust.

As soon as the gunfire let up, he chanced a quick glance at where he was. It was a narrow wooden shack that was barely wide enough to fit a man. It may have been where a foreman checked in the miners or counted loads as they went down the hill. He was penned in and needed to move. He would be as good as dead if he stayed there for long.

He chanced a look over the rim of the ridgeline. The gradual slope from the mouth of the mine was just to his left, maybe twenty feet away. He might be able to make it inside if he could see where the shots were coming from.

"Hello up there," an unfamiliar voice echoed through the camp. "That you, Jeremiah?"

Halstead swallowed a curse. He had been foolish enough to allow himself to walk into a trap.

"What's the matter? Didn't they teach you manners in that Injun school of yours? It ain't polite to ignore a man when he's talking to you."

Halstead refused to take the bait as he took off his hat and inched closer to the edge. He peered down the hill and saw movement in the broken window of one of the old shacks. It was only the top of a man's head, but it was enough to help him peg where the shooter was hiding.

Halstead brought his Winchester to his shoulder and took careful aim.

His tormentor called out, "No call for you to be unfriendly about it. I know I didn't hit you, so you might as well answer me, because you and me are gonna be here a nice long while. Talking might do you some good. It's been known to help ease a man's passing, and considering yours is at hand . . ."

Halstead fired. His bullet struck where he was aiming, which was just below the broken window frame. He watched for any sign that he had hit someone. A cry of pain or a body falling into the doorway. But nothing happened.

"There you are," the man mocked him. "You didn't even come close with that one."

A bullet struck the ceiling of Halstead's meager shelter. A trail of gun smoke trailed up behind the shack. The shooter had been outside.

"See? I'm still here."

Halstead levered a fresh round into his rifle. He would need to have a clear shot before he risked wasting another bullet. He only had fourteen in the rifle, twelve in his pistols, and another six on his belt. He had a feeling he would need each round before this was over.

His attacker kept talking. "I know what's keeping you so quiet. You don't like talking to strangers. What if I told you we ain't strangers? That you and me already met?"

Halstead remained still. He refused to mark his position by asking any questions.

The man's laugh echoed through the camp. "The name's Warren Riker. I'm Alan's boy. Emil's brother. You remember my daddy, don't you? The man you killed after yourself got sprung from prison early."

Halstead kept his Winchester fixed on the shack. He knew Emil Riker was Battle Brook's new sheriff, but he had not counted on him bringing one of his brothers with him.

Halstead had never met Alan Riker's oldest son, but he'd heard plenty of talk about him. None of it was good. Warren was scouting for the army for years before Halstead was named the deputy in El Paso. He had heard the man lost his family in an Indian raid on a wagon train on its way to California but never paid the story much mind. Such tales were as common as they were tragic.

If Warren wanted to talk, they would talk. "Heard you lost your family in an Indian raid. Guess you must've been hiding somewhere when the shooting started."

Warren responded with two quick shots. One hit the rocks in front of him, while the second hit the doorway.

Halstead held his fire and looked at the angle of the bullets while Warren shouted, "Me and some of the other men were riding down the heathens that stole some of our cattle. It was just a trick to lure us out so they could double back and hit the train. I learned a bitter lesson about you people that day, but one I'll never forget."

Another shot struck the right side of the doorframe at almost the same height as the first. Warren was firing up at him from a steep angle. An angle that kept him from seeing the narrow ledge to the mouth of the mine. It might just be the chance he needed to get out of the coffin-size cutout.

"Want to know what I learned?" Warren called out. "That a man can't go against an Injun until he's lost most of his soul. You have to live like one and think like one if you want to kill one. And I killed plenty. That's why I'm gonna kill you today, Halstead. I know how you think and what you'll do next even before you do."

Halstead fired as soon as he saw the barrel of a rifle appear around the right side of the shack. The bullet went through the ruined window and sliced through the thin wood on the side.

Warren fell forward, losing his hat and revealing a thick mop of gray hair. Halstead crawled to the edge of the hill and fired again just as the man scrambled backward. His bullet struck the dirt where Warren's head had been.

The man rewarded Halstead's efforts with another cackle that carried through the deserted mining camp.

"You sure can shoot, can't you, Jeremiah? I heard you were good, but that was some fancy shooting."

Now that Warren had ducked for cover, it was time to move. He used his elbows and knees to move as he crawled toward the mine. He remained as flat as he could to keep Warren from seeing him. He hoped he had gotten the angle of his sight right. If he was wrong, he would probably be dead before he got there.

But he reached the mouth of the mine as Warren called out to him again. "You're making this a lot more fun than it ought to be, Halstead. I didn't have any great love for my daddy. Him and me didn't always agree on things, but that doesn't mean I'm going to let his death go unanswered. When a man's father is butchered by a lowly breed, he's expected to do something about it."

Halstead crawled into the mine and did not stand up until he was well inside. He got to his feet at the edge of the shadows and stood against the right side of the wall. Cool air rushed up at him from the bowels of the earth as he inched forward to get the best look at Warren's position.

"I know what you're thinking, Jeremiah," Warren yelled to him. "You're just waiting for me to climb up there and rush you. You've got the high ground, so you figure I'll do something stupid. That you can pick me off as soon as I start up that hill. Well, I hate to disappoint you, son, but I've already made my mistake for the day. And I never make the same one twice."

Warren Riker's constant mouth was beginning to get on his nerves. "I know better than to expect a Riker to come out and fight in the open."

Another laugh from Warren grated him. "Well, sounds to me like someone has found his way into the mine. Guess you made a run for it while I was taking shelter. That's fine. No harm done. I figured you'd make your way in there eventually. It doesn't change anything. You've still got nowhere to go but down, either in this life or the next."

Halstead cursed himself for not keeping his mouth shut. Now Riker knew where he was. He also happened to be right. He might be able to stand up and move around more in the mine, but he was still trapped. Warren would have a clean shot at him if he tried to move.

Halstead chanced a quick look down at the shack below. From his new position, he could see that it cast a long shadow on the left side. But Warren's shadow was not behind it. The man had moved, too. He could be anywhere among the buildings that dotted the hillside.

A bullet ricocheted off the left side of the mine, causing Halstead to jump back.

"That's right, Jeremiah," Warren called out. "You're not the only crafty one up here. You've got nowhere to go and all day to get there. All night, too. See, I'm not going to kill you right away. What would be the fun in that? No, sir. I'm going to use something I've got plenty of and you don't. Time."

Halstead remained next to the wall as he listened to Warren speak. He tried to figure out where the voice was coming from, but the echo made it difficult to know exactly where he was.

He kept listening as Warren kept talking. "The two things I've got plenty of is bullets and time. You don't have either. I aim to use an old Injun notion on you. I'm gonna keep you pinned down up there and wait you out. You won't get away with crawling out of there again. I'll sit here all day and all night if need be. But I don't think I'll have to wait too long. You'll get impatient sitting up there and you'll make a move before long. Maybe try to crawl back the same way you came in. I hope you try it. I sincerely do."

Halstead took another quick look down at the camp, hoping a shadow or something would give away Warren's position. He saw nothing.

Warren said, "You could try to go back in the mine, of course, but I wouldn't chance it. A mine is a mighty dangerous place in the dark, and the owners don't seem to have kept the place up. You could just as easily trip and break your neck as find another way out. Which you won't. I spent the morning checking around and didn't find anything."

Halstead had never enjoyed cramped spaces and always steered clear of such places when he could. Exploring the mine was pointless. There was only one way out of this mess and that was through Warren Riker.

The man continued. "Have to say, it feels awfully good to use an Injun tactic on an Injun, even if he is just a breed. You're full of spark now, but after you've been trapped up there a while, you'll make a mistake. And that's when the real fun begins."

Halstead knew he was a dead man if he did not find a way to turn the odds in his favor. He could wait until dark to sneak out, but Warren would be waiting for that. He could just as easily sneak up the hill as Halstead could sneak out. He could not allow this to go on that long. He had to find a way to change his own luck, and he had to find it fast.

As he began to search the mine for options, he wanted to keep Riker talking. The more he talked, the better chance Halstead had of figuring out where he was.

"Why don't we quit this hiding like a bunch of kids and end this like men? We look each other in the eye. We can use our pistols if you want. Or our knives."

"Didn't think to bring a knife with me," Warren answered. "And I'm not fool enough to go toe to toe with a gunslinger like you."

Halstead walked into the shadows and bumped into something large and heavy. He pushed on it, but it wouldn't budge. It was one of the ore carts the mining company had used to send rocks down to the camp below.

"Then we can leave our pistols aside," Halstead offered as he felt around the cart. There had to be a way to get it rolling. "We can fight Indian style if you like."

Warren laughed. "I didn't see you toting a tomahawk or a bow with you just now."

Halstead put his shoulder against the cart and tried to push it forward, but the wheels did not budge. "I was thinking more with fists and legs." He felt another cart on the rail next to it and pushed against it. The wheels squealed but moved a few inches.

Warren said, "If I didn't think you'd shoot me the first chance I gave you, I just might take you up on your offer. But seeing as how we can't trust each other, we'd best do it my way. What do you say?"

Halstead strained to put all his weight behind the ore cart. He was glad when the wheels began to slowly turn.

He would have been willing to trade quite a bit for some bacon grease at that moment.

But the wheels slowly turned and he was able to push it just to the edge of the shadows at the mouth of the mine. He did not know what he would do with the cart, but it was nice to finally have an option.

Halstead leaned against the wall and took a rest. He hoped Warren made a stupid mistake before he decided what he would do next.

CHAPTER 17

Had the circumstances been less dire, Sandborne might have enjoyed sitting in front of the jail with Aaron Mackey. He remembered how the marshal liked to sit with Billy in front of the jailhouse back in Dover Station. Mackey in his rocking chair, while Billy rolled smokes and casually watched over the town.

But with Jeremiah somewhere up in the hills alone, Sandborne felt more of a sense of dread than any hint of enjoyment.

And while Mackey seemed content to sit in silence, Sandborne felt the lack of conversation discomforting.

"Think there really were ten men up in the hills looking to jump us?" Sandborne asked him.

The marshal kept his eyes moving over the thoroughfare. "We'll know soon enough."

Sandborne saw the shadows had begun to grow longer now that it was getting later in the day. No one dared walk on their side of the street. They preferred to cross over to the other side and quicken their pace if they had occasion to pass the jail.

"Think Billy will find him?"

"Billy will find him," Mackey said. "He'll track him as

far as the rocks and maybe a bit farther. He's the finest tracker I know."

Sandborne knew he was, but Jeremiah was not like some of the men he had tracked. He was crafty, especially if he did not want to be found. "Guess I should've sent word to you about how bad he'd gotten. You might've been able to do something before it got this far."

"You're still learning this job, Joshua. Regret doesn't do anything except make you feel worse. Billy will bring him back if he can find him. Then I'm going to have a long talk with him. There's a chance I can make him listen to reason." Mackey held up a finger. "Listen to what I said. There's a chance. That's different from a foregone conclusion."

Sandborne was not so sure. "I know he took Zimmerman's pardon bad, but it's like he's not even the same man anymore. All he thinks about is Valhalla and Zimmerman all the time. Guess all those men looking to kill him for money makes it hard to forget. Maybe things will be different once we get him back to Helena."

Mackey's scowl was deeper than usual. "You remember that trellis they used to have on the JT Ranch?" He explained further, "That curved wooden doorframe he had in the field behind the house that had all the vines growing on it."

Sandborne remembered it but hadn't known it was called a trellis. He would look it up in his dictionary later. "I do. Why?"

"I remember when John Tyler's wife made him put it up before their daughter's wedding," Mackey said. "I thought it was a waste of time, putting something like that out in the open only to allow vines and such to grow all over it. But for a couple of weeks every spring, it had the prettiest red and white flowers I've ever seen."

Sandborne remembered it that way, too, though he had not thought about it in years. "It burned along with everything else on the ranch when Darabont put the place to the torch."

But Mackey did not seem to care about that. "You've got to think about Jeremiah being a lot like that trellis. Just because he's got some weeds covering him now doesn't mean he's not still the same man underneath. He's still a Halstead, and trust me when I tell you that means something."

Sandborne had never heard the marshal be so thoughtful. He did not know if "philosophical" was the right word, but it seemed to fit.

"His father was always a melancholy sort," Mackey continued. "Sim stopped talking after his second wife and child died."

Sandborne had known Sim back in Dover Station, but they were never close. "I thought he lost his tongue back when he was fighting the Apache with you and Billy."

"A lot of people thought so," Mackey kept explaining. "Sim's last words were begging them both not to die. He never saw a reason to say another word after that. Didn't make him any less brave or change the grit he had. It just made him different. Hurt in a way a man gets when he loses something important to him. I imagine Jeremiah's going through that same thing right now. He thought he had Zimmerman caught. He'd done everything right, and Zimmerman should be in prison right now, waiting for the hangman to call his name. He doesn't have enough years behind him to know life doesn't always turn out like it's supposed to. Some men don't come back from a disappointment like that. At least not the way they used to be."

Sandborne thought he understood what Mackey was talking about. He remembered how he was after Dover

Station had burned. "You did. You came back from it, I mean. You're the same."

Mackey shook his head. "Don't be so sure."

Sandborne saw Mayor Phil White toddling toward them along the boardwalk across the street. He had a phony grin pasted on his face and waved to the lawmen.

Mackey looked away. "What's that coming toward us?"

"Mayor White. And he looks like he wants a word with you."

Mackey lowered his head. "Just when I thought this day was bad enough already."

Sandborne watched the mayor step down from the boardwalk and come toward them. "Marshal Mackey, we haven't had the opportunity to meet yet. I'm Philip White, mayor of Battle Brook, and I just wanted to tell you it's an honor to have a man such as yourself here in town."

Mackey spoke to Sandborne. "Deputy, who is this man and why is he talking to me?"

"He's the mayor. It sounds like he wants to welcome you to town."

Mackey looked away from him and not at the mayor.

White said, "I've tried unsuccessfully to contact you several times, but there's a great deal we need to discuss."

"I've got nothing to say to you. Get out of my sight."

Sandborne knew the marshal could be prickly when people got too familiar.

The mayor did not take it well and stood his ground. "There are some important matters pertaining to the safety of Battle Brook we need to discuss. As mayor of this town, it's well within my rights to—"

"You the one who hired Emil Riker on as sheriff?" Mackey asked without waiting for an answer. "A man who hates one of my deputies and blames him for killing his father?"

The mayor cleared his throat. "He came with the highest recommendations."

Mackey's head snapped in his direction. "Whose recommendations? Zimmerman? His lawyer? Who thought it was a good idea to hire a man who'll only antagonize Jeremiah Halstead?"

The mayor fumbled for an answer as Mackey rose from his chair and stepped toward him. "You say you're concerned about the peace and safety of this town. If you were, you wouldn't have hired a sheriff who wants to see my deputy dead. You wouldn't have put this town in a dire situation, but you did. You're taking orders from Zimmerman and now you're taking them from me. You will turn around and crawl back to wherever you came from. If I have anything to say to you, I'll send for you. And if I want anything from you, I'll ask Zimmerman. I don't waste my time with middlemen. Now, get out of my sight."

Sandborne enjoyed watching White scurry across the thoroughfare and back to his shop.

Mackey pointed at the deputy. "Don't get any ideas. I can do that. You can't. Understand?"

Sandborne was beginning to learn there was a lot about life he still needed to learn. He found himself wishing for silence again when he spotted Billy Sunday atop his horse round onto Main Street. "Billy's back."

"He surely is."

The two men watched Billy ride toward the jail. Judging by his expression, Sandborne could tell he had not found Halstead.

"I tracked him up into the hills," Billy told them as he climbed down from the saddle and wrapped the reins around the hitching rail. "Lost his track up there just like I imagined I would. I paid Corrigan a visit before I went looking for Jeremiah, but the directions he gave me were worthless. I searched the ground between here and Valhalla, too. My guess is Jeremiah's still up in those hills somewhere."

Sandborne thought that was good news but waited for Mackey's reaction to know if he was right.

"See any sign of riders between there and Valhalla?" Mackey asked.

Billy began building a cigarette. "Not from what I saw, and I would've seen them if there were. I looked for Corrigan just now to ask him why he lied, but he's long gone. Someone said he stole a horse from the livery and tore out of here riding west."

"He's probably going to Valhalla to beg Zimmerman to protect him," Mackey observed. "He'll get a bullet in his belly for his trouble."

The news only made Sandborne feel worse than he already did. "I should've hit Jeremiah in the head instead of letting him ride out like that. This is all my fault."

Mackey grabbed the deputy's shoulder and shook him hard. "That's enough of that talk. He didn't give you much choice and you did the right thing. It's not always easy to know what to do, but you made a decision. It also happened to be the right one."

Sandborne felt himself begin to redden. He knew compliments from the marshal were rare.

Billy smiled, too. "Look at what you've gone and done, Aaron. You made the kid blush."

Mackey slapped Sandborne on the shoulder. "You'd better go fetch dinner for those two we have in the back. Do it quick. After Billy's horse has rested some, the two of us will ride up to look for him. Corrigan lied for a reason and I aim to find out why before Jeremiah gets it into his head to do something wild."

Sandborne got to his feet. He had almost forgotten about the prisoners until the marshal reminded him, but he remembered them now. And he remembered something Jeremiah had said earlier that morning back in the dining room. Something that might change things in their favor for once.

Mackey must have seen the strange expression on his face. "What's wrong?"

But Sandborne kept his thoughts to himself. The marshal was right. It was not always easy to know what to do, but Sandborne thought he had finally found a way to give Jeremiah the peace he sought and end this once and for all.

CHAPTER 18

As day began to slide into night, Halstead knew he had to make a move soon. He had been holed up in the mine for far too long. Either he or Warren would have to act first before sundown and whoever did would have the advantage.

Halstead had kept a close eye on the old mining camp below since managing to get the ore cart to move. He had chosen good cover for Halstead had no idea where Warren was. He hoped what he did next would change that in the next few moments.

He had spent much of the time thinking about Alan Riker as he waited for the opportunity to kill his son. He could almost see the man's face in the clouds that rolled by the entrance of the mine.

He remembered the kind, fatherly way he coaxed him along. How he appealed to Halstead's sense of right and wrong to push an aging sheriff out of office and take the star for himself. How the promise of a long career blinded him to Riker's true goal. The El Paso mayor had not cared about Jeremiah Halstead's future. He cared only about his skill with a gun, a skill given to him by Aaron and Billy. A skill Riker had used to get him to kill the troublesome Cortez and take his cattle ranch for his own.

A skill Riker turned against Halstead when he not only charged him with murder but testified against him at his trial. Halstead's foolishness had cost him three years of his life.

No, Jeremiah Halstead was no longer a fool. And Alan Riker would never use anyone again. Halstead had seen to that personally before leaving Texas to come to Montana.

Despite the weak sunlight that filtered into the mine, Halstead was able to look inside the cart and found it was empty. It was certainly deep enough for him to fit inside after giving it a good push down the track. Its heavy iron sides would easily deflect Warren Riker's bullets.

But that was only half the problem. The other half of it was stopping its momentum when he reached the bottom of the hill.

There was no brake on the cart, so stopping it would be impossible. And the end of the track led to a couple of sturdy boulders to stop a load from running off the rails. It looked like the previous operators had used a pulley system to gradually lower carts and bring them back up again to the mine. They might have used donkeys to make the whole thing work.

Halstead did not have any donkeys or even a rope to help slow his speed as the cart raced down the hill. It would slam into the boulder and scramble his brains before it pitched over. He would either be knocked out by the impact or thrown clear of it. He dared not risk either with Warren Riker waiting to cut him down.

The best Halstead could hope for would be for Riker to *think* he was in the cart when it came rumbling down the hill. He might break cover long enough to watch it roll or, even better, mark himself by shooting at it. Halstead could use the distraction to move out of the mine or get a clear shot at him.

He admitted it was not much of a plan, but it was the only one he had.

Warren called out to him for the first time in hours. "Hope you got yourself some rest, Jeremiah. You're going to be needing your strength for the fight ahead. I've got something real special planned for you and it ain't biscuits and gravy."

Halstead had no doubt he did. And he had no intention of finding out either.

He picked up his rifle and moved to the back of the iron cart. Once again, he put his shoulder against it and used the wooden railroad ties to give himself decent footing. They were cracked and split in places and groaned under the sudden weight. But the forgotten cart slowly rolled on rusted wheels until it reached the mouth of the mine, when Halstead gave it one final shove before dropping to a knee and watching it go.

The wheels shrieked and sparks flew as the great iron box picked up speed, rocking slightly back and forth as it rumbled down the track. It kept building momentum until it slammed into the boulder blocking its path, sending up a great sound like a church bell as it bucked on impact and spilled over on its side.

Now.

Halstead bolted as fast as he could back the same way he had come. He knew it was not far—only forty feet or so—but with a man like Warren after him, each step felt like a mile.

He chanced a look back down the hillside and saw Riker dash out from one of the dugout buildings on the hillside. He dove behind a shack with his rifle ready to fire as soon as Halstead rolled out of the cart.

Halstead made it to the same spot from which he had first surveyed the camp and brought up his rifle.

He aimed carefully as Warren stood and peered out from

behind the shack to see if Halstead had been thrown free in the crash.

He stopped when he saw the cart was empty.

Halstead's first shot went wide, striking the side of the shack instead of Warren. The old scout fell as he tried to move back to cover.

Halstead's next shot caught him in the right shin just below the knee.

Warren Riker's screams echoed through the camp.

Halstead grinned as he kept his rifle trained on the shack. *Who's laughing now, you bastard?*

"You think you got me?" Warren shouted up at him. "It ain't hardly a scratch."

Halstead remained quiet. There was no advantage in answering him. Let him guess, as he had made Halstead guess.

"This ain't over, Halstead!" Warren yelled to him. "Not hardly."

No, Halstead agreed. It was not over until Warren Riker was dead.

The sun sank below the western mountains as darkness began to settle over the camp. He heard boots scraping on dirt and knew the wounded man was getting ready to move. He heard a stifled cry as he threw something out from around the back of the shack.

At first, Halstead thought it was a knife, but when it landed on the rocks at the base of the mine, he knew what it was.

A stick of dynamite.

The explosion rocked the side of the hill and the ground gave way beneath his feet. He skidded down the hill on his side until he reached the smooth rocks and slid down the rest of the way on his stomach.

He looked back up to where he had been standing and saw a great column of dust rising from the other side of the hill. The blast had caused a rockslide that had brought down the whole hill.

Halstead's ears were ringing from the blast and he shook his head to try to clear it. The dynamite must have been the special surprise Warren had bragged about. He had intended to use it while Halstead was in the mine. Why he had not, only Warren Riker could say.

The ringing in his ears finally stopped and he tried to get to his feet. He was sure someone must have heard the blast and was bound to come see what had happened. And since he still had a price on his head, he did not want some miner looking to try his luck.

He tried to get to his feet, but the ground tilted and he fell over again. He held on to his rifle but slid even farther down the rocks on his backside. When he reached the grass, he got sick to his stomach and wretched.

His hat had fallen off his head while he was getting sick and he quickly snatched it up. The world turned again and he rolled onto the grass flat on his back. He shut his eyes and tried to will himself steady. He had felt dizzy before, but not this bad. The blast had scrambled his senses.

He did not know how long he had been lying there when he finally felt brave enough to open his eyes. The darkening sky remained above him and he hoped the spell had passed him by.

He gingerly raised his head and was glad the forest did not move before him. He used his rifle to help sit up before getting to his feet. He was still a bit shaken but did not think he would fall over. When he placed his hat back on his head, he felt much better. Grounded. Centered.

Which was why he was able to hear horses coming his way.

Halstead staggered into the overgrowth and crouched

low. He kept his rifle down until he had something to shoot at.

He saw two men trailing a third horse ride into view. Their pistols drawn as they looked up at the rising smoke from the hillside.

He had never been so glad to see Aaron Mackey and Billy Sunday before.

"It's Jeremiah," Halstead shouted as he stumbled through the overgrowth. "Don't shoot me."

Mackey dropped to the ground and rushed to his side. "We heard the explosion. What happened?"

Halstead asked, "Sandborne tell you about Zimmerman's bunch being out here?"

"He told us," Mackey said as Halstead weaved. The marshal grabbed his arm. "Now tell me what just happened."

"It wasn't Zimmerman." His own words echoed in his head. "Corrigan lied. The only one out here was Warren Riker, Emil's brother. He had me fixed to get trapped in that mine, but I managed to get away. I got him, though. Drilled him right through the leg. Pretty fine shooting, if I say so myself." He looked at Mackey. "Just like you boys taught me."

The marshal shook him by the shoulders. "And the explosion?"

"He tossed a stick of dynamite at me. It didn't come close, but it was enough to bring the whole hill down. I've been feeling poorly since. I can't seem to stand up straight. Kinda feels like I'm drunk."

"You're not drunk," Billy said as he kept an eye on the area, "but it sounds like you got your bell rung pretty good. It should pass in a while."

Halstead squinted at the horse he was leading. "That Col?"

"Found her running the other way right after the explosion

happened," Mackey said. "She was scared out of her mind. So were we over what might've happened to you out here alone. You shouldn't have run off like that, Jeremiah. Abby's worried something awful. Sandborne, too."

Halstead did not want to argue with him. Not with Mackey or Billy or anyone. He just wanted to climb into bed and go to sleep for a while until his stomach settled down.

He tried to shake some feeling back into his head, but it did not do any good. The entire day seemed like a bad dream. Everything blurred into the other. "You sure I'm not drunk?"

Billy said, "Could explain your behavior if you were."

Mackey took him by the arm and brought him over to Col. "Climb up there and see how you are. If you can sit up straight, we'll take you back to town nice and slow. Get you something to eat to replace what you lost over there."

Halstead sat in the saddle and his head lolled back. But another shake of his head cleared his senses a bit. The fog in his head thinned out and the buzzing died down. And when he took hold of the reins from Billy, he felt something close to normal.

Mackey kept a hand on his back until he was sure he was steady. "Think you can ride?"

"Just not too fast." He remembered something he had forgotten to tell Mackey. "I think Warren Riker got away."

"I'm sure he did," Mackey said, "but we can worry about him later. Now it's time to get you back. You left some worried people behind."

He watched Mackey climb back atop Adair and led them back to the road to Battle Brook. He was glad the marshal kept the pace slow and steady. He did not want to get sick again.

CHAPTER 19

Sandborne waited until Mackey and Billy had ridden out to find Jeremiah before he dared to put his idea to the test. He hoped to save himself some embarrassment if it turned out to be nothing, but he had to try.

It began as a whisper in the back of his mind that had quickly grown into a roar in his ears. Something Jeremiah had said back in the dining room that morning repeated constantly in his head: *Run them back to the jail. I'll be over to question them in a while.*

Only Jeremiah had not taken time to question the prisoners. And Sandborne was too busy guarding them against Halstead to think of talking to them himself. So much had happened since that morning, he had never thought to try. Neither had the others, even the marshal.

He had served the men two meals already and never spoken a word to them. In his mind, Randy's words twisted with Halstead's. *Please don't take me back there. Mr. Zimmerman will kill us. I've seen him do it.*

Randy knew something that could put an end to all this business with Zimmerman. And it was up to Sandborne to pull it out of him.

He took the key ring down from the peg and opened the door to the cells. As he went in the back, Mule jumped to his feet and rattled his cell door. He hurled curses as Sandborne found the key to Randy's cell and opened it. The prisoner was curled up on his bunk with his pillow over his head. He did not stir when Sandborne grabbed hold of him.

"On your feet," the deputy said as he tossed the pillow aside and pulled Randy off the bunk. "You've got some questions to answer."

The boy moved like a beaten dog as Sandborne steered him out into the office.

Mule cut loose with a fresh string of curses before lunging at Sandborne, but his thick arms were too thick to reach him.

Sandborne grabbed the outstretched wrist and twisted it, bringing Mule to his knees. "Next time you do that, I'll break it, and I won't send for the doctor. Understand?"

Mule whimpered that he did and Sandborne let him go.

The prisoner pulled his arm back into his cell as he yelled, "Don't you tell him anything, Randy! Mr. Zimmerman will send some boys to come fetch us soon enough. Don't you turn yellow! Just keep your mouth shut!"

Sandborne shut the door, locked it, and pushed Randy against the wall. He had wasted too much time already and wanted to have some answers waiting for the others when they got back to town.

Sandborne tried to make his voice deeper than it was as he put the question to Randy. "Back in the dining room, you said you were afraid of Zimmerman. Why?"

Randy's body was like a rag doll. "You've seen him, ain't you? You know why."

"You said he'd kill you and that you'd seen him do it. What did you mean by that?"

Randy's head lolled around as he began to mutter to himself. "Mule's right. Mr. Zimmerman's got some boys coming for us right now. They'll get us out of this mess. I don't have to tell you anything. I've just got to keep my mouth shut until they get here, then everything will be fine."

Sandborne grabbed Randy's shirt and pulled him off the wall, just as he had seen Mackey do to suspects. "The marshal's already told Zimmerman what you did. He said you could rot in jail for all he cared. He doesn't think much of men who try to steal women, especially without his permission."

Randy continued to shake his head. "That's not true. It can't be true. I'll just keep my mouth shut. Just go back to sleep and wait for Mr. Zimmerman to spring us, just like Mule told me to."

Sandborne shook Randy hard enough to smack his head off the wall. He had to get him talking. "The only one who's coming for you is the hangman."

"The hangman?" Randy finally seemed to hear him. "I didn't kill anybody."

"But Zimmerman did, and you saw it. If you don't tell me who, you're as guilty as he is." Sandborne was not sure if that was true, but it sounded good. "We'll put you on trial for murder the same as him. And the marshal will see to it that you hang. Do you want that?"

Randy's lips quivered as he tried to find the words, but he gave up. "Mule said to keep my mouth shut and that's all I have to do."

Sandborne could count on one hand the number of times in his life when he had lost patience with someone, but Randy was about to make him add to that number. "Don't listen to what Mule told you. Because after I'm done with you, I'll pull him out here and offer him the same deal I'm offering you. And he'll take it. He'll take it and put your head in the noose right next to Zimmerman's and won't think twice about it."

Randy pawed at his neck. "They'll hang me?"

"It's what hangmen do, Randy. It's your choice. Talk to me or I talk to Mule. This is your last chance to save yourself. Tell me about the man you saw Zimmerman kill."

Randy lowered his head again. "I didn't mean anything when I said it. I was just scared. Seeing Hec get shot like that rattled me. I don't even remember what I was saying."

Sandborne pulled him off the wall and pushed him down into Halstead's chair. It rolled backward on its casters until it hit the wall.

Sandborne crowded him by leaning on the armrests. "Enough lies, Randy. I'm the only friend you've got right now. Tell me what you saw Zimmerman do and I promise I'll help you. This is your last chance before I put you back there and bring out Mule."

"Help me?" Randy moaned. "How can you help me by keeping me locked up?"

Sandborne had already spent a good part of the afternoon thinking about that. "Lots of ways. You didn't hurt anyone. I don't think you even laid a finger on Miss Abby, right?"

Randy shook his head. "No. I didn't so much as touch her. I just held a gun on some people. We didn't even have any bullets."

"Which means I can help you even more. Halstead can get Miss Abby to not press charges if you tell me about the man Zimmerman killed. You'll sign a sworn statement and testify against him at his trial in Helena. Then you'll go free. You can start over somewhere else."

Randy kept shaking his head while Sandborne spoke. "It won't work. Mr. Zimmerman's got friends everywhere. If he finds out I'm going to speak out against him, he'll have me killed."

Sandborne strengthened his grip on the prisoner's collar.

"He won't get near you unless we let him. And if you don't talk, we're going to drop you off to him in Valhalla, just like the marshal did with your friend Hec. I'll tell him you told us about the man you saw him kill. You won't be dead when we do, but you'll sure wish you were."

Randy's eyes grew wide. "You can't do that. I'm your prisoner. There's a law against that kind of thing, ain't there?"

"The law doesn't matter much to a man like Zimmerman." He pulled Randy closer to him. "You going to talk, or do you want to go back to your cell?"

Sandborne could sense the boy was close to breaking. He let his last words hang between them. He could almost see the wall the prisoner had built up begin to crack and crumble.

Randy hung his head and shut his eyes as he offered a slight nod.

Sandborne let go of his collar but kept leaning on the armrests. He kept the pressure on and willed the boy to talk. It was what Mackey would do.

Randy began. "I've only been a watchman for a few weeks. I only got the job because one of the men who had it before me fell asleep when he should've been watching the town."

Sandborne could tell he was getting close. "Go on."

"His name was Meachum," Randy told him. "Bob Meachum. Nice fella, but he liked to drink too much. He never drank on duty, but he was suffering something awful the night he fell asleep." Randy shut his eyes. "I was the one who found him like that. If I'd just kept my mouth shut, Bob would still be alive, but I wanted that spot for myself. I've never been anyone important in my whole life and I wanted to be somebody Mr. Zimmerman knew and trusted. That's why I went and got Weasel and showed him where Meachum was."

His lower lip began to quiver again, and Sandborne sensed he needed some gentle prodding. "I understand. Keep going."

Randy's voice cracked. "I thought Mr. Zimmerman was just gonna throw him out of town, like he usually did. Maybe give me his job on account it was me who found him. If I'd known what he was going to do, I never would've said anything. I would've kept my big mouth shut, just like I ought to be doing now."

Sandborne was so close, he could not allow Randy to stop now. "It's you or Zimmerman, Randy. You've seen what he's done to men who fail him. You failed him when you went after Miss Abby. Stop protecting him and save yourself by telling me what happened next. Tell me about what happened to Meachum."

Randy kept his eyes closed. His tears washed away any resistance. "Mr. Zimmerman had me and some of the others wake up the whole town and bring them out to Main Street. It was the dead of night and most people were asleep, but he made us do it anyway. As soon as we turned out the entire town, Mr. Zimmerman dragged Bob into the middle of the street. He'd already beaten him something awful. He said Bob was guilty of laziness, drunkenness, and cowardice. He said a couple of other things I can't remember, but he said he had no choice but to make an example of him. To show what happened to any man, woman, or child who put themselves before Valhalla."

Randy's eyes grew vacant as he held up his hands and curled his fingers. "Everything kind of slowed down by then. He took hold of this long piece of lumber and set to beating Bob with it. It was the first time I'd ever seen anyone die and I never want to see anything like it again.

That's why we didn't have bullets in our gun for Miss Abby. I knew where the key for the bullets were, but I didn't want to see anyone else get hurt. Then I saw Halstead shoot Hec dead and that was even worse."

But Sandborne did not care about what had happened with Miss Abby just then. He only cared about what had happened to Meachum. "You said the whole town saw it?"

Randy nodded weakly as he lowered his hands to his lap. "Everyone was there. Even the kids. They started crying and burying their little faces in their mothers' skirts while it happened. Mr. Zimmerman gave us orders not to let anyone leave until he told them they could. Me and Mule and Hec saw to it." His eyes grew vacant and wide as he relived a horrible memory. "The sounds we heard. Those terrible sounds. I thought I was gonna be sick."

Sandborne finally knew how Mackey and Billy felt when they got a man to finally talk. He felt like he just struck gold but kept as calm and steady as he had seen the marshal act in similar circumstances. "You did fine, Randy. You did just fine. Do you know how to write?"

"I can write some." Randy sounded like he was dreaming. "My spelling's none too good, but I know how to sign my name. My mama taught me that much before she up and left us."

Sandborne knew he had to get this on paper while Randy was still in a talking mood. He needed a witness and fast.

He left the prisoner in the chair and ran to the door. He searched the street for anyone who might be able to help him. A couple had just strolled arm in arm past the jail and Sandborne called out to them. "You folks going by The Standard Hotel?"

The man turned and said, "My wife and I are staying there. We're headed back there now." He looked at the star on Sandborne's chest and pulled his wife closer to him. "Is there a problem, Deputy?"

"No, but I need you to get back to the hotel and ask Mr. Holland to come here as soon as he can. Tell him it's important and I need him right away. It's a matter of life and death."

The couple quickened their pace to the hotel as Sandborne shut the door. He found Randy was still muttering to himself as he relived Meachum's murder in his mind.

Sandborne went to the desk and pulled out some paper and a pencil. "Did Mule see this, too? The beating, I mean."

"He was right next to me when it happened, making sure no one left. Only I'm pretty sure he didn't look away like I did."

"That's good." He would give Mule the chance to cooperate, too. It would be nice to add his statement to Randy's, but he already had all he needed.

Sandborne set the paper and pencil on the desk and rolled Randy back to it. The prisoner did not seem to know what was happening. "I think I'm going to be sick."

"We don't have time for that, Randy. You've got the rest of the night to be sick. Right now, I need you to put everything you just told me down on paper. Then I'll read it back to you and you can sign it."

Sandborne didn't realize he had forgotten to lock the door until Bill Holland walked in. He was holding an old Walker Colt at his side. "I rushed over as soon as I heard."

"You're just in time. Randy here would like to make a formal statement and I need someone to be a witness. Since the marshal and the others aren't here, I figured you could do it."

"I can do better than that." Holland slipped the pistol in

his coat pocket and pulled the pencil and paper to his side of the desk. "I can write it for you."

Sandborne struggled to remain as calm as Mackey would have been had he been there. "That'll be just fine, Mr. Holland. Just fine." To Randy, he said, "I want you to tell Mr. Holland everything you just told me. Don't leave anything out."

When Randy began to speak, he repeated his story word for word, just as he told Sandborne only a few moments before.

Sandborne went over to the stove to check if there was any more of Billy's coffee left in the pot. It was only about a quarter empty, so he poured himself a mug. Then he decided Mr. Holland might need it more and placed it next to him on the desk as he wrote down every detail Randy told him.

He poured himself a mug full and was glad the pot was only half empty. He smiled as he put the pot back on the stove. It was not half empty. That night, it was half full.

CHAPTER 20

Emil Riker slipped back into The Blue Belle Saloon the same way he had left it earlier. Unseen and through the back door. He had made himself scarce when he saw Mackey walk into the saloon and, after pausing to listen to him threaten the cowboys, rode out of town until dark. He had not wanted to risk the marshal seeing him in the saloon out of fear he might remember him once White announced him as sheriff. If Warren succeeded in killing Halstead, Mackey might blame him for putting Corrigan up to a lie. The bartender Purdy would remember him, of course, but a few dollars should be enough to buy his silence for a while.

Riker had spent the hours observing his new town from a safe distance. He was watching when Aaron Mackey and Billy Sunday rode off toward the hills, probably to try to track where Halstead had gone. He considered riding after them in the hopes of ambushing them somewhere along the way, but decided it was foolish to risk going up against both men alone.

Besides, he wanted to see if he might be able to stir up trouble of a different sort.

He remained on the outskirts and watched the town grow steadily quieter as darkness began to fall. The saloons were doing a decent business and the various cafés along

Main Street were full. He was glad Hubbard wasn't lying when he assured him the town would fall in line behind him as their sheriff.

He had come back to The Blue Belle because the window in the back room offered the perfect view of the jail. Keeping an eye on the place would give him the best way to know when Mackey and Sunday returned. Only then would he know if Warren had been successful.

Riker saw the table he had been sitting at earlier that day was still empty. And the same loudmouthed cowboys who had been frightened by Mackey were still there. They were standing together at the bar like a herd of forgotten cows.

And much to Riker's surprise, they appeared to be reasonably sober. They were certainly a sullen bunch. Each man stood quietly, lost in the depths of their own thoughts while the beer in their mugs went flat. They were probably still sore from the scolding the marshal had given them earlier. Wounding a man's pride sunk deep and did not heal quickly. Riker hoped a bit of salt might work to his advantage.

He stood away from them at the end of the bar and got the bartender's attention. He dropped some coins and said, "Whiskey for me and my five sulking friends here."

The prospect of free liquor snapped the cowboys out of their mood and each man came to life. The loud one he had pegged as their leader was the first to speak. He remembered the others had called him Warstler.

"You're the same fella who was sitting over at that table before, when the marshal came in."

"I am." Riker forced an easy smile. "It's nice to be remembered."

One of the other men said, "I seem to remember you were nowhere to be found when Mackey started threatening us."

Riker thought of how to answer that as the bartender placed six glasses on the bar and filled them up. By the time the barman collected the coins and moved away to tend to other customers, Riker had his answer.

"A man decides to leave a place for all sorts of reasons, boys."

"Such as?" prodded one of the others.

"Could be he doesn't want to get himself cornered by the law. Maybe he doesn't want to be recognized."

Warstler seemed interested. "Any reason Mackey would recognize you?"

"Could be," Riker allowed. "Could be he's the reason I came to Battle Brook in the first place. Could also be because of Halstead, too."

The tallest of the group stepped forward. "Could be don't make it so. Speak plain or don't speak at all."

Riker's smile grew. "Could be maybe I need to know more about you fellas before I can cut you in on why I'm here."

Warstler rapped his hand against the taller man's chest. "What did I tell you boys? I knew there was something dangerous about this guy. I just knew it, and I'm rarely wrong about such things."

"Neither am I." Riker took his glass and raised it. "Here's to men like us. Men who are right about all the wrong things in this world."

Warstler gladly clinked Riker's glass with his own. The four others joined them in the toast but were far more wary of the stranger as they drank.

"Seeing as how you left before," a fourth man said, "why'd you come back now?"

"It's after dark, ain't it?" Riker asked. "Figured it was past the marshal's deadline about coming and going in town."

Warstler placed his empty glass on the bar and drew his

sleeve across his mouth. "Plenty of other saloons in town you can drink in. Nicer, too. Why'd you come back here?"

Riker made sure they saw him glance over at the window facing the jail. "Could be because this place has something the others don't have." He looked at Warstler. "Could be because I see some promise in the kind of men who drink here."

"There's that 'could be' again," the tallest man in the group repeated. "I don't trust a man who doesn't speak his mind plainly." He turned to his friends. "This guy reminds me of a snake oil salesman I met once. Always spoke in questions and never had any answers. Come on, boys. This fella is looking to rope us into something stupid."

Riker was glad Warstler held his ground. "Don't be so nasty, Lou. This man bought us a drink and he didn't do it out of kindness. He's got something on his mind. The least we can do is take the time to listen to what he has to say. It ain't like we've got anywhere else we have to be."

Riker shrugged. "Only you men can decide if I have anything worth saying. I just remember how you were talking about riding out to collect that bounty Ed has on Jeremiah Halstead."

Warstler stood a little straighter. "Ed? As in Zimmerman? You sound like you know him."

Riker could almost see the hook dig in deeper in Warstler's gullet. "It just so happens I do. And I know a way you boys might be able to meet him, too, if you're interested in such a thing."

Lou said, "I know how to meet him, too. By riding over to Valhalla tomorrow morning and introducing myself to him. I've heard he's got a warm welcome for any man willing to work."

"Sure," Riker agreed, "if hauling lumber and nails all day long is your idea of work. I had you boys pegged for men who had other skills Ed might find useful. More profitable, too."

"We're drovers, mister," Lou told him, "and proud of it. We've ridden every cow trail between here and the Rio Grande, and some south of it, too."

Riker played along. "There's nothing wrong with that. It's good, honest labor for decent pay, as long as you don't mind staring at a bull's backside for a thousand miles or so."

Warstler set his glass on the bar. "You telling us Zimmerman might be willing to hire us for a different kind of work. And if the next words out of your mouth are 'could be,' my friend here is liable to get cross with you. Quit nibbling around the edges and bite into the meat of the thing."

Riker could tell the time for playing coy had passed. It was time to lay one of his cards on the table to keep them interested. "You can ride over to Valhalla tomorrow and ask for jobs if you want. But he'll be a whole lot happier to see you if you bring him a gift."

Warstler leaned on the bar. "What kind of gift?"

Riker could see all the men were listening to him now. Their greed was beginning to take hold. "Let's make that two gifts. And they're both sitting in that jail over there right now."

Warstler and the others joined Riker in looking out the window at the jail across the street. The door opened and a tall man with gray hair stepped outside and hurried up the boardwalk. Riker could not swear to it, but Deputy Sandborne looked like he was smiling.

Lou was the first one to speak. "You mean you expect us to go over there, kill the deputy, pull those boys out of their cells, and bring them to Zimmerman in Valhalla?"

Riker acted as if he was impressed. "There's no flies on you, Lou. None at all."

The other men looked at one another while Warstler scratched the stubble on his chin. "We saw Mackey and Sunday ride out of here more than an hour ago. And with Halstead already gone, that leaves Sandborne the only one inside."

"They really that valuable?" Lou asked. "To Zimmerman, I mean."

Riker knew Zimmerman would not trade a dead skunk for them, but Warstler and his friends did not. And since Zimmerman wanted him to stir up trouble in Battle Brook, these men were the surest bet.

"You boys passed on your chance to get Halstead," Riker explained, "but I imagine, if you were willing to help me get those men free, Mr. Zimmerman would be grateful. Not as grateful as he would've been if you'd handed over Halstead, but I can probably talk him into giving you a reward for your trouble. Maybe even some jobs as watchmen, or even constables."

Warstler snapped his fingers as if he had just had an idea. "That's why you were sitting over at that window before. Zimmerman sent you to get those kids out of jail."

Riker might have felt sorry for the drunkard if he was not so useful. "You're a smart man, Mr. Warstler."

But Lou was not entirely convinced. "Just what kind of help would you need from us?"

"Nothing too dangerous," Riker allowed. "The same kind of idea you were planning to use on Halstead, except now you'd only be going after one young deputy. We kick in the door, shoot Sandborne if need be, and bring the prisoners back to Valhalla."

He could tell by Warstler's expression that he was warming up to the idea, but Lou threw water on it. "And just what will you be doing while the five of us are doing all this freeing for you?"

Riker had an answer ready for that, too. "I'll be watching the street to make sure no one tries to stop you. And lending a hand if you need it." He saw a way to sweeten the pot. "Of course, if I do anything, your share of the reward will be a bit lower. My share, you see."

"Don't worry about that," Warstler said. "Just tell us what you have in mind."

"Gather around and I'll be happy to tell you." Riker dumped more money on the bar and signaled the bartender to come over.

The piano by the door started up and a man started singing.

Riker was hopeful the night might not be a total waste after all. It might even be fun. At least for him.

CHAPTER 21

Even through the closed door of the jail, Joshua Sandborne could hear the bawdy sounds from The Blue Belle Saloon carrying along the street. Someone was banging out an unfamiliar tune on a piano while the drunks did their best to sing along.

He had just finished checking on the prisoners and found them both fast asleep in their cells. But not even the dank air in the jail was enough to dampen his spirits.

He looked at Randy's confession for the tenth time and it still gave him a thrill. His signature, along with Bill Holland's, meant it was legal. It had weight and could be used to finally get a warrant to arrest Ed Zimmerman.

Sandborne had won. He might not be as fancy as the marshal or Billy or Jeremiah with a pistol, but he had done serious work that day. He no longer felt like the kid Mackey had felt sorry for and hired on. He finally felt he deserved the star pinned on his shirt. A star that meant everything to him.

He felt good. No, better than good. He felt right at home.

He could not wait to see their faces when he showed them Randy's statement. Mule had refused to give one, but he had expected as much. The marshal would be able to lean on him enough to get him to sign if he thought it was necessary. But Randy's sworn statement would be enough. Sandborne had helped save Jeremiah the only way he knew how. His way.

The waiting for the marshal to return with Billy and Jeremiah was beginning to wear on his nerves. And although Mackey had ordered him to keep the door closed, he needed some fresh air. No, he decided he deserved it. His humble reward for a job well done. He had broken a prisoner just like Mackey would have done it. He had nothing to fear from grabbing a little bit of fresh air just outside.

Sandborne took his rifle down from the rack, opened the door, and stepped out onto the boardwalk. He knew the marshal might be angry with him if he rode up and saw him standing outside, but he was sure Randy's sworn statement would be enough to earn his forgiveness.

He had found another way to go up against the likes of Ed Zimmerman and his kind. Times were changing, and Montana was changing right along with them. He hoped to find a place for himself in keeping it safe.

He drew in a deep breath of cold night air and let it out slowly. Yes, sir. Confidence was a fine feeling for a man to have. Not cockiness or arrogance, just a belief in himself. He had passed a test before he realized he had been taking one and felt good about it. He was no longer the lowest hand of the brand. He had earned his place.

The ruckus from The Blue Belle began to grow even louder, and he squinted in the direction of the saloon. Oil lamps burned on each side of the thoroughfare, casting an uneasy, flickering light on the street. But the windows of The Blue Belle always burned brightest until the small hours of the morning and this night was no exception.

Sandborne did not understand why the place was so popular. He was never one to frequent saloons but knew there were nicer places to drink in town. Places that had better games of chance and prettier girls working the floors. Better pianos, too. It had always been a mystery to him why men picked one saloon over another, but he supposed the reasons did not matter. If they kept their fun inside and no one got out of hand, it was no concern of his.

But Sandborne took notice when five men stepped out of The Blue Belle. They were steadier on their feet than he might have expected given the amount of noise coming from inside. He watched them buckle their pistol belts while they tucked rifles under their arms. They did not go near the horses hitched to the rail like he expected them to.

And when the last man finished adjusting his rig, he watched the five of them begin to walk toward the jail on the other side of the boardwalk. One foot right in front of the other. No hint of stagger from drink.

A sour feeling crept into his stomach.

Sandborne kept his rifle at his side as he moved closer to the post of the boardwalk roof. He could tell by the angle the shadows played on their faces that they were looking straight at him, too.

"Well, would you look at what we have here," one of the men said loud enough for Sandborne to hear him. "That looks like a federal star with a boy pinned to it."

It was difficult to see much in the darkness, but Sandborne thought the man looked familiar. He had seen him a few times in the past week during his patrols through town but had never had any reason to pay him much mind except in passing.

"I do believe you're right, Jimmy," one of the other men said loudly. "Unless my eyes deceive me, that looks like Jeremiah Halstead's shadow. Sandborne, ain't it?"

"Newborn would be closer to the mark," called out another. "And since Halstead's not around, the poor little fella looks just plumb lonely."

"Maybe Mackey and that deputy of his forgot to leave some milk for him before bedtime," the one called Jimmy said. "That what happened, little fella? Left outside all alone on a cold night?" He stopped directly across from the jail. The others stopped with him. "Come over here like the good kitty you are. I've got something for you."

The five men proceeded to call out to him as they would an alley cat.

Sandborne brought his rifle to the crook of his shoulder but kept it aimed down at the street. "You boys had better go on with your drinking before I run you in for disturbing the peace."

The five men laughed in unison, but not as he had heard drunkards laugh. They did it for effect. They were trying to intimidate him.

Jimmy spoke first. "Just listen to that little kitty cat growl. No need for you to trouble yourself, Newborn. We were planning on coming over there anyway to keep you company."

One of the other men said, "You just let us take them prisoners off your hands like a good little boy and we won't have to put you over our knee."

Sandborne raised his rifle and aimed it at the leader. He did not have to rack it. They always kept their rifles ready to fire. He kept the tremble out of his voice as he told them, "First man off that boardwalk gets shot."

The men were not laughing now, but they began to slowly fan out on either side of the one they called Jimmy. Not quickly, but quick enough to flank Sandborne if he was not careful.

"I guess Mackey didn't teach you manners before he stuck that star on your chest," Jimmy said. "About how to speak to your elders properly. Now, you'd best be a good boy and step aside before you get yourself hurt. There's no shame in being smart."

The men continued to spread wider. Sandborne knew the danger increased with every step they took, though he did not dare move. He had made a mistake by coming outside and he had to live with it now.

If he did not die because of it.

Jimmy pointed a finger at him. "You'd best lower that rifle and run off while you still have the chance, boy. I know you want to."

"Let him stay," the man at the far right of the lengthening line said. "He'll just curl up into a ball and cry like Halstead's woman when he rode out. Won't you, Newborn?"

Sandborne turned when he saw the man on his far-left sidestep into the thoroughfare.

"The name's Sandborne."

He aimed at the center of the man's chest and fired.

The bullet struck the man just below the neck. He clutched his throat as he dropped to the ground.

Sandborne went to his knee as the four remaining men reached for their guns. He levered in a fresh round as he saw Jimmy begin to dive behind a water trough. Sandborne fired and hit him in the left side of the chest before he dropped out of sight. He cried out from the impact as he fell.

Rushed shots from the remaining three gunmen began to pepper the front of the jail and boardwalk as Sandborne levered in a fresh round and moved backward to the protection of the doorway. He knew one man was still off to his left and two were on his right side. If he backed all the way into the jail, he would lose any hope he had of hitting them. If he shut the door and locked it, they would break in eventually and he would be trapped.

He kept his eyes moving between both ends of the boardwalk as he looked for another target to shoot at. He knew they would be coming for him. He had not given them any choice.

From behind the trough, Jimmy yelled, "The brat got me, boys. When I give the word, rush that little bastard and get them prisoners!"

One of the men called back, "Where the hell is Riker?"

Sandborne remembered the name. *Riker? The sheriff?*

He dove to his left when he saw Jimmy's pistol appear over the top of the trough before firing blindly in the direction of the jail.

As bullets struck all around him, Sandborne saw the last man on his left break cover and run into the street. Sandborne's first shot went wide, but his second hit him in the chest. He kept running for a few more steps before he twisted and fell to the ground.

Three down. Two to go.

Rifle fire broke out from the remaining two on his right as Jimmy's pistol clicked dead. Dust and splinters filled the air as Sandborne rolled onto his back, trying to remain as flat as he could amid the barrage of bullets.

He forbade himself from panic as he levered another round while the last two men darted across the street. He rushed his next shot, which went between both men just as they reached the alley on his side of the boardwalk. Between him and the alley, the jailhouse door hung open and unguarded.

Sandborne remained flat on his back, knowing he only had a few precious seconds before their wounded leader behind the trough reloaded his pistol. If he tried to get to cover, he would be an easy target for the last two men. If he rolled into the street, Jimmy would cut him down.

He was still on his back, deciding what he should do, when a shot rang out from the mouth of the alley. The bullet struck the same chair Mackey had been sitting in earlier that evening and knocked it over. Sandborne remained flat, keeping his Winchester low, and aimed in the direction of the alley.

"I think I hit him that time," the man in the alley called out. Sandborne watched him sneak a quick look up the street before he ran toward the open door.

Sandborne sprang upright and fired. The shot caught the man under the chin and snapped his head back as his momentum caused him to pitch forward and drop to the boardwalk.

Four down. One left.

There was still one able-bodied gunman in the alleyway. He knew he could hold out inside the jail against one man. He got to his feet and was about to duck inside when a bullet slammed into the left side of his back. The impact threw him hard against the doorframe and caused him to drop his rifle inside the jail. More shots struck all around him as he tried to hold himself upright, but it was no use. He collapsed to the boardwalk and found himself once again on his back.

Fire burned in his left shoulder as the sound of his own blood roared in his ears. He struggled to lift his head in time to see the fifth man approaching him on the boardwalk. He must have run around the back and come up the other side of the alley. Sandborne's vision blurred, but he saw a pistol still smoking at his side.

Sandborne used all his strength to keep his head up as he heard the man call out, "I got him, Jimmy." The man sneered down at him. "Stupid kid."

Sandborne's vision blurred and went double as he heard Jimmy yell back, "You hear that, Riker? We got him. Get them prisoners free. We've . . ."

Sandborne pulled the pistol on his hip and fired into the center of the illusion where both shooters met. He kept squeezing long after the man fell from his view. Long after the hammer hit spent bullets.

The empty pistol became too heavy to keep raised and, try as he might to fight it, his hand dropped to his side and the gun fell into the thoroughfare.

He felt a great weariness overcome him as the pain in his left side slowly began to fade. He tried to blink his eyes clear when he sensed another man drawing near. A sixth man he knew he had not seen yet. He could barely make out a blurry silhouette as he stood over him.

"You did better than you should've, kid. Halstead will be proud."

Sandborne squinted up at the man. "You . . . Riker? Jeremiah was right." He coughed. "You don't look like much."

Sandborne heard Riker laugh as the man aimed a pistol down at him. "That may be so, but I'm enough for right now."

And as Joshua Sandborne slipped into the welcoming darkness, he thought he heard more shots being fired. But he slid away into nothingness and it did not seem to matter.

CHAPTER 22

Halstead pulled his pistol from his belly holster as he heard shots come from the other side of Battle Brook. He dug his heels into Col's flanks and launched the horse into a full gallop down Main Street. Mackey and Billy followed close behind.

Halstead peered down Main Street and saw a rectangle of light spilling out onto the boardwalk in front of the jail. Several men were down in the street. The jail door was wide open as he saw a man walk past it.

He called out to Sandborne, though he knew he was still too far away to be heard. He was still far out of pistol range, too, but fired at the man anyway. The figure dropped to a crouch before running across the thoroughfare before disappearing in the shadows.

Halstead saw another man stagger out from the same side of the street. The man's pistol was half-raised at the figure lying in front of the jail. He steered Col toward the man and barreled him over before bringing the horse to a skidding stop in front of the jail.

Halstead saw the man on the boardwalk was Sandborne, and blood had begun to pool beneath his left shoulder.

Halstead dropped from the saddle and ran to his fallen friend's side. The left of Sandborne's shirt was soaked in red, and he placed his hands over the bleeding wound. "Somebody get the doctor!"

His hands began to shake as the blood continued to flow. *There's so much blood. Too much blood for him to still be alive.*

Billy Sunday pushed Halstead aside and tore open Sandborne's shirt as he dug his hand behind him. "The bullet went through, but he's still bleeding bad. Help me get him inside."

Halstead lifted Sandborne and carried him into the jail. Billy took the keys from the peg by the door leading back to the cells and opened it. Halstead carried Sandborne into the last cell on the right, opposite Randy and Mule, and placed him on the bunk.

"Aaron's gone to fetch a doctor," Billy said as he pulled a sheet from the bunk and placed it over the wound. "Go fetch me that pot of coffee off the stove."

Halstead did not know why he'd made such an odd request and did not pause to ask. He ran into the office, grabbed the pot, and brought it back to Billy.

The deputy had ripped a sheet and tied it around Sandborne's upper chest to stop the bleeding, but the amount of blood showed it was not working.

Billy dumped out the remaining coffee and dug his hand into the pot. He scooped out a handful of grinds and used them to pack the front of the wound. He took another handful and packed them in the wound at his back.

Halstead looked away when Sandborne cried out in agony. The sight of gore had never bothered him before, but this was different. This was Sandborne's blood. His friend's.

"Scream all you like, Joshua." Billy's voice remained steady and soothing. "I'm right here with you. You did good out there, boy. You did real good. The devil won't be getting you tonight. Not if I have anything to say about it. No, sir. Not you. Not now. This old Indian remedy will fix you up in no time."

Halstead stepped aside when Mackey returned with Doc Potter. The frail old doctor moved with purpose as he carried his black medical bag to the cell where they brought Sandborne.

Billy told Doc Potter what had happened. "Bullet struck him in the back left side and came out the front here, Doc. I packed it with coffee grinds to stop the bleeding. I've seen it work before."

Doc Potter grunted as he examined the chest wound. "Interesting remedy. Are you a doctor?"

"No, but I've had to act like one from time to time."

Halstead watched the doctor take a metal tool from his bag. "Is he going to make it?"

"Ask me in a couple of hours," Potter said. "Now get out of here. We have much work to do." He looked at Billy. "I hope you'll agree to assist me, Deputy."

"You don't even have to ask. Just tell me what you need me to do."

Mackey grabbed Halstead by the arm and pulled him out into the office.

Jeremiah felt the rage begin to build inside him again, and any trace of the control he had felt only a few moments before disappeared.

"This is Zimmerman's doing, Aaron. I'm going to kill him for this. I'll kill him with my bare hands!"

Mackey snatched him by the throat and slammed him hard against the wall.

"Zimmerman didn't do this," Mackey seethed through

clenched teeth. "Five drunks from The Blue Belle did this. The same five drunks who were talking about following you up into the hills this afternoon. I recognized them lying out there in the street. This happened because Sandborne was alone." His grip on his neck grew tighter. "He was alone because we were out looking for you."

Halstead did not try to break Mackey's grip. His words had landed too heavily on him to move.

"If you hadn't run off," Mackey continued, "the four of us would've been in town and this never would've happened."

The marshal released Halstead with a shove and turned away.

Halstead remained against the wall. The thought of moving did not occur to him.

Mackey was right. This was his fault. Sandborne had been shot because of him. "I'm sorry, Aaron, but what if Corrigan had been telling the truth. What if Zimmerman really had . . ."

Mackey turned on him. "I'm sick and tired of hearing you use Zimmerman as an excuse for everything you do. I told you—no, I *ordered* you—to stay here until we got back from Valhalla. But you knew better, didn't you? You just had to ride out there alone to show Zimmerman and his men that you're not afraid of him."

Halstead was ashamed to speak.

"You disobeyed a direct order, Deputy. My direct order, and now a good man might die because of it. I hope you're proud of yourself."

Halstead looked away as Mackey's words struck home.

"I knew your daddy, so I know bouts of melancholy run in your blood," Mackey said, "but you're not just Sim Halstead's boy anymore. You're one of my deputies.

You can't allow your emotions to take such a hold on you. I chose you to go after Zimmerman because I knew you could handle him when things got thick. I was counting on you to keep your head even if everything around you fell apart. If I'd thought you would've turned out like this, I would've sent someone else."

Halstead's pride might have been wounded, but it was still intact. "You're preaching to me about controlling emotions? After what we did at Dover Station?"

Halstead saw Mackey's expression fade from annoyance to something else. The way a wolf looks at a pack member who challenges his position. Someone on his side of the line finally had dared to stand up to the great Aaron Mackey and he did not like it.

Jeremiah Halstead had never thought of running from a fight in his life and would not start now. But he was suddenly aware that his back was against the wall. And Mackey now stood between him and the front door. Halstead was not afraid but felt trapped. He did not like that feeling. He did not want to think about how he could change it.

The marshal slowly began to move toward him. "I can preach about controlling emotions because I know how rage can destroy everyone and everything in its path. You were there, remember? You saw it happen. You saw what it cost me. You're supposed to learn from my mistakes, Deputy. You learn from them so you can become better than me."

Mackey stopped about a foot away from him. Close, but not close enough for Halstead to feel cornered. "And after all that blood and all that burning, do you want to know what Dover Station taught me? That this"—he poked the star on Halstead's chest—"isn't always about *this*."

Mackey snatched the Colt from Halstead's belly holster before the deputy realized he had touched it. He had seen Aaron shoot steady and true plenty of times but had not known he could move that fast.

Mackey slid his finger through the trigger guard and allowed the pistol to dangle harmlessly in the space between them. "And when this isn't enough?" He laid the pistol on the desk. "You need to use this." He tapped a finger hard against Halstead's temple.

The marshal sat on the edge of the desk. "You can't expect to be able to shoot or kill your way out of every problem, Jeremiah. The star we wear means we do whatever's necessary to maintain law and order. Not just in our work but in how we act. Not just for Montana but for ourselves, too. Sometimes we need a gun to do the job and sometimes we use our minds. Zimmerman isn't free because of anything you did or didn't do. He didn't outfight you. Instead, he outthought you. He outthought all of us, including me. You can't beat a man like that with a Colt in your hand. You need to find another way. A way within the law. Otherwise, it's just murder, and a lot of good people might get hurt. People like Sandborne."

Halstead lowered his head. Mackey was right about most of it but not all of it. "I didn't ride out of town today because I lost my temper. I rode out because Corrigan told me there were five Valhalla boys waiting to ride into town to start trouble. I was angry about going back to Helena, but it wasn't just about that. I haven't been myself since the pardon, but I need you to believe me, Aaron. I had a solid reason even though it was the wrong decision."

Mackey looked down at some of the papers on the desk. "I know you believe that." A piece of paper alone in the middle of the desk caught his attention and he squinted as he looked it over. "Did you see this?"

"No," Halstead admitted. "What is it?"

Mackey picked up the paper and began to read it. "It's a sworn statement from one of the prisoners back there. Randy. And Bill Holland served as the witness." He handed the statement to Halstead to read. "Looks like Sandborne got Randy to confess to witnessing a murder in Valhalla. He must've done it while Billy and I were out looking for you."

Halstead read through the statement twice to make sure he had understood it properly. "Says he saw Zimmerman beat a man to death in front of the entire town. His name was Bob Meachum. Says the whole town saw it. " He thought this was great news. "Think this will be enough to get a judge to sign a warrant for Zimmerman's arrest?"

"Depends on the judge," Mackey admitted. "But I know one or two in Helena who would be happy to sign it." He placed his hands on his hips as he stepped back from the desk. "That kid must've been over the moon when he pulled this off. Explains why he was outside against my orders."

Halstead knew what should happen next, but he had already tested Mackey's patience as far as he dared and made no assumptions. "What'll you do now?"

"How many telegraph clerks do you have in this town?"

"Three that I know of," Halstead told him. "Two regulars and one that fills in for the others on their days off. Why?"

Whatever Mackey was planning, he kept it to himself. "Lock that statement in your desk and don't open it again until I tell you. If the doc comes out before I get back, send someone to get me at the telegraph office. I'm going to see about getting an answer tonight."

Mackey left before Halstead could ask him anything more.

He placed the statement in the top drawer of his desk and locked it. He did not know what Mackey was planning, but he hoped it brought an end to this nonsense once and for all.

CHAPTER 23

Emil Riker watched Zimmerman hurl his glass against the wall of The Iron Horse Saloon. None of the customers so much as flinched.

He watched Zimmerman's face grow scarlet. "I told you to start trouble, not round up a bunch of drunks to kill Halstead's pet deputy. What were you thinking?"

Cal Hubbard flicked shards of glass from his coat. The banker seemed more disturbed by the stains on his clothes than the thought of a dead lawman. "Honestly, Ed. There's no call for being destructive. What's done is done."

Riker had heard about Zimmerman's temper, so he was expecting such a reaction. "All I said was that Sandborne was shot up pretty bad. I don't know for sure that he died."

Zimmerman turned on him. "What difference does it make? Even if Sandborne doesn't die, this mess will just stir up Mackey and Sunday to do something about it. Hell, you saw Sunday blow Weasel's head off this morning. Once they find out you were behind Sandborne getting shot, what's to keep them from sitting out in the rocks waiting to pick me off, too?"

"No one's going to tell them about me." Riker was surprised he had to spell it out for him. "The only men who know for certain who were there are dead."

"Including the bartender?"

"No," Riker admitted, "but he won't say a word. He knows what'll happen if he does. Besides, no one's going to care about the details after tomorrow."

Zimmerman threw out his hands in confusion. "Why? You think they'll just wake up and forget about eight men getting killed in one day? They'll be talking about this for decades."

"Because Mackey and Halstead will have bigger troubles on their hands. Everyone in Battle Brook knows Halstead ran off this afternoon, but they don't know why. They saw his woman beg him not to go but rode off anyway. The reason how Sandborne got shot won't matter as much as the reason why he got shot. No one was around to help him. Not Halstead and not the great Aaron Mackey, or Billy Sunday either. The town will be angry at Halstead for letting such a nice boy get hurt. Come this time tomorrow, after Mayor White announces me as sheriff, I won't be the only one telling Halstead to leave. The whole town will be demanding that Mackey get Halstead out of there as soon as possible."

Zimmerman was not convinced. "That might've happened if it was just Halstead, but Mackey and Sunday being around changes things."

"I'm not saying people will march up and down Main Street with torches, but the damage already has been done." Riker sat back in his chair. "That's when I'll ride in as the new man, ready to do the job their way. To bring peace to their quiet little town. A few hours ago, I was just the mayor's choice. By this time tomorrow, and with Mr. Hubbard's help, I'll be the answer to a problem Battle Brook didn't know they had."

Zimmerman's scowl only deepened, but Cal Hubbard was intrigued.

"Riker might have a point, Ed," the banker said. "This mess just might help us put Riker in solid with the people. He'll be brave where Halstead, Mackey, and Sunday look weak. That kind of popularity will come in handy for our plans."

Zimmerman pounded the table in frustration. "Everything is happening too fast for my taste. Halstead was shaky before Mackey came in to prop him up. Now, they'll talk some sense into him. The marshal can be persuasive when he wants to be and he's got a reputation to back him up. He won't take kindly to being run out of town, even if he thinks Halstead is the problem. His pride won't allow it."

Riker could see Zimmerman was not the kind of man who could be convinced. He only trusted an idea if he had thought of it himself. "It might be a good idea to quit thinking about what Mackey might do and start thinking about what you're going to do. You've already got the ball rolling, Mr. Zimmerman. No reason to stop now. This is the opportunity you've been looking for, assuming you're willing to take it."

Zimmerman's scowl softened, "You're sure it was Halstead who took a shot at you on Main Street?"

"He used his pistol from half a town away," Riker said. "There's no way he saw me, but I made sure I got a good look at him from the alley. Mackey, Billy, and Halstead were all there, just like I told you."

"Looks like your brother failed," Zimmerman said. "Doesn't say much for his chances, does it?"

"Warren's not so easy to kill," Riker reminded him. "If he was dead, they would've brought his body down from the hills with them, just like they did with Hec Garvey earlier."

Zimmerman took his seat and dropped his head into his hands. "You'd better hope that bartender in The Blue Belle doesn't get chatty."

"And I already told you not to worry about him," Riker said. "I'll talk to him tomorrow. A few coins should be enough to buy his silence."

Zimmerman sneered. "You better hope you're right because I've seen plenty of men get themselves hanged because someone who should've kept their mouth shut didn't."

Cal Hubbard leaned forward to interrupt. "Don't be so sure, Ed. The Belle caters to a rough crowd for a reason. If word got out that they told Mackey anything, the place would have to close. No one would ever go in there again."

Zimmerman shook his head. "I'll try to remember you said that when they lead me up to the gallows." He pointed at Riker. "When anyone asks—and they will—we're going to tell them you were here all night. I'll make sure all the boys swear to it. Tomorrow morning, when you get back to Battle Brook, find that bartender and make sure he keeps his mouth shut."

"That's sound reasonable, Ed," Hubbard said.

"I'm glad you like it," Zimmerman said, "because you're going with him. I want you to make sure the mayor announces Riker as the new sheriff. It'll keep Halstead and the others off balance and make the mayor look like he's doing something for a change."

Hubbard said, "I'll have my coach ready at first light. We'll bring your horse in tow. It'll do well for the people of Battle Brook to see their new sheriff arrive in town in grand style."

Zimmerman got up from the table. "It's getting late. I'd better get to bed before you tell me something else that annoys me. If something else happens, like a plague of locusts, send someone to get me. I doubt I'll sleep much tonight."

When Zimmerman left the saloon, the banker and the sheriff were alone.

Riker decided to test Hubbard a bit. "He always that prickly?"

"He has been lately," Hubbard told him. "Building a town isn't easy, especially with a man like Halstead always at his heels." He lifted his glass of whiskey. "Here's hoping tomorrow's events serve to give him peace of mind."

Riker raised his glass and sipped it. "Can't hurt to hope, but I've seen plenty of men under worse pressure who didn't act like that. He seems brittle to me."

Hubbard flashed a look of agreement but quickly recovered. "Careful, Mr. Riker. Zimmerman controls everyone and everything in this town. You'd do well to choose your words with greater care in these parts."

Riker slowly turned the glass of whiskey. "I always choose my words carefully, Mr. Hubbard. My actions, too."

"I've noticed," the banker remarked. "I thought that remark about your brother might've thrown you a bit. He was trying to get a rise from you, but you took it well."

Riker shrugged off the compliment. "Warren's fine. Probably hurt some, but he's alive. He had the jump on Halstead and that would be enough for him. There's a lot of men below ground who thought they had my brother beat. I won't believe he's gone until I see his body."

"It's good for a man to have brothers," Hubbard observed. "I have five sisters. All of them married to prominent men, of course, but it's not the same as having a brother you can rely on to pitch in and do the hard work on behalf of the family. Times are changing quickly out here, but blood still counts for something."

Riker could tell the banker was working up to something. "You're working up to telling me something, aren't you? What is it?"

"Just that alliances are important, even when blood isn't

involved. Blood helps, sure, but when there's too much of it, it can stagnate progress."

"Depends on who's doing the bleeding."

Hubbard grinned. "You have a point. There's been too much bleeding in this valley lately for my tastes. I was thinking we might be able to reach an agreement. You and me and Warren and Mr. Mannes."

Riker had wondered how long it would take before they had this kind of conversation. He thought Hubbard would wait until he was sworn in, but he supposed now was as good a time as any. "Why would I trust you?"

"Because I did you a good turn." Hubbard took the bottle of whiskey and poured himself a drink. "Remember, I'm the one who recommended you as sheriff to Mayor White."

"That doesn't count. Zimmerman told you to do that."

"True in part, except that I'm the one who told him to send for you in the first place."

Riker still did not see the need for gratitude. "Because you wanted to throw Halstead off his feed."

"That was part of my reason." Hubbard set the bottle on the table. "But that doesn't explain why I told Halstead that he could find Zimmerman in Wellspring all those weeks ago."

Riker had not known that. He looked at the banker in an entirely new light. "Why would you tell me that?"

"Because I want to establish trust between us," Hubbard explained. "You're a man who looks out for his own interests and so am I. For that matter, so is Mark Mannes. Our interests lie in a prosperous Valhalla, not in one temperamental lunatic's quest for revenge on another."

Riker admired the way Hubbard thought. "So, you're not loyal to Zimmerman?"

"He and Halstead can kill each other as far as I'm concerned. I'm neither an outlaw nor a lawman. I'm a banker. I'm interested in making money and I'm not all that particular about how I do it."

"Or who with," Riker added.

Hubbard smiled as he raised his glass to toast him again. "Precisely." He sipped his drink, not downing it in one shot. "I think you and Warren are the right men in the right place who can help me make an awful lot of money in this valley. With Mannes and me here in Valhalla and you in Battle Brook, we would have the control Zimmerman's been dreaming about for some time."

Now Riker understood completely. "Only without Zimmerman."

"You're very perceptive, Mr. Riker. Mannes has influence in the capital. I control all the finances here in the valley. You'll control Battle Brook once Halstead's gone. You can even hire Warren as your deputy if you like. Between the four of us, we'll control everything worth controlling in this part of the state."

Riker looked around the saloon. The place was empty except for a few men standing at the bar. They were well out of earshot, but Riker kept his voice low anyway. "Crossing a man like Zimmerman isn't smart."

The banker's bushy eyebrows rose. "But Mackey and Halstead will be taking care of him for us. I'm not talking about an outright betrayal of him. I'm just not particularly concerned about stopping the wheels of justice grinding him down."

When the saloon door banged open, Riker went for his gun as he got to his feet. He feared it was Zimmerman returning and cursed himself for being foolish enough to allow Hubbard to speak so freely.

But he stopped reaching for his gun when Warren hobbled into the saloon. He was covered head to toe in blackened dirt and grit. His left leg was tied between two thick branches and his pants leg was brown with dried blood.

Riker got to his feet and ran to his brother as he dropped into a chair by the door.

Warren had been left winded by the effort. "Good to see you, brother. Had me quite a night."

Riker grabbed his brother's left leg and pulled it onto a chair. "What happened?"

Warren spoke through clenched teeth as Riker began to untie the branches keeping his leg in place. "Halstead's not the scared young pup you told me about, Emil. He's a smart one. I had him just where I wanted him, but he wriggled free. I was planning on keeping him holed up in that old mine we saw, but he got away. Put a hole in my leg before he did. Might've finished me off, too, if I hadn't had that stick of dynamite Zimmerman gave me before I left. I got out, though."

Riker threw the branches aside and tore the pants leg at the seam. The bullet had gone straight through the calf muscle but did not look to have struck the bone. "I numbed it with some whiskey I was carrying, but it's hurting something awful now."

Riker called out to the bartender, "Get me a bottle of whiskey and a clean towel."

Hubbard looked over Riker's shoulder. "The whiskey won't be a problem, but I'm afraid anything clean is in short supply in Valhalla."

Riker was no longer in the mood for Hubbard's mouth. "We'll take what we can get."

The bartender brought a bottle of whiskey and three towels to the table.

Warren grabbed the bottle first, pulled out the cork, and

drank down a couple of healthy swallows. "Figure it'll do as much good on the inside as it will on the outside."

Riker imagined it would. "Have another pull, then give it back to me." He asked Hubbard, "You have a doctor in town?"

"None that I'd trust with your brother's care," Hubbard admitted. "But I'll be glad to bring one here if you want."

"No need. I'll take care of it." Riker took the bottle from his brother and poured whiskey onto the wound. Warren's body tensed as the alcohol soaked in, but he did not scream. Riker boys had a high tolerance for pain. "You got a stove in here?"

Hubbard winced, obviously knowing what would come next. "Back in the kitchen. They usually keep a good fire going."

Riker handed the whiskey back to his brother as he got to his feet and then walked into the kitchen. There was no sign of a cook, but the stove was still plenty hot. He used a towel to push aside the cover and place his knife blade on the flame. He held it there until he was sure the steel was hot enough to do the job.

When he walked back into the saloon, Hubbard had already begun to make his exit. He was standing by the door as he said, "I enjoyed our conversation, Sheriff. I look forward to continuing it early tomorrow morning on the ride to Battle Brook."

Riker took the whiskey from his brother and set it on the floor a good distance away. The searing pain of the blade would hurt and he knew his brother would kick something awful.

"I'll be right here keeping an eye on my brother," Riker told him. "I won't be getting much sleep tonight."

He had never seen a banker move so fast as when he

placed the hot blade on Warren's skin to seal the wound. His brother was already unconscious when he placed it on the second hole. Hubbard was long gone by then.

Some men did not have the stomach for unpleasant duties.

CHAPTER 24

Despite being clearly exhausted, Doc Potter did not take the chair Halstead offered him. Billy took the seat instead. "How is he?" Halstead pressed the doctor.

"As well as can be expected," he explained. "The bullet missed his heart by the tiniest of margins but may have pierced his left lung. The lung may have filled with fluid, which I've managed to drain. Billy's use of coffee grinds to stop the bleeding may very well have saved his life more than anything I could have done." He nodded to Billy. "My compliments, sir."

Billy said, "I saw it work on a couple of patrols and didn't see any harm in trying it now. Glad it helped."

Doc Potter continued, "The internal bleeding may have stopped for now, but the deputy's heart is very weak. It is beating at a concerningly slow rate due to the amount of blood he's lost. The only reason I have even the slightest hope he might recover is his youth. I'm not normally this blunt, but I fear the occasion calls for it. Deputy Sandborne is stable for the moment, but he may fail quickly."

Billy glared up at Halstead. "Would've been better if he hadn't been shot at all."

Halstead steadied himself on the desk. "Is there anything

else we can do? Are we just supposed to sit here and hope he gets better?"

"Prayer might help," Potter offered. "It certainly can't hurt."

Mackey asked, "What about a blood transfusion? I've seen it done in the cavalry."

"It's possible." Potter went to the basin next to the stove and began to wash his hands. It was the same basin Halstead and Sandborne used to shave. "I have all the necessary equipment for it, but it's a dangerous procedure that doesn't always work."

"I know," Mackey said, "but I've seen doctors do it. They've used my blood a time or two."

The doctor continued to wash his hands. "Did it work?"

"Both of them died from gangrene," Billy answered for him, "but not for several days afterward. They seemed to take Aaron's blood just fine before that. Guess all that meanness he's got in him does a weak body some good."

Potter took the towel beside the basin and began to dry his hands. "It might work, but it's still a risk. His chances are slim enough as it is and a transfusion may only make matters worse if complications set in. Do you think Deputy Sandborne would approve of such a drastic step?"

"Joshua's a fighter," Halstead said with pride. "He'd want us to do it if you knew how."

Potter folded the towel and placed it beside the basin. "I'm willing to do it provided you understand there are no guarantees. Even if the procedure is successful, he may die anyway. I don't want any resentment toward me if he does."

Mackey unbuttoned his sleeve and began to roll it up to his elbow. "Don't worry, Doc. We won't shoot you if he dies." He walked back toward the cells. "We'd best get started. I've got an early day tomorrow."

Potter followed the marshal, leaving Halstead and Billy

alone in the office. Billy had not taken his eyes off Halstead since he had come back from the cells.

Halstead wanted to do anything to change the mood. He did not like the way Billy was looking at him. "You going to clean yourself up? I can get you something to eat if you want. I think the kitchen in one of the saloons is liable to still be open."

But Billy made no sign that he had heard him. "We've got to get a few things settled, you and me. There'll be trouble coming after this. For me and Aaron. For you, too. We're going to need you to be the old Jeremiah. The sharp, strong Jeremiah, not whoever you are right now."

Halstead hung his head. "I know. I'm better, I promise."

"This town needs you," Billy went on. "Sandborne's going to need you. If you can't find a way to get your head and your heart pulling in the right direction, a lot of good people are gonna end up dead. A lot more people are going to get hurt."

Halstead moved away from the desk and folded his arms. He had expected Mackey's anger. He had deserved it, but hearing Billy talk like this cut even deeper. "I already apologized to Aaron and now I'm apologizing to you. I know I was wrong for running off like I did, but I had my reasons. I thought keeping a fight from coming to town was a good idea."

"I don't care what you thought and neither should you. You need to do what you're told. You're not a boy anymore, Jeremiah, and Zimmerman's not your only concern. Everybody loses something in this world. The longer you're in it, the more you lose. It ain't fair, but it's the way it is. And if that brave boy in there dies because of you, you're gonna lose me as a friend and there won't be any going back. Not ever. I'll hold his death against you for the rest of my life. That's a promise."

Halstead did not want to think of that. "Let's just hope it doesn't come to that."

Billy continued to glare at him despite Halstead's embarrassment. "I heard you and Aaron talking about Randy swearing out a statement against Zimmerman."

Halstead was glad to be able to change the subject, even a little. "I hope it'll be enough to get a warrant."

"There's nothing any of us can do about that," Billy said. "But I'm going to tell you something Aaron hasn't mentioned yet. He hasn't told you for your own good. I'm telling you for the same reason."

Halstead did not like the sound of that. "Go on."

"Zimmerman plans on swearing out a warrant of his own for your arrest. He's charging you with the murder of those Valhalla boys you shot over in Wellspring."

Halstead placed his hands on his hips. Zimmerman never ceased to amaze him. "You've got to be kidding me."

"I'm not in a joking mood," Billy reminded him. "I'm telling you now so it doesn't come as a shock later. I don't know if Randy's complaint against Zimmerman or Zimmerman's complaint against you will be enough to get a warrant, but no matter what happens, you'll accept it. You've got plenty of time to make peace with either, so I won't be happy if you kick up a fuss if things don't break our way. You understand?"

Halstead was still getting used to the idea of Zimmerman's complaint against him, but he meant it when he said, "I understand. I'll keep a tight grip on my temper. You have my word."

"I had it before for all the good it did anyone," Billy said. "Your place is to stay right here to watch over Sandborne and the prisoners no matter what happens. That new sheriff they've hired is liable to be here any day now. I know you and Riker have history, but none of that's important. Joshua is all that matters, even more than this whole town."

Halstead looked up at the ceiling. He might have prayed had he thought it would do any good from the likes of him. "Joshua's all that matters. I know."

"See to it that you don't forget it this time. I've taught you a lot of things over the years, Jeremiah. I hope I don't have to teach you what happens to a man who finds himself on the other side of me."

Halstead's breath caught. Billy had never threatened him before. He had never had a reason to threaten him before and that stung more than anything. "I know that, too."

The chair creaked as Billy rose and went over to the basin to clean up. When he was done, he dried his hands and walked back to the cells without another word, leaving Halstead alone with only his prayerful regret to keep him company.

He went for his Colt when he heard a loud rapping at the jailhouse door.

"It's Bill Holland," a man called out. "I've got Abby with me."

Halstead rushed to the door and flung it open as Abby rushed into his arms. She held on to him tightly.

"Thank God you're not hurt, Jerry. I was so worried when you left."

"I'm fine," Halstead lied. "Hardly a scratch on me."

She pulled away from him to look him over for herself. "How is Sandborne doing?"

"He's doing as well as can be expected. Doc Potter is in with him now."

He moved her farther into the jail as Bill Holland stepped in and shut the door behind him. "I didn't think it was a good idea to bring her here after all that's happened, but Abby can be quite insistent when she wants to be."

Halstead stroked her cheek. "She surely can."

She leaned her face into his touch. "People all over town are awful, Jeremiah. They're blaming you for what happened to poor Sandborne, as if it was your fault."

Halstead had not bothered to think about what the people of Battle Brook might say about the shooting. He did not care what they thought either. He said to Holland, "I saw Randy's statement. Thanks for your help, Bill. It might go a long way to bringing Zimmerman to justice."

"I just moved the pencil while Randy spoke," Holland said. "I'm glad I could help, especially if it benefits the both of you."

Halstead appreciated the sentiment but knew it was more complicated than that. "I hope helping us doesn't cost you if things get ugly for me here in town."

"I'll be fine," Holland said. "But Phil White's been fanning the flames in your direction. He's saying you're the reason why this happened to Sandborne. That it never would've happened if you had been in town. It doesn't help matters that Mr. Fitzgerald has corpses stacked up in the yard behind his mortuary. He says he doesn't have any more room inside to keep them. 'Eight men, one day' seems to be the refrain I've been hearing. White has the people saying they've had enough bloodshed. He's not having any trouble getting people to agree that it's time you left town."

"I'll go when Aaron tells me to go," Halstead said. "And not before."

Abby looked up at him with tears in her eyes. "Do you really mean that, Jerry? Back in the room, you were so angry about it that I never thought you'd agree to it."

He remembered what happened in their room as though he were watching it happen to someone else. The hurt, frightened look on Abby's face as he ran down the stairs. Her cries that followed him as he rode out of town.

Bill Holland looked uncomfortable. "I'll step outside to give you two some privacy. You've clearly got quite a bit to talk over."

"It's not safe outside," Halstead told him. "Stay in here so you can take Abby back to the hotel with you."

"I'm never going to leave you again," Abby said. "My place is right here with you where I belong." She reached up and took his face in her hands. "You're you again, aren't you? It's just like you were our first day in town, isn't it?"

"I'm better." He took her hands and gently lowered them. "But I can't go back to Helena with you. Not right now. Sandborne's in a bad way and someone needs to stay behind to watch over him until he's fit to travel." He did not dare think he might not get well.

"I can help," Abby said. "I can tend to him when the doctor isn't around. I can look after you, too. You haven't done a very good job of taking care of yourself lately."

But Halstead would not hear of it. "A jail full of lawmen and prisoners is no place for a lady. I'll be fine if I know you're safe." He looked at Holland. "And you can keep her safe, can't you, Bill?"

"No one will harm her," Holland said. "You have my word on that."

Abby began to argue, but he said, "I don't know what Aaron's got planned for us, but just be ready to do whatever he says. He knows what he's doing, and if there's one thing I've learned today, it's that he's usually right. That's why I need you to stay in the hotel and be ready to move if he gives the word. You've got to promise me that, Abby. I can't do my job and worry about you at the same time."

Abby frowned. "How in the world do you expect me to be safe if you're not?"

He stroked her hair and cursed himself for being so blind for so long. So many wasted mornings spent out on the hilltop looking at Valhalla. So much time spent in anger while ignoring so much love.

Holland said, "Jeremiah's right, Abby. He can't help Sandborne if he's worried about you, too."

"I belong with him. I don't care if it's in Helena or on the moon."

Halstead placed his hands on her shoulders and eased her away from him. "Take her back and make sure she's safe. If anything happens, you'll find me here. Come get me any hour of the day or night."

His stomach sank when he saw her face was streaked with tears. He softly brushed them aside with his thumbs. "I know I haven't been right since the pardon, but that's all over with now. I promise."

She pulled his face down to her lips and kissed him deeply, much to the embarrassment of Bill Holland.

And when their kiss ended, Abby said, "I'll do it. I don't like it, but I'll do it."

Halstead gave her a final embrace, wishing it could go on forever but knowing he had kept her too long already. To Holland, he said, "Thank you."

He could not bear to look at her again as the hotel owner offered her his arm and led her out of the jail. Halstead had almost closed the door when Abby said, "I love you, Jeremiah Halstead."

"I love you, too." He quickly closed the door before he could say something foolish.

He went over to the stove, loaded it with some wood, and set it aflame. He tried to remember how Billy had made the pot of coffee earlier and did his best to follow his directions. They would be needing coffee. The night ahead would be a long one and the day that followed promised to be even longer.

He looked up when he heard Mackey step out from the cells, buttoning his sleeve. "That was quite a speech. You mean it?"

Halstead nodded. "Yes, sir. Every word."

"Good. I want that coffee ready by the time I get back."

Halstead watched him and Billy walk to the door. "Where are you going?"

"To see a man about a telegram," Billy said. "And you might want to get a couple of those cells ready. We'll be expecting some company later."

He did not have the chance to ask what he meant before the two men left the jail. Things being as they were, he was glad Billy was talking to him at all.

CHAPTER 25

Early the next morning, Zimmerman woke with a start and saw it was still dark outside. He had not planned on falling asleep, but his body clearly had other plans. He did not know how long he had slept, but given it was not yet sunrise, it could not have been long.

Nor had it been deep enough to have been considered sleep. His mind had not rested as questions and concerns plagued him throughout the night.

He had risen the previous morning with a clear sense of purpose and direction. Valhalla was getting stronger every day. Riker's installation as sheriff of Battle Brook would give him more influence over the neighboring town and Mannes's warrant would further sow the seeds of Halstead's destruction. The future was so close to being well in hand.

But that future seemed less assured now. The events of the previous day had changed everything. First, those three fools had taken it upon themselves to steal Halstead's woman in a foolish attempt to impress him. Then, Mackey and Sunday had come to Battle Brook just in time to save Halstead from himself. Finally, Riker's attempt to raise havoc the previous night had failed and now a deputy US Marshal may die because of it. All his plans were now in jeopardy. He was losing the thread that bound everything together. He was losing all sense of control.

He groaned as he rubbed the sleep from his eyes. *If people just did what I told them to do, this wouldn't be happening.*

This was his town. His valley. Nothing happened here without his permission. There were dire consequences for disobedience. The time had come to remind everyone who was in charge. He would have to think of a way to reassert his authority without driving them away. Balance remained at the heart of the empire he was trying to build.

But first, he had to visit the privy. He was certain the longest journey did not start with a single step but with a pause at the outhouse.

He lumbered out of bed and looked out into the area behind his home. The sky had begun to brighten just enough to allow him to see the outline of the outhouse. He was reasonably sure the yard was clear. At least he could answer the call of nature with some expectation of peace.

Still, he took his gun belt from the bedside table and placed it on his shoulder. He saw no sense in putting it on only to have to take it off again in a few moments.

He had stepped out the back door and begun the short walk to the outhouse when he heard the unmistakable click of a hammer being thumbed back.

He reached for the pistol on his belt, but a hard blow to the back of the head forced him to his knees as the belt was pulled from his shoulder.

Exploding stars and lights filled his brain as he tried to shake his vision clear.

"Morning."

Zimmerman recognized that voice. He had heard it the day before. Clear and strong.

"Mackey?"

"I'm touched you remember. The man who just brained

you is Deputy Sunday. Edward Zimmerman, you're under
arrest for the murder of Robert Meachum, late of Valhalla,
Montana."

He recognized the name. The fool who had fallen asleep
at his post. "And if I refuse to submit to arrest?"

"I've got a warrant from Helena with your name on it,"
Mackey said, "so you're going. Straight up or over the
saddle. It makes no difference to me."

Zimmerman drew in a deep breath to let out a cry for
help, hoping one of the watchmen would come to his
rescue, but another heavy blow to the back of his head
knocked him flat on his face.

A knee across the back of his neck stuck his face further
into the mud, stifling his cry as his hands were pulled
behind his back and quickly bound with a rope. He tried to
keep his hands apart to give some slack to the rope, but
Deputy Sunday was practiced enough to know that trick.

Mackey led a horse to him as he was grabbed by the
arms and hauled to his feet. He did his best to try to struggle free, but their grip on him was too tight. His legs went
weak when they slipped a noose over his head and pulled
the knot tight around his throat.

The black deputy held him fast as he spoke directly in
his ear. "The other end of that rope is tied to the saddle horn
of your horse. It's got just enough slack to let you climb
aboard and stay there. Spook the horse, you'll fall and snap
your neck. You shot or dig your feet into his flanks, you get
bucked off and snap your neck. Anyone shoots at us, the
horse bucks and you snap your neck. Understand?"

Zimmerman did not dignify the threats with an answer
but did not resist as they forced his bare left foot in the stirrup
and steadied him as he set himself in the saddle. The cold
air cut threw his long underwear and made him shiver. He

told himself it was only from the air and not from Sunday's dire warning.

He watched the two men get on their horses. He made sure he pitched forward as Sunday pulled Zimmerman's horse behind him on a short lead rope.

It was still too early for anyone to be going to work and the quiet streets were empty. *Where are my watchmen? Where are Tote and the others? Why isn't anyone doing anything to stop this?*

Zimmerman wanted to ask them where they were taking him but dared not risk his own life. He got his answer when they broke east instead of west and knew they were taking him to Battle Brook. Knowing Mayor White would be announcing Riker as the new sheriff of Battle Brook would make for an interesting day.

The horses were moving at a near gallop as they put as much distance between themselves and Valhalla while the darkness held out. Even if he had been able to let out a cry for help, he doubted anyone would have heard him.

And as the sky began to slowly brighten, he saw the short length of rope from the knot around his neck down to the saddle horn. Sunday's threat had not been an empty one.

His thigh muscles began to burn as he did his best to remain upright atop the swiftly moving horse. He wondered if that morning's sunrise would find Halstead standing on the hill, glaring down at Valhalla not in anger but in triumph.

Zimmerman hoped he did. He hoped he enjoyed his victory while it lasted, for Emil Riker would not be the only man in the valley to avenge a wrong. Edward Zimmerman would make Aaron Mackey, Billy Sunday, and Jeremiah Halstead bleed for this.

* * *

As Cal Hubbard watched Emil Riker tie his horse to the back of his private coach, he felt like he was watching history in the making. It was the first day in a new era for the valley and he was watching it unfold before his very eyes.

The banker was proud that his coach would play an important role in ushering in Battle Brook's new age. The coach had become a reflection of Hubbard's fortunes over the years. It was a source of pride for the town back when Hard Scrabble Township had first been successful. Few people in the territory could afford to ride in such luxury, which was why Hubbard had spent a great deal of money to do so.

Its reddish-brown paint was chosen for its richness, which was enhanced by black trim. Brass lanterns on the sides gave the coach a refined look and inspired Hubbard to make the lantern the symbol of his bank. He had arranged for "H. Calvin Hubbard—Banker" to be painted on both doors, as if there was any doubt who owned the carriage.

Appearances meant everything on the frontier. People believed what they saw. And if Hubbard was wealthy enough to have his own coach, he must be successful in business. People felt their money would be secure with him and his bank prospered.

But when the valley's favor later moved toward Battle Brook, the coach—like Hubbard's bank—had fallen into disrepair. Its varnish slowly faded. Its rich brown paint cracked and flaked away. The glass of the brass lanterns broke. The axels surrendered to rust. Unable to make any of the necessary repairs, the wagon was parked and forgotten in the back of the abandoned livery. Its interior soon became a dusty haven for spiders and other vermin to call home.

But then a couple of outlaws named Ed Zimmerman and

Rob Brunet walked into his bank one day and decided to buy themselves a town. They used their ill-gotten gains to change the old Hard Scrabble Township into Valhalla.

Hubbard made a point of using his newfound wealth to restore the grand carriage to its former glory. It was an undertaking as expensive as it was extensive, but he was pleased with the results. It was a smart-looking coach and the brass fittings gleamed. The interior still smelled of new leather and its seats were softer than before. The brass-handled walking stick he carried was more for show than use.

He even insisted his driver wear a brown uniform with brass buttons that complemented the color scheme of the livery. It may have seemed absurd extravagance to some, but that was the point of extravagance. And to H. Calvin Hubbard, it projected the desired effect of class and elegance. Of permanence.

Hubbard was admiring his coach when he heard the hooves of several horses out on the thoroughfare. Riker heard it, too, and drew his pistol as he ran out to the front of the yard to see what was happening. Even Pip, his driver, climbed down from the box and followed Riker to the front.

But for all his cunning in matters of banking and business, Cal Hubbard had always been more cautious than curious. He was content to let the sheriff and his driver investigate while he climbed into the comfortable safety of his coach.

The wagon rocked as Pip climbed up into the driver's box and Riker joined him in the carriage, sitting opposite him.

"Well?" Hubbard asked him. "Who was it?"

"Three riders heading east at a good clip. It was too dark for me to tell for certain, but I'm pretty sure it was Mackey and Sunday trailing Zimmerman on a rope."

"Interesting." Hubbard tapped the roof of the carriage

with his walking stick, signaling Pip to start moving, which he did. "Quite interesting indeed. I didn't think Mackey would be so subtle."

Riker leaned forward as he straightened out his coat. "Don't know what you're so happy about. They were headed straight back to Battle Brook. Throwing Zimmerman in jail will throw the town into a lather and pour cold water on my announcement as sheriff."

But Hubbard did not think so. "Nonsense. They might be intrigued at first, but soon they'll be fearful of a reprisal from Zimmerman's men. They'll look to you to put their minds at ease. Zimmerman's arrest will only solidify your perception as a savior." Now that he had said it aloud, he was sure of it. "Mackey did us a favor without realizing it."

Riker grunted as he looked out the window. "You still want me to prod them about moving out of the jail? As sheriff, I'll have a right to demand it back."

"We'll see the mood of the town once we get there. I don't want your first act in office to be a defeat. Mackey and Halstead are under foot. There could be more to be gained by showing restraint." He tapped Riker's boot with the tip of his walking stick. "Restraint in all things, Sheriff. For both of us."

Riker slid his boot back. "What's that supposed to mean?"

"It means that you and Halstead have a history of animosity between the two of you." He quickly added, "The man killed your father, so I can hardly blame you. I just need you to remember that he's no longer the gullible young man you may remember from El Paso. I've dealt with him several times and I've seen how he works. He has a way of grating on a man's nerves to his own advantage. You can't let him bait you into losing your temper."

Riker sat back on the bench. "He'll follow Mackey's lead and Mackey's a cool customer. You don't have to worry about me. Warren's always been the one with the bad temper."

Hubbard had almost forgotten about Riker's older brother. "How is he doing? Did you dress his wound properly?"

"I did the best I could with what I had," Riker said. "He won't lose the leg, but he'll be off his feet for a day or two. I was going to ask if Mr. Zimmerman would mind letting him rest up in the saloon's storeroom, but I guess he won't have a say from a cell."

"I'm afraid he'll have a great deal to say as long as he's alive." Hubbard sighed. "We're fortunate that Mannes is already in Wellspring, waiting on the train to Helena. I'll have to get word to him about this once we reach Battle Brook. I don't want him wasting time coming back here even if Zimmerman sends for him. Filing that complaint against Halstead is far more important."

Riker looked out the window. "You said bringing me here was your idea. I guess that murder charge was your idea, too."

"Mannes deserves most of the credit," Hubbard allowed, "but Zimmerman thinks it was his idea. I'm just as anxious to get Halstead out of this valley for good as I am to see Zimmerman gone. I doubt there's twelve people in Montana who would convict him, but it'll be enough to get him out of our hair for good, which suits my designs nicely. A trial will establish bad blood between Mackey's office and the valley, which will make Mackey think twice before crossing us again. Between that and Mannes's connections, I'm confident of our prospects." He tapped his stick on the floor of the cab. "The valley is effectively ours."

"Yours," Riker said. "Not mine."

"For now," Hubbard said, "but it won't be that way for long. And stop worrying about your position, Riker. I've already explained that you're the cornerstone of our plans.

You and Warren. You serve a purpose. Zimmerman and Halstead don't."

Hubbard joined Riker in looking out the window of the coach as it rumbled through the early morning. The sky was even brighter now and sunrise was only a few minutes away.

"Just don't try to play this same game on me and my brother as you're playing on them," Riker said. "I'd hate to have to kill you, Cal."

The banker smiled. "I'll be sure to keep that in mind."

CHAPTER 26

Halstead sat on the boardwalk in front of the jail, enjoying some of Billy's coffee as he waited for a new day to begin. A new day in so many ways. His old friend had been right. A mug of good, strong coffee was a fine way to start the day.

It was the first early morning he had spent in Battle Brook for weeks. He had insisted on starting each day by riding out to the hill overlooking Valhalla, feeding his hatred by renewing his oath of vengeance against Ed Zimmerman. By digging up the sins of the past to give his present anger some meaning.

By allowing the dead to take hold of his life, he had put so much in jeopardy. Sandborne's life and Abby's love. Aaron's faith in him and Billy's friendship.

Halstead's stomach tightened as he sensed a change in the air, and it was not just the approach of colder weather. The change he felt came from within himself. He felt as though he had just woken up from a long, restless sleep. He had allowed his rage to make him too blind for too long to see what it had cost him, but he saw it all so clearly now. Today was the start of a life where the likes of Zimmerman had their place. He would never allow his anger to grip him so completely again. He only wished it had not taken his friend getting shot to make him realize it.

By this time yesterday, he had been forced to kill two men looking to collect on Zimmerman's bounty already. The day ahead promised to be a busy one, but he refused to dwell on it. Anticipation was as pointless as vengeance and regret. He would face whatever came at him as he had faced every man who tried to kill him. Head-on and on his feet.

He set his mug on the boardwalk when he heard horses approaching from the west. He stood when he saw Mackey and Adair riding out front at an even trot. Billy Sunday followed with Ed Zimmerman in tow. His hands were clearly tied behind his back. The rope around his neck was tied to his saddle horn.

As he watched the three riders draw closer, he waited for the old feelings to return. The contempt and hatred. The satisfaction of seeing his enemy laid low.

But he felt nothing except happiness that Aaron and Billy had made it out of Valhalla in one piece.

Mackey brought Adair to a halt in front of the jail, climbed down from the saddle, and tethered the mare to the hitching rail. Billy did the same for his own horse and the one bearing the prisoner.

Halstead felt Mackey eyeing him carefully. "What do you want me to do, Boss?"

"Help Billy and take charge of the prisoner," the marshal told him. "You're in charge of Battle Brook, Deputy. Do your duty."

Zimmerman tried to spit at Halstead but only succeeded in drooling on his shirt. "This is a banner day for you, isn't it, Halstead? Too bad you had to send your friends to do what you weren't man enough to do."

Halstead helped Billy ease Zimmerman off the horse

and down to the ground. They each took an arm and led him into the jail.

Zimmerman kept up the abuse as he fought every step. "The great Jeremiah Halstead. The brave Jeremiah Halstead, content to hide behind Mackey's skirts."

Halstead took the keys from the peg and opened the door leading back to the cells.

Zimmerman placed a foot on the doorframe and tried to push off it. "I'm not going in there with those traitors."

"You're going where we tell you to go." Billy kicked Zimmerman's foot down and helped Halstead push him inside.

Zimmerman struggled against their grip as they led him to the cell next to Mule's and across from where Sandborne was recovering.

"You boys think this is over?" Zimmerman shouted. "You think my men will let this stand? You don't know Valhalla. They'll lay waste to this place like it was Dover Station. You're about to get a lot of innocent people killed, Halstead!"

Halstead opened the door to his cell and shoved him inside. He was about to lock the door when Billy said, "Wait a minute. Sandborne needs his rest."

Halstead was not sure what he meant until Billy reached into Sandborne's cell and took a long strip of bandage Doc Potter had left behind. With his arms still bound behind him, Zimmerman backed up as far as he could and charged like a bull. Halstead fired a hard right hand, which caught him in the jaw. The blow staggered him and Halstead kicked him down onto the cot.

Billy moved inside and wrapped the bandage around Zimmerman's mouth. "That ought to keep him quiet enough for Sandborne to get some sleep."

Zimmerman shook his head and tried to speak through the gag.

When Billy stepped out of the cell, Halstead locked the door. "What do you want me to do now?"

"He's your prisoner," Billy told him. "That's up to you."

Halstead waited until Zimmerman recovered some from the punch. "We're going to keep your hands tied until you calm down. If you don't calm down, they'll stay tied. We can treat you well or treat you poorly. You decide how it's going to be."

Zimmerman hurled muted curses at him as Mule went to the side of his cell and began to console the new prisoner.

Randy gripped the bars of his cell and pleaded, "You can't just leave me in here with him, Mr. Halstead. He's gonna try to kill me."

"I've got nowhere else to put you and he can't get you from two cells over. Just sit down and shut up. If he makes too much noise, stick your fingers in your ears."

Halstead went back in the office and shut the door. Mackey was leaning against the desk, sipping a mug of coffee. "You handled that better than I thought you would, Jeremiah."

Billy was at the stove, pouring himself a mug. "I'd have put even money you were going to blow him out of the saddle on first sight."

Halstead had been glad to disappoint them. "Guess I'm growing up. You find any trouble in Valhalla?"

Billy said, "Just a couple of scared kids playing guard. They probably already got someone to cut them loose by now." He looked across at Mackey. "Zimmerman's right about his men coming after him. They'll be here soon enough."

"Let them try," Mackey said. "Zimmerman's not going anywhere except to Helena."

Halstead admired Mackey's grit but knew it would not be as simple as that. "Even if they don't try to take him in town, it's a good half-day's ride to Wellspring. It's unforgiving country. Plenty of places they could try to ambush us."

Mackey looked at him over the rim of his mug. "Seeing as how you've been here a while and know the land some, I was figuring you might have some ideas on the subject."

In fact, Halstead had thought of little else since Mackey returned from the telegraph office with the judge's warrant for Zimmerman's arrest. "There's a stretch of flat track a couple of hours away. The train stops there to fill up on water for the boiler before pushing on to Wellspring. I was thinking you could bring Zimmerman there, flag the train to stop, and get on board. That way, you're already on the train before any Valhalla boys can stop you. They'll be left watching the road while you head back to Helena."

"You?" Billy asked as he set the pot back on the stove. "You mean 'we,' don't you? You'll be coming with us."

Halstead shook his head. "A wise man once told me my place is here with Sandborne. He's the priority. And since he won't be fit to travel for a week or more, I figure I'll be staying on here with him until he's better."

Mackey and Billy exchanged glances as Billy joined him at the desk. "Sounds like someone's regained his senses, Aaron."

"Sounds that way," Mackey said. "What about Abby? You asking her to stay here with you?"

He had thought about that, too. "I figure she rides out this morning with the luggage wagon from the hotel, not the stage. That way she'll already be in Wellspring before Zimmerman's boys can watch the road. And seeing as how you two will be on the train when she gets aboard, she'll be in good hands the rest of the way."

Billy's grin warmed him as he raised his mug to toast him. "Welcome back, Jeremiah."

Halstead remembered he had left his mug on the boardwalk and went outside to retrieve it. He saw a six-team coach pulling onto Main Street from the west. Its brown paint and brass shone in the early morning light. It wasn't the stage from Wellspring bringing passengers to and from the train. That was painted all black and wasn't due in town until later that morning. This was something else.

He watched the coach as it rumbled to a stop directly across the thoroughfare from the jail.

He saw the name painted on the door of the coach. "H. Calvin Hubbard—Banker."

He picked up his mug and watched as the door opened and two men stepped out. He recognized Hubbard right away. His white muttonchops had been trimmed some in the weeks since he had last seen him, but otherwise he looked the same.

He recognized the other man who stepped down from the coach as well. He had changed some in the years since El Paso but moved with the same arrogant nature of his father. He finally had managed to grow in the black mustache he always wanted, but his eyes were as dead as ever. It was Emil Riker, the new sheriff of Battle Brook.

The two men put a great deal of effort in not looking his way as they stepped up onto the boardwalk and headed toward Mayor White's haberdashery.

It seemed Riker was about to be named sheriff much sooner than expected.

He brought his mug inside the jail and hoped Billy had not been too hasty in welcoming Halstead back to his senses.

CHAPTER 27

"I'm not sure the time is right for such an announcement," Mayor White told his guests in the cramped back room of his haberdashery. "I'm afraid I've just heard some rather unsettling news."

Cal Hubbard always found the mayor to be at his most entertaining when he was flustered. "No reason to be afraid, Phil. We're here now. What's this news that has you so upset?"

White's chins waggled as he cleared his throat. "Mackey and Sunday have just brought in Ed Zimmerman. They have him over in the jail right now."

Riker looked at the bolts of fabric on one of the shelves around the room. "So?"

White blinked at him. "That means the town will be consumed by the news. I don't know if my message reached you last night, but Sandborne was gunned down and is clinging to life."

"I received your message, for what it was worth," Hubbard said. "The sheriff and I decided to come to town anyway. I fail to see why that should stop us from making Riker's announcement as planned."

White explained, "Everyone was already unsettled by yesterday's events. I talked a few of the hotheads to take to the streets to call for Halstead's scalp today. Now we have Zimmerman in town, there's liable to be panic over what his men might do. That will steal away all the thunder we'd hoped your announcement would bring us."

"Nonsense." Hubbard pulled his gloves tighter on his hands. "The people have a right to be upset by so much killing. Eight men shot dead all because of Halstead's reckless behavior. He shoots first and asks questions later. A man like that attracts danger to him like honey draws bees. What happened to Sandborne only makes our case that much stronger. They'll welcome Riker as sheriff. Things are clearly getting out of hand and they'll look to him to make things right."

Hubbard smiled at White's confusion. "Everything is as it should be, Phil. Don't worry. The stage is set and our timing is perfect."

But White would not be easily buffaloed. "They'll expect us to say something about Zimmerman's arrest. They'll want to know how we're going to keep the peace if his men try to spring him."

Riker said, "Tell them I won't abide a single trouble-maker within the town limits. Not from Valhalla or Battle Brook or from Helena either. My family knows a thing or two about putting Jeremiah Halstead in his place. That's why you hired me for the job. Tell them that and they'll welcome it."

Hubbard was encouraged by Riker's thinking. Perhaps he was more than just a hired gun after all. "See that, Phil? Spoken by the man himself. Well done, Sheriff. Now, before news of Zimmerman's arrest spreads any farther, let's get out there and give your constituents the good news. Put their minds at ease that law and order has finally been restored in dear old Battle Brook."

White took his bowler hat from his desk and put it firmly on his head. "I still don't think this is a good idea."

Hubbard ushered him toward the door. "Don't think, Phil. That's my job, remember?"

Halstead opened the jailhouse door when he heard a crowd beginning to gather outside. The few snippets of conversation he heard told him Mayor White was about to make a major announcement.

They began to cluster in front of Cal Hubbard's fancy coach. His driver had climbed down from the box and was keeping the people a respectful distance away.

Mackey and Billy joined Halstead in the doorway.

"Looks like something's about to happen," Mackey observed.

Billy sipped his coffee. "Looks like we'll have the best seats in the house, too."

Halstead leaned against the doorframe. "I hear Mayor White's going to make an announcement. That coach belongs to Cal Hubbard, the banker over in Valhalla. Got himself a piece of the bank here a while back, too. I saw them pull up outside a while ago. Hubbard had Emil Riker with him. They headed off to White's store as soon as they hit town. I figure they're about to swear him in as sheriff."

Mackey said, "I didn't know that. You seem to be taking the news well, considering your history with Riker's family."

"There's no sense in getting worked up," Halstead admitted. "I can't do anything to stop it. I just need to know what you want me to do about it in case things get out of hand."

"Battle Brook's your post, Jeremiah," Mackey reminded him. "Billy and I are here to help you if you need it."

Billy asked, "Want us out here with you when the show starts?"

Halstead shook his head. "I figured you boys would want to rest a bit before you push off for that water tower. You'll want to get there in plenty of time to flag down that train on the straightaway."

Billy clapped his hand on Halstead's shoulder before he and Mackey stepped back inside. He could feel they were acting differently toward him now that he had shown how calm he could be. Sandborne's condition had likely improved their mood. He had begun to mutter in his sleep, but there was no sign of fever. According to Billy, it was an encouraging sign.

He saw Bill Holland walking quickly toward him along the boardwalk. He had an old Walker Colt held low against his leg.

When he reached him, the hotel owner said, "I just found out Cal Hubbard's in town, and he brought Emil Riker with him."

Halstead kept leaning against the doorway. "I know. I saw them."

"They're about to swear in Riker as the new sheriff," Holland told him. "They're planning a reception at my place this evening."

Halstead allowed the information to pass through him without resistance. There was nothing he could do to stop it, but there was one important step he had to take.

"Ought to be quite a time. You hear about Zimmerman?"

"No. I was busy with the mayor, Hubbard, and Riker. What about him?"

"The marshal and Billy hauled him in here early this morning," Halstead said. "I'm going to wagon run Abby down to the station early, before Zimmerman's men can block the road. I don't want anyone trying to use her to get at me again."

"I'll see to it personally," Holland assured him. "I'll keep her hidden until the train pulls into the station. I'll make sure the train detective escorts her on board."

Halstead did not tell him Mackey and Billy would be there. It was better for Holland if he did not know all the details. "Thank you, Bill. I'll rest easier knowing she's safe."

"Just make sure you keep yourself safe, Jeremiah. That young woman cares about you a great deal."

He did not think he could answer that without his emotions getting the better of him. He was glad Holland quickly turned and hurried back to his hotel.

Halstead tried to put any thought of Abby from his mind as he watched the crowd around Hubbard's coach begin to build. They had managed to fill in half the thoroughfare since Holland had talked to him and more people were on the way. Most of the people looked away from Halstead when they saw him leaning against the doorway of the jail. No one tipped their hat or offered a polite nod in his direction. It was as though they might catch something just by looking his way.

He knew that was natural. He had not expected much bravery or gratitude from the good people of Battle Brook. As one of the nuns in the mission school in El Paso used to say, "Eaten bread is soon forgotten."

He looked to his left, where he saw a large knot of citizens moving toward him along Main Street. He had not realized how much Cal Hubbard and Mayor White resembled each other until that moment. Hubbard was a bit taller and a few pounds lighter, but otherwise, the two men could have been brothers.

Hubbard had acquired a walking stick and rose it up

and down like a bandmaster on parade as the mayor trotted close behind him.

Emil Riker brought up the rear, ignoring the many people slapping him on the back or offering their hand to him. His skin was darker than it had been in El Paso, his face thinner. His eyes were much harder, which gave him a look some men might describe as dangerous. His eyes still darted constantly as he moved. He had always had an excitable nature, which had caused his daddy no end of heartache in his youth.

It was clear that Riker was no longer the soft, spoiled brat Halstead had known when Alan Riker was still alive. He was an important man's son back then. A bully who leaned on his father's name whenever it gave him an advantage. Now he moved with confidence. He was clearly his own man now, at least as long as men like Zimmerman and Hubbard allowed him to be.

Halstead looked to see if there was any sign of Warren hobbling along, but there was only an enthusiastic crowd following along behind him.

Then, amid the noise of the crowd, a lone voice began to chant, "Down with Halstead. Down with Halstead."

The chant grew louder as many in the thoroughfare took up the refrain and yelled as loud as they could manage. "Down with Halstead! Down with Halstead!"

Hubbard and his driver helped Mayor White climb up in the wagon box of his coach, and it was only then that Halstead saw the Bible in his hand.

Emil Riker finally looked across the thoroughfare at Halstead. Despite all the years and the miles that had passed between them since, his dead eyes were alive with hate.

Jeremiah remained leaning against the doorframe. He hooked his right thumb over his belt buckle, bringing it close to the butt of the Colt jutting out from his belly holster.

Riker had seen it. He was meant to see it.

Cal Hubbard raised his walking stick as Mayor White stepped up to the roof of the carriage and called for the crowd to quiet. The chants died away as the people gave him their full attention.

Mayor White held the Bible against his chest, as if he was about to begin a sermon. "Good people of Battle Brook. Gather round, for I have great news to share with you today. We all remember the deep and tragic loss we suffered not so long ago when our beloved sheriff, Jack McBride, was cut down in the prime of life while trying to stop a bank robbery. We've been fortunate enough to have good men take his place while we looked far and wide for someone who could fill Jack's shoes. I would be remiss if I did not take this opportunity to pause and give thanks to United States Marshal Aaron Mackey for offering the services of Deputy Jeremiah Halstead and Deputy Joshua Sandborne to keep us safe these many months since."

A few in the crowd applauded, but most looked back in awkward silence toward the jail. Some began to elbow each other when they noticed Riker was staring at Halstead. And Halstead was staring right back at him.

Mayor White spoke over a growing chant of "Down with Halstead." "It took a great deal of searching to find a suitable replacement for Jack McBride, but after considerable effort, I am pleased to report that we have found the best man for the job. We had to reach deep into the heart of Texas to get him but get him we did. Ladies and gentlemen, I ask you now to give a boisterous Battle Brook welcome to Emil Riker, our new sheriff!"

Hubbard thumped his walking stick on the boardwalk as the crowd began to cheer. Riker was too busy staring at Halstead until Hubbard shook him out of it. Riker easily climbed up on the roof of the coach and shook White's hand.

Halstead looked on as townspeople threw their hats in the air to applaud their new lawman. Shouts of "Down with Halstead" mixed with "Hurrah for Riker" as Mayor White held out the Bible to Riker.

"And now," White said as the crowd once again grew quiet, "I will administer the oath of office."

Riker placed his left hand on the Bible and his right hand in the air and repeated the words Mayor White said. To defend Battle Brook and its people to the best of his ability. To act within the law and to enforce it with prejudice toward none.

The crowd cheered again as White tucked the Good Book under his arm and took a star from his pocket. He held it up for the people to see before pinning it to the lapel of Riker's coat.

The two men shook hands as cheers of "Hurrah for Riker" rose from the townspeople, as though they were speaking in one voice.

Yesterday, Halstead had been their hero. A man to be respected. Today he was forgotten. Old news.

Mayor White cleared his throat again before waving for the crowd to grow quiet again. "Sheriff Riker, perhaps you'd like to say a few words to commemorate the occasion."

A good number of people took a few steps back so they did not have to strain their necks as much to look up at their new sheriff as he spoke.

Riker said, "I know you've all had a hard time of it as of late. It's gotten so that decent men and women are afraid to walk down the street out of fear of getting shot by desperate men trying to kill Jeremiah Halstead."

A few looked back toward the jail. Most kept looking up at Riker.

"I'm glad to tell you that those dark days will be over soon enough," the new sheriff continued. "It's time for Battle Brook to have its own law and order. Our way by a man accountable to you, not some man hiding behind a desk all the way over in Helena."

A smattering of "Down with Halstead" rippled through the crowd.

Riker continued. "When I got to town today, I heard a lot of you good people talking about how Aaron Mackey and Billy Sunday just brought in Ed Zimmerman from Valhalla. I know many of you are worried that some of those Valhalla boys won't take too kindly to us having Zimmerman in our jail. You're afraid they'll ride in here and make trouble. They might even try to burn us out. I understand why that worries you. You all remember how the great Aaron Mackey lost Dover Station to the torch a while back. But I'm here to tell you that this ain't Dover Station, and I'm not Aaron Mackey. My name is Riker, and if you ever find yourself down in Texas, you can ask anyone about my family. They'll all be glad to tell you that a Riker man knows how to put Jeremiah Halstead in his place."

The crowd cheered, and Riker raised his voice to yell over them. "And I aim to do that this very day when I walk over to that jail and tell Mackey that we've had just about enough of his way of doing things. I'm going to tell him we want him out of our jail before dark or, by God, we'll throw him out. And he'll take Halstead with him."

Halstead had expected the crowd to match Riker's enthusiasm and was surprised to hear them only grow quieter.

Halstead grinned up at Riker. The good people of Battle

Brook were glad to cheer a notion, but carrying it out was another matter entirely.

Mayor White had since climbed down from atop the coach and joined Hubbard on the boardwalk. He pointed over at the jail and said, "Did you hear that, Halstead? You've been put on notice."

Halstead remained leaning against the doorframe. He kept his voice at a normal level as he gave his answer.

"No."

"No?" White repeated. "What do you mean, 'no'?"

"It's a simple word, Phil. Two letters. Says a lot. I've got a jail full of prisoners and a wounded deputy in there. You can shout all you want, but we're not going until Marshal Aaron Mackey tells us to go and not a second sooner."

"'Occupied' is more like it," Riker shouted to the crowd. "Held against the will of the good people of Battle Brook by a lunatic hell-bent on a vendetta against a leading citizen of this valley."

Some of the townspeople cheered at Hubbard's urging, but most quietly began to drift away to go back about their business.

Halstead looked back up at Riker as the crowd gradually moved on. "They don't seem to think much of your idea, Emil. Maybe you ought to listen to them, seeing as you're now a man of the people and all. Don't let it bother you, though. You can always count on the good people of Battle Brook to let you down when you need them the most."

Riker began to climb down from the roof of the coach as Mayor White sprang on his tiptoes in a bid to get their attention. "You're all welcome to join us over at The Standard Hotel around noon today to meet Sheriff Riker in person. He's mighty eager to make the acquaintance of each and every one of you. Compliments of the town, of course."

Riker jumped down from the wagon box into the thoroughfare. Halstead had seen that look before. He knew Riker was about to come straight at him until Hubbard stepped in front of him and used his walking stick to block his path.

"Not here and not now," Hubbard said loud enough for Halstead to hear. "Our time will come and this isn't it. You just had a great start. Don't ruin it by letting Halstead rile you."

Halstead watched the vein in Riker's neck bulge the way it always did when he decided to throw someone a beating. Or have his father's men hold a man down while he did it.

Mayor White took hold of his arm and tried to shake Riker out of it. "Let's go, Sheriff. There's a lot of important people who are anxious to meet you."

Riker went with him, but only broke off his glare when White pushed him farther along Main Street.

Halstead made sure he was not the first one to look away.

Cal Hubbard was left standing in the street with his driver by his side. "You can't do anything the easy way, can you, Jeremiah?"

"I'm not the one who brought him here. That's your doing. And when he beats some old drunk senseless or drills a man for looking at him too long, that'll be on your head, not mine. Pretty soon, you'll wish I'd shot him in El Paso when I had the chance."

Hubbard placed his hands behind his back as he walked toward him. "You always think you know best. It's your way or no way. Guess you got that from Mackey."

"I got it from surviving the likes of Riker," Halstead told him. "There's only one way to deal with a man like that and pinning a star on him isn't it. Ask him what they used to call him behind his back in El Paso. It was 'Sparky,' on account of that flinty temper of his. You'd do well to keep that in mind if you're going to let him run around loose."

Hubbard stopped several feet in front of the jail. Close enough to be heard, but not close enough to be considered a threat. He always struck just the right balance. "What'll you care? You'll be long gone before that happens."

Halstead shook his head. "Riker's changed, but not that much. If he goes a day without putting someone on their backside, it'll be a miracle. Just make sure you don't come at him with that walking stick when he does. You won't like where it winds up once he gets a full head of steam built up."

"What makes you think it'll be me?" Hubbard asked. "It's more likely to be you."

"He tried that once," Halstead told him. "Took a swing at me in front of the whole town on Robert E. Lee's birthday."

"And?"

"He wound up on his back looking up at the sky before he knew what hit him."

"He probably remembers it differently."

"Only one way to remember it. Why do you think he didn't rush me when he had the chance?"

Hubbard looked around him at the jail. "How's Zimmerman doing? I hear you've got him locked up right now."

"He's not taking visitors at the moment. Come back later, maybe after Riker's party. You can bring him a piece of cake. I'm sure he'd appreciate the gesture."

Hubbard smiled. "I imagine the only man angrier than Riker right now is Zimmerman. I guess I don't have to tell you that getting him in that jail was one thing but getting him on the train to Helena is something else entirely."

"And here I was, thinking Sheriff Riker was going to keep us safe from all those bad men in Valhalla. Zimmerman's our concern, not yours. And now that I think of it, we're doing you a favor, aren't we? You've wanted him out of the way for a long time. There's nothing standing in the way of you controlling this entire valley now."

"Perhaps," Hubbard said. "Except for you."

"Careful, Cal. Threatening a lawman is against the law. You don't want to wind up in the next cell to Zimmerman."

Hubbard shifted his weight as he took a step back. "You only see something one way, don't you? It doesn't count unless you can slam a door in a man's face or hear the trapdoor of a gallows open beneath a man's feet. You did something rare out here, Jeremiah. You did something no one else has been able to do. You gave Ed Zimmerman a real run for his money. You had him beat, in a fashion. But that wasn't good enough for you. You had to keep on pushing him until you broke him and caused a whole lot of hurt and pain in the bargain."

Halstead felt old memories begin to gather inside him. "Men like Zimmerman are supposed to be broken if this place is going to be fit for decent people to call home."

"Is Valhalla really so bad? Is Battle Brook?" Hubbard waved his walking stick over Main Street, as if he was presenting it to him. "Behold the starving, naked children huddled in doorways. See the painted women peddling themselves like shovels in front of a dry goods store. Just look at all the drunkards passed out in the ruins of all these burned-out houses."

He lowered his walking stick and slowly shook his head. "But you don't see any of that and neither do I. You know where I saw it? In Hard Scrabble, before Ed Zimmerman came along. I had no choice but to sit by and watch while Battle Brook fed off that town like a leech, growing fat and happy with each passing day. We call it Valhalla now, and before I'm through, it'll be a place worthy of the name."

He held up a gloved finger. "But this time I won't do it at Battle Brook's expense. This valley is big enough for two prosperous towns, Deputy. You just can't abide the fact that it'll happen whether you're here or not. Zimmerman was the same way."

Halstead felt the old dark clouds begin to close in on him.

Hubbard raised his chin as he looked him over. "I often wondered what kept you warm on those cold early mornings out on that hilltop. I imagined it was your hatred for Zimmerman. Your dream of finally bringing the big man down once and for all. But Mackey and Sunday took that from you, didn't they? They swept in and took that glory for themselves. All those mornings and all that hate and what do you have to show for it? Nothing except a fine young man shot to pieces because you wanted to be a hero. You wanted to be the one who rode up into the hills and stopped the bad men from destroying another town."

Hubbard took another step back. "What'll you do now that it's all gone? How can you go on living when everything you've wanted has been taken away from you? If you weren't so stubborn, I might manage to have some pity for you. Such a waste. I used to think we could've run this valley together, you and me. I'll make do with Riker, though. And you'll have the rest of your life to think about all the things that could have been."

Halstead fought the spike of rage that rose inside him. He kept himself still while he focused on what was truly important. "How did you know?"

"About what? Regret?" Hubbard laughed. "I'm a banker. I consider myself something of an expert on the subject."

"No," Halstead said. "How did you know I rode up to the hill to fight off Zimmerman's men?"

Hubbard's left eye twitched. "Everyone knows. The entire town knows."

"No, they don't." He pushed himself off the doorframe and stepped down into the street. "No one knew that except for Aaron, Billy, Sandborne, and Abby. None of them said a word about it to anyone. You knew it would happen because you were there when Riker and his brother planned it."

Hubbard began to back up quicker toward his coach. "Now just hold on, Jeremiah."

But Halstead kept talking as he got closer to Hubbard. "You either gave Riker the idea or you were there when he planned it out. You knew I'd take the bait and ride out there to head off trouble. You're the reason Sandborne got shot, aren't you?"

The coach driver moved between them just as Halstead heard Mackey shout, "Jeremiah. That's enough."

Halstead stopped stalking Hubbard and watched the banker step up on the boardwalk. "Who's the pitiful one now, Hubbard?"

Halstead turned and walked back toward the jail as Hubbard and his driver walked toward The Standard Hotel.

Halstead looked at Mackey as he went inside. "I was in control."

Mackey closed the door. "Didn't look that way to me."

"Of course I was," Halstead said. "He's still alive."

CHAPTER 28

Zimmerman had never known such pain. The rope binding his hands did not hurt him nor did the gag in his mouth. The sounds of the town's celebration of Riker's oath of office drifted into the jail and hit him like a slap in the face.

This was supposed to be his celebration. His moment to shine. His glory at watching the first nail being driven into Halstead's coffin. He should have been out there instead of that preening fool Hubbard or that mindless puppet White. He deserved to see the look on Halstead's face as all he had fought against for so long happened before his very eyes. How the ghosts of his past stepped out from the shadows to stare him down.

Instead of seeing his foe beaten, he was sitting bound and gagged in a wretched cell with that pleading imbecile Mule blubbering apologies while Sandborne babbled in his sleep across the way.

He vented his rage into his gag as he tried with all his strength to snap the rope that bound his hands. He stopped when his wrists began to burn and his shoulders felt as if they might come out of their sockets.

"I sure wish you'd let me help with that, Mr. Zimmerman," Mule said from the next cell over. "I don't know if I can undo the knots, but I'd be happy to take that gag off your mouth."

Perhaps the fool might prove useful after all.

He pushed himself backward on his cot until his head was against the bars of his cell. Mule's clumsy fingers worked on his gag first and, when he pulled it free, Zimmerman drew in a deep breath of rancid air. The cells stank of blood and sweat.

Zimmerman flexed his jaw as he tried to get the feeling to return to his face.

"Good work, Mule. Now see what you can do about these ropes. I think I've got a way of getting us out of this mess."

He leaned against the bars while Mule began pulling on the knots. "I knew you'd be coming for us, Mr. Zimmerman. I kept telling Randy here that you wouldn't just give us up without a fight. Getting thrown in here with us is all part of your plan, ain't it?"

"Of course." Zimmerman wished the lumbering oaf was as good with knots as he was at spewing nonsense. He felt the pressure on his wrists begin to let up. "How're those knots coming along?"

"I'm almost done," Mule said as he continued to work. "How are you fixing to get us out of here? I'll help you any way I can. You know I always do."

"That's what I always said about you." Zimmerman kept an ear out for any sound of Halstead or one of the others checking on them. "All the boys said Mule was the one to watch. There was even some talk of making you a constable. A man like you with a gun on his hip would be a force to be reckoned with. Now, about my hands . . ."

"Almost there, Mr. Zimmerman."

He felt the knot give and his hands were free. He held them up before him as he got to his feet. He flexed them into fists and, for the first time since Sunday brained him that morning, knew he had a chance. A fighting chance, which was all he needed.

Mule gripped the bars between their cells, almost as excited about his freedom as Zimmerman. "What'll we do now, Mr. Zimmerman? You just tell me what you need doing and it's done."

Zimmerman slowly turned to face him. Yes, Mule would play an integral part in his next step toward freedom.

"I'll tell you," Zimmerman said, "but I want you to keep an eye on Randy while I do it. He's the weakest link in our chain. He's liable to tell Halstead everything we say. Turn around and I'll whisper it to you."

Mule quickly turned around and pressed his back against the bars. "I'm watching him, Mr. Zimmerman. He won't double-cross us this time."

Zimmerman enjoyed Randy's fear as he watched him close in on Mule.

Zimmerman slipped his arms through the bars and brought his right forearm tight around Mule's thick neck. He reached through with his left and strengthened his grip on the bigger man's throat.

Mule bucked and struggled to break free once he realized Zimmerman was slowly choking him to death, but the older man held fast. His grip was too tight and only grew tighter as Zimmerman pulled him back against the bars with as much strength as he could manage.

Mule's desperate gasps for breath reminded him of how long it had been since he had taken a man's life. He did not count beating Meachum to death as a challenge. The drowsy old drunk had not been able to stand when he delivered his sentence against him.

But Mule was different. He was a challenge, or at least

he might have been had he not allowed his desperation for approval to cripple him.

Zimmerman kept squeezing as hard as he could manage until he heard a muted crack before Mule's body went limp.

Zimmerman pulled his arms back into his cell and watched the body drop to the floor.

Randy looked at him in slack-mouthed terror and disbelief.

Zimmerman smiled as he brought a finger to his lips. "Quiet, Randy. Now the fun begins."

Zimmerman brought his hands to either side of his face and yelled, "Help! We need help in here! Something's wrong with Mule!"

He brought his hands behind his back and waited. The door to the office swung open and Halstead stood in the doorway. Mackey and Sunday looked on over his shoulder.

"What happened?" Halstead asked.

"Something's wrong with Mule," Zimmerman said. "He started twitching and banging his head against the bars. I think he's choking on something."

Halstead cocked his head to one side as he looked down at Mule's body. "Looks like his neck is broken. Look that way to you, Aaron?"

Mackey nodded. "Looks broken to me. What do you think, Billy?"

The black man craned his neck. "I've seen a broken neck a time or two and I'd say it was Zimmerman who did it. Old Randy here doesn't look up to the task."

Zimmerman kicked the door of his cell. "He's not dead, just sick. Get him a doctor."

"Doctor won't do him much good," Halstead said. "Mr. Fitzgerald's going to be glad for the business, though. It's been a slow day for him, seeing as how no one's tried to kill me yet."

Zimmerman felt his hopes for an easy escape run through his fingers like sand.

Mackey said, "I think we were supposed to run in there to help Mule so Zimmerman could grab one of us in the confusion."

Billy looked appalled. "No. He wouldn't do something like that, now would he?"

"He might," Halstead allowed. "He's been in there a long time. He just might've thought that's how it would work. Should've kept his gag on, though. Would've been more convincing if Randy gave out with the cry."

"Maybe," Mackey said, "but not much."

Billy let out a long breath. "Shame to see a big fella like that go to waste. The warden will be mighty disappointed. A boy like Mule could've broken a lot of rocks."

"He could indeed," Mackey said. "Come on, Billy. I'll buy you a free cup of coffee."

Halstead remained in the doorway as the others went back inside. His grin cut through Zimmerman's guts deeper than any blade. "It was a nice try, though. We'll be sure to add another murder charge against you. We didn't know if Randy's statement would be enough to convict, but this pretty much seals it."

Zimmerman brought his hands from behind his back and pounded the bars. "Too bad you can only hang me once."

"True, but once will be enough for me."

Halstead shut the door and locked it, leaving Zimmerman standing next to a dead man.

CHAPTER 29

Halstead watched Doc Potter step out into the office from Sandborne's cell. His lips were moving, but he was not saying anything.

Halstead locked the door to the cells and went to the doctor's side. "You feeling poorly, Doc?"

Potter's troubled expression did not change. "That prisoner was alive last night and earlier this morning. Now he's dead. You say Zimmerman did it just to set a trap for you and the others? To make you release him from jail?"

Halstead was glad the doctor was not ill, just disgusted. "It's been known to work a time or two, but it didn't work today."

Doc Potter lowered himself into the chair behind Halstead's desk. "He killed that young man purely on the hope that it might help him go free. That's something an animal would do."

"An animal kills because it needs to," Halstead corrected him. "Zimmerman does it because he likes it." He knew Mackey and Billy would want a final report on Sandborne's condition before they rode out to meet the train to Helena. They were over at the livery, getting their mounts fit to make the trip, but would be back soon.

"How's Sandborne doing?"

"Remarkably well," Potter said. "He's a strong young man and he's healing nicely. At this rate, I think he might be fit to travel in ten days or so. That's assuming he regains consciousness, of course. He's still groggy, but he's mumbling in his sleep. That's an excellent sign. The best we can do is give him as much peace and quiet as possible until he wakes up. And when he does, send someone for me immediately."

"Peace and quiet are two things we're in short supply of around here, Doc," Halstead said. "Especially now that White and Hubbard have hired Riker as sheriff."

"Fools," the doctor spat. "I never thought much of Phil White before today and after seeing that spectacle on the street earlier, my opinion of him has dropped considerably. Allowing Riker to demand the jail back. He knows Sandborne can't be moved yet. I've told him as much. He was just grandstanding. Wasting time, and I hate waste."

Potter walked over to the basin next to the stove and began to wash his hands. "Battle Brook is an odd little town, Jeremiah. It talks big but fights small, if it fights at all. The people love conflict if it doesn't darken their door. They want a quiet, safe place as long as they aren't inconvenienced too much."

"Sounds like every town I've ever seen."

Potter continued to soap up and soak his hands. "I'm just sorry you're caught up in the middle of it. You and that young man in there have sacrificed a great deal for this town. I'm sorry we showed our gratitude by hiring a sheriff who wants you dead."

Halstead grinned as he sat behind his desk. "Riker's in good company. A lot of people want me dead. Always have, come to think of it."

"Keep defying them, son." He grabbed a towel and began to dry his hands. "The best medicine for adversity is to thrive within it. Like Zimmerman has, despite all your efforts to bring him down. Like you have thrived despite all the men who've tried to kill you lately."

Halstead imagined he had a point. "I don't mind the danger when it's coming at me, but it's a different story when it hurts my friends."

"You mean to blame yourself for Sandborne's condition, don't you?" Potter finished drying his hands and folded the towel. "Any man who pins a star on his shirt is always in danger. No one made him do it. He got shot doing the work he loved. If he heals—and I expect he will—he'll have a couple of nasty scars the ladies might find interesting."

He set the towel next to the basin. "You didn't pull the trigger, Jeremiah, and you didn't cause those men to hurt him. You've all made decisions that led to this, and not all of them were your own. It's not always easy to know what to do in the moment. And while I haven't known you long, I can testify that you usually do the right thing when the occasion calls for it."

Halstead remembered Zimmerman's murder complaint against him. "Careful what you wish for, Doc. I may be needing that testimony sooner than you think."

The doctor closed his black medical bag. "As soon as I leave here, I'll be going to that ridiculous reception they're having for Riker at The Standard. I plan on having a long, stern talk with the mayor that Sandborne cannot be moved without my permission. I'll make sure I have plenty of witnesses when I tell him. That should throw some water on the situation and give cooler heads time to prevail."

Halstead doubted it would work but admired his willingness to give it a try. "I'd wish you luck if I thought it would do you any good."

"I won't need luck. I can be very persuasive when I put my mind to it." He offered a comforting smile. "Be good to yourself, Jeremiah. This town still needs you, even if they're too stubborn to admit it."

Doc Potter opened the door to leave just as Mackey and Billy wrapped their reins around the hitching rail in front of the jail.

Mackey asked about Sandborne's condition and Potter repeated what he had just told Halstead. He shook hands with the marshal, then with Billy.

"Coffee grounds as a poultice. I never would've thought of it. An inspired choice, Deputy."

Billy had never been one to accept praise well. "Glad you found it useful."

The doctor touched the brim of his hat and moved down the boardwalk as Mackey and Billy stepped inside the jail.

Mackey said, "He seemed like he was in a hurry."

"Riker's reception," Halstead reminded him. "They're having some kind of event for him at The Standard Hotel."

"You're not going?" Billy asked as he began to build a cigarette.

"Guess my invitation got lost." Halstead laughed. "Though I'd love to see Riker's face when I walked in the door."

Mackey sat on the edge of the desk. "You want to go?"

Halstead had not considered it. "I can't leave Sandborne, Aaron. And you two ought to get going if you want to catch the train at the water station."

"We've still got more than enough time for that," Mackey said. "You think you could be in the same room with Riker without causing a fight?"

Halstead was confused. Ever since he came to Battle Brook, Mackey had been warning him to remain calm. Now that he finally had been brought to his senses, Mackey was suggesting he do the opposite. "I'm sure I could, but why risk it? I didn't think you'd want me anywhere near that hotel."

Mackey explained, "We saw Abby ride out on the luggage wagon when we came out of the livery with the horses. In an hour or so, Billy and I will be gone, too. And with Sandborne still out of it, that means you'll be here on your own. Someone might get it in their head to test you like they tested Sandborne."

Billy added, "If you think you can control that temper of yours, showing up Riker the way he tried to show you up out there could make him—or anyone else—think twice about coming at you. You'd be showing the flag, as they used to say in the army."

Halstead saw their point and knew they were right. He did not want to be a prisoner in his own jail. Going to the reception might help push some folks back, just like Hubbard's driver had pushed back everyone who tried to crowd the coach before Riker's swearing-in ceremony. Even if it only deterred one hothead, it would be one less gun pointed in his direction.

"I'm calm enough to go if you think it'll do any good."

"I'm glad to hear it," Mackey said. "But make sure you leave your irons here. I don't want you pulling on him in a civilized setting."

As usual, Aaron was probably right. He stood up and slipped off his belly harness and laid it on the desk. Then he unbuckled his gun belt and placed it next to it. "Mind if I keep my knife?"

"I don't see why not." Billy thumbed a match alive and lit his cigarette. "As long as you promise not to carve a steak out of him."

"I'll use it to bring you back a piece of cake," Halstead said on his way out.

* * *

Halstead saw a large crowd in front of The Standard Hotel. He was quickly reminded of the previous morning, when another crowd had gathered because three boys had tried to take Abby. But now that he knew she was safely away from Battle Brook, he could tend to other urgent business.

None of the citizens waiting for a chance to meet the new sheriff acknowledged Halstead as he milled around at the back. He craned his neck to look inside and saw a receiving line had formed. People lined up, shook Riker's hand in the dining room, and moved on to a table of refreshments on the opposite side of the room.

He judged it might be half an hour or more before he had his chance to meet Riker. He knew Mackey and Billy wanted to get on the road with Zimmerman before then. He could cut the line, of course, but what would be the fun in that? He knew a better way.

He walked down the alley and rounded over to the back door of the dining room. He walked up the back steps and found the door was unlocked. He moved inside, careful not to make much noise as he did.

Halstead saw the dining room was packed with Battle Brook's leading citizens, who had stolen a few minutes out of their day to make the new sheriff's acquaintance. Shopkeepers, tradesmen, attorneys, and their wives. A reporter from the town's newspaper—*The Battle Brook Bulldog*—wrote furiously in a notebook as guests told him all they hoped the new sheriff would accomplish. Several members of the Bank of Battle Brook were there, as well as Mr. Fitzgerald, the undertaker. Considering all the bodies he still had to bury, seeing the death merchant there was a bit of a surprise.

Riker's back was to him and no one seemed to have noticed Halstead had entered through the back door. The new sheriff was flanked by Mayor White on the right and Cal Hubbard on the left. Both the mayor and the banker appeared as relaxed with the public as Riker was uncomfortable. He shook hands with every man who offered and bowed to every lady on their arm. Halstead remembered the only time Riker liked crowds was when he was surrounded by the painted women he paid to laugh at his lousy jokes.

Halstead knew he still had a while before Mackey and Billy had to head for the train, so he decided to see how far he could push things. He kept his hands in his pockets as he strolled toward the three important men greeting the public.

It was only when one of the town's three barbers gasped at seeing Halstead's approach that Hubbard, Riker, and White turned and spotted him.

A hasty silence descended over the room.

Halstead held out his hands from his sides, showing he was unarmed and his hands were empty. "I didn't come for trouble. I'm just here to offer an old acquaintance my best wishes on his new position."

Riker's right hand balled in a fist, while Hubbard forced a smile for the benefit of those watching. "Well, isn't that nice, Sheriff? What a thoughtful gesture." He looked at the line of well-wishers as they decided if they should run before the shooting started. "It looks like we may have peace in our humble valley after all."

Some of the guests forced a laugh out of politeness.

Mayor White cleared his throat. "I'm all for you boys burying the hatchet, as long as it's not in each other."

Halstead extended his hand and saw the rage brewing in Riker's eyes. He hoped he took a swing at him.

Mayor White pulled Riker toward Halstead and lowered his voice as he said, "Shake his hand and get him out of here. Don't make a spectacle of yourself. We still have several important people you need to meet."

Riker shook Halstead's hand and squeezed hard. "You've got a lot of nerve showing your face here."

"Serves you right for keeping your back to the door." Halstead matched the pressure Riker applied to his hand. "Thought I'd see Warren here. Caught him playing with matches up at an old mine yesterday. Hope he didn't get himself blown up."

Riker's right eye twitched like it always did when he was angry. "Don't worry about him. You'll be seeing him real soon."

Halstead squeezed harder until he heard cartilage pop. He did not know if it was from his hand or Riker's. "I'll be looking forward to it. And Mr. Fitzgerald will be glad for the business."

Riker shoved Halstead's hand away and took a step closer. His eyes brimmed with hate as the two men stood face-to-face.

Halstead grinned. "If you're going to do something, now's the time. I'm not armed, so you might have a chance."

Riker's jaw clenched. "You killed my father. I'm gonna make you pay for that."

"Wouldn't it be nice to think so."

Hubbard slid his walking stick between them and nudged Riker back toward the receiving line. "Come on, Sheriff. We can't allow the deputy to monopolize all your time. There are several people who've just come in that I'd like to introduce to you."

Halstead saw Riker was teetering and hoped a small push might send him over the edge. "Still doing what old men tell you, eh, Sparky? Glad to see some things never change."

Hubbard had managed to push Riker back far enough for him to step in between them and guide him to the waiting guests on the receiving line.

Halstead was left standing alone behind them and made a point of meeting the eyes of every citizen who looked at him. They quickly turned away, often beginning a conversation with whoever happened to be standing next to them.

Yesterday, they'd looked at him as a dangerous but necessary man. Today they looked at him as though he was a leper. A marked man who had death hovering over his shoulder.

Since their discomfort was their own doing, he decided to let it last a while longer. He moved through the crowd to the side table, where Mr. Fitzgerald was helping himself to a piece of cake.

The mortician flinched when he realized Halstead was standing next to him.

Halstead grinned. "Guess making a man in your business jump is quite an accomplishment on my part."

"Forgive me, Deputy." Fitzgerald gestured at the cake on his plate. "I was so taken by the food that I wasn't expecting anyone to talk to me. People seldom talk to me unless they have a specific reason." His false smile fell as the truth of his own words reached him. "Good Lord. You haven't killed someone else, have you?"

"No, but Zimmerman did. One of the kids I brought in yesterday. Mule. The body's still over in the jail. Since I've got Deputy Sandborne resting back there, I'd appreciate it if you could stop by to pick up the body."

"Of course." Fitzgerald bowed slightly at the waist. "I'll tend to it personally as soon as I can. My men are busy . . . burying the other men . . . from yesterday's unpleasantness."

"It was only unpleasant for them," Halstead noted.

"Yes, I suppose you're right." He lowered his voice as he said, "You know, not everyone here disapproves of you, Deputy. For my part, you've proven to be very good for business."

Halstead had to take compliments where he found them. "At least someone in here likes me."

Halstead could feel the dozens of pairs of eyes following him as he headed for the back door. They could not face him, but now that he was leaving, it was safe to talk about him behind his back. Let them talk. He had given them much to discuss.

And as he walked through the back door of the dining room, he could have sworn he heard a sigh of relief follow him into the courtyard.

CHAPTER 30

Since becoming a United States Marshal, Aaron Mackey insisted his men follow a strict protocol when it came time to move a prisoner. It did not matter if it was from a holding cell to the courtroom or clear across the state. It was always the same. There was predictability in uniformity. Each step ensured the prisoner was secure and ready to be moved.

Which was why Halstead led Mackey and Billy into the back, where they stood together outside Zimmerman's cell.

Billy held the same noose they had used on Zimmerman in Valhalla.

Mackey gave the order. "Deputy Halstead, prepare the prisoner for travel."

"Get up off your cot," Halstead told Zimmerman. "Get up and place your back against the bars of the door."

Zimmerman sneered up at him. "And if I refuse?"

"Then the three of us will come in there and pound you into powder," Halstead told him. "We'll be happy either way."

Zimmerman cursed as he got to his feet and threw his shoulder into the bars in defiance before placing his back against them.

Billy slipped the noose over Zimmerman's head and pulled it tight between the bars, roughly jerking Zimmerman's head back.

Billy spoke into his ear. "Deputy Halstead is going to reach in there and put a nice pair of shackles on your wrist. You fight him and I'll pull on this rope until you pass out. We'll hog-tie you and you'll stay that way the whole trip to Helena. Understand?"

Zimmerman grunted and Halstead was able to secure the prisoner's hands behind his back without incident.

Mackey checked the shackles and confirmed they were tight. "Open the prisoner's cell."

Halstead slipped the key into the door and pulled it open. Billy moved with it, ensuring Zimmerman did the same. Halstead took the prisoner's arm and pulled him into the aisle as Billy readjusted his grip and took hold of the rope on this side of the bars.

Mackey said, "We're transporting you to Helena. That rope around your neck will be tied to the saddle horn. Same rules that applied in Valhalla will be applied now. If you behave yourself, I'll allow you to ride with your hands chained in front of you. Give us any problems, you'll spend the rest of the trip like you are right now. Do you understand?"

Halstead expected Zimmerman to curse or spit, but he did neither. "I understand. And now you understand something, Marshal. My lawyer's going to meet us in Helena, and when he does, he'll blind you with so much paper, you'll think it was a snowstorm. I'll be out of there in time for supper."

Mackey did not look worried. "Deputy Sunday, escort the prisoner outside and get him on his horse. We're moving out."

Billy pushed Zimmerman into the office as he held a tight grip on the rope.

Once they were out of earshot, Mackey said, "I want to take a last look at Sandborne before I go."

The marshal moved past him and looked in at Sandborne. Most of his color had returned and he was resting peacefully. Halstead might have feared the worst if he had not seen his chest rise and fall several times beneath the blankets.

"He's probably through the worst of it now," Mackey said. "You get word to me as soon as you're able."

"I will," Halstead assured him. "And I'll wait to leave until you give the order."

Mackey thumbed his hat farther back on his head. "I appreciate the gesture, but I want you two out of here as soon as possible. The next train for Helena is in three days. I know he's still mending, but I'd feel better if you two were on it. Put him in a wagon if you have to. I don't like leaving you alone like this, but the longer we let Zimmerman's men get set, the more time they'll have to do something. Bringing Zimmerman before a judge is too important."

"I promise I'll keep you posted."

That was good enough for Mackey, who walked up to Randy's cell. He was not technically a prisoner, so the rules were more relaxed. "Open it up, Jeremiah."

Halstead unlocked the door and Randy stepped out. He moved like a beaten dog.

Mackey said, "You're not a prisoner, Randy. You're a cooperating witness. No one's tying you up or putting a rope around your neck unless you do something stupid. Can you ride a horse?"

"Been riding since before I could walk," Randy told him. "It's the getting there that worries me." He looked down at Mule's corpse. They had thrown a blanket over him to hide the eyes Randy swore kept looking at him. "I'm in for a rough time of it, ain't I?"

"Not nearly as rough as Zimmerman's going to have it," Mackey assured him. "Come on. We've got a horse waiting for you outside. Best climb aboard."

As Randy walked through the office and outside, Mackey and Halstead followed behind him.

"I hate leaving you here by yourself," Mackey said as they walked outside, "but I think you're in better spirits since we got here yesterday."

"Feels like you got here a week ago," Halstead admitted. "But in a good way. I want to thank you for helping me snap out of that bad spell, Aaron."

"You can thank me by getting yourself and Sandborne back to Helena in one piece." He extended his hand to him. "Don't let Riker pull you down. Sandborne needs you and so do we."

Halstead shook his hand and stepped outside to bid goodbye to Billy. He had already secured Zimmerman in his saddle and had backed the mounts away from the jail. He threw Halstead a wink. "See you back in Helena, Jerry."

"You surely will."

Zimmerman forced a laugh. "No tender goodbye for me, Halstead?"

"I'll say my goodbye to you at your hanging."

Billy clicked his teeth and got the horses moving, pulling Zimmerman's mount on a lead rope. Randy ducked his head and fell in behind them.

Halstead watched Mackey climb atop Adair and pulled the reins to make the mare step backward. She truly was a majestic animal.

Mackey brought his fingers to the brim of his hat and gave him a final nod. "Deputy Halstead."

It sounded good to hear him say it. "Marshal Mackey."

Mackey brought Adair around and quickly closed the gap between himself and the others.

He felt a surge of pride as he turned to watch them ride away. He knew the road to the water tower would be tough going, but they were tough men who could handle it. He was proud to know them. Proud to be counted as their colleague. Their friend.

He did not feel as if they were leaving him behind. He felt good, and he vowed he would not allow himself to let them down.

He leaned against the doorway and watched the way the gentle afternoon light fell across Main Street. The town was quiet for now, but he doubted that would last long.

And when called upon, Jeremiah Halstead would be ready.

He watched Mr. Fitzgerald lead his mortuary wagon onto Main Street and head for the jail. He had almost forgotten he had told him to come pick up Mule's body.

Cal Hubbard thought he saw a spring in Mayor White's step as he came back to the private alcove of the dining room, where they were enjoying an early supper with Sheriff Riker and Doc Potter.

"I have good news," White told the small party. "Mackey and Sunday have just left town with Zimmerman and that boy from Valhalla. Saw it with my own two eyes."

Riker stopped chewing his steak and set his silverware on his plate. "What're you so happy about? I don't see how that helps much."

White tucked his napkin into his shirt collar. "It means Halstead is all alone with a sick man to tend to. We finally have what we've wanted, gentlemen. Halstead is vulnerable for the first time since he rode into town all those months ago. And once Mannes and his family work their magic in Helena, our new sheriff here will be able to arrest him on a charge of murder."

Hubbard glanced at the doctor as he told the mayor, "Phil, perhaps we should mind what we say in front of mixed company."

Doc Potter did not look up from his plate of ham and mashed potatoes. "Don't mind me, gentlemen. I've always been content with the treatment of corporeal ills, not political ones."

"That's a foolish way to look at it," Riker said, "considering how political ills often lead to corporeal ones. People get killed from them all the time."

Potter continued to cut into a slice of ham. "By the time the situation is that far gone, it's a matter for Mr. Fitzgerald, not me."

Hubbard regretted allowing Potter to dine with them. He had extended the invitation only as a courtesy. Most of the others he had invited had been gracious enough to turn him down. But the doctor was all too happy to enjoy a free meal at Hubbard's expense.

Perhaps it was time for him to sing for his supper. "You've spent quite a bit of time in that jail lately. How's young Sandborne doing?"

"My clinical opinion?" Potter chewed his food. "He's a tough kid. Five men tried to kill him and he put down every single one of them. Took a back shot to knock him down. He might've been young before the shooting started, but he's a full-grown man now in my book. He's lived this long and I expect he'll pull through, barring any unforeseen complications, such as infection."

Hubbard was not pleased to hear it. He bore Sandborne no ill will, but he knew how close Halstead and he had become. His death would only weaken a man who was already on the edge. "And what of Deputy Halstead? How's he faring?"

He thought it over as he continued to chew his ham. "If Sandborne is tough, I don't know what you'd call Halstead. I'd put him in the same class as Mackey and Sunday, whatever class that is. He sounds like them. Dresses like them and, from what I've seen, fights like them."

Hubbard did not like to hear what he already knew. "What of his mind, Doctor? I hear he's been under a considerable strain since Zimmerman's pardon."

"He's fine now that he knows Zimmerman will never breathe free air again." The doctor looked at each of the three other men around the table. "I take it you haven't heard. Zimmerman strangled someone in his cell."

White was the first to register surprise. "He what?"

Potter explained as he cut through more of his ham. "He choked the life right out of him. Broke his neck, which is no easy feat considering that young man had a neck like—well, like a mule. I didn't get into the particulars since he was already beyond my abilities to help him when I got there, but Zimmerman's done for. I know Randy's complaint against him was flimsy at best, but Mackey will see to it that he swings for Mule."

Hubbard set his silverware on his plate. He had lost his appetite. "Why in the world would he do something so stupid?"

Riker resumed eating, unaffected by the news of Zimmerman's fate. "Probably thought someone would rush in to help him and, when they did, he'd try to grab hold of them and make them let him loose. And if they didn't, maybe there'd be one less of them to handle him. It would even the odds a bit in his favor. I've seen it done. I've seen it work, too. Never in one of my jails, of course. I'd have been surprised if Halstead or the others fell for it."

Hubbard ran a finger across his brow as he tried to order his thoughts. Zimmerman was always an impulsive man, but his violence always had a reason. A purpose. Killing Mule burned down all their plans. He should have known they never would have allowed him to go free. What was he thinking?"

Riker laughed as he pointed a fork in Hubbard's direction. "You should see the look on your face right now, Cal. You don't know why he did it, but I do. Being locked up behind bars changes a man. Makes him do all sorts of things he wouldn't think of doing on the outside. He wasn't thinking when he killed Mule. He went back to what he's always been. A thug. It got him this far and he hoped it would get him farther. Don't waste your time trying to understand it. You've got more important concerns."

"Such as?"

Riker cut off another piece of steak. "Such as getting Mannes's kin to sign that murder warrant against Halstead. You said you wanted him out legally and that's the only way we're going to do it. Nothing Zimmerman's done has changed that."

White threw up his hands. "Killing Mule changes everything. Do you think any judge will read a murder complaint made by a man who has not one but two murder charges of his own leveled against him? Mannes might have been able to fight off that Meachum mess, but breaking a man's neck in jail with the federal marshal for the state as a witness?"

Riker popped a piece of steak in his mouth. "He's only a witness if he saw it happen, which I'm betting he didn't. They likely only came in when one of them called out for help. That leaves Randy as the only one who saw Zimmerman do it." He held up two fingers as he chewed his meat. "The only witness for both the Meachum and the Mule killings. I heard plenty of talk about that boy when I was in

Valhalla. Unless he's managed to grow a spine in that jailhouse, which I doubt, we can get to him."

Hubbard normally enjoyed the musings of dullards like Riker, but in this case, it was a dangerous distraction. "There's no way Mackey will let anyone get near him."

"Where there's a will, there's a way," Riker said. "And if you've got the will, my brother and I will find a way. But first things first. Have Mannes get that warrant signed against Halstead so we can get him legally like you want. If they charge Zimmerman with Mule's murder, Mannes can probably make it look like they're trying to make a jailhouse accident look like revenge for his complaint against Halstead."

Hubbard began to look at Riker in an entirely new light. He had brought the man to Battle Brook in the hope he might push Halstead to further extremes. He had not counted on the Texan to have a brain.

"That's good," Hubbard said. "That's very good."

"It's weak," Mayor White said. "Mackey won't let that stop him. There's too much at stake here."

Riker pounded the table, which made all of them jump except for Potter, who was still enjoying his free meal.

"I want Halstead gone." The new sheriff glared at Hubbard and White. "You want him gone legally, so we're trying it your way. If that doesn't work, Warren and I will try ours. Every day that half-breed sits in that jail is a slap on the face to me. I won't abide it, boys. Not for one second longer than I have to. You'd better hope Mannes can pull this off because if he can't, I'll handle it my way."

Hubbard had suffered enough surprises for one day. Riker would not be satisfied until he had some real authority behind him.

He spoke to the mayor, who was still recovering from Riker's outburst. "The sheriff has a point. I'm going to talk to the owner of The Blue Belle and let him know that the back of his saloon will serve as the town jail for the moment. The bank owns the mortgage on the place, and since I control the bank, I'll be able to make him listen to reason. I'll need you to get some men to build a wall separating the two. The sheriff will use the back door to come and go without bothering the patrons. Ask the blacksmith how long it might take to install iron bars in a corner of the room. I imagine it will take more time than we have, so perhaps a stout iron ring installed on the wall would do the trick."

Riker frowned. "I ain't setting up shop in the back of a whorehouse."

"The Blue Belle is a saloon," Hubbard reminded him. "The few women who work there ply their trade in cribs in the back alley."

Riker shoved asparagus stalks around his plate. "Still don't like it."

"Neither do I, but we all need to be flexible for the moment." Another thought came to him. "How is Warren doing, anyway? I remember he was shot in the leg."

"Just a scratch on his calf," Riker said. "He'll be fine in a day or so."

Hubbard had seen the wound the night before and knew it was more than a scratch. But there was no point in arguing. "Let me know when he's ready to ride. I have a feeling Mr. Mannes might be able to use his help." The banker smiled. "In Helena."

Riker and White appeared pleased with the idea. Only Doc Potter remained immersed in his meal throughout the conversation.

"We've discussed a great deal in front of you today, Doctor," Hubbard said. "I hope we can rely on your discretion."

Potter shoveled a forkful of mashed potatoes in his

mouth. "I hope you boys find a peaceful solution to all of this."

"And if we don't?" Riker asked.

"Then I'll do my best to patch up your holes and hope you don't die." He swallowed his food and dug in for more. "But I won't let you move Sandborne until he's well enough to travel. That means he'll be in that jail for a week or more."

Riker slowly raised his head. "I thought all you cared about was patching holes."

"I do," the doctor declared. "And I'd demand the same treatment for you or any man here who found himself in the same condition. Violence is your concern. Mine is what follows. The rest of it is really none of my business."

Hubbard was glad to hear it. At least one man at the table knew his true place in the grander scheme at play.

CHAPTER 31

"How long was I out for?"

Halstead kept Sandborne's head propped up as the wounded man drank more water. "Only a few hours, but it seemed longer."

Sandborne managed to finish half the cup before he rested his head back on the pillow. "My left side is burning up something awful."

Halstead placed the back of his hand against Sandborne's forehead. "You don't have a fever. It's probably just your body working to heal itself."

He saw no point in telling Sandborne how close he had come to death. If the bullet had struck him an inch to the right, it would have hit his heart and killed him on the spot. An inch lower and he might have lost his lung. But none of that mattered now. He was awake, which Doc Potter had said would be an excellent sign.

"It all happened so fast," Sandborne said. "I didn't have time to think. I just did it."

Halstead understood all too well. "The time for thinking ends when the bullets start flying. A man can get himself killed if he thinks too much at a time like that. This time, it was you who did the killing."

Sandborne's brow furrowed as he remembered what had

happened. "I only winged the leader. He dove behind the trough before I got a clean shot at him." He gripped Halstead's shirt. "He might still be out there."

"He's over at Fitzgerald's place right now," Halstead assured him. "Col and I buffaloed him when he tried to finish you off. He died soon after, but it was your bullet that finished him. He was too stubborn to let death take him just yet."

Sandborne blinked hard as the ugly memories slowly returned to him.

Halstead pulled his hand from his shirt and lowered it to his side. "Put it out of your mind, Joshua. Just work on getting better. Don't trouble yourself with that now."

Sandborne shut his eyes tighter. "Keeping it inside is even worse. There was another man at the end. A sixth man I hadn't counted. I can see the others as plain as day. It's like they're right there in front of me now. There were only five. I know there were. Where'd that sixth fella come from?"

Halstead did not know how much he should tell him. He needed rest, but it was clear he would not find peace until he had an answer. "We'd just reached the far end of Main Street when we heard the shots. We came running, and I saw a man standing over you. He ran off when I got close, but I have a pretty good idea of who it might be."

"A couple of the others kept calling out for someone," Sandborne went on, "like they were waiting for him to help. I just can't remember the name. I feel like I'm hearing them with cotton in my ears."

Halstead knew the name, though he hoped for his own sake he was wrong. He did not want to tell him out of fear he would be proven right. Out of fear of what he might do if Sandborne told him he was right.

But his friend was suffering, so he said, "Riker."

Sandborne's eyes sprang open. "That's the name. That's the sheriff they hired on to irk you, isn't it?"

"'Irk' is a mild word for it."

He steadied himself as Sandborne continued to tell him how the shooting unfolded. He steadied himself as he waited for the old anger to return. He remembered his solemn promise to Mackey about keeping Sandborne's safety his main priority.

But Halstead never had been good at lying to himself. He knew the rage he felt toward the Riker men was always just below the surface, coiled and waiting. Thinking Riker had played a role in Sandborne's shooting had been one thing. Knowing it would be enough to cause the rattler from its den and strike before he could stop it.

But as Sandborne went on, Halstead quickly realized he felt nothing. Fury did not well up inside him. The hate and urge for violence did not appear. Sandborne's confirmation had not shocked him and had not changed his course. He had been shot and now he was alive. It was up to Halstead to keep him that way until he was well enough to travel back to Helena.

His oath to Mackey held.

Sandborne snapped him back into the present by lightly tapping his arm. "Well? Aren't you gonna answer me?"

Halstead brought his hand to his eyes and squeezed the bridge of his nose. "Sorry. Guess I drifted off there for a minute. I haven't gotten much sleep the past couple of nights."

"I asked about the marshal and Billy. I'd like to see them. Did they see I got Randy's statement? I left it on the desk before everything happened."

Halstead spent the next couple of minutes telling him how Randy's statement had been enough for Mackey to get a warrant for Zimmerman's arrest, about Zimmerman killing Mule, and how Randy, Zimmerman, Mackey, and Billy had headed for the water tower to flag down the train to Helena. About Riker being sworn in as sheriff. About how Abby made it to Wellspring early, before any of the Valhalla boys could block the road.

As he finished his tale, Halstead said, "I imagine Mackey and the others are already on the train by now. Abby will be soon."

Sandborne seemed saddened by all he heard. "I sure wish I could've seen the boss when he read that statement. I would've liked to see his face when he saw what a dumb kid like me could do."

"He saw it," Halstead assured him. "He was proud of you. As proud as he'd ever let on, anyway. And you'd better quit thinking of yourself as a kid. You're the one who keeps reminding me I'm only about five minutes older than you. After the way you handled yourself against those five cowboys, no one'll ever call you a kid again. You went and got yourself a reputation, Joshua. Just like you always wanted."

Sandborne winced from pain in his left side. "Here I am talking about me and I haven't asked how you're doing. You seem different."

"Normal?"

Sandborne looked him over. "Yeah, normal."

"Don't tell anyone," Halstead said. "The people here think I'm a mad-dog killer. If they think I've changed, they might try to take advantage."

"I wasn't out of it long enough for anyone to get that stupid." He laughed at his own joke and paid the price in pain. "Think you could get word to the doc to take a look at me? I'd like to know when we can get ourselves out of here and back home, where we belong."

"Home" had always been a strange notion to Halstead.

He never had one worth the name and had come to believe he never would. He had allowed himself to think Battle Brook might be home to him, but it no longer felt that way. Abby was not there. She was on her way to Helena. And if the bleak past several weeks had taught him anything, it was that he was always better with her by his side. Wherever she was, his home would be, too.

"I'll have someone fetch the doc. I'll be right back."

As Halstead walked into the office, he heard a loud chorus of hammering and banging from outside the jail. His mind flashed to the same sounds he had heard echoing across the hill from Valhalla.

Someone was building something and, given it was approaching dark, it sounded like they were in a hurry.

He opened the door and found Emil Riker across the thoroughfare, directing two men on ladders as they positioned a wooden sign in place. Someone had used a hot poker to burn the letters into the wood. "Battle Brook Town Jale."

Halstead stepped out onto the boardwalk and leaned against a porch post. He hooked his thumb on his belt buckle again. It was close to the Colt on his belly in case Riker decided to get frisky.

"Nice sign," he called out to the sheriff.

Riker glanced back at him as he directed one of the men on the ladder to lift his side an inch higher. "Thanks. I scorched in the letters myself."

"I can tell. You spelled 'jail' wrong, you stupid bastard."

Riker ignored the insult. "Not everyone's as particular as you, Jeremiah. They'll know what it means. So will you before long. I'm fixing it up real nice, just for you."

"Don't waste the effort. I'll never set foot inside."

"We'll see." He told the man on the right ladder to raise his side and declared it was perfect. Despite the cold air, the men were sweating from the effort and happy to start nailing it to the porch roof.

"It's still crooked," Halstead told him.

Riker slowly turned to face him as he clapped his hands as though he had hung the sign all by himself. "So are we."

Halstead could not argue with him on that score.

Riker placed his hands on his hips as he looked around the town. "I can see why you took to this place. Montana, I mean. It's a tough place to get a hold on. An easy place to get lost in. Not big enough, though, seeing as how I found you."

"You didn't find me because you were smart enough not to look," Halstead told him. "You were brought here because you were summoned here by Zimmerman. And you came running, too, just like the lapdog you've always been."

The hammering from inside the saloon continued, but the men on the ladders stopped working when they realized they were in an awkward situation in the event of a shooting.

Halstead saw the anger in Riker's eyes, but the storm quickly passed. He looked up at the men. "Keep hammering, boys. Nothing's going to happen. The deputy here is just trying to rile me in front of witnesses." He looked over at Halstead. "You've gotten tricky, Jeremiah. You used to be a lot plainer. I can remember a time when you never would've let me stand here like this. You would've started shooting right on sight and worried about the trouble later."

Halstead would not allow him to pull him back to memories of El Paso. "That's the same time you had your father's men to fight for you. Never understood how a man could live with himself like that. Needing his daddy's name to prop him up wherever he went."

"Who's propping you up now, Jeremiah? It sure ain't

Mackey or Sunday. They've ridden off with Zimmerman. Where'd they go, anyway?"

"They didn't tell me and I didn't think to ask. But you can go looking for them if you want. I'm sure they'll have a warm welcome for you if you find them."

"Hot lead would be my guess," Riker said. "But don't worry. If they want Zimmerman so bad, they're welcome to him. I've got my eye on a bigger prize." He pointed across to Halstead. "Seeing you sitting in my jail awaiting trial for murdering those brave men in Wellspring. I'm gonna bring you to Helena myself. Maybe pay a visit to the lovely Miss Abby Newman while I'm there. Help her through her grief, knowing you'll be swinging from the gallows real soon."

Halstead did not allow the thought to trouble him. "That's thoughtful of you, Emil, but she'd never give you the time of day. She likes an independent man, not a lapdog."

The men scrambled down from their ladders and left them behind as they quickly moved farther up Main Street and out of the way of trouble.

Riker watched them leave. "Looks like it's just you and me now, Jeremiah. I could cut you down right here and be within my rights as the lawfully appointed sheriff."

Halstead kept his thumb hooked on his buckle. "You can die trying."

He knew there were over a thousand miles between El Paso and Battle Brook and more than three years since Halstead had last seen a Riker man. But now, as they glared at each other across the wide expanse of Main Street, time and distance ceased to matter, and Halstead felt as if they were back in that harsh, sun-bleached town. The only difference was that Riker was alone and Halstead was not a naïve young man anymore.

Riker kept his hands on his hips. "I must confess it's mighty tempting."

If his hands so much as twitched, Halstead would kill him. "I'll see to it that Mr. Fitzgerald gives you a fine burial."

A freight wagon rattled up Main Street between them, blocking each man's sight of the other until it passed.

Halstead thought he would see Riker's pistol in his hand. In fact, he hoped it.

But the sheriff had not moved and neither had Halstead.

Riker smiled at the passing freighter. "A spiritual man might call that divine intervention."

"I don't need anyone intervening for me."

"No," Riker agreed. "I imagine you don't. Our time will come soon, Jeremiah. Sooner than you want. I still haven't decided if you're going to hang yourself in your cell or if I'm going to shoot you while you're trying to escape. But when that glorious day comes, it'll happen my way, not yours."

"It won't matter when. The result will be the same."

Riker slowly turned and stepped back up onto the boardwalk and began to walk down the alley. The same alley he disappeared in when Halstead scared the sheriff off from shooting Sandborne.

And he could not let Riker go without knowing that. "I'm going to kill you for what you did to my friend, Emil. You're going to die like your daddy did. Alone and afraid."

When Riker stopped walking, he thought that might have been enough to cause him to turn around and fire. It would have been a good way to end things. Death usually was.

But when Riker continued to walk into the alley, Halstead knew it would not be that easy. Nothing in Montana ever was.

CHAPTER 32

In the storeroom of The Iron Horse Saloon in Valhalla, Riker refused the bottle of whiskey his brother offered him. He could have used the drink. His run-in with Halstead still stung.

"It's best if I keep a clear head," Riker said. "How's the leg?"

"It hurts." Warren took a healthy pull on the bottle. "But this helps. Thanks for patching me up, little brother. Just give me a couple of days and I'll be riding into town with you. That lousy half-breed got the jump on me once, but it won't happen again."

Riker did not doubt Warren believed that, but he was not so sure. "He's changed since El Paso. It's like he's a completely different man."

"He's changed. We haven't. We're still Rikers and, by God, that means something. Doesn't matter if it's Texas or Montana or anywhere else. He's got to pay for what he did to us." The pain in his leg arced again and he took another long drink from the bottle. "Heard you got yourself sworn in as sheriff today. I'd expect you to be in town celebrating."

"Not much to celebrate in Battle Brook yet. I'm saving that for when I have Halstead in a cell. The day that happens, I'll drink this whole town dry."

Warren set the bottle aside. "What's troubling you, brother? You only talk about drinking when you're working up to something unpleasant."

Riker had been trying to find a way to break the news to him but just came out with it. "Hubbard wants you to go to Helena to take care of a problem for him."

"What sort of problem?"

"The two-legged kind that sings. Seems one of Zimmerman's boys from here in Valhalla has turned on him. He's going to testify at Zimmerman's trial."

"They're worried about what some kid says?"

"Worried enough to see if you'd be willing to go to the capital and handle it for them."

"That's lawyer's work," Warren said. "That bald, shifty-eyed rodent he's got working for him should just pay him off. They don't need me to traipse all the way to Helena for that. My place is here with you until this mess with Halstead is finished."

"Hubbard thinks different. He's looking at the future. He wants to make an example of the kid and I almost agree with him." The more he talked, the more he liked the idea. "This valley's wide open to us, Warren. Men like Hubbard and Mannes only look at the world one way. They can spend all they want and make deals all they want, but none of it's any good without men to back their play."

Warren grunted. "Men like us."

"Men willing to do the killing they don't have the stomach for," Riker added. "There's always going to be another banker and another lawyer to do what they do. But there's only a few men like us smart enough to know our limitations. I think it's a good idea for you to do this favor for them if you think you're able. They think they're paying us, but all the while, we'll be looking to get an angle on them. We'll watch what they do. We'll see why they do it. We'll learn. And once we know we're finally ready, we surprise the heck out of them."

Warren's eyes grew distant. "Or pull the house down around them. Just like Daddy did down in El Paso."

Riker was glad his idea had begun to take hold in his brother's mind. "A man like you wouldn't have a problem handling a kid like Randy. And Mackey's got enough pull in Helena to make sure he goes on trial anyway. If Mannes gets him clear, we'll worry about that then. But if not, we just make sure we make the most of the chances we have."

He nudged his brother's right leg. "It's just a train ride either way."

"I hate trains," Warren said. "They're cramped and noisy and smell something awful. But I suppose I could tolerate it for a greater cause."

"That cause is us, big brother. Us."

Warren sloshed the whiskey in the bottle as he thought about taking another drink. "When would I have to be ready?"

"There's a train bound for Helena the day after tomorrow if the schedule is to be believed. I can have Hubbard wire ahead to make sure Mannes knows you're coming. It'll give him time to find out where they're keeping Randy until the trial starts. It'll be up to you to decide where it happens and how."

Warren raised his bottle and examined its contents. "Let me drink on it a while. But if Hubbard agrees to let me do it my way, you can tell him we have a deal."

Riker knew it was best to quit while he was ahead. He left his brother with his bottle and stepped out into the saloon. They were standing two deep at the bar and he had never seen the place so busy. He wondered if Zimmerman's absence had anything to do with it.

Tote, one of Zimmerman's constables, grabbed Riker's

arm as he headed for the door. "You hear what they did to the boss? You have any hand in this?"

Riker could tell the man was drunk but was not in the practice of allowing anyone to paw him. "Get your hand off me."

Tote pulled Riker toward him. "I asked you a question and you'll answer it or I swear . . ."

Riker brought his right heel back into Tote's left knee, causing the big man to buckle. He twisted his arm around his back, and by the time the rest of the saloon noticed, already had the barrel of his Colt jammed against the base of the constable's skull.

Every man in the saloon took a step forward until Riker thumbed back the hammer. "One more step and he dies."

A fat, bearded man Riker had heard Zimmerman call Gordo pushed through the group to the front of the crowd. "I don't know about you boys, but that just about settles it as far as I'm concerned. Tote was right. Everything was moving along just fine until these Rikers showed up. Didn't think much of it at the time, but it all makes sense now. Riker comes here, Mackey comes here. Riker gets named sheriff and the boss is on his way to Helena. They win and we lose."

The men around the saloon grumbled their agreement.

Gordo continued. "Don't need to be a fancy man like Hubbard or Mannes to see things for what they are. They're working with Mackey and Halstead. Today it was the boss and tomorrow it'll be us."

Riker forced the barrel of his pistol hard enough into Tote's neck to make him yell, "Quit talking and get him off me."

Riker kept the Colt pressed against Tote's skull. "I'm not working for anyone except Ed Zimmerman, same as all of you. He figured there'd be trouble soon, which was why my brother and I are here. We draw wages from him, same as all of you."

"A lot more than us by my reckoning," one of the men called out to the agreement of the others.

"And what would any of you do with more money in your pocket?" Riker shouted at them. "Spend it in here, drinking away your troubles. Zimmerman hasn't even been gone a day yet and just look at you. I rode in here seeing a town on the rise. You were building things and making them better. And look at how fast you all folded. You're like a cheap canvas tent without a pole to hold it up."

The constable with the square jaw and flat expression—the one he had heard Zimmerman call Stoneman—said, "Maybe what you say is true, but it sure don't seem likely. It's awfully funny how everything fell apart when you two showed up."

"Things were already falling apart when Zimmerman brought us here." Riker looked over the men, trying to see if any of them was willing to be the first one to die. They were listening to him, so he kept talking. "He kept you all so busy, you didn't have the chance to see all the cracks, but they were there. He wouldn't have sent for me and my brother otherwise."

Riker sensed, rather than saw, some of the anger leave a few of them. Their faces changed as his words made sense.

"I'm not looking to take anything from anyone, and neither is my brother." He let go of Tote's arm and pushed him over on his belly. He held his pistol level as he slowly turned to face each man who had formed a circle around him. "We're here to help, not hurt. To build, not destroy. There's only one man all of us can call an enemy, and he's the same one who's been stalking this town for weeks. His name is Jeremiah Halstead and he'd have himself a good laugh if he could see all of you right now."

Riker flinched when a shotgun blast boomed through the saloon and bits of plaster and wood rained down from above. The men scattered farther into the saloon and away from the bar.

Riker saw Warren had gotten hold of the double-barreled shotgun in the storeroom. He stood propped against the corner of the bar, favoring his left leg.

Now that he had their attention, Warren said, "There's three types of men in this world. Rikers. Those who ride with us and everyone else. We don't have much use for everyone else, so you'd best decide what kind of man you want to be. You want to fight? My brother and I will give you all you can handle. But if you want to ride, you can ride with us. You can ride with us against Halstead. What's it gonna be? You'd best decide now because my baby brother and I ain't known for our patience."

A tense silence spread throughout the saloon as the men thought it over. Riker had already tilled the soil, but Warren planted the seeds. They were giving way. He could feel it.

His suspicions were confirmed when one of the men called out, "Ain't known as much of a marksman either, I'd reckon."

The men laughed as one, with Warren laughing loudest of all. "I'd wager there's a couple of dead birds in the attic who might disagree with you."

Warren looked through the crowd at Riker as the men closed in around him. Not in anger but in friendship.

No, Riker knew it was not friendship. It was more permanent than that. It was deference. The Riker boys had bent Valhalla to their will.

He holstered his Colt and accepted handshakes from men who only a few moments before wanted to tear him to pieces. Even Tote joined in, leading three cheers for the Riker men.

And as he allowed himself to be moved along a human tide toward the bar, Emil Riker knew this was how empires were built.

CHAPTER 33

Halstead poured himself a mug of coffee while he put the question to the doctor. "How long until I can move him?"

The doctor sagged in the chair across from Halstead's desk. He looked worse than tired and could hardly sit up straight.

"Medically speaking? A week at the soonest."

Halstead caught his meaning. "Is there another way you'd speak, Doc?"

"As a man," Potter offered. "As a man who you might consider a friend."

Halstead knew something more was coming and it was not good. "All right. As a friend, how soon can I move him?"

"It may already be too late. And not for Deputy Sandborne but for you."

Halstead sipped his coffee but did not put it on the desk. "What have you heard?"

Potter folded his hands across his belly as he sought the right words. "I haven't been in this town long, but I've been in other towns just like it. I've seen how they can come together around a man like you. I've also seen them come apart and leave such men flat. Vulnerable, even, though that's not exactly the word I'd use to describe you."

None of this was helping. "What have you heard, Doctor?"

"I hoped Zimmerman's arrest would calm things down for a while. Give everyone a chance to breathe while we grew used to a new situation. A new way. But Hubbard isn't a man who likes to wait. He's not one to allow for a single breath unless it benefits him."

Now Halstead had a clearer view of things. "What's he planning?"

Potter raked his lower teeth over his lip. "I found myself involved in this kind of thing once before, and I vowed I'd never get caught up in politics again, but I can't sit by and let a good man get grounded beneath Hubbard's heel. Riker has proven to be more than just a hired gun to scare you off. He's a thinking man, Jeremiah. And a thinking man with a gun on his hip is most dangerous indeed. He's gunning for you, and not the way you're accustomed to. He's smart and he's going to get a lot of people in Valhalla and here in Battle Brook to support him very quickly. Hubbard has wealth and influence, but without Zimmerman around, Riker has power. He knows that. I watched him feel it today after the luncheon. This valley is there for the taking and he intends to take it, whether Hubbard likes it or not."

Halstead did not know Doc Potter well. He did not know if he was a man to be trusted or had been sent to give him false information. Worse, he did not know if he was a troublemaker who enjoyed watching rival factions battle one another for his own amusement.

No, Halstead did not know Potter, but he knew Emil Riker. And a Riker man was never content with what he was given. He preferred to take what he wanted. Potter was telling the truth.

"Did they tell you when they're coming for me?"

"No," Potter admitted, "but I think it'll be soon."

"Yeah. That sounds about right. Lucky me."

The doctor said, "There is a way out of this, you know. You won't like it, but it's for the best."

Halstead had already ruled it out. "I can't run."

Potter leaned forward in the chair. "It's not running. It's a tactical retreat, and there's a difference. If you stay in here in this jail, you and Sandborne will be trapped. I believe Riker has gone back to Valhalla with Hubbard for the night. He wanted to see how his brother is recovering from his leg wound. After we move Sandborne to my office where I can watch over him while he recovers. You can ride out of town. I can get the general store to open up and give you supplies for the trip to Helena. You can probably make it in a week or so. I can guarantee Sandborne's safety. The town has embraced him since his shooting and no harm will come to him."

But Halstead had already made his decision. "I can't do that, Doc. I made a promise to Mackey to watch over Joshua and I'm living up to it. Even if I hadn't, I don't run out on my friends. They already tried to grab Abby. What's to keep Riker from threatening to kill Sandborne to force me to come back? No, there's no way around this except straight through the middle of it. I'm not going anywhere."

Doc Potter lowered his head. "Yesterday, you blamed yourself for what happened to him. That you almost cost him his life. You were wrong then and you're wrong now. Don't let your pride cost him his life."

"I said I'm not leaving," Halstead said. "Sandborne's a different story. No one will try to hurt Sandborne if he's already dead."

Doc Potter sat back in the chair as if he had been slapped. "What?"

Halstead explained. "I want you to go get Mr. Fitzgerald

for me. Have him—and only him—bring his wagon here. I'll help him carry Joshua out of here with a sheet over his head. But Fitzgerald won't take him to his mortuary. We'll bring him to your office instead. We'll spread the word that Sandborne is dead. You'll look after him and keep him alive until this is over. As far as the rest of the town is concerned, he's dead. As for what happens after that, we'll worry about that later."

Potter raised an eyebrow as he thought it over. "It's risky. I see a fair number of patients in my office. I can't guarantee one of them won't discover he's there. And what if they want to have a service for the boy?"

The doctor's constant questions were beginning to annoy him. Halstead got up from the desk and walked over to the high, narrow window facing Main Street. He saw Riker's ridiculous sign mocking him from across the thoroughfare. The hammering from The Blue Belle Saloon had stopped some time ago.

Potter said, "I'm not trying to be difficult, Jeremiah. I'm just not used to this sort of thing. Maybe I should've just kept my mouth shut, but I don't want to see good men like you and Sandborne hurt by the likes of Riker."

Halstead wished it was only his pride talking. He could push it aside and do what was right for Sandborne. But this was not a matter of dignity. It was about more than that. It was about survival.

"You don't beat a man like Emil Riker by running from him, Doc," Halstead said. "From men like Hubbard and Zimmerman. I tried running when I left Texas. Thought I could put all that blood and misery behind me by moving to someplace new. With friends I could trust and who trusted me. But a man can only run for so long before he gets tired, and I'm tired, Doc. Tired of letting things from back then bleed into right now. Tired of letting the dead grab hold of my life. Eventually, you need to stop running and stand your ground against whatever's chasing you. You need to put it down before it runs you into the ground."

The more Halstead looked at Riker's misspelled sign, the more it bothered him. "The Rikers have pushed me far enough for one lifetime. This ends here in Battle Brook, one way or the other."

Doc Potter's chair creaked as he stood up. "I'll go get Mr. Fitzgerald and have him bring the wagon around. I'm not very good at lying, so I'll allow him to spread word of Sandborne's demise if you don't mind. People are liable to believe it more if it comes from him."

Halstead kept looking out the window. "Fine by me."

He heard the doctor begin to leave. "I wish you'd listen to me about running, Jeremiah. Riker won't go down without a fight and he won't fight fair."

Halstead rested his hand on the Colt at his hip. "Fine by me."

CHAPTER 34

Hubbard refused to listen to Riker's bluster. "Have you lost your mind? You want to lead an army of drunken rabble into Battle Brook? Tonight?"

Riker crossed his legs. The chairs in Hubbard's bank office were much more comfortable than the chairs in Mannes's office. "Any man too drunk to set a horse or sit up straight gets left behind. We don't need them and we don't want them."

"Who is 'we'?"

"Me and my brother."

Hubbard could tell the man was serious. He had hoped he was drunk, but he did not reek of whiskey. "Do you have any idea what a horde of angry men could do to that town? You might be after Halstead, but it'll lead to chaos. You're using a shotgun to kill a gnat, Emil. And you won't be able to stop them once they get started. A mob takes on a life of its own."

Riker shrugged. "Who cares if a few windows get broken? You want Halstead gone and so do I. I was willing to go along with the warrant idea when I thought it was the only choice. But all that changed when I saw those boys in the saloon tonight. They're mad, Cal. They're fighting mad, and they're scared, too. Scared of what'll happen to this place now that Zimmerman's gone. I say we go after him now while their blood is up. End it quick and blame it on Mackey's kidnapping of our leader."

"He had a warrant!" Hubbard exclaimed. "And Zimmerman's absence doesn't change anything. We have plans for Battle Brook. We don't want it destroyed. We want it strong. Halstead's not more important than that. He'll be gone in a couple of weeks. Until then, we need to keep our powder dry and keep those men in that saloon working here in Valhalla."

Riker lowered his head. "I hate to put it to you this way, Cal, but the only reason me and Warren came here was to kill Halstead. It would've been nice to do it legally, but the result's the same. I'm just getting the job done quicker than you plan to."

Hubbard saw the time for reasoning had passed. "Sheriff Riker, I forbid you from leading anyone into Battle Brook. Do not force me to take actions tonight that you will regret tomorrow."

"You forbid me." Riker looked out the office window. "You gonna forbid them, too?"

Hubbard looked up as riders with flaming torches began to pass his window. He stood up and watched as a long line of men rode by and gathered in the street in front of the bank.

He quickly counted the number of torches he saw. "There have to be twenty men out there."

"Eighteen at last count," Riker said. "Not including me and my brother, which makes it twenty."

"Your brother has a hole in his leg," Hubbard said. "He's in no condition to ride."

"He was in good enough condition to get here when the wound was a lot worse," Riker said. "He'll come in mighty handy for the work we have ahead."

Hubbard felt as if the floor of his office was shaking and steadied himself against the desk. "You can't do this, Riker. You'll ruin everything for the sake of one man. Our plans . . ."

Riker bolted from his chair and stuck his finger in the banker's face. "Your plans, Hubbard. Not mine. Not Warren's. And nothing will be ruined. I'll ride in with them, but I'll hang back when they head into town. Warren and I will keep them to the jail and only the jail. If Halstead comes out, we'll try to grab him."

"He won't come out," Hubbard said.

"Then we'll just have to go in and get him. And if he keeps us out, we'll burn the jail to the ground and only the jail."

Hubbard was on the verge of pleading with him. "You can't control fire once it's started, Riker. Not in those men's minds and not in Battle Brook either. Flames jump to the oddest places, and need I remind you a burned-out town doesn't need a sheriff." He brought his hand down hard on the desk. "You can still stop this madness, Riker. Bring them back to the saloon. Get them good and drunk. I'll pay for the whole thing. But if you bring them to Battle Brook, it's going to turn into more trouble than even you can handle."

He thought Riker might hit him. He hoped he would. It might help him stop and see the horror he was about to unleash on the valley.

But Riker did not hit him. He withdrew his hand and stood straight. He rolled his neck, causing the cartilage to make a sickening crack. "We won't burn anything. You have my word. As for the rest of it, we're already committed and so are our men. I'll try to send word back to you once it's done."

Riker walked out of the office and did not bother to close the door behind him.

Hubbard raised his voice as loudly as he could. "If I see a trail of smoke in my valley come morning, Riker, don't bother coming back. Not even God will be able to help you then, do you hear me? Not even God will protect you from Halstead if you don't kill him."

Riker left the front door of the bank open, too, as he stepped outside, climbed into the saddle, and led the men to Battle Brook.

Hubbard dropped into his chair. *How could it all have gotten so out of hand so quickly? How had Riker rallied them to violence?*

Hubbard held on to the armrests of his chair as his office began to spin as his dreams unraveled before his eyes. "What have I done?"

"I don't want to go anywhere," Sandborne protested from the cot as Mr. Fitzgerald helped Halstead slide the canvas stretcher under him. "If there's a fight coming, I want to be here with you, where I belong."

"Quiet," Halstead scolded him. "You're supposed to be dead, remember?"

With the canvas under Sandborne, Fitzgerald laid a sheet over him. "This is most extraordinary, Deputy. I'm not accustomed to this sort of thing. I'm grateful for all you've done for my business, but this is beyond what I normally do."

"Nothing extraordinary about it," Halstead told him. "You're just picking up a body from one place and moving it to the other. Only difference is that Sandborne's going to Doc Potter's place and not yours. Now, lift."

Halstead and Fitzgerald used the poles of the stretcher to lift Sandborne from the cot and carry him outside.

Halstead spoke through the strain. His friend was heavier

than he looked. "Pull the sheet over your face, Joshua. And don't move."

Sandborne grumbled as he did as he was told.

Halstead and Fitzgerald carried him through the office and outside, where they slid Sandborne into the waiting wagon.

"Wait here," Halstead told him. "I've got to get some things. I'll just be a minute. Be ready to go as soon as I get back."

Fitzgerald continued to fret as he climbed up into the wagon box.

Halstead took his Winchester down from the rack, and remembered he already had a box of bullets in his saddlebags from the previous day's ride into the hills. He took another box just to be safe.

He was about to leave when he saw Jack McBride's double-barreled shotgun in the right side of the rack. He had not touched it since the night McBride was murdered by Zimmerman's robbers but had seen Sandborne clean it a time or two. He had not been able to bring himself to touch it again out of respect for the brave man who had once owned it.

He tucked the Winchester under his shoulder and took the shotgun down. He pocketed a box of shells and left the oil lamp burning as he closed the jailhouse door behind him. Perhaps for the last time.

He slid the rifles into the wagon bed next to Sandborne's stretcher and climbed in beside him. He pulled the tailgate closed and told Fitzgerald, "Let's get going. And let's hope this is the last trip I take in this wagon tonight."

Fitzgerald cracked the reins and the old nag began pulling the cart into a wide turn back toward Fitzgerald's mortuary. It shared a common alley with Doc Potter's office, so no one would see them carry Sandborne to the doctor's place instead of the mortician's parlor.

From beneath the sheet, Sandborne asked, "Can I take this thing off my face yet?"

"No and stop talking. You're still dead."

"I don't like this."

Halstead smiled. Even with a hole in his chest, his friend was nothing if not predictable. "It's for your own good."

He pulled his coat tighter around his neck as the nag completed the turn and a cold wind kicked up along Main Street. He could almost smell the trouble it carried with it.

For he knew the dead would be the only ones who had nothing to fear in Battle Brook that dark night.

Doc Potter had decided to keep Sandborne in his own bed, where his patients were less likely to see him. Once he was sure Sandborne was as safe as he could have hoped, Halstead took his rifle and shotgun and crossed Main Street to go to the livery. It was time to get ready for whatever trouble the night might bring and he would need Col to help him survive it.

He was in the middle of the thoroughfare when he saw a lone rider lope into town from the west. He ran to the boardwalk and took cover beside a water trough. Halstead left McBride's shotgun on the ground and brought the Winchester to his shoulder.

Once his eyes adjusted to the darkness, he saw that the rider was not Riker. He was much smaller and rounder than either of the Riker boys. The oil lamp still burning on the boardwalk in front of the jail showed it was a small native woman wrapped in a blanket.

Strange.

Halstead stood up and beckoned the rider to come

closer. When she got within range of his pistols, he set the Winchester against the trough.

He placed his hand on the Colt on his hip as he told her to stop.

If the old woman was frightened, she hid it well. The leather strap that lay flat across her face where her nose had once been explained why. "You Halstead?"

He wrapped his fingers around the butt of his pistol. "I am."

The old woman's eyes moved over him. "You are not one of my people like they say."

That wasn't important. "Who are you?"

She replied in Spanish. "I'm the woman who takes care of the outlaw Brunet in Valhalla."

Halstead had heard Brunet had been laid low from a bullet in the back during the bank robbery in town. He liked to think it was McBride's bullet.

He answered her in Spanish. "Why are you here?"

"The outlaw Brunet is not as sick as he seems," the old woman told him. "He knew Zimmerman might kill him if he was awake. He wanted to wait until the right moment to prove this to the town."

None of this mattered to him and he had things to do. "Last time I ask. Why are you here?"

"The outlaw Brunet sent me to tell you there are many riders coming to Battle Brook tonight. They bring fire and blood. They are coming to kill you. A man named Riker is leading them. The outlaw Brunet does not want this to happen."

Halstead looked beyond her to the west. To see if anyone was coming. "Why does he care about what happens to me?"

"The outlaw Brunet does not care about you. He cares about Valhalla. Zimmerman is gone. He does not want Riker to take his place. He fears this will happen if Riker kills you. That is why I am here. He wants you to have time to prepare so you can kill Riker instead, but there is not much time. My horse is old and so am I, but we came as quickly as we could."

Halstead saw no reason why she would lie. "What does he want for this warning?"

"He only wants Valhalla left in peace in exchange for your life."

"I don't know what good it'll do him after tonight, but tell him I agree."

The old woman clicked her teeth and the horse resumed its slow pace along Main Street.

Halstead picked up his Winchester and McBride's shotgun before running to the livery. Now that he knew for certain trouble was coming, he had much to do.

CHAPTER 35

Riker was impressed that the men were able to keep up the quick pace he and his horse set. Zimmerman had chosen Valhalla's citizens well. None of the men fell behind and none of them uttered a single complaint on the ride to Battle Brook.

He enjoyed the feeling of riding through the night with torches. It triggered a brave and proud feeling inside him. He imagined soldiers felt this way as they marched into glorious battle. He had grown up hearing his father's stories of the War Between the States and the gallant cause against northern oppression.

Riker saw this as his war and Halstead's corpse a treasured prize.

As they had reached the outskirts of Battle Brook, Riker resisted the urge to halt his men and give them one last word of encouragement before they rode into town. But Halstead might see the torches if they stopped too long and be alerted to their arrival. The sooner they cornered the rat, the sooner they could kill it.

Riker moved his horse to the side of the road and waved the men on. The man called Tote led the way. "Head straight for the jail and call for Halstead to come out. I'll be right behind you."

The men picked up their pace as they brought their horses to a full gallop into Battle Brook. Riker remained at the side of the road until Warren caught up. He had been guarding the rear from any stragglers.

"They all made it, little brother. Every last one of them. Where do you want me?"

Riker had already thought that far ahead. "Ride around to the eastern edge of the men. Don't let anyone past you. Hubbard will never forgive us if trouble spreads to the rest of the town."

"After tonight, no one will care what that old dandy thinks." Warren dug his heels into his horse's flanks and rode on toward town.

Riker allowed himself to watch the spectacle of the men—his men—forming an arc in front of the jail. His jail. Maybe he would let them burn it down after all. He could have Hubbard build him a new one in its place, with an office just as fancy as his own in the bank.

But there was work to be done before that. He had a dead father to avenge and an old score to settle.

He checked his pistol to make sure it was loaded, then spurred his horse on toward Battle Brook. Toward a new Riker destiny.

Riker brought his horse to a halt at the edge of the riders who had stopped in front of the jail. He tied his horse to the rail in front of the café next door and got down from the saddle.

Tote was in the center of the group. "We called out to him, but he ain't answering."

Gordo, who was on Riker's edge of the group, said, "He's probably inside hiding in one of them cells."

Riker could tell the men were getting restless. So was he. "Stoneman, climb down and see if the door is locked."

He might have expected the man to hesitate, given Halstead's deadly reputation, but Stoneman did as he was told. He kept his rifle in his right hand as he stood to the side of the door and pounded it with the heel of his boot. "Come on out, Halstead. We know you're in there."

He looked at Riker as he waited for a reply.

Nothing.

Perhaps Halstead was readying himself to make a final stand inside the jail. It was time to find out.

He told Stoneman, "See if it's locked."

Stoneman reached over with his left hand and worked the latch. The door creaked as it swung inward.

All the men on that side of the group aimed their rifles at the jail with their free hand. The other kept the torches high.

Stoneman chanced a quick look inside. "He ain't there. The door back to the cells is open, too."

Riker could hardly believe his luck. There was no back door to the place and Halstead would never leave Sandborne alone. Did he think he could hold them off from the cells?

"Go in and see where he is."

Riker watched as Stoneman gripped his rifle in both hands, ready to round the corner and start shooting.

But then he looked past him farther up the street and noticed something curious.

None of the oil lamps on Main Street were lit. And all the buildings were dark, even the saloons.

His blood ran cold when he heard a voice behind him say, "You boys looking for me?"

A flash from his right and a shotgun boomed. Riker

dropped to the ground. Men and horses hit by buckshot screamed.

The fight was on.

By the time Riker and his men reached town, Halstead had spent the previous half hour practicing how to reload the shotgun as fast as possible. It was tricky with only two barrels per pull, but he had broken it down into five steps.

Shoot. Open. Dump. Feed. Snap.

Repeat.

His first blast was with both barrels aimed in the center of the group. Before the first man fell amid the blood and surprise of his ambush, Halstead had already opened the shotgun and dumped the spent shells on the ground as he pulled two more from his left pocket. He slid them into the barrels, snapped them shut, and was ready to fire into the cluster of remaining riders struggling to bring their frightened mounts under control.

The group had loosened some amid the chaos but had dropped their burning torches as they tried to keep from being thrown from the saddle. The flames at their hooves only served to make the animals more terrified.

Halstead brought the shotgun up to his shoulder and cut loose with one barrel. The men to his left spilled to the ground as the horses fed off one another's panic. One man who had been hit but did not fall was crushed as his horse lost its footing and rolled over him.

A single shot rang out as riderless animals broke away and ran from the flaming ground back toward Valhalla.

Halstead went to one knee as he aimed at the riders to the far right of the group. As soon as the fleeing horses were clear, he gave the men a blast from the second barrel.

Three men dropped as Halstead heard a shot from one

of the few survivors. He opened the shotgun and dumped out the spent shells as he ran down the alley, back to where he had Col ground and ready to ride. He slid when he reached the cover of the corner of the saloon and fed two more shells into the barrels.

He flicked the barrel shut and waited. His eyes were well adjusted to the darkness by then, better than Riker's men would be.

The scene at the mouth of the narrow alley was one of flame and dead men. He had been too busy to count how many he had hit, but at such close range it did not matter. He knew he had culled them down by at least half, perhaps more. He had taken them by surprise, but now that surprise was gone.

"He took off down the alley!" one of them shouted to the others. It might have been Riker, but he was not certain. "Gimme one of them torches."

Halstead did not move as he saw the mouth of the alley brighten and one of the men tossed a still-burning torch into it. It landed almost between the two buildings, but Halstead's position remained in shadow.

He heard muffled sounds of men whispering among themselves and knew they'd be coming.

Pistol fire started up, forcing Halstead to flinch as a bullet slammed into the building only inches above his head.

He heard their boots scrape the dirt of the alley as soon as the shots stopped. Halstead rounded the corner and gave them both barrels at close range.

More screams went up as the men fell forward onto the torch. He dropped the empty shotgun and ran back to where Col was waiting. He jumped in the saddle as he gathered up the reins and sped into the street that ran parallel to Main.

Pistol shots and rifle rounds filled the air behind him as he fled as quickly as he dared to allow the horse to run.

They quickly cleared the edge of town and continued on until they reached the road that led up into the hills and mines above.

He listened for anyone who might be chasing him, but all behind him was quiet.

He brought Col around and they inched back closer to Main Street. He was too far away to see much detail, but even from that distance, the street in front of the jail looked like a battleground. Torches still smoldered among the bodies of the dead and wounded still on the ground. He hoped Riker was among them but doubted he would be that lucky.

He watched the street for any movement as he pulled his Winchester from its scabbard. No one moved. No one stepped out into the street to take care of their wounded or dead.

He knew it was not over yet. He steered Col toward the right side of town and quietly rode through the darkness, listening and waiting for someone to shoot at. He heard the stifled cries of frightened citizens failing to remain quiet amid the carnage. He hated having to do this in town, but Riker had forced his hand.

He had just passed the first alley next to the dry goods store when a single shot broke the uneasy silence.

Col reared up on her legs and screamed, dumping Halstead on his back. Instinct caused him to roll away as soon as he hit the ground, fearful the horse might have been hit and might fall on him.

But he heard her trot away and stop. The bullet had come close enough to scare her, but she might not have been struck.

He had dropped his Winchester in the fall and did not dare look for it now. He remained in a crouch and let the silence settle in. The man could be one foot or half a block away. He must have heard Col's approach and fired blind.

The other man was just as quiet as Halstead. He was either very cautious or a practiced hunter of men. He hoped it was Riker, but imagined it was Warren.

He had not made a sound that might give away his position in the dark. Their run-in at the mine had taught each man how the other fought.

Halstead slowly pulled the Colt from his cross draw rig. He wanted the pistol out and ready when he needed it.

He flinched when another shot rang out and heard Col take off again. But she stopped only a few steps later. Her gait sounded normal, so he did not think she was hit.

Halstead knew the shot had come from the alley right in front of him. He had seen the flash and knew he must be close. And he was still firing blind. But he had taken a bullet to the calf and could not move quickly.

Halstead kept his eyes moving, listening for any sound as he felt around on the ground. He was looking for a stone or pebble to throw in the hope it would trick Warren into firing and revealing his position. But the ground had been pounded flat and was almost frozen. He would give himself away if he tried to pull a stone loose.

But he did have something he could throw. He slid a bullet from a loop on his gun belt and hoped it made enough noise to cause Warren to shoot.

With his left hand, Halstead tossed the bullet to his right like he was skipping a stone across water. The round hit the ground three times and drew a single shot from Warren.

The flash pierced the darkness between them.

Halstead fired three times at the center of the muzzle flash. Warren cried out before Halstead heard his boots scrape dirt as he hit the ground.

It was too dark to confirm he was hit and Halstead knew

it might be a ruse to draw him in. And when he saw torch light and heard voices coming from Main Street, it was time to get going.

His boot struck the Winchester he dropped when Col dumped him off her back. The rifle scraped across the frozen ground and Halstead stopped moving. He slid his Colt back in its holster and felt around for the rifle. It would have much better accuracy than his pistol. The angry orange light stopped moving and he knew the men must have heard him. The torch cast three long shadows into the street before they melted into one. They knew someone was out there.

Halstead cursed his luck as he felt the ground around him for the rifle. He knew it must be somewhere close.

He kept searching blindly as he heard Warren's gravelly voice. "Careful, boys. I'm shot. He's out there right now. Get him like he got me."

"Deke," one of the men said. "Grab hold of him and pull him back here."

Halstead's fingertips grazed the wooden stock of his Winchester. He followed the shape of it and picked it up. He was glad he did not have to lever a round into the chamber. Mackey insisted each deputy's weapon always be ready to fire.

He brought the rifle to his shoulder and remained on one knee as he heard Warren's groan, followed by a scraping sound on the dirt.

Now that they had gotten the wounded man out of the way, Halstead knew they would be coming.

He saw two shadows grow longer in the street as the torchbearer threw it end over end in Halstead's general direction.

He scrambled to his feet and broke into a run as it

tumbled through the night, only to land a few feet from where he had been crouching.

One of the men cried out, "There he is, Gordo! Shoot!"

Halstead dove to his right and tumbled as rifle fire echoed along the darkened street. He rolled flat on his belly and brought the Winchester to his shoulder.

The burning torch revealed a fat man and a taller one, firing their rifles as they moved forward, shooting at where they had last seen him.

Halstead took careful aim at the fat man and squeezed the trigger.

His first shot hit the fat man in the middle of his chest. He staggered back from the impact of the bullet but remained on his feet.

Halstead levered in a fresh round as he rolled back to his right twice while the taller man shifted his aim and fired at where he saw Halstead's muzzle flash. He had almost moved out of the light when Halstead fired.

The tall man cried out when the bullet struck him in the left shoulder and rocked him backward.

"Get him, Gordo. He's . . ."

Halstead's next shot struck the tall man in the head. He dropped his rifle before falling beside the burning torch.

"Tote!" the fat man shouted. He began to go to his friend but stopped well short of him. He stood on the edge of the light and peered into the darkness. "You killed Tote!"

Halstead got to his feet and kept the Winchester aimed at him. "And I'll kill you, too, if you don't put the rifle down. You're already hit. No point in getting dead."

Gordo weaved on his feet as he looked down at the bloody hole in his chest. "I'm dead already."

The fat man tried to fire the rifle from his hip. Halstead's next shot put him down for good.

He knew he had been in one place too long already.

He did not know how many might still be out to kill him, so he backed up in the direction of where he had last heard Col. He found her when the mare snorted and rattled her bridle.

He climbed into the saddle and rested the Winchester on his right leg as he rode her up the street. He kept her at a walking pace as he listened for anyone who might be stalking him in the darkness. He reached the end of town and steered her toward Main Street, careful to remain in the shadows.

Some of the torches were still burning in front of the jail. He counted six men lying dead in the thoroughfare, along with two horses. The dead horses bothered him. The animals had not chosen their riders. They deserved a better fate.

He remained at the edge of town as he watched and listened for signs of more gunmen looking to kill him.

He heard the creak of a door and saw the bartender from The Blue Belle come outside. More customers followed and were soon joined by other townspeople, who began to light the oil lamps Halstead had extinguished. He remained where he was until he saw enough people on Main Street. Judging by the way they began to cluster together, no one else seemed to be waiting to kill him.

It was time to find out.

He lifted the reins and moved Col into town. She fussed a bit at the scent of death and the sight of flame but did not fight him. He rode past the jail and by the people who had come out of their warm beds to look at the carnage on a cold night.

He looked down at the bodies, hoping to see Emil Riker among them, but did not. All the men were strangers to him.

Halstead kept looking at both sides of Main Street as he

rode by. Someone might still be lurking in the shadows, waiting to take a shot at him.

"Murderer!" one man in a long bed shirt yelled at him as he passed. "Halstead the murderer!"

A woman took up the cry. "Down with Halstead! Get out of Battle Brook, butcher!"

Halstead ignored their jeers as he reached the middle of town, near where he figured he had shot Warren. If the old scout was still alive, he would be eager to die fighting.

He slowed Col's pace when he saw a red slick leading from an alley and across Main Street. He followed the trail with his eyes and saw that it led to the front door of Doc Potter's office. And the lamps inside were lit.

He slid the rifle into his saddle scabbard and climbed down from Col. He wrapped the reins around the hitching rail in front of the office and drew his Colt from his hip. He stepped up onto the boardwalk and stood to the side of the door as he tried the knob. It was unlocked and he pushed in the door.

"Jeremiah?" Doc Potter called out. "That you?"

His voice sounded odd. "Yeah."

"Don't come in here," Potter answered. "Please don't come in here now."

Halstead kept his Colt at his side as he walked in.

The bloody trail led inside to where Emil Riker was on the floor, cradling Warren in his arms. Doc Potter was kneeling beside the old scout, though it was clear Warren had no further use for a doctor. His eyes were half open and his jaw was slack.

Doc Potter spoke to Riker. "Sheriff, you've got to let me tend to you now. That shoulder's in a bad way. Warren wouldn't have wanted you to suffer."

Halstead saw the ruined mess that remained of Riker's shoulder. His brown shirt was shredded and dark with blood. He had caught a fair amount of buckshot from one of Halstead's blasts. His gun arm was ruined.

And he was glaring up at Halstead from behind his dead brother.

"You," Riker seethed. "You did this to him."

Halstead grinned. "That's right. And I'm gonna do the same to you. Get up."

Doc Potter's knees cracked as he stood up and got in between the two enemies. "Not in here, Jeremiah. Not now. The sheriff's wounded and he needs care."

Halstead looked beyond the shorter, older man. "I know. I'm the reason he needs it."

Doc Potter surprised him by pushing him backward. "Get out of here right now. This isn't the time for that."

Riker slid back from his brother and began to get to his feet. "Move aside, Doc. Let's finish it."

But the doctor kept pushing Halstead toward the door. "The sheriff is my patient now, Jeremiah. I told you I won't let any harm come to my patients and I meant it. Leave now."

Halstead looked down at the elderly man. "For a man who says he doesn't want to get involved, you're sure involving yourself now."

Riker cut loose with a guttural cry and launched a left hook over the doctor that caught Halstead on the jaw.

He was rocked back by the blow but easily kept his feet. He drew back his right hand to throw a punch of his own, but Potter grabbed him and pushed him back toward the examining table as he yelled, "Stop it, Riker. He'll kill you!"

Riker sagged against the table and Potter pushed him on it. He lifted his legs and laid them out straight. The sheriff offered little resistance.

Halstead felt a warm trickle of blood on his lip and

wiped it away with the back of his hand. "That one was free, Riker. Next one will be expensive."

Riker raised his head to answer, but Potter reached across him to tear away the right shoulder of his matted shirt.

Halstead holstered his Colt on his hip. There would be no further gunplay that night.

"Get out of here, Halstead," the doctor ordered. "You've done enough damage for one night."

Riker's eyes flickered but never left him as he stepped closer to Warren's body. "You get away from him!"

Halstead pulled his Colt from his belly rig and opened the cylinder. He palmed the spent shells and looked at Riker as he allowed each one to drop on his corpse.

Riker tried to push Doc Potter out of the way but was too weak to do it.

Halstead pulled a bullet from his belt and slid it into an empty chamber. "I know it's not over, Riker. Not by a long shot. When you're ready to try to get even, you let me know. I'll be waiting. Give you a nice reunion with the rest of your family."

Riker cried out from the pain of his wounds as much as from the pain in his soul. "Why don't you just do it now? Get it over with. You already let one man get away from you."

Halstead fed the last bullet into his Colt.

"Good idea."

He spun the cylinder and flicked it shut, then aimed it at Riker.

Potter threw himself across his patient.

"Jeremiah!" Sandborne shouted. "Don't do it."

Halstead saw Sandborne keeping himself propped up on the walls on either side of the hallway.

"He can't fight back," Sandborne said. "If you kill him

now, it's murder plain and simple. You don't want that. You don't want to become that."

Halstead moved his finger to the trigger. Even with Potter in the way, he could take Riker clean. He had spent enough of his life worrying about the Riker clan. Grieving over what they had done to him. All he had to do was squeeze and put it all behind him.

Sandborne stumbled closer. "Please, Jeremiah. You've come so far, but if you shoot him, you'll never come back from that."

Halstead lowered his gun as Sandborne collapsed. He holstered the pistol and went to help his friend. Some things were more important than vengeance.

CHAPTER 36

One month later

It had begun to snow already as the guards led Edward Zimmerman into the prison yard. The sight of his old enemy in shackles warmed Halstead on a cold wintry day. The hangman's noose swung idly in the wind. A gray day for a gray deed.

Zimmerman had grown thin and pale since his conviction. He had not shaved in weeks and his hair was long.

A photographer stood behind a camera tripod. A reporter from the *Montana Herald* was next to him to document the condemned man's final moments.

Billy Sunday was standing to Halstead's left. "Funny how prison garb and shackles have a way of taking the starch out of a man. This time last month, he was sitting in Valhalla on top of the world. Now he's just another outlaw about to die."

Mackey said, "He deserves it." He placed a hand on Halstead's shoulder. "You put him there, Jeremiah. And you did it the right way."

Halstead watched in silence as the guards led Zimmerman up the thirteen wooden steps to the top of the gallows.

A preacher trailed behind him, reading passages from the Bible.

Sandborne rubbed his left side. "I never thought it would happen. I figured his friends would've found a way to get him out of it."

"They didn't even try," Billy said. "He expected them to save him, but they're content to let him swing. Brunet and Hubbard took his town and threw him away. It almost makes me feel sorry for him." He looked at Halstead. "Almost."

Halstead watched the guards position Zimmerman on the trapdoor. The hangman stood behind him with the noose in hand.

One of the guards began to read from a sheet of paper. "Edward Zimmerman, having been found guilty of murder by a jury of your peers, you have been sentenced to hang by the neck until you are dead. So ordered by the Honorable Judge Niles Crowe of the great state of Montana." The guard lowered the paper. "If you have any final words, son, now's the time to say them."

"I ain't your son," Zimmerman sneered. He squinted as he looked out over the small group who had gathered to watch him die. He had no trouble spotting the line of black-coated lawmen at the front and his eyes fell on Halstead.

"There he is." Zimmerman laughed. "I knew you wouldn't miss this, Halstead. The Butcher of Battle Brook himself, just like the papers called you. You never did manage to get me, did you? Had to rely on that pup next to you to do it for you."

Halstead could hardly remember the hatred he had once felt for the man who was about to die. The hate. The vengeance. But he had left all that behind him in a small jailhouse in a little town known as Battle Brook. He had left a part of himself back there, too. Perhaps the part that had allowed him to let such a man pull him so low.

"I'll be waiting for you in Hell, Jeremiah Halstead!" Zimmerman shouted. "Mine will be the first face you see when you get there."

Halstead felt nothing for the man as he said, "Wouldn't it be nice to think so."

The reporter quickly scribbled down Zimmerman's last words in a notebook as the photographer ducked beneath the cloth hood of his camera. The powder he held high flashed as he took a picture of the grim scene.

The hangman slipped the noose over Zimmerman's head and pulled the knot tight under his chin. He positioned the knot just behind the left shoulder and took his place at the lever that controlled the trapdoor.

Judge Niles Crowe stood to the left of the lawmen, by the door leading back to the prison. The preacher finished his prayers, closed his Bible, and stepped back, head bowed in continuous, silent prayer.

Halstead saw the hangman look at Judge Crowe, who closed his eyes and nodded once.

Zimmerman shouted, "Down with Hal—"

The hangman threw the lever and the trapdoor opened. Zimmerman dropped. The rope held and the knot did what it had been tied to do.

Halstead looked on until the last twitch of his enemy's shackled legs. "No. Down with Zimmerman."

Judge Crowe went back inside and the rest of the witnesses followed a guard's directions to a door in the wall that led out to civilization.

The guards climbed down the steps to retrieve Zimmerman's body.

Halstead closed his eyes. *It was over. It was finally over.*

Mackey said, "Joshua, you'd best head back to the office. Deputy Lynch has something he wants to talk to you about."

Sandborne looked confused. "But I thought we were all going over to the . . ."

Mackey looked at the ground as Billy barked, "Deputy Sandborne. Get back to the office like the marshal told you."

Sandborne ducked his head as he quickly followed the other witnesses out into the street.

Halstead watched him leave. "You were a bit short with the kid, Aaron. He was only going to ask if we were still going to lunch after this."

Mackey kept looking at the ground. "He's got to get used to things changing fast, and not for the better. We all do."

Halstead knew Mackey never took a hanging lightly, no matter how much the man deserved it. "What do you mean by that?"

Mackey's mouth moved, but no sound came out.

Halstead's stomach sank. "Aaron, what's wrong? Is it Katherine?"

Billy had moved away from them and stood off to his right. "It's not Katherine, Jeremiah."

It took Halstead a moment to realize Billy had not just stepped aside. He was flanking him.

Mackey scratched the side of his face with his thumbnail. "You remember Zimmerman's lawyer, Mannes?"

"Yeah. How could I forget that miserable weasel?"

"He's been busy these past few weeks. He wasn't saving Zimmerman. He was building a case against you."

Halstead was relieved. He had not entirely forgotten about the murder complaint they had threatened, but he had put it out of his mind. "That was Zimmerman's complaint. He's dead. The complaint died with him."

Mackey toed the ground of the prison yard with his

boot. "It should've, but it didn't. That mess in the papers didn't help. That Butcher of Battle Brook nonsense they wrote about you kept it alive."

Halstead felt alone among his two oldest friends. "That was all justified, Aaron. Those boys came to town to kill me. Everyone knows that."

Billy said, "You killed nine men, Jeremiah. And Riker lost his arm."

"They were trying to kill me. What was I supposed to do? Let them shoot me? Let them shoot Sandborne?"

Mackey finally looked at him. "I know it was legal, but it gave Mannes the chance to paint you as a cold-blooded killer. All those mornings up on the hill. All the bad blood between you and Riker. All the killings. I know you're in the right, but Billy and I are the only men who think so. Mannes used all that to get a judge to see it his way."

Mackey's voice caught again and he looked away.

Halstead knew the news was bad, but he had to hear it. He wanted to hear it from his friends. "And?"

Billy spoke for them. "And Judge Owen signed a warrant for your arrest about two hours ago. He's charged you with murder, Jeremiah. You're officially a wanted man."

Halstead raised his head and looked at the gray sky. It was a grim day for grim business after all.

He watched two of the guards take hold of Zimmerman's legs and lift him so there was enough slack in the rope for the hangman to loosen the knot. "I guess he wins after all."

He felt the blood begin to flow through his body again. He had heard the words. After a month of peace, he was a wanted man again.

He slowly flexed his fingers. "You boys gonna try to take me in?"

Mackey shook his head. "No. I know I should, but I

can't do that. Not because of this. The papers haven't been filed yet, so it's not official, but it's coming. Now that Zimmerman's dead, Mannes is going to use every bit of pull he's got to see you swing. He wants to show everyone what happens to any man who's ever crossed him and he's got the influence to see you hang. Billy and I might be able to get the governor to stop it, but that'll take time we don't have right now."

Halstead heard the words but was not sure what Mackey was trying to say.

Billy said it instead. "We need you to run, Jeremiah. Don't tell us where you're going. We'll delay them as much as we can, but they'll be expecting that. Word is Mannes is ready to hire Pinkertons to go after you."

Halstead felt numb as Billy took him by the collar and shook him. "Aaron and I served with a man named Schneider. A Matthew Schneider. He's been dead for a long time, but you need to be Schneider now. You need to use that name to send us a telegram from wherever you are. Send it to me on the first of every month. Nothing fancy, nothing a telegraph clerk will remember. When we see a message from Schneider, we'll know it's from you, and you'll wait for our answer. If we say it's still cloudy, you keep moving. If we say the weather has lifted, you come back."

Billy shook Halstead hard. "And you will come back, Jeremiah. You'll come back here to us and to Abby. We can't promise you when, but we promise you that."

Halstead knew running would be the worst thing he could do. "We can fight this together, Billy."

"And we are," Billy said, "but not with you here. Not where Mannes's men can get their hooks into you. Now, Katherine's arranged a packhorse full of supplies waiting for you at the general store over on Second Street. You get on Col, take that horse, and ride on while you still can."

Halstead had not expected this. Not today. Not now.

And Mackey still could not look at him. "Say something, Aaron. Please."

But Mackey continued to look at the ground.

Billy said, "He can't bring himself to say anything, Jeremiah. Your daddy helped him a lot over the years. Helped us both, and it tears him up something awful that we can't help you now. But help's coming. You've got our word on that."

Halstead looked at the marshal, hoping he might say something before he left. But all he saw was the flat brim of his hat.

He pulled the deputy star from his coat and held it out to the marshal. "Guess I'm not a deputy anymore."

Mackey closed Halstead's hand over the badge. "You keep it. Might come in handy. Do what Billy told you. Keep your head down, your horse fast, and your guns loaded. We'll fix this."

He finally raised his head enough to look Halstead in the eye. "Now run."

Halstead dropped the badge in his pocket and went past the guard holding the yard door open to the street. He made sure to keep his head down as he walked quickly through the bustling city of Helena.

He shut his eyes tight as he passed by Abby's hotel out of fear he might see her and change his mind and stay. The past few weeks with her had been more than he could have hoped. It was all gone now. At least he would have the memory of her to warm him on the cold nights ahead.

He kept walking fast until he reached the livery where Col was kept and quickly got her ready to ride. He pulled her from the stall and swung himself into the saddle. He rode her to the general store, where a clerk brought out the packhorse from the yard in the back and handed the reins up to him.

"Guess they're sending you out after another passel of bad men, eh, Deputy?"

Halstead felt a knot in his throat. "Yeah. I guess you could say that."

"You're a credit to Montana. Where you off to this time?"

Halstead pulled the packhorse behind him as he brought Col around and headed west.

He had not answered the clerk, for he did not know what to say.

But at least he was free. He had a chance. And, so far, a chance had been enough for him.

KEEP READING FOR A SPECIAL EXCERPT!

DISTURBING THE PEACE
by Terrence McCauley

US Deputy Marshal Jeremiah Halstead keeps the peace
in the mining town of Silver Cloud, Montana.
But an old enemy has declared war against him.

Ruthless and clever, Ed Zimmerman would have
become the leader of one of the West's
deadliest and hell-bent outlaw gangs.
Zimmerman has offered a generous bounty to every
desperado willing to put a bullet through
the US Deputy Marshal's heart.

A death sentence won't stop Halstead from enforcing the
law. The sheriff of Battle Brook needs a hand dealing
with some hell-raising badmen in the surrounding hills,
threatening to take over the frontier town. Joined by
Deputy Sandborne, Halstead rides hard for Battle Brook,
only to discover manhunters aware of the price
on his head are in town, guns cocked
and ready to collect the reward.

And Zimmerman has joined the outlaws in the hills,
waiting to catch Halstead in his sights . . .

Look for* Disturbing the Peace *on sale now!

CHAPTER 1

"Jeremiah Halstead!"

Halstead drew his Colt from his belly holster as he turned around on the crowded street to see who had called his name.

He spotted a fat man in the thoroughfare, beginning to raise a rifle in his direction.

Halstead fired and struck the man in the belly. The impact of the bullet caused the would-be assassin to stagger backward a few steps, but he managed to keep his feet.

He kept his rifle in hand, too.

Halstead's second shot struck him in the head, which sent him flat on his back.

As more rifle shots filled the air, Halstead dove for cover behind a horse trough. Bullets pelted the dry goods store where he had been standing and punched through the trough, sending a steady trickle of water onto the boardwalk.

The citizens of Helena, who had found themselves in the middle of a gun battle, screamed in panic as they scattered for the nearest cover they could find. All of the noise prevented Halstead from being able to tell where all of the shots were coming from.

"Keep firing, Luke!" a man yelled out above the gunfire and chaos. "We've got him now!"

Halstead pegged him. Left side, across the street. In front of the spectacles store.

When the gunmen stopped to reload, Halstead sat up and aimed his pistol at the gunman on the left. His target was in the process of levering in another round into his rifle when Halstead fired twice. One round missed. The second hit him in the chest.

Another rifleman on his right began to cut loose with a primordial yell before he began firing again. That yell had given Halstead time to lay flat behind the cover of the leaking trough. The screaming man's rifle went empty after three shots. When he heard the rifle hit the compact of the street, Halstead rolled over onto his stomach to see a man charging at him as he pulled his pistol from his holster.

Halstead squeezed off a round, and the bullet hit the charging man in the left hip, causing him to spin as he fell forward.

He landed facefirst on the ground but had not dropped his pistol.

Halstead quickly got to his feet as he kept the Colt Thunderer aimed down at the fallen man. "Push the gun away from you, mister. You don't have to die today."

But instead of pushing the gun away, he tried to raise it.

Halstead's shot hit him in the top of the head. His body went limp as Halstead watched life leave the stranger.

As he walked over to the man he had just killed, Halstead could hear the stifled whimpers of the citizens who had scrambled for shelter wherever they could find it. He stepped on the dead man's hand and picked up the gun. A rusty old Walker Colt. Halstead was surprised the gun had not blown up in his hand.

Halstead stood over the dead man, cracked his cylinder,

and dumped the dead brass on the corpse. He was in the process of taking rounds from his gun belt and reloading his pistol when a boy from across the thoroughfare shouted, "This one's still alive, deputy!"

Halstead spun the cylinder and snapped it shut before he looked at a boy of about nine years old pointing down at the second man he had shot in front of the spectacles store.

He kept the Colt at his side as he walked toward the fallen man.

The boy backed away as Halstead drew closer, but he did not run off.

Halstead aimed his pistol at the fallen man as he approached. The gunman was barely still alive. His right shoulder was a ruined, bloody mess and getting worse by the second. The bullet must have hit an artery. He would bleed out in a matter of minutes. Not a lot of time for him, but more than enough time for Halstead to get the truth out of him.

The wounded man was still pawing for his rifle with his left arm when Halstead's shadow fell across him. He squinted up at the deputy marshal and laid his head flat on the boardwalk. "Go ahead, you bastard. Finish me. I'm done for anyway."

Halstead had no intention of letting him off that easy. He already knew the answer to his question, but he had to ask it anyway. "Who sent you?"

"Go to hell," the man spat as he struggled to raise his head. "You've already killed the others. Do the same to me."

Halstead placed his boot on the man's ruined right shoulder, causing him to scream.

"Last time I ask nicely," Halstead told him. "Tell me who sent you."

"Zimmerman, damn you!" the man cried out. "It was Ed Zimmerman."

Halstead removed his foot. He had been afraid of that. The ten-thousand-dollar bounty the outlaw had put on Halstead was double the bounty the territory had placed on Zimmerman. It had caused the lawman more trouble than he could have imagined.

He heard the citizenry mutter and scatter as they saw another man approaching with a rifle. But there was no reason to worry for the young man had a deputy marshal's star pinned to his shirt. It was his friend, young Joshua Sandborne.

"You hurt?" Sandborne called out as he aimed his Winchester down at the dying man.

"I'm fine," Halstead told him. "He'll be dead in a minute, so no need to go for the doc. Just keep an eye on him and let me know when he goes. Keep an eye on the street in case anyone decides to help him."

Halstead went to check the other two men he had shot. Both men were already facing whatever justice awaited a man in the hereafter. He just wanted to see if he knew them.

He heard some of the women on the boardwalk gasp at the sight of such death and carnage in broad daylight. They made a great show of clutching their pearls and turning their heads, but not their eyes. In his brief time in the territory, Halstead had learned that blood was a popular sport in Montana. Helena might have been the capital of the territory, but it was no different from Dover Station or Silver Cloud or any other frontier town in that regard.

Halstead looked down at the fat man he had shot first. His beard was long and sported a healthy amount of gray and white mixed in with brown. He looked to be about forty years old. What little hair he had left atop his head was also streaked with gray. His skin was weathered and had clearly seen more than its share of the sun. His overalls were faded and stained with sweat and grime that no amount of soap and water could ever wash out.

He looked less like a gunman and more like a farmer, which Halstead expected he was.

Halstead walked over to the last man he had killed. He looked to be younger than the fat man by about a decade or so, but decided he had been a farmer, too.

He had been forced to kill a lot of farmers and shop-keepers and drovers and cowboys and wanderers of every description over the past few weeks. Foolish, desperate men who had taken a gun in hand in the hopes of being able to claim what had been called The Outlaw's Bounty; the one Edward Zimmerman had placed on Halstead's head.

Halstead had to admit some admiration for Zimmerman. Not many men had the gall to openly put out a price on the head of a lawman, much less a federal lawman. Most people were appalled by the notion. Public officials and newspapers around the territory denounced it as a hindrance to the territory's efforts for statehood, which was assured to happen in less than a month or so.

But public condemnation of the bounty had only made word of it spread farther and wider than it otherwise might have. Which was why Jeremiah Halstead had spent every moment of the past several weeks on a knife's edge. His hand was never far from one of the two Colts he wore on the fancy black leather gun rig he'd had made specifically for himself. One on his right hip and the other in the holster on his belly. The fancy two-gun rig normally drew attention wherever he went. Now he drew attention for a different reason. Men looked at him like they were watching ten thousand dollars walking right by them.

He remained in the thoroughfare as he heard a horse and rider approaching from around the corner. He did not draw either of his guns for he could hear the chatter among the crowd that Sheriff Aaron Mackey and his first deputy, Billy Sunday, were approaching.

He watched Mackey round the corner first, atop the black Arabian he called Adair. The marshal of the Montana Territory was tall and lean and about thirty-five, which put him ten years older than Halstead. The dark hat and clothes he wore also served to make him look older.

As usual, Billy Sunday was right behind him, prodding a man along at the end of a Winchester. The black man was as tall and lean as Mackey and about the same age. The two men had ridden together in the cavalry, and Billy had been Mackey's deputy in Dover Station and now here in Helena. Dover Station did not exist anymore, but their friendship had endured.

Halstead noticed the prisoner was a sandy-haired man who looked to be on the verge of tears. Halstead had seen many a man cry when they found themselves at the wrong end of a gun where Mackey or Sunday were concerned.

Halstead watched Mackey draw Adair to a halt in front of the corpse at his feet. The black mare caught the scent of blood in the air and tossed her head. Halstead knew the smell of death did not spook her. If anything, it brought her to life. Adair was a warhorse in every sense of the word.

Halstead touched the brim of his hat to Mackey. "Good morning."

Mackey looked around at the two corpses in the thoroughfare. "Wasn't for them." He nodded over toward Sandborne. "Looks like you left one alive."

"Not for long," Halstead told him. "I hit an artery. He'll bleed out in a minute or two."

Billy stood up in the stirrups and cut loose with a low, long whistle as he kept the sandy-haired man covered with his Winchester. "Looks like it took two shots a piece to finish them off. You losing your touch already, nephew?"

Halstead expected some ribbing from the man he considered an uncle. "Just being thorough is all."

But Mackey had not been in a kidding kind of mood as of late. He was responsible for a territory larger than some European countries, which left little time for jokes. "They come at you because of Zimmerman's bounty?"

"That's what the dying one over there told me." Halstead looked at the sandy-haired prisoner whose eyes were already welling up. "Who's your new friend?"

"We came running as soon as we heard the shots," Billy said. "We found this one creeping up the street heading this way. Rifle in hand."

Halstead looked at the sandy-haired prisoner. He was trying really hard to look straight ahead instead of looking down at the corpse on the ground.

He grabbed the prisoner by the neck and bent it, so he had no choice but to look at the man at his feet. "You were with these boys, weren't you?"

"I was." The prisoner swallowed hard and shut his eyes. "But I don't want to see them like this, please. They were my brothers."

"Where'd you ride in from?" Mackey asked.

The man shut his eyes tight, forcing tears to stream down his cheeks. "We rode in here from Bisbee, Idaho, last night. We'd heard about that bounty the outlaw fella put on your head. Zimmerman I think his name is."

"Zimmerman." Billy frowned.

Halstead asked him, "You hear about the bounty from Zimmerman personally or from someone else?"

"We heard it from four men we met who rode through Bisbee about a few weeks ago. Said they were riding up here to put a bullet in a man named Halstead and collect the reward." The prisoner chanced a look at Halstead. "Seeing as how you're Halstead, I guess they didn't collect."

Halstead remembered them. Four loudmouthed drunks who took him on after spending half a day in The Wicked Woman saloon drinking some courage. They had collected plenty of lead for their trouble, but no gold. "You boys farmers?"

The prisoner shut his eyes again and shrugged. "Tried to be. Ain't got much to show for it except aches and blisters and bills. When those boys rode into town on a Saturday night bragging about how much money they'd get for killing you, a bunch of us figured we ought to have a go at that reward money instead, so . . ."

Halstead waited for more but realized that was all the man decided to say. He was smarter than he looked. If he had kept talking, he would have talked himself into a noose. As it was, he was looking at ten years hard labor.

"Open your eyes," Mackey ordered him.

The man did as he was told and held a hand to his mouth as he saw Sandborne slowly lower his rifle. There was no need to cover a dead man.

"That's Reb," the prisoner said.

"Not anymore." Mackey beckoned Sandborne to come over to them. When the young deputy got there, he said, "Take this man into custody and lock him up. Send word for the coroner to bring his wagon. I'll keep watch over everything until they get here."

The young deputy grabbed hold of the prisoner and shoved him in the direction of the jail.

As they watched Sandborne do his duty, Halstead looked up at Mackey and Billy. "The kid's really grown up this past year or so, hasn't he?"

"We all have," Billy said. "Guess we've had to."

Halstead could not disagree with them. In the span of

about twelve months or more, they had gone from being the law in Dover Station, Montana, to being the law for the entire territory and with only a few more men than they'd had with them in Dover Station.

Mackey had gotten married and watched his hometown burn in the same fire that took his father. It was a lot of a change in a short amount of time. Most men would have buckled under the pressure or at least shown some signs of strain. But Aaron Mackey was not most men.

Mackey had always been older than his years, even when Halstead remembered him as a cavalry lieutenant in Arizona where Sim Halstead, his father, served as his sergeant. Mackey had been stern back then. The years since had only made him grow more so.

The marshal looked over the three bodies spread out before him. "Any sign of the constables?"

Halstead shook his head. "Guess they're too busy planning the big statehood celebration with the mayor."

Billy grinned. "Never let a shooting get in the way of a good party."

"This is bad business," Mackey said. "Zimmerman's bounty has turned out to be more trouble than I thought. I figured the five-thousand-dollar reward would help people do our work for us. I didn't think he'd respond with a ten-thousand-dollar bounty on you."

"Neither did I," Halstead admitted. "And I never thought anyone would try to collect based on a rumor."

Mackey looked down at the dead man lying in the thoroughfare between them. "We've been lucky that no real hardcases have come for you, but luck doesn't last forever. Even people who look like you are getting killed."

Halstead winced at a memory that still ate at him. The week before, a man who bore a passing resemblance to him and wore all black was killed by a traveling fabric salesman looking to cash in on the bounty. The man he had killed had been an undertaker just arrived in town to look at opening a business in Helena. He could still hear the cries of the man's family as they gathered around his body. The salesman had shot himself in the head upon learning of his mistake.

"Seems like dead people follow me wherever I go."

"Knock it off," Mackey said. "You didn't do this. Zimmerman did. And it's going to keep on happening while you're in Helena. Good thing we caught a break this morning."

Halstead was suddenly interested. "What kind of break?"

Mackey deferred to Billy. "We got a letter from Jack McBride, the town marshal of Battle Brook and Hard Scrabble. Battle Brook is a boomtown in the western part of the territory. Hard Scrabble used to be a jumped-up mining camp, but now it's a town on the decline."

Mackey added, "Our old friends Mr. Rice and Mr. Ryan are building up Battle Brook to serve the mines they have up in the hills."

Halstead held his tongue until they told him what all of this had to do with him.

Billy went on. "McBride wrote to tell us he's heard rumors from the miners that Rob Brunet is in the area. That name mean anything to you?"

"Sure does," Halstead said. The man was wanted throughout the West for a series of stagecoach robberies and homestead raids he and his gang had pulled. He was known for striking in Montana or other territories only to jump the border back into Canada. He'd also had more than a few run-ins with the Mounted Police north of the border. "I thought that bastard ran back to Canada last year."

"He's back now," Mackey told him, "but we don't know if it's just him or his gang is with him. McBride says he's heard rumors that he's fallen in with some bad company, possibly Ed Zimmerman."

"Zimmerman." Halstead said the name as if it was a curse. "Seems too far away from civilization for Zimmerman's tastes."

"Which makes it a perfect place for a man with five thousand dollars on his head to hide out," Mackey told him. "McBride thinks he's hiding out around Hard Scrabble. Makes sense since everything's relocating from there to Battle Brook."

Halstead felt a mixture of dread and excitement begin to spread through him. "Guess you'll be sending me out there to get him."

"I am," Mackey said, "but it's not my first choice."

Halstead frowned. "Thanks for the confidence, boss."

Mackey's jaw tightened. "It's got nothing to do with you and everything to do with the terrain. Those hills are dangerous for anyone, especially for someone like you who's still new to the territory. They're bad in summer and even worse now in late fall. Normally, me and Billy would go, but with all this statehood nonsense going on, we're needed here. That's why I'm sending Sandborne with you."

Halstead's dread overcame whatever excitement he had been feeling. He had nothing against Joshua. If anything, he was too fond of him to risk his life going against a man like Zimmerman. "Aaron, I don't think that's a good idea. He's a bit green and—"

Mackey looked down at him, and Halstead felt his throat go dry.

"Josh is young, but he's capable. He grew up here and knows how to handle himself in the snow and the mountains. You don't, so he's going with you."

Halstead knew all that, but there was more at stake here than just knowing how to handle the elements. "Zimmerman's not the kind of man you cut your teeth on, Aaron. He hits hard and he hits fast."

"So do you," Mackey reminded him, "and he's excellent at following orders. Unlike you."

The look Billy gave Halstead told him to stop arguing. And he had learned from experience that Billy was rarely wrong.

Halstead said what he knew Mackey wanted to hear. "Sounds like we'll be able to learn a good bit from each other."

Mackey nodded. The discussion was over. "McBride's a good man. Billy and I served with him a bit in Arizona. Tall man and tougher than he looks. And I'd appreciate it if you didn't give him the same kind of greeting you gave Sheriff Boddington in Silver Cloud."

Halstead closed his eyes. He wondered if Mackey would ever let him live that down. "That was different."

Billy said, "McBride's different, too. You two will get along just fine."

Mackey went back to looking over the bodies in the thoroughfare. "The train leaves in three hours. The journey lasts a couple of days, depending on the conditions of the tracks. You'll get off the train at a place called Wellspring. It's barely a town, and the sheriff is an old fool named Howard. No need to check in with him when you get there. If all goes well, you won't have to deal with him."

Halstead would remember that. "Anything else?"

"There's a stage that can run you up to Battle Brook," Billy told him, "but with the price on your head, I'd avoid it. That means you boys will have to travel off the road to get there. You'd best get busy outfitting yourself. Get a mule from the livery and put two tents and provisions for a three-day ride on our account at the general store."

Mackey added, "I'll give the warrants on Brunet and Zimmerman to Sandborne. He'll help get the animals loaded on the train for you. The governor would like to be able to announce we've captured Zimmerman and Brunet at the statehood celebration in a week or so, but don't let that rush you. Stopping them is more important than his announcement."

Halstead was glad Mackey saw it that way. "Sounds like I have a lot of work to do. Best get to it." He touched the brim of his hat as he began to head toward the general store when Mackey called out to him.

"One more thing. Best start getting in the habit of picking up your brass. I spend more on bullets for you than the rest of the marshals combined. It's cheaper to reload them than to buy new."

Halstead had no intention of reusing a bullet he had spent killing a man. But he saw no reason to argue with Mackey about it. "Guess it's a sign of how popular I am."

"Expensive, too." Mackey looked away as he stood watch over the carnage. "Bring back Zimmerman and Brunet, Deputy Halstead. Straight up or over the saddle. Makes no difference to me."

But it made all the difference in the world to Halstead. He had promised to kill the man once and that was exactly what he planned to do.

CHAPTER 2

In the dense forest just outside of the dying town of Hard Scrabble, Edward Zimmerman led Rob Brunet through a snow-covered thicket and into a sparse clearing. The sky was slate gray, and the morning sun was blinding despite the thick clouds.

"Don't know how the hell you hope to find anything out here with all this snow," Brunet said. "If I didn't know better, I'd think you were setting me up to stop a bullet."

Zimmerman smiled at his fellow outlaw's angst. "Never fear, Robert. The only thing I'm setting you up for is success."

Zimmerman's mount, a skittish bay gelding, caught the scent of death lingering in the air and shied away from it. A spur to the belly and a sharp tug on the reins brought the animal back into submission. "Be mindful of your mount around here," Zimmerman cautioned. "I'm afraid I had to leave a couple of bodies behind when I was here last."

Brunet followed Zimmerman's lead. "As long as you don't aim to leave another one now, we'll be fine."

Realizing they were close enough to the spot; Zimmerman climbed down from the saddle and wrapped his horse's reins around a nearby bush. He reminded himself to get a better horse when he got back to town. The gelding was a bit too mild for his taste and purpose.

He stepped over the skeletal remains of a leg poking out of the snow and approached a heavy rock that stood out in the middle of the clearing. He bent at the knees and, with little effort, rolled the heavy rock aside so his guest could get a good look at what was beneath it. He took a couple of steps back and gestured down to the deep hole in the ground.

"Voila, mon ami," he said to Brunet. It was all the French he knew, but enjoyed putting it to good use. "Behold the treasure I promised you."

Brunet produced a pistol from beneath his coat and aimed it squarely at Zimmerman's head as he looked over his horse's head and into the hole. "All I see is a sack in the ground, Zimmerman. Pull it out real nice and slow. And if you pull out anything more than money"—he thumbed back the hammer—"it'll be the last thing you do."

Zimmerman dramatically held up his hands and ducked his head. "Robert, my friend. Where's the trust? I already told you there's a pistol in the bag for emergencies, but I won't go near it."

The burly outlaw with the wild black beard grinned. "I didn't get this pretty by doing manual labor." He gestured with the pistol as he said, "You pull it out, leave it on the ground, and step over there where I can see you. And you'd better be as unarmed as you said or . . ."

"Yes, yes, I know. I'll be the next one left out here," Zimmerman said. "You've already threatened me enough for one day."

Zimmerman reached into the hole and hefted out a yellow bank satchel. The stenciling on the side of the bag had read "Wells Fargo" once, but the lettering had faded after repeated burials.

His treasure now out in the open, Zimmerman backed away and kept his hands visible as per his earlier agreement with Brunet. He was also unarmed, save for the rifle on his saddle more than twenty feet away. All of these precautions were taken at Brunet's insistence.

Zimmerman did not much like all of these measures. In fact, he found them quite insulting. True, the two men only knew each other by their respective reputations, but Zimmerman preferred to think they were somehow bonded together by their greed. Their mutual lawlessness. Their unending desire for more. Always more. More of what was a question he often asked himself. The answer was as unimportant as it was consistent. Just more.

Zimmerman was sure to stand particularly still as he watched Brunet climb down from the chestnut Canadian he rode. It was a fine-looking animal and better suited for this climate than the fretful beast he had.

Zimmerman tried to find the best word to describe Brunet as he watched him walk toward the last remaining testament to the Hudson Gang. Like Zimmerman, he was just shy of six feet, but not by much. And, like Zimmerman, he was a broad and powerfully built man. His physique came about naturally and was not the result of hard work. Both men were healthy and far from fat, but their size gave them a more menacing quality than a miner or farmer or other workingman might possess.

That was where the similarities between them ended. Zimmerman preferred to shave every morning when he could. Brunet's thick black beard covered the upper part of his heavy buffalo coat. The floppy brim of his weathered brown hat served to keep the wind and the rain out of his face. The large brown eyes beneath it had a wild, almost feral quality to them.

Zimmerman regarded himself as a planner, while Brunet was a man who got things done. He often acted rashly and killed without purpose. Every man Zimmerman had either killed or allowed to live had been for a reason.

Zimmerman watched the outlaw descend on the bag of money like a wolf on a fallen elk. His greed had overtaken him, but like the wolf, not enough to make him careless. He opened the bag with his left hand while he kept Zimmerman covered with the pistol in his right.

Zimmerman took this to be an excellent sign. Wild men were not always careless men. And with the right influence, they could be tamed. Alexander Darabont had taught him that. He had taught him so many things by his example. He had learned as much from his former leader's mistakes as he had from his successes. Perhaps more.

And all he had planned for the past three months had led to this moment. To this grubby, monstrous man pawing all the money Zimmerman had in the world.

Brunet found the pistol Zimmerman had placed in the bag and tossed it aside as he dug his hand into the bag. His eyes grew wide as he lifted his hand full of coins and allowed them to slip from his fingers back into the bag as if they were grains of sand.

He looked at Zimmerman with toothless delight as he dug his hand deeper into the bag and came up with even more coins.

"Remember our agreement," Zimmerman cautioned him. "You can see the money. You can even count it. But all of it stays here. Neither of us takes a cent."

But Brunet seemed too consumed with the treasure to hear Zimmerman. "There's got to be a million dollars here."

Zimmerman prevented himself from laughing. If he had a million dollars at his disposal, even a quarter of that, he would have no use for Brunet's talents. "It's ten thousand to be precise. I joined my money with the loot of the

Hudson Gang's after their unfortunate demise in Silver Cloud."

Brunet grabbed a single coin from the bag and bit it with one of his few remaining teeth. "It's genuine, by God." He allowed the coin to drop back into the bag and looked up at Zimmerman. "I'll admit I had my doubts about you, boy, but you're a man of your word. That much is certain."

Zimmerman thought it low praise coming from a mountain brute, but he feigned sincerity when he said, "Given the source, I take that as a compliment. Now, if you'd be so kind as to place the pistol back in the bag and put the bag back in the hole, I'll place the rock back on top of it so we can continue our discussion."

Brunet surprised him by not only doing as he asked but also pushed the heavy stone back on top of the hole as if it were a pebble. He was obviously much stronger than he appeared. Perhaps even stronger than Zimmerman. He took note of that.

Brunet stood upright and opened his buffalo coat just long enough to tuck his pistol away inside one of the hide's many pockets. He stood looking at Zimmerman. His short arms hanging from his sides like an ape. "You took a hell of a risk bringing me out here to see all this. I could shoot you now and take off with all the money."

Zimmerman shrugged. "If you did, you'd be riding away with ten thousand dollars and riding away from ten million. You doubted my sincerity, which is understandable. At least now we know we can trust each other."

Brunet nodded his head down toward the skeletal foot sticking out of the snow. "That fella trust you, too?"

Zimmerman had wondered how long it would take Brunet to ask him about that. "There's another man about ten yards to your left. They were prospectors who had a donkey I could use to bring the gold up here. Once they had dug the hole and placed the rock over it, they had served their purpose. Like the Good Book says, "Three men can keep a secret if two of them are dead."

Brunet ran his thick tongue around the inside of his mouth. "T'ain't any scripture I've ever heard."

Come to think of it, Zimmerman doubted it was from the Bible, but it sounded good. "Well, if it isn't there, perhaps it should be." He gestured toward the horses. "Now, I don't know about you, but I think we've been out here in the cold long enough. What do you say we get back to the cabin where we can continue our discussion?"

Brunet showed his agreement by walking back toward his horse and climbing up into the saddle. Zimmerman made sure he was mounted and comfortable first before he did the same. He was aware that the outlaw was fully capable of killing him and taking the gold for himself but doubted he would do that. For if Brunet agreed to what he was proposing, the contents in the hole would be pocket change compared to the riches that lie ahead for each of them.

The two men descended the rocky hilltop in silence until they reached the flatland that led to the trapper's cabin they shared as their mutual hideout for the past day or so. The place had been a ruin when Zimmerman had stumbled upon it as he fled Halstead and Silver Cloud and had remained so until he had been well enough to fix it.

Zimmerman tried not to think of all he had endured in the days and weeks following his run-in with Halstead. How the gaping hole in his left side had almost crippled him in his mad scramble for the freight train as it stopped to take on water. How even breathing set his entire body on fire. How the saddle and saddlebags he carried with him only made it worse.

He remembered the feverish days he had been forced to

spend in that wretched boxcar, surrounded by five forgotten men who looked at him as hungrily as Brunet had looked into the Wells Fargo satchel just now. He had counted himself fortunate that he'd had the good sense to shoot them all before the pain and the fever robbed him of consciousness. He had no doubt they would have done the same to him— and worse—as soon as he had passed out from the wound in his side.

He only regretted that the dead men were as poor as the lice and rats who dwelled in the boxcar. Their corpses had yielded little except to serve as a distraction for the vermin to feast on while he slowly recovered.

The only thing of value any of them possessed had been coffee and the fixings to make a small fire in a tar box they had found somewhere. The coffee grinds served as a poultice he used to fill his wound and the fire kept him warm on the cold, endless nights when fever dreams haunted him amidst the endless rocking of the westbound train.

He remembered how weak he had been when the train stopped and one of the crew decided to check the boxcars for stowaways. He had not wanted to kill the man who opened the unlocked car, but he could not afford to allow himself to be taken prisoner, either.

He could not die or be arrested for he had unfinished business to tend to. Business that could not afford to be delayed by a lengthy stay in prison and the inevitable end he would meet on the gallows.

He could still hear the gunshots of the remaining members of the train crew echo in the distance as he struggled over hard ground, hauling his saddle and bags across the frozen land and through the unending forest that surrounded him. By the time the sun had dipped well below the horizon that wretched day, Edward Zimmerman knew he was done for. The cold Montana day had almost killed him. His fever was raging. The unforgiving night would surely finish the job.

He had thought his eyes had been playing tricks on him when he spotted the ragged darkness in a clearing just ahead of him. He did not know if it was real or if this was Death itself come to collect his soul before his body grew too cold. He stumbled toward it anyway. He'd had nothing left to lose.

He found it was an abandoned trapper's shack. It was little more than several dozen planks of wood nailed together and a slanted roof that kept the snow from piling too high atop it. The rusted steel traps that adorned its walls showed its past purpose.

He remembered a great plume of dust rose up as he collapsed on the crude mattress stuffed with crushed leaves and dried grass. The place had a door and a roof that did not leak much and a stove where he could make fire.

It was where he had spent weeks recovering. The same place to which he rode with Brunet now. The place that had saved him from death and allowed him to carry on the last bit of unfinished business he had left in the world.

That business being the slow death of Jeremiah Halstead. The man who had wiped out his gang. The man who had put the gaping hole in his side. The man who had put him through a living Hell as he fought to survive.

Now, upon reaching the shack, the two outlaws stowed their mounts in the tangle of pine branches and wood Zimmerman had cobbled together to serve as a place to stow their horses. The animals were just as susceptible to the cold as humans and required some shelter from the elements. It was not much, but it was better than standing tethered to a porch post all night.

Brunet followed Zimmerman inside the shack. They had kept the fire in the stove burning before they left to see the

gold, and Zimmerman quickly fed it more sticks and wood
to make it even hotter.

Both men shucked their coats and warmed their hands
by the growing warmth of the stove.

Brunet stomped his feet on the wooden floor Zimmerman had done his best to repair following his recovery.
"Showing me that gold up there bought you a lot of stock
with me, Ed, but I still need some answers."

Zimmerman had been expecting that. "And I'll be glad
to give them to you."

"How'd you manage to find me?"

"By word of mouth," Zimmerman explained. "Once I
was healthy enough to move around, I spent my time vis-
iting the various mining camps in the area. I make a circuit
of about ten of them or so. The big mines run by the mining
companies and the smaller claims by Hard Scrabble. I told
them I was just a simple trapper, so they paid me little
mind. I'd play cards with them and drink with them. I'd
listen to what they had to say. I even added a bit to that bag
you just hauled out of the ground as a result of it. That's
when Dippy pulled me aside one night and told me he thought
I was Zimmerman. I was worried at first until he asked me
if I wanted to meet you."

Brunet nodded at the memory. "Poor old Dippy. He
never did know how to keep his mouth shut. Didn't like
him letting on about me like that. Always looking to show
the world how big a man he was." He looked at Zimmerman. "You did me a kindness by killing him for me like
you did. He was the last one of my old bunch who stuck
around."

"Killing him was the least I could do," Zimmerman
said. "If he brought me to your hideout in the mine, he'd
eventually lead someone else there, too. Maybe someone

not as friendly as me. And, since he had figured out who I was, it was only prudent to kill him."

"True." Brunet rubbed his hands over the stove. "Though it'll put you in a bad way with the miners. When they notice Dippy is missing and you quit coming around, they might say something about it to the sheriff."

"My time with them served its purpose," Zimmerman explained. "I learned all about their operation. I know what shifts they work and, most importantly of all, when and how they get paid. They're particularly fascinated about all of the wanted men said to be hiding out up here in the hills. They love to talk about what they'd do with all the money they'd collect by bringing down a man with a big price on his head. Men like you and me." He laughed. "My scalp alone would bring five thousand dollars."

"That's nothing," Brunet sniffed. "I've got two countries hunting for me. Either one would bring twenty thousand easily. But I'd wager you already knew that."

Zimmerman did not bother hiding it. "As you already knew about the reward out for me. So I decided to play a game with them. I let them know that I'd heard Zimmerman was alive and well in California. Not only that, but he had placed a bounty on the head of the marshal who chased him out of Montana. Ten thousand to the man who killed him. All they had to do was make sure the killing got mentioned in the papers and Zimmerman would make good on his claim. Either to him or the man's family, if he had any."

Brunet laughed. "Heard that one myself. Mighty good thinking on your part. Putting out a bounty on the man who put one on you. What happens if someone comes to collect?"

"I'd gladly pay it," Zimmerman admitted, "though I doubt it'll ever come to that. No bounty hunter worth his sand would dare take on Halstead. He'd be finished for life.

But I knew the amateurs who think ten thousand is a godly sum would gladly take a gamble, especially if they had nothing to lose. A few seconds' work with a gun beats a lifetime spent digging gold and copper out of the ground to men with few other prospects."

Zimmerman felt himself growing warmer and not just from the stove fire. "Word has spread far and wide and, last I heard, about ten men have tried to collect on my offer. They're all dead now, of course. Halstead isn't likely to be taken down by desperate farmers or miners or cowhands." He sighed deeply. "Still, I live in hope. And even if they miss, it keeps Halstead on his guard and distracted."

"Distracted," Brunet repeated. "You mean distracted from hunting you."

"Distracted until I am ready to hunt him," Zimmerman said.

Brunet ran that thick tongue of his along the inside of his mouth again as he thought that over. "I've got no more quarrel with him than I've got with any other man toting a badge, Ed. If we join up, I'm in it for the money, not the blood. I've never minded the killing part of it. You know that. But I'd just as soon let a man go if I can."

But Zimmerman had already surmised all of that. He knew Brunet killed whenever the occasion called for it. And he knew that, if they went up against Halstead, the occasion would certainly call for it. "I never thought different, Robert. I see men like you and I as shepherds in a way. We don't enjoy killing, but it's an unavoidable circumstance in our line of work."

Brunet thought about that for a while. "Could always get ourselves honest work."

The two men looked at each other across the stove before breaking out into laughter that filled the tiny shack. Brunet had a high-pitched cackle that did not fit such a deadly man.

As the Canadian pawed away tears of laughter from his eyes, he said, "Let's say you and me throw in with each other. We're going to need men."

"We most certainly will," Zimmerman agreed. "Good men and lots of them, too, if we're going to put my plan into place."

"About that." Brunet wagged a gloved finger at him. "You've been going on about this plan of yours for the past couple of days. You ever going to get around to telling me what it is or am I going to have to guess?"

"That depends." Zimmerman extended a hand to him across the stove. "Are we partners?"

Brunet regarded the hand for a moment and the man extending it to him. "I think we can do better than that."

Zimmerman watched him produce a knife from somewhere inside his buffalo hide. The large blade caught a glint of firelight before he pulled off his glove and drew the sharp edge across the palm of his right hand.

Zimmerman pulled the blade he kept tucked in the back of his pants and did the same. The two men clasped hands until their blood was intermingled. Some of it sizzled as drops hit the stove between them.

"A pact sealed with blood is the only pact I honor," Brunet told him as he gripped Zimmerman's hand tightly.

Zimmerman matched the strength of his grip. "All right, then. Now we can finally talk about how we're going to take over the territory."

Visit our website at
KensingtonBooks.com
to sign up for our newsletters, read
more from your favorite authors, see
books by series, view reading group
guides, and more!

Become a Part of Our
Between the Chapters Book Club
Community and Join the Conversation

Betweenthechapters.net

Submit your book review for a chance to win exclusive
Between the Chapters swag you can't get anywhere else!
https://www.kensingtonbooks.com/pages/review/